IF *You* REALLY KNEW ME

A Novel

By

Jeffrey McClain Jones

Book 1 of the series

Anyone Who Believes

If You Really Knew Me

Copyright © 2015 by Jeffrey McClain Jones

All rights reserved. No part of this book may be reproduced in any form by any electronic or mechanical means including photocopying, recording, or information storage and retrieval without permission in writing from the author.

John 14:12 Publications

www.john1412.com

Cover photos from ShutterStock and Dollar Photo

Cover Design by Gabriel W. Jones

For Dave Frederick: a fearless champion of truly free grace.

Opening Prayer

Dixon Claiborne uncrossed his legs and planted his feet flat on the floor. Somewhere, in the fuzzed echoes of educational memory, he had learned that this posture enhanced concentration, or something. Actually, maybe that was for typing.

He inhaled with purpose, sighing out his exasperation about letting his mind wander. Perhaps as an act of penance, he clasped his hands together—fingers interlaced—and wedged his nose between his thumbs, his head bowed and eyes closed. This posture came from another region of his early indoctrination. Sunday school, of course. Who was his kindergarten Sunday school teacher? No. He refused to follow that rabbit trail.

"Lord," he said aloud, half prayer and half expletive.

"Lord, you gotta help me to concentrate here." Then, noticing a lack of humility to this demand, he edited. "I mean, I need your help. Show me how to pray." He paused here to fend off an internal critic that thought it was pretty lame to pray for help with praying. Dixon subdued that rebellion quickly.

"Lord, lead me in my efforts to bring glory to you, to do your work, to protect your church from deception, to deliver us from . . ." His voice faded when the phrases all sounded too familiar and his anxiety level overpowered his confidence in the effect of praying at all.

"But I know this is right. I know you are true and men are all deceivers," he said, jump-starting his petition again. "Lord, let your truth come out. Let me say it right. Don't let me get my own ideas or interests mixed up in this. Yes, have your way, Lord. Not my way, but yours."

He paused to wonder whether he hadn't hit it right on the head with that. As he did so, he looked at the corner of his office, where a gap in the paneling revealed the painted drywall beneath. That snippet of pale blue dug into his mind and expanded into wondering whether he should stay at this medium-sized church, with its limited budget and aging congregation.

And that was it for praying, at least for that afternoon. He had to meet with the committee before the big meeting that night, when the whole town, and hopefully national media, would be watching.

Rising from the old nylon couch that used to be the centerpiece of his living room at home, Dixon stepped over to his desk. He wore his new navy blue suit, white dress shirt and red and blue striped tie. The words "power suit," would never pass his lips, but that's what he was wearing. His fit, six-foot-three, physique wore it well. He grabbed his cell phone off the corner of the desk and punched the wakeup button to check for messages. That's when he realized that he had been praying for only about three minutes, or at least trying to pray. An unspoken curse aimed at himself punctuated his turn toward the plain oak door of his office. The wood grain on that old door formed the figure of a woman, crippled by some distorting disease, one shoulder larger than the other, her neck twisted to the side, her head bowed as if ducking. The image appeared twice, mirrored where the wood had been cut and glued together to build the door.

Once through that door, he said to his secretary, "I'm heading home now, Connie."

The compact woman at the reception desk, with the dyed black hair, looked up at him and smiled. Her admiration beamed at Dixon, even if he didn't pause to notice. "Okay, I'll stay here a bit longer and then get ready for the meeting myself," she said, her voice the perfect tone for a preschool teacher, as usual.

"Good luck tonight." She nearly shouted this, as the outer office door eased shut behind the retreating pastor.

Home Sweet Home

A low May sun sharpened every leaf and grass blade in the yard. Sara Claiborne sat on the cushioned patio chair with her toes splayed, waiting for the fire engine red polish to dry. The curlers in her hair were her mother's idea. The fiery nail polish was hers. She rarely suffered an indignity from her mother that she didn't counter with some small retaliation.

Who cares what the daughter looks like, anyway? she thought. It's not like he's running for president or something, needing the perfect family as a backdrop for his campaign, along with the bunting and banners. That was it. She felt like so much decoration. Now she was asserting her own sense of taste into that familial décor. She was, in fact, getting the idea that her parents had ambitions, if not political, at least on a bigger scale, a bigger stage.

She wasn't going to have to be on stage, was she? That would definitely prove that this was more than church, more than worshipping God. Or, rather, less.

Behind her, she heard a vigorous slide of the patio door, complete with the vacuum hiss as the out-of-doors penetrated the seal of the air-conditioned house. Out stepped her twelve-year-old brother, Brett, sucking on an orange Popsicle with exaggerated gusto. His mother's voice sounded from behind him, siren-like but inarticulate to Sara's more distant ear.

"I can get ready in a couple of minutes." Brett yelled back into the house.

That same distant voice, somewhat muted, said one more thing, but Brett cut that off by sliding the door shut. He didn't need to catch every syllable to know the point.

Rounding the chair on which Sara sat, Brett slurped his desert and commented. "I see you're painting your toes (slurp). I bet Mom doesn't know."

Sara's first instinct, to threaten her little brother, bowed to her need for an ally. "She's really about to lose it, isn't she?" Sara said.

Brett slurped and nodded. "What do you think the big deal is about this meeting?" He shifted easily into ally mode. On the verge of teen age, Brett had begun to allow a bit more respect for his older sister, whom he had discovered was something of a queen among the teenagers. Guys, especially, worshipped Sara. Though Brett couldn't catalog them accurately, he knew that she had qualities that attracted attention, like the gawking looks of gapers at a toll way collision. Still too young, and too much a brother to really see, nevertheless he knew that her face, her body, her clothes and her attitude commanded respect among her peers. He knew power when he saw it.

"I don't know." Sara exhaled. "It must be something big. I mean, meeting at Calvary, instead of our church, and making sure that the press are gonna be there." She began to pick at the curlers in her hair, like a small boy picks at a scab, knowing that he shouldn't, but driven by some unstoppable urge to do what is forbidden. Of course, that forbidden thing lay right at the feet of her tense and over-attentive mother.

"I bet it's the stuff he's been finding about that kooky healer," Brett said. Brett was good at games of strategy, a solid chess player for his age. Sara was more book smart, knowing how to please people per the stated rules, not so perceptive of what lay behind the rules and facades. Brett's speculation struck her as more likely than the political nightmare she had been window-shopping.

If You Really Knew Me

"That could be it," Sara said. "Do you really think he's so bad?" She was willing to let down her guard a bit more, with no adults around.

"Heck, he thinks he's like an angel or something," Brett said, catching a line of drips with a particularly lengthy inhalation.

"Hmmm. Yeah, I guess that *is* pretty weird," Sara said, one curler now entirely free from her golden hair. She smiled slightly at the sun glistening through her freshly washed hair. "I wonder why Dad has to be the one to say something about him, though."

Brett withdrew his left foot just before a drip landed on his white sock, the orange droplet turning a spot on the light gray pavement dark as blood. "He's a leader. A lot of people listen to what he says. He has that radio show and all."

Hearing the respect in her little brother's explanation warned Sara to lower the intensity of her questioning. "I wonder what he's gonna say about those people. There must be more to it than just that they're weird."

The patio door slipped open again. This time Brett's mother confronted him from short range. "Okay, kiddo, you get in here and get dressed. Drop the Popsicle in the sink. You can get another one when we get home tonight."

Kristen Claiborne, the mother of these two catalog model children, wore a pink silk blouse over a white slip, her skirt waiting to be added later, after she had sat down for the last time before leaving, minimizing wrinkles. She thought of things like that …all the time.

Brett and Sara both silently added the concession of a second Popsicle as further evidence of the magnitude of the evening. No one ever purposely threw away good food in that house. That she was willing to sacrifice even that pointy remnant of a frozen desert bespoke desperation. Both children experienced a slight elevation in adrenalin at that tip-off.

"Ooookaaaay," Brett said, his voice twisting toward his lowest register in expression of his victim status. He knew he was overplaying the sacrifice demanded of him, but habits like that are hard to overcome at a moment's notice.

Kristen's attention turned to her daughter who was facing away, but whose half-liberated hair glowed over the top of the patio chair. "What are you doing now, Sara?" It wasn't an information gathering type of question, more of an inquisition.

Sara stood, realizing her mistake, but hoping to use it to avoid a direct confrontation over the nail polish. "I'm sorry. I was just talking to Brett, not even thinking about what I was doing. I think it's pretty well curled, though," she said, as she slipped past her slender mother who was still standing in the door, the two women fitting stomach-to-side in a space that the average American would have to occupy alone.

Kristen turned to watch her daughter mince through the kitchen, catching a flash of red that a vigilant mother recognized immediately. Even as the words—full of angst and authority— formed in her mind, she waited a beat and recognized something else, a battle not worth fighting. Instead of a yell, a sigh whispered through her lips, and she just shook her head and closed the patio door, flipping the latch to lock it.

Getting the Platform Ready

At the edge of the stage, Kyle Mauler pushed the Bluetooth headset close against his right ear, to be sure he was hearing correctly. "You said *what* isn't gonna be ready?"

"*The video clip from the meeting in L.A. isn't loading, it looks to be corrupted, or something.*" This reply sounded pinched, a machine-like attempt at patience tempering the answer.

"'Corrupted or something?'" Kyle said in disgusted disbelief. He swore, cutting the phone call off in the middle of his short string of four letter words. His voice faded just as someone approached him from behind.

"How are we doing, Kyle?" That too perky inquiry came from a tall, athletic man in a new blue suit.

"Oh, it's all under control, Pastor," Kyle said, spinning the truth without a microsecond of forethought.

"Good to hear. We're countin' on your magic tonight, buddy."

Kyle simply smiled in return, editing and deleting verbal responses as automatically as the hand movements of a deli sandwich maker at lunch hour. He headed for the control room to check on that video clip. Though he wasn't the man to explain the theological importance of what that clip contained, he knew that the movers and shakers behind this meeting wanted that evidence to seal their case against the bad guys, whoever they happened to be this week.

Skipping down six stairs to the main floor, and striding up the aisle nearest him, Kyle pulled his phone from his pocket to see who was calling him now. Claire, his fiancée. That one he would ignore. He needed to stay focused on what he was doing here. This was a big stage, a public opportunity to show what he could do, the sort of spectacle he could produce. Up the narrow stairs to the control booth he hopped, beginning to feel a bit winded. There was something to be said for running systems and events at a smaller venue, like Pastor Claiborne's church. But, then, if he was in charge over here, at Calvary, he wouldn't be the one doing so much running.

On the other end of the cell call, Claire Sanchez hit "End" before Kyle's voicemail kicked in. She shook her head and stared at the screen on her phone, trying to think of who else to call. She brushed the black hair hanging over her right cheek behind her ear again, her dark brown eyes still locked on the phone.

"Sara," she said aloud. "She'll answer." But she hesitated. Calling the pastor's daughter might not be fair to *her*, putting her in the middle, or even lining her up against her father. No, that wouldn't be right.

Claire grunted her frustration and lowered the phone to her lap. She sat sideways in a big recliner at her mother's house, where she would live for the next few months, before the wedding. For the first time, she glanced at the possibility that a wedding might not be in her immediate future. That Kyle didn't take her call in the middle of setting up for the big event wasn't the problem, or even a particular symptom. No, what had begun to sprout inside her soul had been planted long before this latest season in the life of her home church.

Instead of following that growing apprehension, Claire swung her bare legs off the arm of the chair, pushing herself up to her feet and hurrying to her room, to begin dressing for the meeting. Despite her misgivings about the reason for the meeting, and the coming campaign, she would have to attend. Maybe she could talk to someone there, to try to get the leaders to think more about what they were doing, before going any further.

One hand shuffled through her closet and grabbed the first acceptable dress from the array before her. The twenty-six-year-old ignored any concern for style or presentation. She was on her way to confront an impending disaster, not primping for a date, or even for a typical church service.

Back in the control room at Calvary Church, Kyle looked at the scrambled tapestry of colored lines that appeared on the multi-media workstation screen. "Did you try this on any other computers?" he said to the bearded tech sitting in front of him.

That tech, Randy Morris, looked at his younger friend next to him for the answer to that question. Pete Stolzer, a twenty-year-old with a Denver Broncos hat hung backward over his bushy head, just shrugged.

"Ah, that's a negative," Randy said, translating that gesture.

"Well, let's see if we can get it running in a different media player or a different operating system and maybe convert it to a format that works on this machine." As Kyle lined up that strategy he barely suppressed his frustration at the incompetent help he'd been saddled with.

Pete and Randy both nodded calmly, as if pleased with Kyle's suggestion, no sign of an apology, no urgency evident. When Pete picked up a silver DVD from the desk in front of him, Kyle spun and headed back out of the booth, counting to ten silently in hopes of exiting before he verbally assaulted anyone.

Down on the stage, Dixon Claiborne stood behind a large metal and glass podium, turning left and right for the stage and lighting crew to set the illumination levels for the TV cameras. His prominent jaw and fat-free face lost and gained defining shadows as the tech crew fiddled with the lights. The host church had their own cameras with which they projected an image of the speaker onto a twenty-foot screen above his head. But the cameras for which Dixon now prepared were from local network affiliates and even national news channels. The crews hauling those cameras maneuvered around each other, laying cables and testing equipment in the aisles and the first two rows of the center section. Seating there had had been replaced by video monitors, computers, and a wide array of men and women wearing jackets with logos from networks and TV stations, people who rarely attended church meetings of any kind.

Having satisfied the lighting mavens, Dixon paused to squint into the relative darkness of the seating area, trying to count the number of cameras present. Then he looked up the aisle for any indication of a crowd gathering at the doors to the huge auditorium. They would certainly come. Who could resist the coalition of prominent local preachers declaring that they had evidence that a famous Hollywood billionaire, and reputed healer, was not who he claimed? Dixon knew he didn't have to say everything that he believed to be true of this cult leader. He was counting on the secular media to do more of the digging for him, collapsing the false church behind that glitzy friend of the stars.

Dixon inhaled a relaxing breath that filled his broad chest and straightened his spine. Now, everything was in place.

Translation Please

Earlier that day, Jonathan Opare buckled his right sandal, stood up and stamped his foot lightly to settle the tan leather footwear in place. He pulled a bright orange, blue and yellow striped shirt over his head, covering the more mundane blue Chelsea Football Club jersey he had been wearing all morning, as he ate his breakfast and read his Bible. The blue of the jersey showed in two inches of the V where the brightly colored shirt stood open slightly on his chest, as he intended. He was dressing for lunch with one of the assistant pastors from his church, as well as for a city-wide meeting of several area churches. The ornate shirt over his dark slacks constituted his usual worship attire.

He glanced at his handsome African face in the mirror on the hallway wall, checking that his hair was symmetrically combed. He allowed a slight smile of satisfaction at the picture that greeted him there. Grabbing his briefcase, which contained his slim new laptop, his phone and his wallet, he stepped to the front door and let himself out, pausing to insert his key to lock the door from the outside. The cool breeze accompanying the midday sun reminded him of early spring back home. Finally, some weather he could enjoy and not just survive.

With his briefcase slung over his shoulder, messenger style, he rode his bicycle to the restaurant on the corner of Colfax and Piedmont, locking it to the bike rack that served the entire strip mall. Jonathan pulled his case off over his head and took the handle in his left hand, carrying it more like a traditional briefcase. As a graduate student of economics, he had acquired a position as a teaching assistant and considered himself a teacher as much as a student. His case symbolized this dual life, in his mind, the shoulder bag of a student and the satchel of a profes-

If You Really Knew Me

sor, all in one. Jonathan had learned to keep this sort of thinking to himself, trusting only Treena, his wife, with such intimate imaginings.

When he entered the Greek-owned family restaurant, specializing in a mixture of American and Greek cuisine, he spotted Darryl Sampras already seated at a small table by the windows, perusing the menu. Darryl was the assistant pastor to Dixon Claiborne, a well-known local religious leader. Darryl bore responsibility for the missions and outreach programs of the church.

Noticing Jonathan's approach, Darryl looked up from his menu, smiled broadly and stood to shake the graduate student's hand.

"Jonathan, so good to see you," Darryl said, holding onto the handshake an extra second.

Jonathan smiled and bowed very slightly, unsure what the pastor's extra-long handshake indicated across the dived between Ghana, his home country, and the United States. He had liked the thirty-something, balding pastor from the start, but assumed he didn't understand him much better than any of the other American Christians he had met in his first year in the States. Darryl had mentioned a desire to have lunch with Jonathan back in October of the previous year. His explanations since then for the delay seemed lacking both detail and remorse, but Jonathan had learned to expect this sort of thing by now, and it didn't sour his attitude toward Darryl particularly.

A rich combination of sweet and salty odors escaped the kitchen and perused the room, awakening Jonathan's appetite even more than the bike ride had.

"Hello, Pastor," Jonathan said, setting his briefcase in the chair next to the window and taking the seat diagonal from Darryl, hoping to avoid his sandaled toes being injured beneath the table.

"Oh, just call me Darryl. No need for titles here."

Jonathan nodded and smiled in response, lifting his menu to look at what he might like. Darryl had suggested the location for their meeting, when Jonathan cornered him after church that week. Growing in comfort among the Americans, Jonathan had decided to pin the friendly minister to making an actual appointment. He felt that Darryl was the person at the church most likely to help him understand the American religious culture.

Darryl set his menu down after another brief look and Jonathan followed, determined to get as many answers as he could, more than finding the perfect lunch order.

"You know why I attend your church?" Jonathan said, launching his agenda.

"No, not really. Why?"

"In my country, we are used to American churches sending people, usually men, to build things, small projects like churches or daycare centers. One of those teams came to my uncle's small village and helped with a medical clinic, bringing their own doctor and a nurse with them. They were from the church that founded your church, Grace Chapel. So, my uncle told me that we should look for a church like them when we arrived in the states."

"What kind of church did you attend in...a...Ghana, is it?"

"Yes, I am from Ghana," Jonathan said. "Our church in Kumasi was really a Pentecostal congregation, I think you would say. Most of the big churches there are like that."

"Oh." Darryl raised his eyebrows. "So we must seem pretty strange to you."

Jonathan laughed, his mind winking past the countless ways that a North American, white Bible church differed from the church he attended as a child in the second largest city in Ghana. "In Ghana, a Bible-believing church is usually a Pentecostal church, so we didn't know there would be a difference here. I am an economist, not a church historian," he said.

Darryl smiled, pausing to thank the waiter for pouring them water and then giving his order. Jonathan followed, ordering a chicken sandwich and iced tea.

If You Really Knew Me

When the waiter left, Darryl followed up on Jonathan's opening comments. "So, are you wondering what you're doing with us?" he said, still smiling.

Tipping his head briefly to the left, while raising his right eyebrow, Jonathan smiled with tight lips. "No, to be honest, we have found a prayer meeting in town that feels more like our home church. But we have made friends at your church and are content to stay among you for our time in the States."

"That's good to hear," Darryl said, sipping his water while keeping his blue-gray eyes on Jonathan.

"But I do have a question about something I heard from the leader of the house group we are attending this spring," Jonathan said.

"What's that?"

"He mentioned that the meeting tonight, with the other big Bible churches in the city, is meant to expose some millionaire guru in California. And he showed me a Web site that contains some pretty outrageous claims about this man."

Darryl's face froze and his color flushed to dark pink and then red. He turned toward the window and scratched the back of his head, looking again at Jonathan in the way a boy would when he's about to admit that he hit the baseball through your living room window.

"Yeah, well that site is probably not the best way to introduce the issue. I know some people are saying pretty crazy things."

Darryl's obvious discomfort with the subject actually reassured Jonathan, who feared that this accessible and reasonable assistant pastor would not see the potential difficulty with this report about the actions of the Church's senior pastor.

Jonathan cleared his throat and continued. "When I asked our house group leader what it was that this man had done to raise this suspicion, all he could tell me was that the man healed some people and claimed to hear from God."

This time Darryl grimaced, seeing immediately why Jonathan would find that characterization problematic, given his Pentecostal background. "No, I don't think that's a very good

19

If You Really Knew Me

explanation of what's caught the attention of some of the local pastors. They're not getting together to attack anyone for claiming to heal people or to hear God's voice. This man is doing something much more questionable, I think."

That little qualifying hesitation at the very end of his reply left both men hanging in a pensive pause, Darryl because he knew he couldn't offer any more certainty, and Jonathan because he wondered if Darryl was hiding something from him.

Leaning forward, his elbows on the edge of the table, Darryl tried to come clean, feeling he owed it to the articulate young scholar sitting across the table. "Look, Jonathan, I don't know all that's gonna be said at the meeting tonight. I do know that some folks have gotten hold of this and made it into more than I understood originally was involved." He shook his head slightly, looking down at the table. "Frankly, I need to attend that meeting tonight myself, just to figure out if *I'm* okay with what's happening here."

Jonathan smiled reassuringly, sorry to see Darryl in such distress about his questions, and inclined to believe Darryl's innocence regarding the kind of witch-hunt that he feared.

"I too will attend with that in mind, then," Jonathan said.

Darryl grinned. "Afterward, we should get together again to compare our reactions." When he saw a doubtful look sink Jonathan's face, he said, "I really mean it. Let's schedule a meeting at my office early next week."

Again, Jonathan smiled, this time showing teeth and breathing a soft laugh, just as the waiter delivered his chicken sandwich.

The Course is Set

In the small room off the side of the stage, where speakers picked up water bottles and Kleenex, Dixon Claiborne stood with Bishop Stephen Jefferson of Emmanuel Holiness Temple, a leading African-American pastor in the city. The bishop filled his pale blue suite with his generous proportions, and his face glistened with the slightest sheen of perspiration.

"Everything set for the choir and the opening music?" Dixon said.

The bishop nodded. "Yes, it is. They're practicing in a room down stairs designed for just that purpose."

Dixon could tell that Bishop Jefferson was as impressed as he was with the Calvary facilities. It was hard not to envy the conveniences, and even luxuries, built into the city's largest conservative church. But Dixon subdued that thought by reminding himself that this evening was not about looking for a position at a bigger church.

"I know your choir will set the right tone for this evening," Dixon said in a conciliatory key. "It's all about the glory of God and protecting his precious church," he said.

"Yes, Pastor, that's exactly right. Let's pray the worldly media doesn't turn it all against us, however."

Though the bishop may have meant those words as a simple statement of hope, Dixon took him literally and started to pray, calling out to God to protect the proceedings that night and to get the glory in everything that happened. Bishop Jefferson, of course, added his voice not only to "Amen" Dixon's prayer, but to contribute a lengthy prayer of his own.

Out in the auditorium, at six-thirty, middle-aged men in gray slacks, white shirts, blue blazers, and maroon ties opened the auditorium doors, even as Bishop Jefferson said his final

"Amen." Dixon peaked out the door to see if a flood or a trickle resulted from opening those doors. He was neither impressed nor disappointed. People of all ages, genders and skin tones sauntered down four aisles, many of them rubber-necking at the expansive meeting space. A few moments later, a string quartet bowed the first notes of, *Onward Christian Soldiers*, a tune that Dixon didn't remember hearing performed by a string quartet before.

Bishop Jefferson excused himself and headed back down the hallway, intent on praying with, and energizing, his church choir before they took the stage.

Up in the booth, Kyle previewed the video file that had raised his blood pressure earlier, now converted to a format compatible with the main multi-media workstation that commanded the projectors around the auditorium. As if immune to any impact from the content of that video, Kyle watched like a factory worker checking that all the widgets on the conveyor belt were right side up. The techs, Pete and Randy, on the other hand, stared with open mouths at a series of startling and audacious scenes, watching the whole video for the first time.

Glancing at them briefly when the video ended, Kyle grunted, mildly pleased that the video impacted the uninitiated as predicted. "Okay, get that cued up for when Dixon calls for it, about fifteen minutes into the meeting.

Down in the auditorium, Kristen Claiborne led Sara and Brett out the door at the right of the stage and down dark red carpeted stairs, her shiny black high heels planting purposefully on each step, her hand white knuckling the railing. In her left hand, she carried a shiny black purse, containing all the essentials: cell phone, tissues, breath mints, wallet, lipstick, face powder, and a hair brush. Sara noticed the way her mother gripped her bag and wondered if it contained some vital state secret or something. But then her mother seemed to be gripping everything extra tight that night. This realization contributed to gastro-intestinal turmoil in Sara that she thought might be forecasting ulcers for the years to come.

Brett just looked around at the crowd, sizing them up like a captain assessing the troops before a battle. Unlike the generals who would take the stage, Brett merely had to show up and follow along, like everyone else. But he still practiced for the day when it would be *his* crowd and *his* platform.

Toward the back of the multitude waiting to enter the auditorium, Claire Sanchez surveyed her fellow attendees more surreptitiously than Brett did inside. The evening still warm and sunny, Claire fanned herself with an old church bulletin that she found stuffed in the outside pocket of her purse. The close crowd robbed her of the cooling breeze that ruffled leaves on the sycamore trees lining the sidewalk in front of the huge edifice. She recognized a few faces from her church and noted the large number of strangers as well. She saw Jonathan Opare, but not his wife, edging forward with the crowd, his head prominent above the shorter people around him.

Jonathan glanced at the crowd but exercised no interest in assessing the audience, pondering, instead, why so many would come to such a meeting—assuming that they knew what this was about. But then, did *he* really know what it was about? Turning his eyes toward the ushers standing by the doors in front of him, Jonathan wondered where Darryl was, whether he was already inside, back stage, or merely mixed in with the general populace.

Darryl had found a seat in the front row, near Kristen and her two children, having entered the church an hour before the meeting. He had wandered in and out of rooms full of a choir preparing to sing, ushers receiving instructions, nursery workers acquainting themselves with unfamiliar facilities, and pastors shaking hands and patting backs. Yet he had felt most drawn to the most sparsely populated rooms, including the auditorium before the doors opened. Darryl sat alone. His wife Karen would be in the cry room with their nine-month-old for the duration of the evening, her turn to miss the main festivities.

A few minutes later, when the choir up the carpeted risers in the back and center of the stage, Bishop Jefferson and Pastor Claiborne followed them, along with six other church leaders. There was no one among them tonight that needed, or deserved, a big entrance. These were the faithful shepherds of local churches, not marquee speakers or musicians. They would take their seats on the stage and preside over a solemn meeting, a gathering for the defense of their collective flock, defense against deceivers who would lure away the weak and ignorant, to devour their souls without regret.

Raising the Flag

A sixty-voice choir singing *God Bless America*, accompanied by piano, organ and a small symphonic orchestra, launched the meeting. Following that rousing anthem, Bishop Jefferson lead in an unscripted prayer of nearly three minutes in length. Kyle timed it in the booth, shaking his head for every second over the two minutes he had allotted the opening prayer.

During the second choir number, *Holy, Holy, Holy*, Claire started to feel like it was a worship service, the prayer and hymn granting some recovery from the patriotic opener. Two thousand voices joined in the last two verses and the building swelled with the sound.

This launched Rev. Luis Cruz into his prayer, which seemed somewhat less spontaneous than Bishop Jefferson's, but still raised the hairs on the back of Darryl's neck, inspired particularly by the phrase, "we gather here as one people, your people, devoted together to the glory of your name alone, O Lord." That was something Darryl could get behind. A united body of Christians stirred him as much as anything could.

If You Really Knew Me

Dixon Claiborne stood, and glanced at his family in the front row to his left, when Pastor Cruz surrendered the podium (now two minutes behind schedule per Kyle's digital stopwatch). As the two pastors crossed paths, they shook hands vigorously, Dixon looming six inches taller than Pastor Cruz. Cameras flashed at the image of unity there mid-stage. Darryl loved it. Kyle counted it against his clock.

Sitting up straight in the plush theater seat, Kristen smiled strenuously at her husband as he took the podium. She had never seen him in front of so many people, and the main speaker at that. Sara could sense her mother's pride, or perhaps just her nerves, in the depth of her breathing and the intensity of that painful smile. Anyone focused on Sara at the time would have thought she was about to dial 911. Brett just took it all in, like a boy at a football game, such as the college and pro games to which his father had taken him numerous times.

"We welcome you, brothers and sisters, neighbors and friends, as well as media representatives," Dixon said, with a grand smile. "Let me thank the Evangelical Ministerial Association for sponsoring this event, an organization represented by these distinguished gentlemen to my right." He gestured behind him, his right hand swinging toward the row of solemn looking pastors and then coming back to rest on the podium.

"For those of you who have speculated about the purpose of this meeting, I want to deny categorically that I am running for President." He guffawed with the chittering response from the crowd. "Although, I must admit, most presidential candidates start their campaigns with exactly that same denial. In my case, it's a safe bet that I'm not one of them." And again, he grinned to punctuate his attempt at humor.

Sara scowled, feeling confused by this joke, given her earlier speculation about a political agenda. She glanced at Brett to see what he was thinking. His gaping spectator posture told her nothing. Her mother's rapid blinking told Sara what she already knew, the woman was as nervous as a drug smuggler at a border checkpoint.

"Seriously," Dixon said. "We are gathered here, as fellow Christians and as fellow Californians, with a common concern, a concern that stretches beyond our fair state. As pastors, we gather united in protection of our church families, in protection of the integrity of the whole church as a body. We have called you here to issue a warning to our people, and to call for action from other leaders who claim the name 'Christian,' bearing their own responsibility for the integrity of God's holy church."

"It is our belief that a wolf has been allowed in among the sheep, that this dangerous creature is even honored in some circles of the Evangelical church, when he should be chased away for the protection of the innocent among us. We want to make it clear to all of our faithful members, and close friends in Christ, that they must stay clear of this man for their own spiritual safety, disassociating ourselves from false teaching and rampant sin."

"Though I could stand up here and list the deeds which have prompted this warning, we would rather let you see for yourselves the kind of behavior that is being tolerated in Christian churches right here in our state, and across the country. We have acquired video footage of the sort of things that this supposed minister of the Gospel is doing in church meetings and in his personal life. So, we'll dim the lights and let this short film show you what I could only tell you about. See for yourself. . ."

Kyle wasted no time responding to Dixon's prompt, anxious as he was to get things back on schedule. Lights faded from a moderate glow to a faint twilight in a single second, provoking a brief "whoa" from members of the audience. But the flashing light from the video clip jumped in to illuminate the room once again.

The opening shot of the film showed a well-known pastor of a large California church holding the door handle of some building, perhaps his church, standing halfway in the door. The handheld camera angle called to mind exposé journalism. An unseen

If You Really Knew Me

reporter said, "Pastor, are we correct in believing that Beau Dupere is a member of your association of churches?"

The gray-haired pastor, looking through designer sunglasses, nodded his head uncertainly. "Yes," he said. "What's this about?" His voice hesitated in a way that would alert the suspicious listener. To most of the viewers in that auditorium, his surprised hesitation made that famous pastor look guilty of something.

A deep, authoritative voice began to narrate. "Pastor Jack Williams acknowledges that his church supports one of the most dangerous men in California, and with no apologies."

Back to the interview, the reporter said, "Do you know, sir, that this man has more than one wife and spends much of his time partying with movie stars and rappers?"

Pastor Williams removed his sunglasses, perhaps feeling that this would make him look less dubious to whatever audience this report was designed to insight. "Well, Jesus was accused of hanging out with some pretty questionable people, as I recall," he said with a small grin.

The reporter pressed his point. "But what about the multiple sex partners, and affairs with several women?"

"I'm not aware that he has multiple sex partners, or multiple affairs," said Williams, beginning to sound a little squeakier. "I know Beau very well. And I'm not sure where you're getting these accusations."

The film cuts here to a picture of Beau Dupere with his arms around two women, with two more women flanking each of these. Dupere, the well-known healing minister, is in top form, perfectly tanned, his dark hair immaculate and his white shirt and gray suit pressed and pristine. The four women could easily be actresses or supermodels—glowing skin, brilliant smiles and luxurious hair of various shades from blonde to brunette.

The voice-over defined the picture for the viewers. "Here is a picture of Dupere with just four of his wives, or girlfriends, attending a Hollywood opening. Later they would all join the party at Daphne Kline's house, the well-known lesbian actress and liberal political activist."

Back to the handheld shot of Jack Williams, we see the pastor trying to extricate himself from the blindside questioning. "I don't have anything more to say. Good day, gentlemen." With that, he scoots inside the building, an assistant or security officer steps in front of the camera, and the shot swings wildly as if forced away.

The voiceover resumes on a picture of Beau Dupere leaning intimately close to Connie Phillips, the actress, famous for salacious movies featuring her nudity. They both hold champagne glasses. "In spite of questions about his moral character and sexual behavior, Beau Dupere continues to be featured in church meetings and special services in his home church, as well as around the world. But many of those who attend those meetings, desperately in need of help, find a rude awakening instead."

A new scene fills the screen, another hand-held shot, but this time it appears to be a cell phone or mini camera, the image less stable and the audio muffled and distorted. A throng of people crowd in close to Beau Dupere, who has shed his suit coat and pushes through the audience in his shirtsleeves, his tan face and arms prominent against his pale shirt.

The audience in Calvary church stare at the jolting images, reacting involuntarily with moans and gasps as Dupere punches a man, who collapses to the ground. The film skips a bit and we see him confronted by a ten or eleven-year-old girl, in a wheel chair, begging in a tearful voice, her hands stretched toward him. Instead of stopping, he just waves his hand at her in what appears a dismissive gesture. The girl screams and we hear her crying and shouting inarticulately as the camera follows Dupere pushing through the crowd, away from the girl. "Not only does he refuse to minister to some, but others he assaults violently," says the narrator. Again, the video skips and we see Dupere reach his hand toward the blouse of a young woman who screams and falls backward. From the viewer's angle, it seems that he may have pushed her over after sexually assaulting her.

If You Really Knew Me

"At times, he seems delirious and disoriented, as if unaware of the great crowds who think he has some hope for them." Another brief hop in the footage lands much closer to Dupere, who is muttering in an unfamiliar language. People around him are calling out and someone seems to be narrating or commentating, but we can't understand what that other man is saying, blocked out by Dupere's meaningless muttering.

The video cuts away to what seems like the same meeting, where a half dozen people squat and kneel around someone lying on the ground, weeping inconsolably. Then they show Dupere on stage, holding a microphone, waving a bundle of money and laughing. The voiceover says, "Though many receive nothing but disappointment in his meetings, Mr. Dupere has become one of the richest men in California, from the donations of desperate and deceived people." An ornate, ocean front home fills the screen, presumably Beau Dupere's home.

The scene switches next to an attractive young woman with long brown hair. "I thought he could lead me to God. But I went to his house, after he invited me there, and he just made sexual advances at me. There was only one thing he was interested in," she says, in a surge of indignation.

Back to that scene in front of Jack Williams's church: they rerun that one grinning excerpt. "Well, Jesus was accused of hanging out with some pretty questionable people." The narrator responds in a scolding tone. "And his own pastor claims his behavior is like our Lord Jesus Christ, a sad confession of blatant disrespect for the things of God."

During the video, Darryl Sampras sat with his mouth open, dodging between shock and disgust. He was shocked that he was seeing this exposé in church, at an event sponsored by *his* church, and his disgust increased at the jarring images of behavior by a man many consider to be a gifted healer. Darryl had spoken to one of his cousins recently who became pregnant after her doctors told her it was impossible. She credited a healing touch she received at one of Dupere's meetings. How could this be? How could any of this be?

Repercussions

When the video ended, Kyle barked direction to the tech crew. "Cut to the live camera feed and raise the lights." At least the prepared video ran on time, and without a glitch. Several people in the booth leaned forward to get a look at the congregation as the lights returned. Even in the booth, they heard crying from several points in the auditorium. At least a dozen people stood and stormed up the aisles, using their feet to communicate what they thought of the video.

In the auditorium, Claire Sanchez sat with her hands over her mouth. She watched as an African American woman she didn't know stomped up the aisle saying something that included, "my Jesus doesn't come to meetings like this." A small girl, with braids down her back, bounced along behind, her hand gripped tightly by the retreating woman.

Dixon Claiborne stood at the microphone by the time the lights revived, ready to direct the agitation inflicted by the video. "I do apologize for the offensive images of this man's behavior. I didn't want to see any of that either. But we must be aware of false teachers in our churches. The Lord himself said that in the last days, people would come along claiming to prophesy and heal in his name, and he says to them, 'I never knew you: depart from me, ye that work iniquity.'" He surveyed his congregation with eyes like polished stone, his jaw set, hands gripping the edge of the podium. "How could our holy God respond any other way to behavior like this?"

A murmur swept across the crowd. One man, to Dixon's left, stood up and shouted, "This is not appropriate among God's people. This is the work of the Devil, the Accuser!" Hands reached for him, as if to pull back into his seat. Ushers ran down both aisles that bordered that section.

Dixon leaned into the podium, his mouth on top of the microphone. "There's no need for us to accuse anyone, his own actions and his own words condemn him." He looked at the disgruntled man, who was now being tugged up the aisle by three ushers. Then his eyes swept across the crowd. "And our task here is only to warn you, our people, to stay clear of this man and those who associate with him. We make no accusation against those who have attended his meetings, or even those who claim that they have been healed by his hand. We only unite here today to warn you to protect yourselves, to stay clear of those who seek to soil the name of our God and King, our holy Lord and Savior and his precious church."

Dixon stood up straight, his head high, and looked down at the gathered crowd, like a father laying down the law and waiting to see acceptance reflected back. Hundreds of heads nodded in affirmation of the warning, in support of keeping the church pure. Still more sat in stunned stillness, not yet recovered from the affront of the video images.

For Claire, that shocked silence sheltered an internal voice which was noting the way the video evidence had been edited. She had attended a couple of healing services such as Dupere and his home church hosted, she knew they could appear strange and dramatic to an outsider like her. A conversation with a coworker who invited her once to such a meeting resurfaced from her mental archives. "The proof of his ministry is the fruit, the results," said her friend, Pam. "People getting well, glorifying God and devoting their lives to God's service because of their experience." This was Pam's response to Claire questioning why people cried out and fell down in the meeting she attended. Though her friend's explanation seemed reassuring, she had declined all subsequent invitations to similar meetings. In her mind, this expression of God's work in the world was just not for her, but she felt very uncomfortable having to decide whether it was wrong for anyone else.

She could imagine ways that the meeting she had attended could have been filmed, and that film edited, to create damning evidence in the minds of outsiders. On the other hand, counter to her internal hesitation, she wondered whether Pastor Claiborne and his colleagues knew more specifics, which caused them to issue so clear an indictment. And she did have to admit that some of the images she saw in the video would be disturbing in any context.

For Jonathan Opare, however, the cultural context for his evaluation of the meeting's agenda had to cross oceans, as well as a big religious divide. In fact, he had attended hundreds of meetings in his life that included scenes similar to some of those offered as video evidence against Beau Dupere. He would have to be convinced of the veracity of *all* of the shocking claims before he could comfortably remain in Dixon Claiborne's church. For him, the confrontational style of the meeting had spun the focus toward the behavior of his own pastor, instead of Beau Dupere. To Jonathan, making unfounded accusations against another Christian was at least as inappropriate as the actions for which Pastor Claiborne judged Mr. Dupere.

Most of the silent majority sitting wide-eyed in that meeting did not ascend to rational considerations as clearly as Claire and Jonathan. Many of them slogged through the miry path that the video laid down and Dixon's words reinforced. They saw no solid ground within reach. Stuck in an emotional reaction to the video evidence, most people swung wildly for any handhold, like a falling climber flailing to clasp anything. Whether he understood this in advance or not, Dixon's conclusions from the video evidence offered most of the shocked audience this sort of desperate vine to grab.

Another pastor, Tim Hanneman, followed Dixon to the podium, providing action items for those unclear about how to respond to the video and Dixon's call to arms. He pointed attendees to a Website, with a catchy name, from which to gather more information, and to track the united effort to warn the church at large about the threat of Beau Dupere.

To the left of the speakers, down in the front row, another woman listened to all this and considered whether she should storm out of the meeting. But, since she was the wife of the meeting's lead organizer, Kristen remained magnetized to her seat. She had been hoping that the full revelation presented in the meeting would relieve her fears and doubts about the wisdom of this campaign. Instead, her insides churned over how her husband could forget that Brett and other children his age would witness the harsh and revolting video images. How could he ignore the traumatic impact of his shock tactics, as if his lofty intentions would cover them in grace?

Though these considerations ran deep, it took only thirty seconds for Kristen to riffle through her options, and she chose the one that her husband would have expected, if he had paused to expect anything. She folded what she saw, along with her emotional response, down into a small tight packet, small enough to fit into one of the little offering envelopes stocked in the pews of her home church. She put that little packet away in her heart for now, to look at some other time, some undefined future time.

Sitting next to her, Sara would have worried about the colors her mother was turning beneath her makeup, if she wasn't feeling bound hand and foot by the unimaginable thing she had just seen; not only in the video, but in the way the video was thrown at her, like the contents of a kitchen garbage can that hadn't been emptied in weeks.

Brett...well, Brett loved it. He could sense the rising war that lay ahead, and looked forward to more new experiences and eureka revelations like the one he witnessed in the video of Beau Dupere. The always-guilty child inside Brett relished the prospect that his parents would be honed in on someone else's misbehavior for a change.

The meeting ended with a few more disruptions quelled by the ushers, and *A Mighty Fortress is Our God,* sung by choir and congregation. Though the size of the crowd wasn't greatly diminished by those who stormed out, or who were ushered up the

If You Really Knew Me

aisles, that final triumphant hymn lacked the gusto of the earlier music.

Dixon didn't notice this. His mind had shifted forward to his press conference following the meeting. And the professional reporters packed into the front of the auditorium seemed just as anxious to move on to that part of the evening, a whirl—like fall leaves in a heavy breeze—rippled across the phalanx of media representatives, as they used the sound cover of the final song to comment to each other and gather notes for questions.

There was a closing prayer, but no one remembered it later, not even the elderly host pastor who spoke it.

Just One More Question Please

Dixon Claiborne stood surrounded by the other association ministers in attendance. A bottle of water gripped in his big right hand, Dixon absently twisted the cap on with his left, as the first question from a reporter reached him at the podium.

"Do you have proof of your claims that Beau Dupere is living with, or even married to, multiple women?"

Nodding before he spoke, Dixon jumped in. "If you go to the Web site we indicated during the meeting, you will see eye witness accounts of behavior that proves that, yes. There's people there that have seen him romantically, or maybe intimately, engaged with at least three of these women, and it seems like there's more than just three."

"How does his arrangement compare to Hugh Hefner's girlfriends?" the same reporter said.

Now shaking his head, Dixon shrugged and said, "Well, I can't tell you anything at all about Mr. Hefner. I'm not a fan of his." His volume faded toward the end of that response, turning away from the microphone and looking at his fellow ministers. At least one skeptical reporter wondered if Dixon was looking for one of the ministers who actually *was* a fan of Hugh Hefner. No one volunteered.

Dixon tried to recover. "We're not here to say anything for or against anyone who's outside of the church, anyone who's not supported by a church and a respected pastor. Our concern is a church that supports this man, and a man that claims to be a minister of the Gospel, whose behavior is not at all Christ-like."

A young woman in the front row, with big tortoise-shell glasses, raised her hand first, but Dixon bypassed her and took another question from a reporter with one of the major news networks, pointing his water bottle at the man before realizing what he was doing. He set the bottle on the podium in front of him while he listened to the question.

"Are you aware of members of your own congregation that are going to meetings that Dupere holds, or who are following his teachings?"

Dixon quickly looked to his right, knowing Ken Bennington had something to say to this, the pastor of the local Assemblies of God congregation. Pastor Bennington, a slim man with dark hair and a pinched nose, squeezed ahead of Dixon and spoke into the microphone.

"I think that most of us are aware of somebody in our churches that has attended his meetings. I particularly have talked to maybe half a dozen people who thought this man was a legitimate minister of the Gospel, and I had to fill them in on the truth about Beau Dupere."

Aside from the video, no one in the meeting had yet pronounced Beau Dupere's name, until that statement. This reflected the preparations for the event, intended to provide the wealthy healer as little free airtime as possible. Dixon glanced at Ken Bennington, who kept his eyes trained on the far wall, to avoid that indicting look from his fellow pastor. He knew that he had slipped off the script.

Again, that young woman in the front row raised her hand, this time more quickly, as if grabbing a fly out of midair. However, Dixon called on someone else, a mannequin-like woman from a local network affiliate.

"Pastor Claiborne, have you confronted Mr. Dupere himself about these accusations? The financial improprieties, the sexual questions, and the legitimacy of his healing claims?"

For a moment, Dixon floated on the syrupy thick tone of that reporter's alto voice, which sounded as good in person as on the nightly news. He had to break away from the momentary hypnosis prompted by her big blue eyes, and curvaceous lashes, to answer.

"Ah, yes, some of us have tried to talk to him, to tell him of our concerns, on several occasions. He fails to take us seriously, I'd say. And, in some instances, he doesn't even bother to deny our claims, just laughing them off as if they don't matter."

That young woman in the front row scribbled in her notebook when she heard the low, introspective voice and saw the distant gaze Dixon fixed while answering. "He seems to be remembering a particular conversation, or conversations," she wrote.

Another reporter received the nod from Dixon, before that young reporter finished writing and could raise her hand again.

"How do you intend to carry this campaign forward from here? Do you plan any kind of action, legal or otherwise, against Mr. Dupere or his church?"

Dixon scowled at the word "campaign," and then yielded the microphone to Bishop Jefferson.

"This is not a campaign, not the formation of any kind of organization, nor the launch of legal action. Rather, this is the effort of a group of united servants of God to alert our fellow believers, even beyond our own flocks and our own city, that there is a predator loose among us—that danger is near." He spoke with his head lifted high and his voice as undulating as the California coastline. "We are issuing a warning, and certainly we will continue to issue warnings, in hopes that good people will make wise choices, and the integrity of the body of Jesus Christ will be restored."

As he listened, Dixon's face shifted from raised eyebrows that bespoke admiration for the articulate bishop, to squinted eyes and a lower lip clenched under his upper teeth. That young reporter in the front row wondered whether Dixon's look was from concern about Beau Dupere, or concern that the golden-tongued bishop was stealing the show? When Dixon regained the microphone, and terminated the press conference, he seemed to confirm her suspicions. Several of the ministers cast squinting inquiries in the direction of their quarterback, but none spoke up to question the play call.

Anna Conyers, that young reporter in the front row, folded her notebook shut and turned to look at a sound engineer next to her. His fuzzy microphone, like the tail of some arctic beast, had brushed against her cheek and she recoiled from the tickle.

"Sorry," said the engineer, reeling in his mic cable and telescoping in the boom.

Anna just waved a hand at him and continued to stare down her little nose through her big glasses, as if a replay of the press conference ran on a small screen there. Though Dixon had shut her out, she was determined to ask her questions, and she wouldn't limit her interviews to only the accusers.

Show Me Where it Hurts

In downtown Chicago, in May, the midday sun warming the uneven pavement between the shoppers and commuters on Michigan Avenue, Beau Dupere settled his sunglasses on his nose. He had finished lunch at a pricey bistro located on that

If You Really Knew Me

prime strip of real estate. He wore pale khaki slacks and a medium-blue dress shirt. His thick hair ruffled in the lake breeze, but an expensive haircut and a moderate amount of gel kept his signature look in place. Next to him stood a much younger man, his son, Ben, who had also donned his sunglasses against the clear spring day. Ben followed his father's gaze up and down the street. He knew that the free time before their flight home would fill up soon, and just waited to see how.

Two middle-aged men in suits approached, apparently arguing about something, though they seemed to be at ease with each other, the intensity of their voices and gestures reaching a low ceiling before settling down. Ben glanced at his dad who nodded. Turning back toward the two men, Ben stepped in their path, as if he might be heading for the curb and a taxi cab. This slowed them down and distracted them from their conversation briefly. Beau seized the opportunity to address them.

"Pardon us, gentlemen," he said, with the precise confidence of upper level management, even as he looked like he might be on the way to the country club. He raised one hand chest high, holding up one finger. "You mind if I ask you something?" he said, removing his sunglasses, as if they had been a mere prop put in place just for this smoothly executed gesture.

The older and thinner of the two, a balding man with an orange complexion, looked at Beau as if he anticipated a sales pitch. Looking like a successful salesmen, Beau was used to that response. "Oh, don't worry, I'm not gonna try to sell you something," he said with a chuckle that seemed to settle both men. The second man, in his late forties, with slicked-back blonde hair and a gray, designer suit, studied Beau, as if trying to recall how he recognized him.

Looking at the first man, Beau said, "I believe you have liver cancer, and have been in remission until just recently. Is that right?"

The man cocked his head back one notch, raising his nose. Now *he* studied Beau more closely. "Do I know you?"

"Not yet," Beau said with a smile. "But you will after I kill off that cancer for you."

"What?" the man said, his voice sharper now.

Ben stepped up. "He can do it. He does stuff like that all the time." He too removed his sunglasses as he spoke, revealing his smiling hazel green eyes.

Compared to Beau, Ben seemed like an All-American Midwestern boy, his tan face under a neatly cropped head of golden brown hair. He was dressed similarly to his father, with gray slacks and a lighter blue shirt that highlighted his bright eyes.

"Kill my cancer?" the man said. His voice had turned from skeptical to plaintive in those few seconds.

"I'm Beau," the smiling healer said.

"Roger," the man said, offering his hand.

As Beau shook hands he hung on for an extra second. "Feel some heat starting?" He pointed toward Roger's midsection.

Roger looked down, glanced at his friend, and then said, "I do feel a strange heat, like inside." His eyebrows rose above his slim glasses and he looked a question at Beau.

"That's what it feels like when cancer gets healed," he said. No intensity or unusual inflection accompanied those words, as if what he said was as indisputable as a second doctor's opinion about that cancer's existence.

Roger reached for his stomach, just below his rib cage. "I don't know what it is, but it really feels good."

Just then his friend swore as he stared at Roger's face.

Roger shifted his attention to his friend, though he kept his hand in place, along with the smile that had begun to bloom. "What are you looking at?" he said, with a slight chuckle.

"Your face...your skin color...it just changed. You look like your old self all the sudden."

Ben and Beau had seen the change too and traded smiles at the truth the other two men had just begun to accept.

Roger stared, his smile falling slack, his mouth open an inch, as if waiting for words he expected to come out. He closed his mouth and started shaking his head. "Are you sure about this?"

If You Really Knew Me

His eyes begged for rescue, as he turned to Beau with questions bigger than what he could formulate just then.

A couple in their twenties stood a few feet away watching and trying to listen unobtrusively.

"I'm sure," Beau said. "You're healed." Sympathy softened his usual confident voice.

With that, the eves dropping couple found their confirmation. "Hey, you're that guy that heals people," the young man said, stepping forward and pulling out his smart phone, as if his hand moved of its own volition.

Even as he moved into position to start filming the four men, he said, "I'm gonna put this video online."

Beau looked at him, smiled and said, "No, I don't think so." As he said that, the young man's hand dropped, though he still clung to his phone. He started to shake from head to toe. "Have a good rest," Beau said, grabbing the young man's empty hand. Ben, apparently ready for such an eventuality, stepped forward quickly, grabbing the guy's other arm, and helped lower him slowly to the ground.

As the young man rested on the pavement, in what seemed like a peaceful seizure, Beau reassured his girlfriend. "He'll be okay. He'll be like that for a few minutes." Then, as he stood up straight, Beau added an afterthought. "And tonight he's gonna realize it's time he finally asked you to marry him."

The girl nodded rapidly, apparently ready to agree with anything Beau said, perhaps hoping not to meet the same fate as her boyfriend. She squatted next to him and glanced back at Beau. "Okay," she said. Then she added, "And thank you."

Beau nodded, as if he knew why she was thanking him, and turned back to Roger and his friend. "We should go somewhere we can talk, before a crowd gathers," he said.

The two men were as agreeable as the stunned girl.

Roger's friend, James, led the way to a bar up the street half a block, the dark interior cave-like compared to the bright midday. There, the four men would talk for nearly two hours about healing and about God. Even then, Beau didn't have to try to sell anyone anything, he just answered all the questions that Roger's instant healing raised. And that conversation spread beyond the little round table, scattered with a handful of beer glasses. The other half dozen afternoon patrons either beat a hasty retreat or leaned closer to listen, until they finally pulled their chairs over. As new customers stepped inside, they made the same choice, either flight or yielding to the magnet of that intense conversation.

Who Stays? Who Goes?

Claire Sanchez hunkered into the embrace of the worn, yellow velour chair, her navy business suit humbled by her wrinkle-producing perch. She noticed none of it. Instead, she strained to excavate the words from the muffled rumble of voices behind the pastor's door. A church denominational magazine in her lap disguised her full attention focused on those voices. The tone said a lot, even if she couldn't discern the vocabulary.

Pastor Claiborne rolled a battalion of defenders over a hill and into the valley, defense turning into full assault, but without artillery. Pastor Sampras offered surrender, and then added a caveat and withdrew his white flag, though still not firing a shot. An uninitiated listener would not have been surprised at which of those voices belonged to the senior pastor, the boss in this exchange.

Of course, Claire knew for certain what they were discussing, she just couldn't yet discern the color of the smoke from their fire, nor decide whether the result would call for an insurance adjuster or barbeque sauce.

If You Really Knew Me

Connie cleared her throat like a '58 Chevy trying to start in winter. Claire realized too late that the church secretary had caught her eyes drifting in the direction that her ears had already been straining. She grinned a mute apology at Connie and returned to her imitation of reading a church magazine.

The unmistakable sound of winding down, if not the sound of reconciliation, vibrated through that oak door, as Darryl Sampras approached it and Dixon Claiborne's voice followed. Claire intensified her *I'm-definitely-interested-in-this-article* act and still listened as the door opened and she heard two clear words not intended for her ears.

". . . another job." That was the end of the sentence spoken by Dixon over Darryl's shoulder, as the assistant huffed through the office door and vanquished the distance to the reception door in three steps, his head down, his face red and his fists clenched. Claire felt she knew the rest of that sentence.

Following Darryl's exit, led Claire's gaze across Connie's desk. There, she found the secretary reproducing her own feigned magazine interest with her perusal of visitor cards stacked next to her keyboard. Connie's version, however, included rapid breathing and a tense shaking of her head, which seemed to be mounted on a spring that had been set in motion by Darryl's stride through the office.

Both Connie and Claire had to decide how to follow that exit. Claire relieved Connie of having to measure how long to wait until announcing the presence of Dixon's next appointment. Claire stood up, dropped the magazine onto the pile on the end table next to her and mumbled something about forgetting something somewhere else. The second exit settled some of the dust stirred by the first, and Connie breathed easier.

The intercom on Connie's phone chirped like a drowning bird and Dixon's voice materialized out of wire and plastic.

"Ah, Connie, let me know when that reporter from *U.S. News* is here, will ya?"

"Of course, as soon as he gets here," she said, her voice sounding more frightened than she intended, like it might have sounded if she suddenly discovered that the intercom system reached into the women's bathroom.

"Ah, thanks Connie," Dixon said, oblivious to the micro dramas swirling out from his grand drama.

So How Do I Find this Guy?

Anna Conyers sat in her Honda Civic holding her small reporter's notebook in her right hand, her left hand pressing a blue ballpoint pen to the paper, the ink remaining poised in its cylinder as she drifted away from the dusty dashboard and cluttered carpet, back to the press conference. She had just realized what had been missing. Beau Dupere. His name was everywhere except in the mouths of his accusers. Did they fear speaking the syllables? Did they fear some nefarious consequence to uttering that name, ricocheting their fire off his bulletproof surface and into themselves?

The man did look bulletproof, so shiny and unscathed, seemingly unmarked by life. Yet he had to be over fifty years old, from what she could gather. Fifty? She stalled at that thought. From there she drifted further afield.

She thought about how much she would rather spend an evening with Beau Dupere than with those self-righteous preachers. Of course, that must be what they hate about him, his looks, his money, his women.

What about those women?

Instantly, she was back to being the reporter who graduated from Northwestern University, with full feminist credentials.

If You Really Knew Me

What about those women? Who are they? What do *they* think of Beau Dupere? Or of his coterie of conservative accusers? That would be her story. Now all she had to do was find out where they lived.

As she discovered, the history of Beau Dupere's real estate was both fascinating and baffling. The oldest address she found placed him in an apartment in Lawrence, Kansas, where he lived with two friends after college. There, he worked with one of those roommates at his uncle's shipping pallet business. That was some cheap real estate.

The next address she could find was Aurora, Colorado, from back when that town was still mostly in the planning stages, in the 1980s, not the billowing metropolis it is now. That apartment, he shared with his brother, who had been released from jail and needed someone to keep an eye on him while he cast around for something to do other than sell marijuana. She couldn't tell what Beau did for work in those days, but found mention of his attendance of a trendy new church.

In fact, that church affiliation connected Dupere to California, transporting him the distance across half the continent, but still not moving him up to his present posh lifestyle. His first place of residence that she could find in Redwood, California, was the basement of a church pastor, as if that was the best the poor drifter from the Midwest could do. The first sign of some kind of career followed: a stint as the manager of a Denny's restaurant, full benefits and a pathway to advancement included. Still, he lived in that basement next to the church, which met in a converted warehouse. The church was on the wrong side of the train tracks, tracks that had once rolled lumber and then prospectors during the last dregs of the gold rush.

Beau Dupere was thirty-two years old before he owned his first house, and that was given him by his deceased grandmother. That she selected him of all his relatives to receive this crown of her legacy deepened his alienation from parents and siblings. And it moved him south toward L.A. That move corresponded with a new church started by Dupere and a few of his friends, a sort of franchise of that warehouse church in Redwood.

Here, she found the first mention of Beau Dupere in conjunction with healing someone. That appeared to be his occasional role in this new church. This was also where she found the first mention of his wife, the one listed legally as his wife, that is—Justine. Interesting that he would marry a woman with a French first name, Anna thought.

When children entered the housing picture, the real estate increased in size and value, in the early 1990s. In those days, Dupere worked his way up in a financial brokerage firm, more of a meteoric rise, really, especially given his lack of formal training. A bachelor's degree in history, from Kansas University, doesn't generally land you in the big office with windows and secretarial support. By all accounts, Beau Dupere had a sort of sixth sense about investments, benefitting himself, as well as his clients, with prescient moves that prompted several investigations into insider trading. He was never actually indicted.

Even with his financial success, the real estate only grew at a pace with the family's needs, as far as Anna could tell. This pattern held until more recently, when Beau Dupere suddenly appeared on the list of California's billionaires. Exactly how, Anna couldn't tell any better than the few financial reporters who had tried to pin this down. One Internet rumor claimed that Dupere had once collected the largest multistate lottery ever awarded to an individual winner, another claimed that he financed an expedition that found the most significant cache of colonial Spanish gold in the Caribbean. Others merely traced a lattice work of investments which escalated his worth in boom years, as well as during downturns.

This is when the Dupere family moved to the cliff-top Malibu estate that Dixon Claiborne and friends now eyed with Puritanical disapproval. During this period, as well, he transitioned from finance to healing, his only apparent employment being a church staff position in a Malibu church affiliated with the other churches he had helped found.

Anna frowned at these "church staff" references and an accompanying lack of preaching or other traditional church professional responsibilities assigned to Beau. Justine, on the other hand, did appear on recorded media preaching or teaching at that progressive West Coast church. She made a name for herself as a teacher, but was generally overshadowed by spectacular claims regarding Beau's healing powers.

Looking at an aerial view of their Malibu mansion, Anna tried to picture herself chatting cozily with the residents. She sighed and closed her Web browser, adding a few more clicks, until she had shut down her laptop.

"Well, I hope they take my interview," she said, as if adjusting herself to the proper professional goal for her contact with the controversial healer.

I Was Hungry and You Gave . . .

At LAX, Beau Dupere stood with his daughter, Joanna. She looked up at the list of arrivals and departures, checking to see that their flight was on time. They had arrived earlier than expected and she could sense her father scoping the people around him for a target.

"You're not gonna make us late again with some spectacular healing, followed by a huge revival, are you?" A hint of strained tolerance in her voice, she lowered her head and looked at her dad under her carefully plucked eyebrows.

Beau saw that look, reflected it back for a second and then burst out laughing. "Would I ever do a thing like that to you, Jo Jo?" He swung close to her and wrapped a muscular arm around her shoulders. She allowed his strength to fold her frame like the

If You Really Knew Me

baby gate they used to keep at the top of the basement stairs when the kids were small. Then she laughed too.

"Hey, I was only thirteen. I didn't have much patience back then," she said.

"Umhmm. And now, six years later, you still remind me of it every time we wait in an airport."

"Yeah, which is a lot of times," she said. "I should check my frequent flyer miles." Beau loved all his children, of course, but Joanna, whom her mother called "Jo," was the one who at least pretended to resist his charisma.

"Tell you what," Beau said, "I won't approach anyone from here to Toronto."

Joanna stepped away from him to look up into his face. They started walking toward their gate, and she said, "This will be something I'll have to see to believe, it would be like fasting for you."

Again, Beau laughed, as they dodged through multivalent traffic in the big sunny terminal. Then Joanna thought of something.

"Wait, are you promising not to *approach* anyone because you know that someone is gonna approach you?"

Great, full-chested laughter splashed toward the distant ceiling and walls, diluted in the expanse of the airport. Beau's children knew him well. They had all travelled with him on various ministry trips for the last ten years. At first, it was to expose them to his work, and to protect him from temptation. He had to travel with someone, to more easily resist the many invitations from lonely women, and even a few men. He knew that travelling with his kids would keep his attention where it belonged. More recently, his children provided added healing power to his meetings, having apprenticed under the master.

"*I* know," Beau said, when they reached their gate, "let's hide somewhere that no one is likely to find us. You pick the spot."

For Joanna, this seemed a twisted game. She was fairly sure that her father had received some advanced insight into what was going to happen in the next hour or so before boarding their

If You Really Knew Me

flight, or after they boarded their flight, for that matter. If he already knew, then hiding might play right into that plan. As she thought about it, Joanna realized that she didn't mind so much getting side-tracked by someone receiving their hearing or eyesight. Maybe it was just the feeling of unpredictability, the sensation of falling without even so much as a bungee cord to soften the eventual landing. Rather than solve the conundrum about whether hiding would actually make them easier for the appointed person to find, she just decided to play along.

"Okay, I'll choose the spot," she said, looking around. She found an empty waiting area where the next scheduled flight was a few hours off. It seemed the least likely place for a chance encounter, even one that wasn't really up to chance.

Beau dutifully pointed his forehead in that direction and followed his daughter's clip-clop sandal steps across the concourse. Joanna plunked her brown leather shoulder bag on one of the gray seats, landing herself next to it. She let one sandal stay on the floor as she pulled a leg up under her and looked out the window at crews preparing jets for boarding. Beau headed for a seat across from her, his back to the window. But, before he sat down, Joanna protested.

"Hey, you can't sit there facing all the people streaming by." She sounded like a ten-year-old protecting the sanctity of a board game's rules.

"Oops," Beau said with a smile. "Caught me cheating."

"That's right. You sit over here and look out at those planes. They won't recognize you and you probably won't see some airplane ailment they need healed." Then she added, "I hope."

As he sat down, Beau imitated a clairvoyant he had seen once. He closed his eyes, pressed a thumb and finger to his forehead and said, "Oh, I think someone here has a wing that needs healing." Then he opened his eyes and gestured toward the line of planes beyond the window. "What d'ya know?"

Joanna shook her head and rolled her eyes, but the adolescent gesture aborted before landing back on her father. A

If You Really Knew Me

movement on the other side of the row of chairs closest to the window interrupted her. A man dressed in an old black suitcoat pressed himself up to a sitting position and attempted to regulate his twisted tassel of hair. Joanna's first thought was a movie about a man who lived at the airport awaiting clearance to return to his war-torn country. Then she realized that a dozen real-life scenarios might explain someone sleeping in the boarding area of a flight scheduled several hours later in the day. The third wave of reactions turned to what sort of healing this man needed. She had chosen this unoccupied space to hide, only to find that it was, in fact, occupied. Glancing at her father, she tried to assess his interest in the stranger. Beau sat looking at the planes and a crew of baggage handlers loading an airliner two gates down, at least pretending not to have noticed the disheveled man.

As she might have predicted, however, the man stood up and walked to where Beau could not ignore him, standing directly in his line of sight and facing him across the row of seats. The man said something to her father in broken English.

"I sorry to bother you, sir, but I am need and must ask help from some . . ." His voice faded as he searched for the right word, weariness dragging him below the energy horizon he needed to humble himself and beg in a foreign language.

Beau looked him full in the face with a winning smile. "I'm sure I can help."

Anyone who has been on either end of an attempt to solicit a handout, will recognize the break from expectations embodied in Beau's open promise. The weary beggar didn't seem to have a follow up to such a transcontinental offer. But, then, he didn't seem to have perfected the craft of panhandling yet either.

"You . . . you will . . . you will help? But I not say what help I . . ."

For Joanna, the reason for the question was as obvious as the reason for the unusual response. Though she couldn't tell you exactly how rich, she knew her father was voluminously wealthy and could easily meet the financial needs of anyone they

If You Really Knew Me

could find in that airport. She had also been present once when her father raised a man from the dead, at a healing service in Mexico City. For her father, sickness, death and poverty were enemies, enemies he didn't fear, but rather expected to flee before him.

"I will tell you what you need, and if I'm right you will let me meet that need and a few others as well," Beau said.

"You tell me?"

Beau nodded. He seemed confident that the man understood English better than he spoke it, so he spoke like he would to any neighbor he might meet at the local latte shop. "You are trying to get to Ottawa, but your wallet was stolen and all that was recovered was your I.D. So now you can fly but you have no ticket and no money. And the reason you're going to Ottawa is because your wife is already there with your kids. You had to stay behind in Los Angeles for a few days, to meet a cousin who was going to help you make a business contact. Your wife's mother is sick, so she couldn't wait and took the kids ahead of you."

It was fascinating to Joanna to watch a human face spill incredulity from each orifice. First, the needy traveler's eyes stopped moving, even blinking. Then his lips parted, and his jaw began to lower like the cargo door of a giant jet, huge hydraulic pistons slowly dropping it to the ground. Next, his nose twitched and then began to run, as tears overwhelmed the listener even before he felt their approach. Finally, the desperate man's eyes blinked and then blinked repeatedly, as if batting away impossibility, in a desperate stretch to embrace the unimaginable.

Beau stood up and reached over the double row of seats between them, addressing the man by name. "Ahmed Naser, I'm Beau Dupere. God has sent me to help you."

Ahmed grabbed his face with both hands, just as grievous gratitude exploded from his eyes and mouth. He relinquished half that hold on his face to take Beau's hand and hang on, as if certain that he would sink down through the floor if he let go. Joanna was sniffling ardently by this time, overwhelmed by sympathy for Ahmed and by renewed wonder at the goodness of God.

When he did finally let go, Ahmed pulled at his jacket lapels and ruffle his mop of hair. He grabbed his tangled beard with both hands and seemed to be trying to pull it off his face, oblivious to what anyone might think. Finally, he crumpled to the ground, his elbows landing on the seats in front of him, his face ensconced in his hands again.

Joanna just shook her head, her eyes dazed, her mouth open and wordless. She had tumbled well beyond the little game that had drawn them to this place.

Ahmed wobbled up to his feet and reached his hand out to Beau again. "Thanks you, brother. You have save my life," he said, a spasm rocking his chest as he recovered from his shock. "You speak my life to me, so I know God has send you to help me."

Beau smiled and nodded, shaking that offered hand. "Yes. God is good."

"God is good," said Ahmed in solemn agreement.

For the next few minutes, Beau gathered information about Ahmed's specific needs. To meet them, they used Beau's and Joanna's smart phones, without any apparent angelic intervention. Not only did Beau purchase the ticket for Ahmed, he gave him all the cash he was carrying in his own wallet, equivalent to a year's wages where Ahmed came from, though not in Canada, where he was headed. Beau also gave Ahmed the name of someone to contact for help getting work once he arrived north of the border.

As Joanna watched the final transactions of this linguistically challenged relationship, she felt a twinge of guilt for her earlier objections to being inconvenienced in the past, even if those objections were as mild as oatmeal. She remembered the blessings in which her life had been showered and relaxed into forgiveness with a silent prayer.

But she didn't let her guilt cloud the wonder of what had happened when God found them where they were hiding and brought them a stranger who needed his help. She grinned at her father, eyes shining with admiration, as if she were a little girl all over again.

A Walk Around the Pool

It took three days of calling contacts, and contacts of contacts, before Anna found a number for the Dupere household. She had tried just showing up at the gate, but two very large, and entirely unmovable guards—in their black pants, black t-shirts and close-cropped hair—sent her away. It wasn't hard to understand their vigilance. On the road, across from the driveway entrance, two dozen protesters chanted and waved signs. The boldly printed slogans said, "Come Clean Mr. Dupere" and "Repent of Your Sin." More obscure to Anna were the signs that merely read, "II Peter 2:2." She had to search the Internet for an explanation, something about depravity and false prophets.

But the protesters were not the only ones trying to get to Beau Dupere. On the driveway, by special dispensation from the guards, a half dozen supplicants begged for Beau Dupere to come out and heal them.

The taller of the guards confided to Anna, when she asked about this mournful lot. "Sometimes he actually comes out and heals them." Her arched eyebrows and downturned mouth bespoke her surprise. She still had questions about whether this enigmatic church leader really *could* heal people.

When she finally did reach the Dupere household by phone, it was Justine that eventually spoke with her.

"Hi, Mrs. Dupere. This is Anna Conyers of Western Horizon News. I was trying to get an interview with Mr. Dupere, to get his side of the story, in light of the public criticism against him."

"Public?" Justine sounded less surprised than simply unfamiliar with the reference.

"Dixon Claiborne, and his coalition of pastors, calling for Christians to stay clear of your husband, because of a list of misdeeds they claim..."

"We don't pay attention to that sort of thing. There's too much to do for us to take time away to figure out what the critics are saying. Nothing good ever comes of that," said Justine, still lacking any interest—let alone emotion—in her tone. "But let me ask Beau and I'll call you right back."

Anna agreed, of course. She breathed a sigh when her cell phone rang ten minutes later.

"He says you should come over tomorrow after lunch," Justine said, skipping any kind of greeting. "Can you do that, say around one in the afternoon?"

"Sure," Anna said, knowing that any conflict with her schedule would just have to disappear.

At home that night, in front of her bathroom mirror, Anna looked at her dull brown hair, her too big glasses and pale, blotchy face. She started to pluck at the three stray whiskers that had reappeared near the corners of her mouth and wondered whether she had time for a haircut in the morning. Though she ignored her own internal inquiries as to *why*, she wanted to make a good impression on Beau Dupere. She pictured a warm smile on his tan face, his perfect white teeth sparkling like a sugarless gum commercial. Then her inner editor broke free from the handcuffs and gag and shouted, "What are you doing? He's a married man, maybe several times over."

Anna cursed, as the last of her dark brown facial hairs popped free from her grimacing lip. She dropped the tweezers and leaned on the sink, scowling at herself—the dreamer facing off with the critic, ready for a no-holds-barred round.

The next morning, Anna forgot about the hair cut when she found out that Beau Dupere was to be in Toronto that night, and had left for the airport. She discovered this by accident, doing an Internet search for recent news on Beau. She found a religious news service clip of his rented limo pulling past the protesters with their "II Peter 2:2" signs.

On her third try, she reached Justine by phone again, having squeezed past the gauntlet of assistants and other unidentified female voices. "I thought I had an appointment to see Mr. Dupere this afternoon," Anna said, trying to tamp down the whine in her voice.

"Hmmm. Yeah, actually, he thought you would like to talk to some of us first. He's coming back in two days. He'll be glad to talk to you then," said Justine.

"Some of us?" Some of who? Anna wondered. *Some of "us" wives?*

Justine filled in the silence. "You do want to find out what's going on in this house, right?"

Anna hadn't said anything like that, which made her wonder whether Justine had been bluffing about ignoring the critics. She must have found what Claiborne and the others were saying, in order to figure out what Anna would be investigating. But, then, that alone wouldn't fill in as much as Justine seemed to be assuming.

This time, Anna answered, before Justine could bump the conversation again. "Yes, in fact, I would like to meet with you and some of the...others," she said.

"Good," Justine said. "That's what Beau thought. See you at one?"

"Sure," Anna said, trying to hike a bit of friendliness up over her consternation.

At five minutes past one, Anna sat in her gray Civic looking up at the expansive chest of guard number two. He leaned down and smiled at her, holding a cell phone to his ear. "Yes, they're expecting you." He maintained that grin as he hung up the call

If You Really Knew Me

and motioned for his partner to open the gate. Anna offered a three-quarters smile in return, trying to disentangle from that All-American face looking in her window. When she turned toward the humming gate that was patiently swinging inward, she thought, "I'm pathetically lonely. There's no way around it."

Parking her car under a palm tree in the circular courtyard, in front of the huge Mediterranean style home, Anna climbed out and then had to duck back in to grab her purse. When she swung the leather bag over her shoulder, she fished out the digital recorder with which she hoped to capture the interview. As usual, her hands shook with the same nerves that constricted her breathing. On a good interview, these nerves would dissipate. During a contentious interview, they would generate adrenalin that usually helped her form challenging questions and keep pressing her point. Not knowing which kind of experience lay ahead of her added to the jitters.

Before she had even stepped onto the front porch, the eight-foot-high door swung open, and a woman slightly taller than the petite reported stepped out into the shade provided by the house. "Anna?" the woman said, smiling as if she were greeting a welcomed guest.

Anna nodded and took the offered hand, almost as thin as hers but much more tan, and bejeweled with diamonds that Anna could only dream of owning.

"I'm Justine," the greeter said, wrapping her other arm around Anna's waist. This maneuver seemed natural to Justine, but made Anna's skin crawl. Here, she confronted her unspoken dread that she would be captured by the bizarre polygamous cult that she feared occupied this house.

Justine sensed Anna's tension immediately and quickly slipped her hand free of Anna's waist, as she gestured toward the door. "Come on in. Can I get you something to drink? Water? Juice?"

Anna was thinking whisky, but kept that to herself.

"Water would be nice," she said. Over the years of interviewing people in their homes, Anna had discovered that accepting an offer of water generally helped reduce the tension of having a stranger in the house. It helped her subjects think of her more as a guest. But she already felt Justine's friendly welcome, with her gently stroking touches and sunshine smiles. Anna just hoped she was a guest that had the option to leave when they were done talking.

As Justine led her across the bright foyer of black and white marble, a nimble teenager strode out of the kitchen toward what appeared to be a living room or great room. "Maggie," Justine said, addressing the girl. "Maggie, I want you to meet Anna Conyer from the Western Horizon newspaper," Justine said, dropping the "s" at the end of Anna's last name, but remembering her employer closely enough.

"Hello, Anna," said the slender girl, who stepped up close to shake hands. For a second, Anna thought that the glowing teen would kiss her on the cheek, but Maggie seemed to change her mind and settle for a penetrating gaze on top of a sparkling smile. That smile reminded Anna of her fantasies about Beau Dupere, and she realized the resemblance was natural.

"This is my daughter," Justine said. "She's just turned sixteen. She's my youngest."

Seeing the two women side-by-side, no one could doubt that they were related, from the gray green eyes, to the fine Phoenician points at the top of their smiling cheeks. No hint of makeup, both women could easily appear in advertisements for cosmetics. Anna couldn't imagine that Justine had children older than this full-grown girl in front of her.

"It was wonderful to meet you," Maggie said with 24-carat sincerity. Then she said, innocently enough, "I bless your time here. Just relax and enjoy." With those words, Anna felt most of her tension drain away. The feeling of that stress leaking from her was so palpable that she instinctively looked down at her feet, as if she might find her anxieties in a pool there on the floor. Here, she noted that the other two women were barefoot and she forgot to question what had just happened.

If You Really Knew Me

When Maggie released her hand, and continued on her way, Anna followed with her eyes, as Justine answered that question she had forgotten to ask.

"Maggie has a gift for relieving people of emotional tension and fear. That's what you just felt when she blessed you."

Maggie glanced over her shoulder, as if to acknowledge her mother's words. She passed from sight, a flash of golden brown locks the last thing Anna saw of her.

"Oh," was all she could think to say.

When Justine handed her a tall glass of ice water, in the kitchen, Anna continued to look around her, unsettled, but feeling a sort of expectancy that she couldn't explain.

"There's some lovely shade and a perfect breeze by the pool today," Justine said, leading the way down a back corridor, toward the ocean side of the house. Anna followed with a smile and unblinking eyes.

As Justine led the way, her athletic hips swaying in her white capris pants, she played the role of tour guide. "Fourteen people currently live in the house. My sons have recently moved out, along with my step daughter. She and Eli went to Argentina, where we have some ministry partners. My older daughter, Jo, is traveling with her father. He likes to take at least one of the kids with him when he's away overnight."

The screen door to the patio hung halfway open, and Anna only noticed the reason when Justine stopped and looked down. A toddler stood holding the door, looking up at her. The little boy must have been between two and three years old, with long brown hair and almond shaped eyes. He wore a tiny pair of swim trunks. Pointing to Justine, he said something that sounded like "Jadeen."

Justine looked at Anna and explained. "That's what he's calling me these days. I guess Justine or Aunt Justine is just too much for him to handle." She smiled as she turned back to the little doorman.

"Did someone send you to find me, Luke?"

This time he pointed outside and said, "Mommy," quite clearly.

Anna raised her eyebrows slightly and smiled, relieved to hear a word she understood. Nothing so far had been much clearer to her than Luke's twisted name for Justine.

Justine caught the door as Luke turned to lead the way at a short-legged gallop, saying, "Jadeen," repeatedly as he scampered ahead. Recovering from her distraction at the funny little herald of their arrival, Anna raised her head to take in her surroundings. Just then, they reached an immaculate glass table surrounded by white metal chairs with green and yellow cushions on the seats and backs. Beyond the table, she could see a woman in a one-piece swimsuit playing catch in the shallow end of the pool with two girls less than ten years old. Across the pool she spotted two women in bikinis sitting on shaded chaise lounges. But all that lost focus, as a totally nude woman walked across her line of vision on the opposite side of the pool. Anna stared.

Justine, who was talking to a very short Hispanic woman about snacks for the children, saw Anna's stare and followed it across the pool to the naked woman.

"Oh, that's Bethany," Justine said, pulling out a chair for Anna. Anna broke from her stare and looked at Justine, hoping for an explanation.

Justine chuckled, aware of the shock Anna was feeling, but completely free from any discomfort of her own. "Have a seat. You'll just have to get used to Bethany like that, at least for now. It's part of her healing process." Justine reached across the table, retrieving a half glass of ice tea and taking the seat next to Anna, who was slowly lowering herself into the chair, as if uncertain whether it was actually there to catch her.

"Healing process?" Anna said, managing to construct a cogent reflection of Justine's phrase, if not a fully formed question.

Bethany had rounded the end of the long, narrow pool and passed within easy earshot. "Okay if I tell Anna about your healing?" Justine said, to the enviably proportioned woman.

Anna tried to look only at Bethany's face, wondering what was hidden in the eyes behind the large sunglasses.

"Of course," Bethany replied, smiling at Anna and nodding a bow of greeting.

"It's only women around here these days, and small children," Justine said. "So we decided it was okay for Bethany to parade in whatever she wanted to wear, or not wear, as you see." She gestured toward Bethany's departing backside as it disappeared through the same door from which Anna had exited the house.

"You see, when she came to us, she barely weighted ninety-five pounds. And you can see that she's a tall woman."

To Anna, Bethany looked like a supermodel, tall and shapely. Certainly, she weighed much more than ninety-five pounds now, though certainly less than most women her height.

"What happened?"

"Well, she was healed of her anorexia when some of the children gathered around and prayed over her," Justine said.

That was, however, not an explanation, as far as Anna was concerned. It was more like a list of questions waiting to be asked. "How did they do that?"

"Beau had an insight into what was haunting her and he knew that the children would drive it away, if they touched her and prayed for her. That was one of his sort of intuitions, you might call them."

More questions. Perhaps Justine and Beau both knew how out of her depth Anna would be there, which would explain why they assumed she would need multiple interviews. Was that one of Beau's intuitions too?

Only because she felt so thoroughly dislocated mentally, did Anna ask the next question. "Is she one of his wives?"

Justine let go of her iced tea and pressed her hand against her lips, as if trying to suppress a laugh. She breathed an answer with the air she had captured from that aborted laugh. "I'm sorry, dear. This must be a bit much for you," she said, her head tilting and eyes resting sympathetically on Anna. "Are you all right?"

Anna took two deep breaths and sat up in her chair, crossing her legs and trying to feel the real world around her, the breeze, the sound of the ocean, the brilliant sunlight. Just as she began to focus on Justine again, Bethany stepped out of the house. This time she wore a large hat and no sunglasses. Anna looked at her and giggled. She couldn't have stopped herself even if she had seen it coming. She was nearly hysterical.

When she did find the edge of a rational thought, Anna feared she might have offended Bethany, giggling at her like that. But, instead, Bethany turned and walked toward Anna. She stopped immediately next to Anna's chair and gently rubbed her upper back.

"It's okay. Be free, little sister. Be free," she said. Her tone was soothing and maternal, not the hallucinogenic tone of a hippy nudist that Anna expected. Bethany's words carried authority, along with their sympathy. She spoke like a guide through a dangerous land that she had repeatedly survived and that Anna needed yet to conquer.

Tears filled Anna's eyes, though she managed to cap off the sobs that lodged in her throat. A wave of hope, like the first cooling wind of a storm front, pushed into Anna, but something inside her pushed back. A thought that seemed foreign to everything she had experienced in the last ten minutes pounced into focus. "Are these people doing all this just to avoid answering my questions?"

Luke returned to the table with a graham cracker in his fist. He stopped on the side of Anna opposite Bethany and pointed to the stranger seated in front of him. "It's okay, Anna," he said with perfect diction.

Her lower jaw came loose and her mouth eased open. "How did he know?" she said in a midnight whisper.

Justine grinned. "He gets that from his father."

The Blind Healing the Blind

Hundreds of people wedged into the space between the front row of seats and the stage, as Beau stepped down the stairs to meet the sick and injured. Next to him, a thin young man, with spiked brown hair, carried a microphone. He held the mic close to Beau when the healer spoke in English, but as the healings started popping on every side, his language changed to a rapid-fire dialect that sounded Slavic or Eastern European. The young man translated as much of that flurry of words as he felt would help the people at hand to know what was going on. He had worked with Beau many times before and Beau trusted his judgment regarding the necessary interpretation.

The sound of crutches clattering together on their way to the floor was familiar to Joanna, who had observed and assisted her dad in dozens of meetings like this. She tried to stay close to him to assist her father, though she would be on her own later as the healing spread. With Joanna at his side, Beau would often ask her to touch someone on his behalf. Once, that night, he asked her to wrap her arms around a frail woman of forty who had the withered frame of a ninety-year-old. That embrace resulted in a deep heating sensation at the site of the woman's lung cancer.

After the number she had touched and healed had become too great to count, Joanna stopped and watched Beau for a few seconds. He was kneeling and holding his hands over the eyes of a little girl, perhaps five years old. He flipped his hands open, like shutters, and asked if she could see. When she said "no" he covered her eyes again and then repeated the move and the question. This time, the girl's hands shot up to grasp Beau's hands, and she shouted. "I can see! I can see!" Her mother, standing behind her, fell into a dead faint, caught by the pressing crowd around them. The little girl jumped up and down and shouted over and over, "He did it! I can see! I can see!"

Joanna stared at her father in that moment. He had seen so many healings that he often appeared unaffected even by dramatic recoveries. But not this time. A glisten in his eye, he remained on his knees laughing at the joy of the little girl. Then he addressed her by name.

"Tina, let's go and heal some more eyes," he said, like a father inviting his daughter to go to the zoo or the circus. Tina nodded and held her hands up for Beau to carry her. Her actual father, standing behind her, nodded his approval when Beau looked his way.

Beau leaned in close to his interpreter. "Jeremy, call everyone who has problems with their eyes up onto the stage," he said. Then he pushed his way back to the stairs and mounted them with Tina held against him by one strong arm.

Though most people heard it when Beau said it, Jeremy repeated the instructions for people with blindness, or other eye problems, to come onto the stage. Dozens followed Beau up the stairs or pushed up the other stage stairs to the left or right of where he now stood. A small handful of the people climbing onto the stage did so with the help of seeing friends or relatives, unable to see at all.

Beau prompted Tina to touch the forehead of the first man who had accepted the invitation. The briefest tap sent him sprawling backward, his hands flying to his eyes as he fell. Tina clapped her hands as if it was a game and she was winning. Beau laughed as she did the same forehead tap for a woman with curly gray hair, and then a young man with a shaved head. After several of these taps, Tina stopped and looked curiously at one tall blonde woman. For this one, she just held her little hand on the side of the woman's face. A jagged scar across one eye socket stood in place of her right eye. Beau commanded the eye to come back, as Tina held her hand there. As soon as he spoke, the woman screamed and tried to step back. She lowered her head like someone who had suddenly lost a contact lens. Tina looked concerned, until the tall woman looked up, a delirious smile on her face and two good eyes staring wide.

Others screamed. A man began to jump up and down shouting inarticulately, and several people raised their hands to their own faces to catch the healing grace that had just landed on them without a touch from Beau or his tiny assistant.

Joanna watched this from below the stage, tears rolling down her cheeks, laughing sobs shaking her torso. She shook her head and continued to weep, as Beau and Tina pushed through the crowd that had begun to resemble a cornfield after a heavy hailstorm. Instead of the dense rows of people pressed all around, great swathes of bodies lay in piles, people stumbling and laughing drunkenly. The power of God to heal all those with missing, blind or severely impaired eyes flowed through the hand of a little girl who had been blind fifteen minutes ago.

The Home Front

Dixon Claiborne stepped out of his five-year-old Toyota sedan onto the cracked asphalt of his driveway. His confrontation with Darryl Sampras at the office still echoed in his head, his brain still working on filtering what he had said, and the tone with which he had said it, so that he could live with the (altered) memory. As a result of this preoccupation, he didn't notice the grass that needed cutting, the proliferation of dandelions and thistles, and the downspout that had split open at the elbow near the ground. Normally, he was the first one in the house to notice any of these things, though the kids would be assigned the remediation work.

Nothing broke through his focus until he dropped his keys in the usual spot on the kitchen counter, near the phone. Sara stood over the island counter arranging cookie dough on baking trays. Dixon didn't notice the cookies. He noticed his daughter. She was beautiful. Even in baggy gym shorts and a pink tank top, she was a remarkable looking young woman. The pride of a father admiring his daughter, however, mixed with the fears of a father with a daughter who looked like that. One of the few things he admired about Islam was the conservative traditions around women and public exposure. He privately thought a burka seemed like just the thing for his fully blossomed eighteen-year-old.

"Hello, Daddy," Sara said, turning from her cookies to kiss Dixon on the cheek.

He grinned for a second and said, "Hello, Dear." Then he noticed the cookies, two dozen already cooling on wire racks. "What're the cookies for?"

"Cheerleaders are having a party tonight, end of year sort of thing. We're all bringing something." She shifted the tray to her right hand and stepped to the oven, opening the door with her left.

Dixon spotted the frosting waiting in two bowls on the counter, one blue and one yellow—school colors. What else would you make blue cookies for?

"Sounds good," he said blandly. "Won't be any boys invited then?" He asked questions like that with no effort whatever, it was as reflexive as wincing when seeing a friend bang his head on something.

"Don't worry, Daddy, just us girls tonight." Sara's response was equally reflexive. What Dixon didn't know was whether telling the truth was part of her reflex.

If You Really Knew Me

He hummed a brief acknowledgement of her answer, glanced at her bare feet with the fire engine red polish and shook his head on the way into the living room. There he found Brett battling zombies with a hand-held Gatling gun. Of course, the Brett on the TV console game weighed well over two hundred pounds and could handle the monstrous weapon. Half the TV screen splashed red as he vanquished another of his vicious enemies.

"How's it going?" Dixon said.

"Good," said Brett.

"Homework?"

"Done."

"Great."

The words that make memories...

Dixon could hear Kristen speaking on her cell phone. From the chirpy tone of her voice, he guessed it was her friend Lauren on the other end of that signal. He caught sight of the briefest bit of Kristen's back as she slipped into the bathroom simultaneous with his step into the bedroom. He crossed the room to the mini-fridge under the table in the corner. He lifted a diet cola from the little black box and closed the door. When they had put that fridge in the bedroom, Dixon was contemplating allowing himself a beer in the evening, wanting to keep that out of the family fridge in the kitchen. But that cooler in the bedroom had never seen anything stronger than colas, which, after all, *have* been proven to dissolve metal.

He settled the soda on his nightstand and sat on the bed to take off his shoes. His heart swam in the placid knowledge that this Friday night would be free of committee meetings. He longed for the rest, actually playing with a fantasy about sitting in the back yard on his anti-gravity lawn chair with a cold drink and a spy novel. A pitiful fantasy, he told himself. Now, with the soft bed sinking beneath his efforts to remove his shiny leather shoes, his desire turned toward napping, instead.

Kristen's voice crescendoed toward goodbye as she walked out of the bathroom. She wore a thin cotton robe that she usually reserved for closed door activities after the kids went to bed.

If You Really Knew Me

Dixon noticed and wondered if there was a hidden message in that wardrobe choice. How long had it been? But he still felt the siren tug of that nap dragging him closer and closer.

"Hi, Honey. How are you?" Kristen said, dropping her cell phone into her robe pocket. Dixon kept his eyes on that pocket, still wondering if the robe was talking to him. This left Kristen to step up to the bed and hug the top of his head between her breasts. The oddity of that position caught Dixon's attention as well, and he looked up, receiving a peck on the forehead as his reward.

He sighed. "I'm fine. Glad to have a night with no meetings."

Kristen stepped back and planted both hands on her hips. "Are you telling me you forgot about the Stimsons?"

Now that she stood a bit further away, Dixon could more easily look into her eyes, scolding eyes, turned to glass in rebuke of his forgetfulness. That whole restful evening thing *had* been a fantasy, as it turned out.

On a fully-charged battery, at the height of emotional health, and with the wind at his back, a visit to the Stimsons' luxurious house in the hills would *still* discourage Dixon. Wally Stimson would want to talk church and politics, and church politics, and punctuate his points with those dark dashes he called eyebrows a full two inches above his eyes, the resulting lines on his forehead like a heating vent. This facial expression would be Dixon's cue to agree with Wally's point. As the single largest contributor to the church, Wally knew he could throw his weight around with Dixon, even though he could never do that literally. Dixon outweighed him by at least forty pounds. Where Dixon's triumphs in college happened between the hash-marks of a football field, Wally's happened in Young Republican meetings, or in the Junior Chamber of Commerce. Fully mature now, Dixon never allowed himself to fully script out the image of knocking Wally unconscious with a clothesline tackle, he couldn't afford even the thought.

If You Really Knew Me

With very little whining, and only a modicum of muttering, Dixon forsook his plan to change into his shorts and UCLA t-shirt. Instead, he opted for Friday evening casual attire suited for the Stimson's. Dock shoes and a crisp polo shirt donned, freshly combed and shaved, he felt like he was going to the yacht club. Not that he had ever been to a yacht club. As a pastor, as a man's man, he had always felt more welcomed in basement rec rooms with a game on the big screen and debates about the qualities of quarterbacks and coaches. Wally knew none of that. Dixon would have to stay awake, however, alert to the policy directions implied in Wally's impromptu position statements. Dixon would need all of his wits so that he could agree with Wally only as far as he absolutely had to, and with no hint of action points to follow. He had to move as deftly as when his offensive line let him down and linebackers and tackles surrounded him deep in his own territory. Too bad he couldn't just challenge Wally to a little one-on-one tackle in the back yard.

Dixon actually envied the kids their reprieve from that evening's obligatory dinner. He dropped Brett off at his friend Mark's house for a sleepover, as Sara headed for her cheerleader party.

Standing in Wally Stimson's living room, Wally's wife May providing Kristen a tour of the newest décor, Dixon nodded with serious eyes and mouth, plotting his reply, what he thought of as his shock-absorber defense. He would hit the bumps, and he would feel the bumps, but he wouldn't feel the *full* impact of the potholes and even curbs. But a full minute into Wally's latest tirade, Dixon realized that he actually *did* agree with the Chairman of the Trustees (an old pastor had told Dixon to give that position to the richest man in the church, because he would know finances).

Wally patted Dixon on the back, and Dixon noted a weight of respect in Wally's look. "We can be on the forefront of something with national implications, Pastor. That is a great strategy for our church. This thing is gonna boost our attendance, I just know it." Wally was, of course, speaking of the initiative to expose Beau Dupere.

If You Really Knew Me

Dixon adopted his most agreeable posture next to Wally, as the two men faced a wall arrangement of Chinese artifacts from some long past century, highlighted by carefully placed track lighting. "I'm not sure we're gonna attract a lot of folks, but I know that people who are inclined to favor his ministry weren't coming to our services anyway," Dixon said.

Pressing for insider information, as he usually did, Wally said, "So have you gotten any serious backlash from folks inside the church?"

According to the church constitution, any pastoral concerns regarding issues of faith and practice would be the responsibility of the elders, not the trustees. But Dixon knew who signed his checks and who contributed almost ten percent of the money backing those checks. Dixon wouldn't, however, tell Wally about the most sensitive backlash.

"Well, of course, we caught some people by surprise. It's not that they disagree with the content of what we said, I haven't heard anyone defending that guy, but it's the fact that we made a public announcement that has them upset."

Wally pulled on his long, thin chin as if he had whiskers. Dixon suspected Wally couldn't grow respectable whiskers, even in his fifties, but he started to lower his guard and allowed his host the gesture without even an inkling of annoyance.

At this same time, on the other side of town, Sara Claiborne sat on a brown suede couch in Patricia Oliver's basement, scrunched together with three other girls, watching video of their cheerleading performances from the past year. Jenny Washington's dad put together the video for the squad, out of dozens of hours of footage from the football and basketball seasons. After about twenty minutes of watching themselves, all nine of the girls tired of it, like people who hit the buffet too hard on the first few rounds and can't find energy to go back for another bite. Sara, the captain of the squad, looked at Jenny to see if it would be okay to stop the video. Fortunately, Jenny's dad wasn't there to be insulted. Jenny sat at the other end of the couch, leaning on her left hand, as if her head was filled with lead and her neck just wasn't suited to the task of holding it upright.

"Ya' know, maybe that's enough for now. We can run the rest later," Sara said, a bit apologetic, but still clear about her preference.

Jenny seemed relieved at first. But, when the other girls enthusiastically agreed with Sara, her face turned sour. Now she did manage to hold her head up straight with no hands.

"It is a lot to take in," Candy Matheson said, trying to soften the pinch on Jenny. A more trained video critic than Sara, Candy knew that they were all getting tired because of the way the images had been recorded and edited. The angles lacked creativity and the framing was always the same.

"We *really* appreciate your dad working so hard on this all year," Sara said. "We'll watch the rest after yearbooks and food." They had purposely timed the party to coordinate with the distribution of the yearbooks that day, which, of course, featured numerous photos of these girls.

Because Jenny was fully aware of the failure of her father's efforts, and because she often wondered about his motives for spending so much time recording and editing video of cheerleaders, the efforts to assuage her bounced off. In fact, the obvious need the other girls felt to try to make her feel better just intensified the bitter taste in her mouth.

"It's fine. I don't care, anyway," Jenny said, blurting her lie in a husky voice.

"Sorry, Jenny," Sara said, responding to Jenny's tone and not her words. "I didn't mean to offend you."

Here, Jenny allowed a switch to flip inside, bringing a deeper resentment to light. "I suppose when you're so perfect, it's almost impossible *not* to offend people."

Sara leaned forward a bit on the couch to see Jenny past the other two girls. She recoiled her neck and her eyebrows popped up. "But, why…" she started to say.

If You Really Knew Me

Kira O'Connell piped in at half volume. "Uh oh, here it comes."

Jenny stood up and Sara's response died on her tongue. Seeing Sara stifled like that stopped Jenny for a second, but then she boiled over.

"You probably don't even know how stuck up you and your father seem to the rest of us," she said, blasting the words with flailing hands that appeared to be illustrating something that no one could translate.

"My father?" Sara said, trying to make the connection.

"See! You're clueless. You probably agree with his little witch hunt, trying to make publicity for himself by pointing fingers at perfectly innocent people."

Sara had finally caught up, just after the words "witch hunt" hit the air. She at least knew the general topic, though she was baffled by the reference to "perfectly innocent people," and most dumbstruck by why this mattered to Jenny. As the only African-American cheerleader, Jenny got special treatment from Sara, who always feared offending her with some careless racial remark. That factored into Sara's paralysis now, sending her looking in the wrong direction for a connection between Jenny and Beau Dupere.

Jenny had always liked Sara, and especially appreciated the efforts the captain of the squad made to welcome her into the inner circle, a circle that Sara had stretched to include the whole squad. Sara was a born leader, like her father, if not the same kind of leader. Seeing Sara so innocently unresponsive cooled Jenny's fire. Her own words came back to her. She realized that Sara *didn't* know, and her father probably didn't know either.

Throwing her hands over her head and plunking back down into the couch, Jenny burst into tears. Now she had a bit of sympathy on her side, even if most of the girls had no idea where the explosion originated. Kira knew.

Kira and Jenny attended the same Catholic church. She knew about how people had prayed for Jenny's mother to recover from cervical cancer for several months. This had ended the previous summer, before Jenny made the varsity cheer squad. Sara knew nothing about it. Jenny's mother looked perfectly healthy every time Sara saw her, starting the previous August.

While Jenny tried to suppress her sobs, Kira spoke up. "It's because of her mother's cancer."

Unfortunately, since most of the other girls knew nothing of Mrs. Washington's cancer struggle, this only confused them more. But Sara made the intuitive leap, perhaps due to her awareness of, and secret fascination with, Beau Dupere's reputation as a healer.

"Wait," Sara said. She turned to Jenny. "Your mother doesn't have cancer now, does she?"

Jenny grimaced and shook her head, frustrated at how tangled the whole thing had become. But Sara helped her unwind the story.

"So she was healed of cancer?"

Jenny laughed a barky little laugh through her tears, relieved that Sara had caught on, and subconsciously noting a lift of excitement in Sara's voice.

Kira, feeling left out of the spotlight, finished her revelation. "Jenny's mom was healed of horrible cancer by Beau Dupere and his wife last summer."

Sara allowed her eyebrows to coast upward even as her china doll lips parted to form a surprised O.

Send them Running for Cover

As on many of Beau Dupere's healing trips, the hosts had arranged for a more sedate and intimate gathering the next morning, after the big healing service. The pastor of the Toronto church had invited some of the most severely handicapped people in the congregation to come for healing in that smaller setting.

Joanna recognized her father's weariness in the way he leaned back and draped an arm on the back of the chair next to him, where the pastor had been sitting before he stood up to open the meeting. Beau's eyelids had sunk a few degrees from wide open, probably due to less than five hours of sleep, after the previous meeting ran past midnight. But she didn't worry that this tiredness would hinder what God planned to do there, any more than she feared that the huge mass of people pressing toward him the previous night would overwhelm her father.

In spite of her confidence in what God could do through her dad, and even through her, Joanna sensed a presence in the room that churned her insides like a hand sifting through a bucket of gravel. She tried to detect some hint that her father was sensing the same thing. Though she could see no outward sign, she did feel an intuitive assurance that he was aware of that presence, as well.

In a twenty-by-twenty-foot room off the corner of the sanctuary sat two dozen people that Beau had not yet met. The senior pastor, with the head of the healing ministry and two other church staff, also sat in the light gray fabric chairs with pale painted metal arms that reached around to support the sitters, like caregivers assisting the handicapped into a bath. No one seemed comforted by those embracing chairs or by the prospect of healing that morning. Many sensed the same resistant presence that worried Joanna.

As soon as the pastor finished his welcoming remarks and opening prayer, Beau awakened from his restful posture. Standing quickly, he strode across the room toward a teenaged boy sitting with his mother. The boy appeared normal until Beau approached. As Beau loomed over him, the boy curled his arms and legs reflexively and twisted his neck around to track something that appeared to be just over Beau's shoulder. The boy's previous inattentive posture turned quickly into what looked like schizoid paranoia, as he recoiled from a frightening attacker no one else seemed to see.

To Joanna, it looked as if her father was in a hurry to help the boy, striding to the rescue. To the boy and his mother, Beau looked like a swooping monster, bent on overpowering and crushing them. The mother screamed a single aborted note and the boy writhed into a full seizure, arms and legs twining together and head rotating around the full range possible for his thin neck.

Beau barked a single order. "You get out of here now!"

At that last word, Joanna thought she saw a shadow move behind the boy, as if some stray sunbeam had passed through a window to his left. But the room had no windows. Everyone in the room startled at the ferocity of Beau's actions, several jumping from their chairs and scrambling away from the pounce on the squirming boy.

When Beau stopped above the boy, and his cowering mother, he turned instantly gentle, reaching down and holding the boy's face in his hands. Suddenly, the boy stopped his writhing. Simultaneous with that calming touch, the mother surged out of her chair, as if to leap on Beau and protect her boy. Though she couldn't explain how, it seemed to Joanna that the woman bounced off of Beau and landed on the floor, her attack entirely thwarted.

With gentle sternness, Beau spoke to the sickness oppressing the boy. "You all go now. All of you out now."

Again, the boy writhed, this time screaming like a tortured animal. Beau waved his hands as if batting away diving swallows trying to protect their nest.

"Leave this building, now!" Beau said, his voice booming, but betraying no panic or rage.

Within a second, the entire room snapped free from a suspended darkness that had held all of them, like invisible restraining bands. Everyone dropped free, back into full awareness

If You Really Knew Me

of the time and place—that plain gray room and the two dozen other people all looking like they had just survived a near miss on the highway.

Joanna followed a compulsion to attend to the mother lying on the floor. When she arrived at her side, the woman was praying, begging for forgiveness. Apparently, she had taken her son to some kind of alternative healer. Her penitent prayers acknowledged how that attempt had not resulted in any improvement in her son, Kurt, and had, instead, added a dark oppression to their lives. After listening for a minute, Joanna declared the mother forgiven and commanded all unholy spirits to stay away from her and her son.

Beau stayed with the boy for several minutes, praying in an unknown language or calling the boy to be present with him, as if his mind had gotten lost in some twisted tunnel leading away from this world. When Beau stood up straight and looked around at the rest of the room, he had restored the boy to a normal posture and full awareness. The boy, Kurt, looked down at his mother with a childish smile, as Joanna helped the older woman to her feet. When she saw him, the mother knew immediately that he had been healed. He hadn't looked at her like that since he was four years old. She burst into tears and wrapped her arms around her son, even as he struggled to stand up and return her embrace.

Beau and Joanna both stood and looked at the senior pastor. He stood next to his chair, still gripping the backrest, looking as if he couldn't decide whether to run from the room or to jump in and help. He smiled and then laughed when they both looked at him.

To everyone's great relief, the remainder of that healing session saw no more fireworks, even though several other spirits had to be expelled.

Joanna laughed to herself at how many times she had returned from these trips exhausted by a constant level of vigilance, along with repeated explosions of relief and joy. At least it was never boring.

The Girl in the Mirror

If a sigh were a taxable act, perhaps for overuse of scarce clean air, Anna would have doubled her tax burden on the ride home from the Dupere house, and the subsequent hours in her apartment that afternoon. She looked at her digital recorder, lying on her kitchen table. She hadn't recorded a single word of her time with Justine. Nor had she taken a single photo; though, if she had, she might have had to blur out sections to keep a PG rating to her article. But her feeling of failure as a reporter that afternoon faded under the layer of swirling emotions at the top of her stomach.

Anna had interviewed dozens of celebrities across a wide spectrum, from political leaders to skateboarders, from Academy Award winning actors to new lottery winners. None of those reporting assignments had ever gone as far off the tracks as her experience among Beau Dupere's family.

She looked in her bathroom mirror, leaning on the edge of the sink, oblivious to her own image there. Her hair stood in two hillocks where she had sat holding her scalp, brown locks arching between tense fingers. Her eye makeup now outlined the bowl-shaped sockets below her weary eyes, with assorted drips spilling from those bowls, down her cheeks and her nose. The cherry-shaped bulb at the end of that nose shone redder than usual. She saw none of that.

Anna sighed instead at what she saw inside herself.

Finally, standing up and scuffing over the tiny white hexagonal tiles of the bathroom floor, she felt as if elastic bands had been attached to all her major joints, anchoring her to the floor and straining against her. She passed through the little hall that linked bedroom to bathroom to kitchen and living room, aiming for the refrigerator. When she swung the textured white door open and looked at the pale faces of food and drink that seemed beyond recognition, she thought of Bethany. The golden curves of her nude body seemed to lead inevitably to her face and to her eyes. Those eyes must not have looked so comfortably and casually set into her perfect face before her recovery. Anna had interviewed anorexic women for a piece on eating disorders in college. They all looked haunted, and not just because of their physical resemblance to concentration camp victims. They all looked desperately hungry for more than food. Fragile, that's what it was. The anorexics she had known personally, and through those interviews, all looked fragile. Bethany seemed strong and whole.

"I wonder how long she's gonna walk around naked," she thought. Anna couldn't imagine Bethany's recovery to lasting much longer. She looked more recovered than Anna felt.

Nothing in the fridge enticed her. Anna closed the door without disturbing the sleeping residents. She hadn't had anything to eat or drink since Justine brought her water, followed by something stronger to revive Anna when she seemed like she might faint. It was good lemonade. Homemade probably. Was it magic, like those women and children she met? Did the lemonade provide all the sustenance she needed, negating hunger?

She forked one hand through her hair again, disrupting the dual lump look in favor of a half-parted look. Her irrational thoughts about magic began to scare her, driving her hands to wreck all earlier efforts at quaffing herself to impress the interviewees. She snorted a little laugh. They didn't seem impressed by her, they seemed to pity her.

Even Rhonda wasn't impressed—the newest resident of the house, the late thirties woman with slack blondish-brown hair and clothes that left her body looking like furniture draped with

If You Really Knew Me

dust covers. Rhonda didn't fit at all. She hadn't gotten very far in whatever recovery she was pursuing. But even Rhonda paused to smile across the kitchen island, a sympathetic smile sealing Anna's realization that she was the most desperately needy person in that house.

Of course, the most stunning thing about Rhonda, was what Justine said about her after she headed out to the pool and a walk along the beach. "We were all like her, and most of us worse, when we first moved in here," Justine had said, a nostalgic squint to her eyes and a grateful smile on her lips.

Anna meandered back through her central hallway sleepwalker-like. But the mirror there caught her attention. She wondered what Justine meant by that, "all like Rhonda." All sad and droopy looking? That was hard to believe of the "wives," often described as looking like a bevy of models or actresses. Then Anna realized something about Justine and company. They all looked fresh and gorgeous even without makeup. Their faces shown with natural luster, their skin smooth and relaxed. That was it. Relaxed. They all had that wonderfully age-reducing look of someone peacefully asleep, but with clear opened eyes and ready smiles. Most actresses didn't look like that when she saw them up close.

But most actresses didn't try to heal your anxiety or wash your fears away with a word or a touch. Maybe those healing touches and prayers would make *her* appear younger and fresher, Anna thought, looking still at her image in the mirror, the low light of the hallway leaving room for imaginative generosity.

She suddenly remembered little Luke's startling pronouncement. She said it aloud to herself. "It's okay, Anna." And she smiled.

After a Miracle

In a café overlooking the Pacific, early lunching customers occupied only three of the dozen outdoor tables. The umbrellas over those tables offered their optimal coverage, as the sun neared its apex, on a day with no clouds and a ten-mile-an-hour wind. The cool breeze off the ocean made long sleeves comfortable, not to mention long pants and shoes.

Beau Dupere had stopped at the shoes. If he didn't really have to, he preferred not to wear shoes. Brown leather sandals sufficed for him, with white linen pants and a pale blue sweater over a light gray t-shirt. Across the table sat a familiar face to American movie-goers. Randy Cooper had appeared in dozens of Hollywood features since he was a teenager. He usually played the bad boy that everyone loved. He usually played himself, in essence. His long, wavy brown hair favored one side of his head, persuaded by the westerly wind. Black plastic aviator sunglasses disguised his eyes, but the deep lines in his forehead and around his mouth offered plenty of expression for Beau to see through his own sunglasses.

Dropping the menu as the waiter arrived, Randy said, "Give me a Corona with lime, and some pretzels."

"Grapefruit juice and tortilla chips for me," Beau said.

The waiter, a slight-built young man with spikey hair and dark eyes, nodded. "Very good. I'll be just a minute."

Randy waved a hand absently, as if sweeping the waiter away, perhaps to assist the young man in speeding their order back to the table. He looked at Beau and said, "You heard anything from Bond since you healed his broken hand?"

Beau shook his head. "No. I think it freaked him out. I'm not surprised he hasn't called or anything."

"You gonna call him?" Randy said.

"I don't plan to, but that could change. Why? Did you hear something?"

"No, I just wondered how this worked." Randy grinned and leaned forward in his chair, brushing a lock of hair off his glasses. "I mean, do you like go in for the kill after you rock somebody with one of those healing miracles?"

Beau laughed. "'In for the kill?' You think I'm collecting scalps or somethin'?"

Randy laughed, but not as comfortably as Beau. "Well, I don't know. I really mean it. I don't know how this works. I mean, do people just say, 'hey thanks for making me not blind anymore' and then just go back to their life of screwing around and getting stoned?"

Beau considered Randy for a second and then looked past him to the blue water, and the first sign of clouds on the horizon. "The healing is free. No one pays for it, not with money, not with good behavior. He didn't have to stop fooling around with other guys wives in order to get healed, he doesn't have to get sober in order to stay healed."

Randy swore and added more awkward laughter. "Okay, I get that. But, I guess I'm asking about human nature here. I'm asking what people usually do after they have this monster miracle knock 'em over. Do they repent and all that..." He stopped himself from another expletive, as if just considering cleaning up his language around the Jesus freak.

The waiter arrived with the drinks and snacks. For Beau, it was about lunchtime, but he knew that Randy had only been awake for a couple of hours, and it was too soon for *his* second meal of the day. This meeting wasn't about eating and drinking, anyway, so Beau would wait until he got home to eat a proper lunch.

Beau thanked the waiter and didn't pause for him to get out of earshot before answering Randy. "People react all sorts of ways to seeing God's tangible power at work. Most of them manage to *deny* it, in one way or another. That's just the place and

If You Really Knew Me

time we live in." He sipped his grapefruit juice and resisted smacking his lips at the satisfying tang.

"You remember Betty Timmerman?" Beau said. "You know, the gorgeous blonde that used to do those swimsuit photos and videos."

Randy swigged his beer and set it down, nodding. "Oh, yeah. Whatever happened to her?"

Beau smiled. "She got healed and decided to keep her clothes on after that. She was active in a church down in Anaheim, last I knew." He raised his eyebrows, checking to see that he had caught Randy's attention. A nod from the wiry actor, assured Beau of his audience.

"She'd been diagnosed with breast cancer when she was only thirty. Imagine a famous swimsuit model with breast cancer. There's all kinds of issues that she's struggling with, like what's gonna happen to me? What am I worth? Some serious questions. So, out of desperation, she comes to one of my meetings at that church down in Anaheim, about five years ago. I actually didn't know who she was when she came up front to get healed, I didn't even know that she had cancer. I just got this feeling that this woman's life was about to change forever. All I had to do was put a hand on her head and call out the healing. At that point, she started to vibrate and bounce like a little kid's windup toy. After a few seconds, she went over backward, taking out a half dozen surprised folks behind her." He stopped to laugh.

Randy laughed too, but still restrained his amusement compared to Beau. He found Beau's whole attitude toward these things completely baffling.

"She came to as the meeting was winding down, her makeup all smeared and streaked, her hair matted and wrecked. And she told me who she was and what had happened to her. It wasn't just the healing from breast cancer, it was this intimate encounter with a God that wanted to love her and care for her no matter what she did or who she was. She got up off the floor believing all that because of the healing, but it was really just the starter."

Beau took another swig of juice and started into the tortilla chips, scooping mango salsa from a tray of three varieties of chunky red sauce. Randy looked away, scanning the other people at the restaurant, as a few more showed up for lunch in the middle of the day. Beau could see Randy's jaw muscles pulse and his neck muscles tighten. With so little body fat, Randy couldn't hide his tension.

"Yeah, well..." Randy started and then lost momentum for a second. He grabbed a couple of twisted pretzels and popped them into his mouth, finishing his thought over his own crunching. "I kinda got freaked out myself when I saw that hand healed. I mean, I was close enough, and just sober enough, to see the swelling go down in like a second." He swore again. "That was some serious CGI sorta stuff. But it wasn't. It was real. And I could tell how real it was by the way Bondo acted too. I mean, Mr. Tough Guy was like trying to keep from crying in front of everybody, like a half dozen women he'd been to bed with and all that." He stopped and shook his head, afraid to say more.

Beau sat back, he took a deep breath. Though Randy couldn't see it, Beau closed his eyes for a few seconds. Then he delivered his message.

"Randy, God has been after you all your life, from the time you went to Sunday school with your sister, at your grandma's church, and the time you freaked out at that Ouija board in middle school, to the time you had a bad acid trip and thought you saw the Devil himself," he paused for impact. "God is still after you. He knows about whose fiancé you slept with last night and he knows what you're gonna do tomorrow. But he doesn't just *know* all that stuff about you, he really *cares*."

Beau and Randy had been acquaintances, and almost friends, for several years. They met at the hottest parties and some Hollywood fundraisers. But Randy had never told Beau any of those details about his life. In fact, he hadn't told anyone, that he could remember, including his mention of his infidelity just last night.

Randy sat frozen in place. His mind focused now on a shivery sort of vibration that had started at the top of his head and had just reached his feet. He was sure he couldn't move, but didn't have the will to test it. He swore again, and then started crying audibly.

Beau looked around and prayed for a wall of protection so Randy wouldn't get distracted by what anyone around them might think. A famous drinker, and seven-time drug rehab veteran, it probably looked like Randy was meeting with his sponsor. Beau knew Randy was in a fragile state and wanted to protect his dignity, as much as possible. Only supernatural intervention could explain a dozen restaurant patrons not noticing an A-list actor sobbing at that corner table, with that other guy reaching a hand for his shoulder and praying aloud.

Finding the Exit

When Dixon and Kristen finally arrived home after ten-thirty that Friday night, they found Sara waiting for them in the living room. Was it parental intuition? Did Sara have a thought-bubble over her head that said she wanted to talk about something important? Somehow, they knew that their cheerleader daughter had a serious agenda when she greeted them from the blue Belshire fabric couch, wearing gym shorts and a t-shirt.

Dixon grinned at his lovely girl, perhaps in an effort to soften the impending blow. Kristen chose a counter-offensive approach. "What are you looking so serious about, young lady?" An edge of rebuke sharpened the tone of that question.

One thing that Sara had learned by the age of eighteen was that she need not fear her parents. Her father practically worshipped at her feet, and her mother was all bark and no bite. The same people-management skills that guided her to the head of the cheerleaders helped her maneuver between her mom and dad. Though she knew she would never get everything she wanted from them, she also knew that she could speak her mind, even if it offended them. She knew this, in spite of the fact that she had very rarely tried, and certainly had not confronted them about an important matter of faith.

"I found out something at the party tonight," she said, sliding her feet off the couch and down to the floor. The couch fit her perfectly. She could place her size-eight feet flat on the floor and her lower back still conformed to the lumbar supporting cushions.

"Yeah, what was that?" Dixon said, lowering himself into his recliner, directly across from Sara. Kristen had taken up a post next to the hallway door, her arms crossed over her chest, one foot planted, the other tilting back on her high heal.

Sara pushed a wisp of golden hair off her forehead and looked squarely at her father. "Jenny Washington's mother was dying of cancer until last summer. It was really far along and the doctors had given up."

Neither of her parents anticipated this preamble to the conflict for which they had braced. But the past-tense verbs in this opening statement left them even more bereft of clues about the purpose of this discussion.

"They're Catholic, you know, and their church was praying for them. But finally, they went to a healing service up in Redwood."

Now Dixon and Kristen could clearly see the eighteen-wheeler rounding the bend, headlights blazing, barreling right toward them.

"She was completely healed. The doctors said they couldn't explain it. They had scans from before and from after and they said there was no way that they were from the same woman, except they knew it *was* the same woman 'cause they were there when the scans were done."

Dixon's mind wandered a bit, thinking that, if Sara applied herself, she could make a pretty good lawyer.

Kristen pulled him back into the beam of those approaching headlights. "Well, dear, tell her why that doesn't change anything." She turned toward Dixon with a mixture of her hard-faced defensive posture and an embryonic shrug waiting in her tight shoulders.

This prompt for a command performance may sound like something certain wives commonly do to their husbands, but Kristen normally wasn't like those wives. That she threw the floor open to Dixon so forcefully, reflected how uncomfortable she was with answering the implied question lodged between the well-publicized meeting, starring her husband, and the healing story about Mrs. Washington. On the other hand, she felt confident that Dixon had an answer ready.

Looking at Sara the whole time, seeing his wife only peripherally, Dixon said, "Oh, I know. I've read and heard lots of those stories. In fact, there are so many of them that I think you can't just say that it's fake, or that it's some kind of group hysteria where people just *think* they're getting healed."

Now Kristen began to slump, her crossed arms loosening, her tight lips parting. Here was another preamble that left her feeling as if she was churning her feet, trying to find a place where the water was shallow enough for her to stand.

Dixon took a preacher's pause, checking that the desired impact had landed on both women. Then he said, "And, really, that's what's most disturbing about this guy." This turned his response more to his wife's satisfaction, though she still couldn't have finished this thought for him.

He continued. "You see, if he was faking the healings and just taking people's money, then we'd just say he was a fake and a thief. But there may actually be something much more...ah...disturbing here." He had considered the word "sinister," but was trying not to pour all of his cauldrons of burning oil at once. Seeing his audience still poised for his big conclusion, he said, "It's much more disturbing to think that a guy like this has some serious spiritual power, 'cause we know that power's not from God. So that leaves us just one possibility."

"How do you know it's not from God?" Sara said, her voice ramping at the end.

Dixon saw the 'X' formed in the middle of Sara's face by her eyebrows and her squinting eyes. He glanced at Kristen, catching only the briefest impression, but it was enough to know that he was losing this crowd. He scooted back in his chair and reached for a higher gear.

"Ah, well, you saw the video, his ungodly lifestyle, his greed and the way he treats people like they don't matter. 'You will know them by their fruit,' scripture says."

Something about that didn't settle right for Sara, but she was not a biblical scholar, or practiced debater.

Dixon could see her unconvinced look and tried another stab. "You know that on Judgment Day the Lord will say to people who claimed to do miracles in His name, 'Go away from me, I never knew you.' So the miracles prove nothing."

This time he turned his head for a fuller look at Kristen. She avoided eye contact, protecting him from a double dose of doubt, there in his own living room. She also avoided looking directly at Sara, unwilling to multiply the dissatisfaction she was already feeling, by seeing it reflected in her daughter's eyes.

Dixon squirmed and called for backup. "Kristen, you know this is right."

Hearing a desperate tone in his voice, that reminded her of how vulnerable her man could be in private, Kristen swung back into engagement, with the conflict laid out before her. When she looked at Dixon, however, an acid resentment at his vulnerability tainted the water. Instead of coming to his aid, she just stared back at him. This released Sara to let fly another challenge.

"It's not that I'm saying we ought to go to this man's church or something," Sara said. "It's not that I necessarily want people I know going to him to get healed. It's just that I don't think it's right for you to make public statements about him that we can't really be sure are true."

"Have you looked at the Web site?" Dixon said. He had hit ramming speed now.

Sara's voice deepened with confidence. "I did. And it's really one-sided. There are a lot of things that look bad for him, but he never gets a chance to answer any of it. I mean, even if the accusations are true, they're done in a sort of sneaky and mean way."

Fortunately, for the future of family unity, the Web site had been constructed by an outside organization, and had only been revised and endorsed by Dixon's group of ministers. Therefore, he didn't feel the full brunt of Sara's rejection of its tone and contents. He wondered now, however, whether he should have fact-checked more of what was published there. It was all well-presented, after the refinements his committee had added, but that assumed that everything in it was true. Of course, feeling as if he was already in full retreat, he wasn't going to give that thought any air time.

The Claiborne household grew cold that night in late May, after a ragged ending to the conversation in the living room. The closest thing to an apology that Dixon would offer was, "Well, let's all give this some more thought, and talk about it another time."

Lacking the motivation and the instinct to go for a kill, Sara allowed that to be the final word on the subject, for now. Kristen nearly staggered on her way to the bedroom, a bit of vertigo spiraling around a growing feeling gripping her head, an increasing suspicion that her husband and his colleagues had miscalculated. Focusing on not lurching through the house kept her from carefully defining just *where* they had gone wrong.

Get Up and Walk

Sitting in his Land Rover, the tinted driver's window rolled down, Beau Dupere joked with one of his guards. "You hear about the shoot-to-kill order?" he said, straight-faced.

The muscular young man raised his eyebrows and curved his lips into an upside down smile. "You serious? We don't have guns."

"Well, then Taser-to-kill it is," Beau said, still stone-faced.

"What?"

"I guess you'll have to just let 'em roast."

The more perceptive guard stepped over to his partner. "He's jerkin' your chain. Mr. Dupere is always jokin' around."

The dumbfounded guard looked at his partner and then back at Beau and said, "Oooohh, I get it. Yeah."

Beau raised his eyebrows at the second guard who just shook his head.

"Well, you boys keep the zombies back, while I go get some supplies." And he accelerated out of the driveway, past a few dozen protesters who had become more subdued since sunset.

The window still down, his hair fluttered as he zipped around the curves on the way to the grocery store. Against Justine's recommendation, Beau had volunteered to pick up the list of ten things they needed at the house. They usually had groceries delivered, but she was baking after supper and realized she was missing two key ingredients.

"Time to rescue the maiden," Beau had said, bypassing Justine's objections.

She smiled at her champion, dressed in t-shirt, long gym shorts and flip-flops. "You think I need rescuing?"

Beau kissed her lifted face and answered. "Well, I gotta take what I can get around all these strong, independent women." He looked at Emma, the blonde five-year-old, who had just entered the kitchen. She was trying to fit the head back on a little dark-skinned baby doll.

Emma held the decapitated doll up to Beau without a word. He took the two pieces from her little uplifted hands and said. "Be healed," popping the head back into place.

"I knew you could do it," Emma said with a satisfied smile.

Beau and Justine both laughed.

"Don't worry, we still have a few good uses for you around here," Justine said, raising one eyebrow provocatively.

"Hmmm. Hold that thought," Beau said, kissing Justine on the lips once more, before kissing Emma on top of the head and heading for the driveway.

On the dark road, lighted by street lamps surrounded by swaying trees, Beau hummed a favorite worship song and listened for the presence that stayed with him wherever he went. He signaled to turn when he reached the first driveway for the small organic foods store Justine favored. He knew it would close soon, but had a few minutes to spare when he pulled into a parking space twenty yards from the front doors.

Still humming as he strode through the aisles and gathered all of the items he could find, Beau began to feel that familiar prod in his spirit, an alert to look out for the next person he was supposed to touch. As he studied the various kinds of dates available, in the dried fruit section, the word "veteran" came to mind. He dropped a carton of pitted dates into his basket and headed for the counter. But, before he reached the end of that aisle, a man in a wheel chair spun into Beau's path. The sun-seasoned man, wearing army green pants and a dark t-shirt with an American flag on it, was looking at the cereal on the top shelf.

Beau stopped. "Can I reach something for you?"

The older man tipped his head toward Beau, looking at him through gold, wire-rimmed glasses. He looked back at the top shelf and pointed to granola boxes beyond his reach. "Sure, that'd be handy of you. Can you get that vanilla kind there? He pointed with a hand wearing a driver's glove. Beau followed that

If You Really Knew Me

hand and located the right box, with the help of a couple of prompting grunts.

"There ya' go," Beau said, handing him the box. "You mind if I ask what's got you confined to that chair?"

The man craned his neck to see Beau's face again, this time to judge what sort of inquiry he was making. "Took shrapnel in the spine in Nam," the man said, still studying Beau.

"My name's Beau," he said, offering his hand.

The man in the chair said, "Rich. Pleased to meet ya." He still sounded uncertain, however, about *how* pleased he was.

"What would you say, Rich, if I told you God was gonna get you outta that wheelchair tonight?"

Rich maintained his surveillance of that tan smiling face. "How's...he...gonna...do that?" he said, the words spaced around sluggish pauses, signaling his skepticism.

Beau waited for a second, hoping for some help with the answer to that question, but his hesitation tipped Rich from the "undecided" to the "opposed" category.

"Some other time, maybe," he said, turning his chair away and heading for the checkout, just as the manager announced closing time over the intercom.

Though Beau had become bolder over the years of increasing success, he still harbored the hesitation of the polite Midwestern boy that his parents raised. Bold, usually, but pushy, hardly ever.

Beau followed Rich to the cashiers and went to the other open lane, keeping his internal frequency tuned in for further instructions, even as he greeted the cashier and watched her run his groceries over the scanner. He noticed that the young Hispanic store employee wore a brace on her right hand.

"That from working here?" Beau said, nodding toward the brace.

The young woman, barely twenty, looked up at him and nodded. "Yeah. I get going and don't even think about whether I've been doing the same thing over and over and getting sore and stiff."

"Let me see it," he said.

Thinking that he might be a doctor, the girl raised her braced hand halfway to where Beau could reach it. But he didn't touch it, he just spoke to it.

"Tendons, be healed right now," he said in his regular voice.

The cashier looked up at him abruptly and then used her other hand to pull at the Velcro straps of the brace. An older woman, with an item in each hand, had just arrived behind Beau and stared incredulously at the odd proceedings. Rich had just finished paying for his food and started past where Beau stood. He coasted to a halt, however, when he saw the cashier pulling off her brace.

She stuttered. "It...it...feels really warm, and all the pain is gone. What did you do?"

"I just healed it by the power of Jesus," Beau said.

Rich stayed where he was, inadvertently blocking Beau's exit from the lane, that is if the cashier would stop staring at her wrist and flexing her fingers. She held the brace in her other hand, oblivious to anything else around her.

The woman next in line cleared her throat.

Beau said, "Put her items with mine."

The cashier and the impatient woman made inquiring noises simultaneously. But the cashier was easily persuaded by Beau just then, so she took the two additional items off the conveyor and scanned them.

"Hey, I didn't agree to that," the woman said, barely acknowledging Beau, and directing her protest at the cashier.

"Consider it compensation for holding up the line," Beau said, his voice consoling, like he was talking to his own dear grandmother. He handed the cashier a hundred-dollar bill as the waiting customer tried to recover her ability to speak.

Rich seized the stage at this point. "You healed her arm?" he said, forming a statement with the inflection of a question. Clearly, the implications of his inquiry stretched back to a refusal he had made a few minutes before.

"Yep," Beau said, nodding once. "I told you I could get you outta that wheelchair right here and now." Beau grabbed his groceries in one hand and reached a smaller bag to the woman with the shoulder-length gray hair behind him. She seemed in less of a hurry as she gathered in the conversation in front of her.

Rich swallowed hard, as if he had gone dry. "I guess you could give it a try," he said, sounding more like a shy boy on his first day at school than the tough war survivor he had played a moment ago.

"Try?" Beau said. "Jesus didn't send me to *try* to heal anyone. He just said to do it." He shifted his bag to his left hand and reached his right out to Rich, as if for a handshake.

By this time, the store manager had come up front to see what was holding up the lines. Now he joined in the audience, barely a puff of breath to be heard among them. Standing next to the other cashier, the manager leaned toward her and whispered. "That's Beau Dupere, the healer." That cashier shook her head, unfamiliar with Beau, or his reputation.

Scooting a bit forward in his chair by placing his elbows on the arms, Rich reached up to take Beau's hand. At first, it looked like a tug of war. Rich's right arm went rigid, cocked at the elbow, his fingertips white with the pressure of his grip on Beau's powerful hand. Beau bent at the knees slightly, his bicep flexed with the effort to lift Rich. But his face showed no strain. Beau looked as if he were arm wrestling one of the little kids at home, a mischievous grin beginning to hatch his straight white teeth.

Rich started to shake, as if every muscle strained and shook with one final effort before collapsing.

"Just let it happen," Beau said. "Don't fight it."

Looking up into Beau's face, Rich fairly grunted his response. "Help me." His bulging eyes and clamped jaws suddenly relaxed and his legs straightened. He fell forward into Beau's arms.

Still holding the paper grocery bag in his left hand, Beau embraced Rich momentarily. Then he stepped back and let go. Rich stood on his own. He looked down, as if afraid to find that his legs had disappeared. Instead, he saw them standing firm, unshaken.

"I can...I can't..." Rich tried to clarify his own disbelief, but seemed to lose momentum for the effort. He took a baby step toward Beau, then he straightened his back and stood up to full height, nearly as tall as Beau.

"Guess you'll be gettin' your own granola off the top shelf from now on," Beau said. He laughed almost theatrically, literally forming the words "Ha, ha, ha," with his exclamation of joy.

"This is a dream," Rich said. "This can't be real."

"Well, it's not much of a dream if you're gonna just shuffle along like an old man," Beau said. "Hell, man you can walk! You can run! You can jump!"

Rich stared at him wide-eyed and then made a little jump in place. Upon landing the minor maneuver, he looked at Beau and laughed that same, "Ha, ha, ha."

"Oh, my God," said the cashier with the healed wrist.

"I don't believe it," said the gray-haired customer, sounding as if maybe she did believe it, in spite of her words.

By the time Beau walked into the kitchen back at home, where Justine sat now at the table reading a paperback book, he apologized. "Sorry it took so long."

"How many did you heal?" Justine said, standing to take the grocery bag from him.

"A couple," Beau said, and he gave her a peck on the cheek, before heading to the fridge for some cold water.

A Wider Reach

When Jonathan Opare listened to his voicemail and learned that Darryl Sampras would not be meeting with him, he lined up an even more interesting meeting. Though Jonathan was not a theologian or church historian, he did know a few things about the state of the Church in America. He arranged a meeting with Ken Bennington, from the local Assemblies of God church. While he knew better than to assume that a minister with a Pentecostal background would totally share his viewpoint, Jonathan needed to hear more of the indictment of Beau Dupere from someone for whom healing was still a current ministry of the church. His political instincts led him to search for the divide between the sides in the conflict that had been presented at the big community meeting, especially since one of the sides was entirely unrepresented there.

Ken Bennington was built like a marathon runner and was as high-strung as a beagle. He swigged his diet cola just as Jonathan stepped through his office door. Nerves over the threat of an impending debate wound Pastor Bennington even tighter. He set down his soda can, stood up and wiped his hand on his khaki pants before offering it to his visitor. They shook hands across the desk, the pastor leaning forward slightly to reach Jonathan's boney hand.

"Mr. Opare, pleased to meet you," said the pastor, pronouncing the name "Oh-pear," having only read it on his email.

"It's Oh-pah-ray," Jonathan said, smiling and shaking hands vigorously. Ken Bennington reminded him of athletes he had known back home, tensed and ready for the starting gun. "You can call me Jonathan," he said.

"Great. You can call me Ken."

Though this latter concession seemed friendly, from Ken's perspective, to Jonathan it was just another awkward cultural

If You Really Knew Me

fence to climb. He never would have addressed a pastor by his first name in his church back home.

Gesturing to a chair across the desk, Ken squatted back into his tall fake-leather chair. "So you're in the U.S. to study? What is it you're studying?"

"Economics," Jonathan answered, still smiling as he lowered his bag to the floor next to his chair. For the next few minutes, Ken tried to size up his visitor, and Jonathan tried to explain exactly what about economics he was studying. This led back to his home country and his family background, including church. Finally, they turned to the actual agenda for the meeting.

"So, you see, I brought this particular perspective to the community-wide meeting this past week," Jonathan said. He crossed his right leg over his left knee at the ankle, resting his right hand on the cross bar formed by his shinbone.

"You mean a *Pentecostal* perspective?" Ken said, to be sure he knew what was coming.

"Yes," Jonathan said. "My wife and I have been attending Pastor Claiborne's church, because of some friendships there, but I am still a product of my Pentecostal upbringing, and some of what was said the other night concerned me. I want to understand how *you* see the criticism of Mr. Dupere."

"Well, of course, I was on the stage because I share some concerns about Mr. Dupere's lifestyle, the same as the other pastors from other denominations and traditions," Ken said. "But I can understand where you might have some questions about the way things went at the meeting. I think I would have said some things a bit differently to my own congregation, for example."

Jonathan nodded. "Yes, I expected that would be the case, because it was hard not to feel that the indictment of Mr. Dupere was an indictment of healing ministers in general."

"That's what I thought you were concerned about." Ken smiled here. He was relieved that he could fit Jonathan into the same group as folks from his church who had been calling him and visiting him all week. "And, I think more people in my con-

If You Really Knew Me

gregation actually respected and followed the ministry of Mr. Dupere than in the other congregations represented there. That's why I felt it important to join in the warning to all Bible-believing Christians, a warning against a wolf in sheep's clothes, even more so for people in our churches."

"I suppose the wolf looks most like a sheep to other sheep that have been following him for some time now," Jonathan said, smiling at his own stretch of the metaphor.

Ken wasn't sure if Jonathan was agreeing with him or criticizing his use of that old saying, but he smiled and let it slide past. He spoke more seriously. "I've had some long talks with people in my congregation that are devastated to learn these things about his ministry."

"People who've actually been healed by him?"

Ken raised both eyebrows briefly. "Yes. In fact, some people are wondering about the healing they received in the past from him. You know, 'How could I be healed, then, if he was so bad?' Or even, 'Does this mean my healing wasn't from God?'"

Jonathan shrugged his shoulders slightly. "So what do you tell them?"

Ken took a deep breath and allowed his gaze to drift away from Jonathan, toward the corner of the room, as he remembered these conversations. "Well, Jesus tells a few people that it was *their* faith that made them whole. So I just tell my folks that maybe it wasn't Mr. Dupere that healed them, it was just God responding to their own faith."

Nodding his head slowly, Jonathan pursed his lips. "And you are confident that the accusations against Mr. Dupere are well founded?"

"I'm sure that at least some of it is true, and there are so many of these misdemeanors that only a few of them have to be right before I tell my people it's best to stay clear of this guy."

After a few more questions and replies, and parting handshakes, Jonathan thanked Ken for his time and his frank responses. He had found what he was looking for, enough to assure him that the case against Beau Dupere wasn't just a disguise for attacking a prominent healing ministry. Even if he didn't join in with condemning Beau Dupere, sins or no sins, this assurance would allow Jonathan to stay with Dixon Claiborne's church until graduation in December, at least that's how things stood when he left Ken Bennington's office.

Back with More Questions

Anna cut off the cell phone call to her editor. He definitely was *not* going to let her drop the Beau Dupere story. Protesters had begun to appear outside his home church and the sign-waving crowds outside the Dupere household had grown larger and more ardent. This was news.

"His wife and daughters nearly crippled me emotionally, what's *he* gonna do to me?" she said aloud, after setting down her phone. Even as she said these words, she knew they were not true words. Any emotional handicap she carried had entered the Dupere house with her.

She looked at the time on her phone. She had to be there in forty minutes, just enough time to drive there after changing into contact lenses and having a little drink. She reached for the bottle of sherry that she often tapped at night before bed, soothing her while she read under low light at the end of a tense day. The two glasses she drank that afternoon were a down payment on the tension she anticipated from meeting the miracle man, or the monster. The contact lenses were just in case he wasn't a monster.

Only the most desperate kind of thinking, of course, would lead Anna to use alcohol to take the edge off her fear of the interview, without any thought to the way it would also take the edge off her driving. At the last major intersection on the Pacific Coast Highway, before she turned down the westward road leading to the Dupere's house, she nearly ran over a cyclist, who inexplicably stopped in the cross walk just in time to let her slip past without a disastrous result. Anna drove ten-miles-an-hour below the speed limit the rest of the way.

This time, when she pulled into the driveway, the guards hit the open switch immediately. Inside the gate, Maggie was waiting for her. Anna parked her car at an awkward angle, as if diagonal parking against the edge of the curved drive. When she stopped the engine, Maggie opened her car door for her.

"Are you okay?" she said, bending slightly and looking like a mother receiving her child home from school after a disturbing call from the principal.

Given her slight intoxication, combined with the shock of the near accident, Anna didn't even pause to wonder how Maggie knew. She just answered. "I'm okay, and so is that guy on the bike, thank God."

"Yes," Maggie said. "We were praying for you. Dad said you were going to have a near miss."

As Anna stood from the car, she felt as if she had misplaced some gravity and was about to float free of the ground. Her head swayed as she tried to absorb Maggie's words. "He knew?" That's all Anna could manage to squeak from her clenched throat.

Maggie smiled sympathetically and took Anna's left arm with both of her hands. "Let's get you inside. I think you could use a glass of lemonade."

Anna just nodded and allowed Maggie to tow her up the two porch steps and into the house. It was happening already, she thought. He's already messing me up. She arrived in the kitchen and accepted a seat at the little table in the corner. Maggie stepped to the fridge and pulled the large handle, throwing her slight weight backward to break the vacuum seal of the tall door.

Watching Maggie, Anna didn't notice a little girl with long sunny blonde hair walk up behind her. Emma stopped next to Anna's left arm and placed one stubby hand on Anna's bare skin.

Unable to understand the words she was using as she spoke under her breath, nevertheless, Anna knew the little girl was praying for her. She felt a subtle warmth descend on her as the shock and the alcohol evaporated. Finally, Anna was fully present in the kitchen, just in time to receive the tall glass of iced-lemonade from Maggie with a humble "thank you."

After delivering the drink, Maggie petted the hair of the little girl looking up at her and said, "Okay, Emma. She's good now."

Emma nodded and hugged Maggie around the hips before waving at Anna and marching back out of the kitchen.

"Thanks," Anna said, her voice fading as she called after Emma. Emma looked over her shoulder and smiled just before she disappeared from Anna's sight.

Anna looked at Maggie, hoping for an explanation of everything that had happened since she pulled into the driveway. Instead, Maggie's green eyes smiled and she propelled Anna toward the reason for her visit. "You'll find my father in Peter's room, I think."

"But..." Anna started to question, but interrupted herself with the thought that perhaps it wasn't good to question this sort of thing. Maybe she should just be thankful for arriving safely, for the purge of anxiety granted her by Emma's prayer. Her hesitation was enough to hand the initiative back to Maggie.

"C'mon, I'll show you where it is."

Anna stood, taking Maggie's offered hand. She mused about the instant connection she felt with Maggie, like a sister or friend, though ten years separated them.

Dodging through the back hallway and up the winding main staircase, Anna followed through the house. She had been in dozens of celebrity multi-million-dollar homes. The elaborate architecture and bright open spaces of the Dupere home were familiar. But it lacked the ostentatious artwork or furniture of the stars, as if the home had been furnished with only the essentials, in spite of its pricey zip code.

On the second floor, padding silently down the main hallway, Anna could hear the sound effects that boys make when crashing and exploding vehicles in their games. She thought she could hear two distinct sets of voices screeching tires and crunching fenders as she and Maggie approached a half-opened door. Anna peered around the door to find Peter, a curly, dark-haired boy of six, on his hands and knees, steering a Lego car over tan carpet. Next to him lay Beau Dupere, stretched out on his side, driving his own Lego vehicle around a pile of blocks that resembled the rubble of a demolished building. Beau was a large, athletically-built man. There on the floor next to Peter, he looked like a giant. He wore baggy tan shorts and a white polo shirt that emphasized the caramel color of his skin.

The boy looked up before Anna or Maggie made a sound, but it was Beau who spoke first, without looking up, in a voice that Anna took to represent the driver of the little car in his hand. "Well, Mack, seems like I'm gonna have to park it for a while. Got some business to attend to."

Glancing at his father, Peter just went back to his noisy driving. Beau fluffed Peter's generous locks and rose to his bare feet. No one except Anna seemed to wear shoes around the house. That made her self-conscious.

"See ya for swimming later, kiddo," Beau said.

"Okay, Dad," Peter said, without lifting his head.

Arriving at the door with his hand extended, Beau Dupere looked Anna over from head to toe. He took her hand and said, "Don't worry about the shoes, you can wear whatever's comfortable for you."

Without thinking, Anna stepped out of her little brown flats and wriggled her toes in the thick carpet.

Maggie stepped in immediately, picking up the shoes. "I'll take them down by the front door, so you know where to find them."

Anna watched as Maggie stooped down and scooped up her size six shoes. When she looked up, she saw Beau still looking at her, reading her, it seemed.

"Sorry, I don't mean to make you self-conscious," he said, when she glanced away from eye contact. "It feels like I'm invading your privacy, I know. But it's just the way I'm used to getting to know people. My family is accustomed to it. We just know we can't have many secrets from each other."

Anna started to chuckle, surprising herself as much as Beau. She hitched her purse up on one shoulder. "I usually have to warm up my subjects to get them to go deeper in an interview," she said, to herself as much as to Beau.

He laughed lightly and said, "Okay, let's start with proper introductions." Once again, he held out his hand, but this time for a handshake, instead of taking her spiritual pulse. "I'm Beau Dupere. You must be Anna Conyers."

Smiling very broadly, Anna added some vigor to that handshake and said, "Pleased to meet you, at last." She suppressed a giggle, realizing how much easier it was to talk to him than to the mystical cult leader in her imagination. The man lying on the floor playing Legos with a six-year-old, and who cared about her self-consciousness over wearing shoes, couldn't be the creepy guru of her darker fantasies.

Then a question occurred to her, as she turned to follow Beau down the hallway. "Does reading people's minds cut out a lot of conversation around here?" she said, again feeling like she was just wondering aloud, but not feeling apologetic for converting her thoughts to words.

Beau looked around his shoulder at Anna, walking slightly behind him in the hall, and said, "I don't really think of it as reading people's minds. To me it's more like reading their souls, almost a level below what's on your mind."

"Oh," Anna said. "That seems a bit more worrying then, like me controlling my thoughts isn't gonna keep you from knowing things about me."

Beau led the way back down the central staircase, his voice echoing slightly in the open space. "I don't worry about it, because I trust the one who feeds me the information. I *have* been uncomfortable sometimes finding things out about people that I would expect they don't want me to know. But I usually discover later that they really *did* want someone to know. Everyone wants to be known, even on the deepest level, by somebody. Personally, I think it's God that they want to know them like that."

Not fully tracking with what he was saying, Anna asked a reflex question in return. "But doesn't God know everything and control everything?"

As they stepped onto the cool tile in the front hallway, Beau replied. "The answer to those two questions is yes and no. God knows everything, but God hasn't been in control of everything since he turned the garden over to Adam and Eve, just before they turned it over to the Devil."

Anna caught up to him in the kitchen. She studied his profile for a second before he turned to face her. "More lemonade?" he said, noting the glass still on the kitchen table.

"Oh, no. This is fine," Anna said. She wrapped one hand around the bottom half of the sweating, cold glass.

Beau nodded, but opened the fridge and pulled the lemonade pitcher out for himself, popping open one of the shiny white cupboards and extracting a glass like the one Anna held. As he dispensed ice from the icemaker and poured his drink, Ann followed his earlier answer.

"So you don't believe God is in control of the world?"

Just as Beau looked up at her, they could hear Maggie calling to someone about Peter playing in his room by himself now. The reply to that news, from a woman's voice further away, made Maggie laugh, though Anna couldn't tell what she was laughing about.

Beau tied onto the momentary distraction. "I know people like to talk as if God has built these little people out of Legos and is walking them around, making them talk and fight or drive their trucks, or whatever. But that doesn't represent the God of the Bible, or the God that I know from my experience."

"So you believe people have free will?" Anna followed him now out the back door to two chairs under the balcony that wrapped around two sides of the pool. Three children threw a big red ball back and forth in the water, laughing and splashing. Two women, one of them Bethany—clothed in a pink cotton dress—appeared to be deep in conversation on the other side of the pool. Another woman sat under an umbrella watching the children play, an infant in her lap, looking as if he had just finished nursing, his little round head lolling drunkenly.

"Sure, without freedom humans aren't human and aren't made in God's image. But that doesn't mean that they exercise their freedom. Most people stay confined in a cage mostly of their own devising."

Anna felt that this conversation was running away from her. She remembered seeing video of Beau preaching at a large church conference in Texas. He seemed to jump from topic to topic in that setting as well. Though she hadn't been impressed by his preaching, he did seem clear about what he believed.

Sitting down across from him, Anna crossed her legs self-consciously, careful of her skirt that fell well short of her knees. She set her lemonade on the glass table and pulled her digital recorder from her purse. She fiddled with the controls and then held it toward Beau's seat facing her. "Okay?" she said.

"You mean we weren't even started on the interview yet?" Beau said, his eyebrows raised in mock horror. "That was some of my best stuff."

Anna laughed. She could see why women fell for him. He was as charming as any actor she had ever met, and certainly as handsome. She didn't expect jokes from him, however, given her image of the mystical guru she had constructed. As she thought these things, she could see him looking at her and turning more serious, crossing his legs with his right ankle on his left knee and his right knee pointing approximately at Anna.

She seized the silent opening, though she couldn't tell why his mood seemed to change. "You started by explaining to me about how you don't really read people's minds, but it's something else." She suddenly wondered whether Beau's sobering had been in response to her inner spark of infatuation.

"Right," he said, his tone lower and more formal, his shiny smile less ready. "It's not that I can hear the thoughts going on in your head, it's more like I'm getting these thoughts in my own head informing me about something regarding you, your past, your present condition, like that."

A puzzled squint approaching the corners of her eyes, Anna said, "Okay, you say 'getting thoughts.' Where do those come from?"

"I figure that at least half of them are just my imagination, my own thoughts. I also think I hear things, or think things, that come from my enemy. But the rest come from The Truth that lives in me."

"'The Truth?'"

"Yes, God's Spirit is The Truth, and The Truth lives inside people who invite him in. We listen to that Truth more or less all the time. I keep going for more."

"More truth?"

"More of God's thoughts communicated to me through The Truth he planted inside me."

"Does that mean people who don't believe in God the way you do, don't have truth?"

"When I say that we have The Truth in us, I don't mean to say that others can't know something that's true, or even teach and live by things that are true. But there is one source of all truth and that's God. To live in that truth, we have to surrender our ideas in favor of the ideas that come from The Truth."

Anna decided to leave a topic that she felt was too theological or philosophical, in favor of more practical issues. "So the things that you know about people, that come from The Truth, what is the purpose of that?"

"God only gives us these abilities in order to benefit the people we meet, not to benefit ourselves."

Anna nodded slowly, she switched her recorder to her left hand and reached for her lemonade. She was looking for more biographical information and less of these explanations of beliefs and practices.

"So how did this all start for you, the healing and the knowing things?"

Beau took a big breath and launched into a brief history of his church attendance and evolving faith, from his childhood conversion in the Evangelical Covenant Church in Kansas, to his connection with the new movement of which his home church was a part. "The transition came for me when I was in a really rough time in my life, realizing that I was just living until I died, disconnected from my faith, with no meaning. I went to a meeting some friends from my old church recommended, and I saw Jack Williams for the first time. The main speaker was Bruce Winters, who was more famous back then, but I got to talk to Jack after the service. That was after I got a huge dose of God dumped on me during a prayer time. Jack sorta scooped me up off the floor and started interviewing me, like he was thinking of hiring me for something. Eventually, of course, he actually did recruit me to take part in new churches he was planting around the West."

"So all these things started happening around then?"

"No, it was really gradual. Like, I never saw anyone get healed for the first four or five years I was in Jack's churches. But sometimes I would get ideas that I shared with others, what we call prophecies or words of knowledge. That's all church talk just for different kinds of messages that God delivers through people."

"What about healing? What changed that for you?"

"Oh, I think of it as two forces coming together, really," he said, stopping to sip his lemonade and glancing at a particularly rambunctious turn of play in the pool. For a moment, he looked as if he would get up and join in the fun. But he restrained that apparent urge. "The first thing was this little guy who used to work with Catherine Kuhlman and sort of communicated some of what she had for healing."

"I went to this conference, really something like an old fashioned revival meeting, and I heard this guy, Jay Hamer, talk about some of the healing stuff he had seen in his ministry. Something inside me was saying, 'that's it, that's what I want,' even though the idea of a healing ministry was far from my conscious thinking at the time." Looking again at the kids in the pool, he paused and then continued. "I figured I would get this guy to give me what he had, so I got in line for him to lay his hands on me. Actually, I got in line about four times. I'd get up off the floor and think, 'I don't feel different yet,' so I'd go back for more. I think the last time he was just ready to call it a night so he put both hands on my head and said something like, 'okay, God he's serious about this, give him everything.'" Beau laughed at his memory of it. "I was out for a few hours. They shut off the lights and closed the doors, just leaving me there in a heap on the carpet." He laughed some more.

"The second breakthrough was this dream I had one night, where Jesus came into my house and told me he had work for me to do, and the tools for my work would be in my own body. When I woke up, my chronic back pain was gone. I got a dozen more small healings like that, just directly from God, in that first year. Those healings boosted my faith to heal others."

"So you just woke up in the mornings and you were healed of something?"

He nodded. "That happened several times, with flat feet, an infected ingrown toenail, a curve to my spine and some carpal tunnel in my right hand, for example. But other stuff was healed during worship songs in church. I can still feel what it was like for my allergies to just disappear in the final chorus of one of my favorite songs. That was a blast." He laughed at the memory of it, such that a tiny tear formed in the corner of one eye.

Anna just shook her head. "And none of these conditions have come back as you get older?"

"Who's getting older?" he said, again with that look of mock horror. He laughed, but then straightened himself up, shifting to better posture in his chair.

Anna laughed obligingly, but Beau constructed a serious answer.

"God had put healing in me by healing me of every ache and pain and condition I ever complained of before that," he said. "In recent years, the children have been praying over me and I've seen changes in my energy levels and even seen the effects of too much sun exposure completely taken away. Justine says I look ten years younger than I did ten years ago."

Staring for five seconds of backtracking and absorption, Anna finally asked for clarification. "You mean, you're not only healed of all your ailments, but you're even getting healed of normal aging?"

"Yeah, well 'normal' in the world as we know it is under the curse of the Devil. Normal in God's Kingdom, like Heaven, is no more pain, no more sickness, and no more death."

The halting shock in Anna's responses might have reminded a neutral observer of a conversation over a satellite link, complete with time delay. When she recovered again, she said, "You think you might not die of old age?"

"Oh, I know I won't die of old age. But that doesn't mean I won't die. And when I do, I fully expect to be raised from the dead by one of my family members. We have a deal that we'll come back if we're called."

"'Called?'" Anna couldn't tell if he was teasing because of the big grin on his face.

"Sure. Jesus sent his disciples out with orders to heal the sick, cast out demons and *raise the dead*. The only problem with raising a Christian from the dead is they might not want to come back from Paradise. But we made a deal that we would come back, so God would be glorified after we get killed."

"'Killed?'"

"Oh, honey, you look like you're seeing a ghost." He chuckled. "I'm not dead yet," he said and slid off into uninhibited laughter.

If You Really Knew Me

Justine came out of the kitchen door and headed toward them.

"Just in time," thought Anna, when she spotted her. Then it occurred to her that this may not be a coincidence. Her face flushed, as her mind tripped over the implications of all that she was hearing.

"I knew you would do it," Justine said.

"Yep, you were right, as usual," Beau said in return. They smiled at each other briefly, with no shame or anger registering on either of their faces.

"Anna, how are you doing with all this?" Justine said, though she apparently knew already that the reporter was overwhelmed by what she had heard, like a weak swimmer in big surf.

That sympathetic question burst open a flood of responses from Anna. "I don't know. How can it be?" She breathed rapidly. "I mean, I know something is different, I know something is happening here. But reversing aging without cosmetic surgery or supplements or whatever, and healed of every ailment and deformity, and planning to be raised..."

Justine knelt next to Anna and wrapped an arm around her shoulders when her guest began panting, as if heading for an anxiety attack.

"Peace," Justine said. Beau rose and stood on the other side of Anna, just lightly touching her near shoulder.

"That's right," was all he said. And Anna felt a warm bliss, like when a doctor or nurse injects a powerful drug into a patient's I.V. The injection of peace swept through her body and stilled the hamster wheel in her head.

When her thoughts fell into line, stepping rationally from one to the next, Anna thought of the contrast between her hosts and the other celebrities she had visited. The similarity in their public appearance masked a deep contrast in their personal reservoir of character. Justine and Beau looked just like actors, with their tightened this and injected that, toned by professional trainers and spa treatments. But the celebs behind the front door of most Malibu mansions revealed an acid leak of fears and frus-

If You Really Knew Me

trations with their lives, once she dug in. The stars always looked confident on the red carpet, on the screen or on the stage. But these odd church folks didn't have to fake it. They didn't even have to try. And the result was unedited honesty that, on paper, would make them sound totally bonkers. Yet they seemed the sanest people she had ever met.

Anna started to standup. A sensation, like some large invisible creature pouncing on her from behind, triggering her flight instinct. But, when it landed on her, overtaking her, it arrived less like a predator and more like a sudden memory. She burst out weeping, as if recalling a lost relative, a lost home or lost love. Yet she couldn't identify any object to this sudden sorrow, a rush of tears beyond even the day she learned her father died. Even as her emotional gauges all swung into the red, she felt a relief, a purging.

Justine just held on through the sobbing spasms and smiled. Beau just said it again, "That's right."

Digging Deeper

For Sara, these last few days of her senior year had begun to drag and stagnate. The days of anticlimax sapped her energy for even *attending* school, for the first time in her life, as if she had been holding off that so-common urge to play hooky all these years and surrendered just at the end.

On top of that, the story about Jenny's mother being healed of cancer hatched a feeling of betrayal that had been incubating in some hidden corner of Sara's heart. Her parents' faith had always sufficed for her, as long as she didn't have to think much about it, or even argue in its defense. Now, she felt no compunction to defend it, but rather an—almost animal—instinct to attack it and see if it could survive a predatory challenge to its fitness, its very right to live. Was this just boredom? Was it a forced rite of passage, from her parents' faith to her own? Maybe it was even more than that, maybe it was a bugle call to take up arms, to choose a side, instead of merely resting behind battle lines defended by others.

At lunch, the Monday after her confrontation with her father, Sara sat with Jenny Washington and Kim Crenshaw. Kim had remained silent at the cheerleader party, uncomfortable discussing church things among her school friends. She attended Ken Bennington's Assemblies church. Quietly, Kim harbored admiration for Beau Dupere, because of a dozen stories of healing she had heard attributed to him. Several of her relatives had attended his healing services and some of them had been freed from pains or afflictions as a result.

Sara chewed inattentively on her tuna sandwich, trying to figure out how to raise the topic without throwing gasoline on any hidden embers. Kim helped her out.

"I'm glad to see you two are still hanging out together," she said, to Sara and Jenny, opening her little carton of skim milk and unwrapping her silverware from the paper napkin.

Sara seized the opportunity. "As far as I'm concerned, the only thing that happened Friday night was that I figured out how clueless I am about this healing stuff."

To the other girls, this constituted an apology, acknowledging Jenny's accusation at the party.

Looking at Sara while she sipped diet cola through a straw, Jenny sensed that her friend jumping beyond the peacemaking surrender of Friday night. "So what changed your mind?" she said.

Sara dropped the corner of her sandwich and wiped her hands on a napkin. "I talked to my parents that night, and they had nothing to say that answered any of my questions. I assumed they had better reasons for attacking Beau Dupere. It re-

If You Really Knew Me

ally felt to me like my Dad was stretching to come up with a reason to hate the guy."

"You think they really hate him?" Kim said. She was looking at a boy at the next table who had turned toward them when Sara mentioned Beau Dupere.

Sara shrugged. She paused to tug at her braid on the back of her head, which hadn't felt right all day, as if she'd woven it unevenly that morning. "My dad practically accused him of being a devil worshipper last night."

"Ooooo," Jenny said, wincing at that sour note. She had always liked Sara's parents, but that had been in the context of nice questions about school and cheerleading, lobbed at her by Dixon or Kristen.

That boy at the next table turned all the way around now, his feet behind the bench on which he sat. "My dad claims Dupere is the Antichrist," he said, with typical teen skepticism twisting his voice around that last word.

Sara looked at the intruder, turning her head ninety degrees to do so. She had seen that junior boy around, he played on the football team, though he spent more time on the sidelines watching the cheerleaders than hitting people out on the field. Her almost graduated persona, however, allowed for interaction with the lower castes in the school now.

"Antichrist?" she said.

"Yeah, the people at our church are always talking about who might be the Antichrist, like saying it's the Pope or that it's the President. Now my dad says it's Dupere 'cause he can do miracles."

Sara twisted her torso to make looking at the guy easier. She was still trying to remember his name, picturing his last name in white letters on the back of a blue jersey. She recalled his number, forty-seven. His medium length brown hair, round blue eyes and small mouth with thin lips barely distinguished him from a score of other underclassmen, as far as Sara's memory was concerned.

"When did they go from saying that he didn't really *do* any miracles to saying that the reason he *does* miracles is 'cause he's a Satan worshipper?" Sara said, bending her gaze from the guest speaker back to her friends.

"That's a good question," Kim said. "Maybe it's so that the people who claim to be healed by him aren't made out to be liars. It's like a political move to get the people on their side."

The unnamed boy nodded vigorously at this, his hair falling over his forehead with the movement. "Yeah, that's what it is. Politics."

Jenny shook her head. "Not for me, it's not politics. It's my mother's life. Why would the Devil want to heal my mother of cancer? Doesn't the Devil want to hurt people and kill them?"

Sara could think of some reasons the Devil would want to heal an evil person, but she knew better than to introduce that angle right after Jenny made the issue personal. Sara really did like Jenny's mom, and was pretty sure that the tall athletic attorney wasn't evil, even if she *was* a lawyer.

Sara noticed that the conversation had begun to catch the attention of more people than she was comfortable including in a discussion about God or religion, so she turned back to her tuna sandwich. Jenny saw this and turned in as well.

"You wanna come talk to my mom about it?" she said more quietly.

Sara thought about that, weighing the awkwardness of such a meeting against how much difference it would make to her. She realized that she already doubted her parents on this and didn't need to hear any more about Jenny's mom. She believed Jenny and Kira, and that was enough. Her own mom and dad had sealed her doubts about them with their weak performance Friday. This cafeteria conversation had added more fuel, raising her suspicion that this was just another case of Christians hating each other for reasons that she couldn't justify, or even explain.

"I don't think I really need to talk to your mom," Sara said. "I think the next thing would be for me to go see for myself. I'm gonna look for videos online that aren't made by people trying to

If You Really Knew Me

make Beau Dupere look bad. Then maybe we can find out if he's doing any meetings around here."

Jenny and Kim both perked up at this last idea.

"I know where to look for his schedule," Kim said. "I'll see if there are any dates or places we can do."

"It shouldn't be too hard to find," said Jenny. "But you'll have to get past all the hater sites first."

Sara liked the sudden coalition with Kim and Jenny, two girls whose faith had remained as unnamed as her own for all the time she had known them.

What Just Happened to Me?

After two interviews at the Dupere home, Anna felt as if she knew what to expect from them, even if she didn't understand everything they said or did. She definitely didn't understand the emotional tremors they were setting off in her own life.

The only person she could think to debrief with, regarding these experiences, was the religion editor at the paper. Anna had been given the story as a contemporary issues piece involving a wealthy celebrity. No one even thought to hand the story to the religion editor.

Marla Kato was about twice Anna's age and seemed far too serious for after work drinks or hanging out together, as Anna did with several of the other reporters and editors, especially the singles. But Marla's Zen-like solemnity counted in her favor when Anna had to decide who to consult about what was happening to her. She didn't expect Marla to be fully sympathetic to the Duperes. But she hoped that Marla would at least be able to help her categorize her experiences with them.

At five o'clock on Friday, quitting time on the day after deadlines for the weekly paper, Anna stopped at the glass door of Marla's office. She started to knock but found the door open a crack and gave it a gentle push. "Marla, are you in?"

A desk lamp was still lit and Anna could see Marla's purse on the chair next to her desk. As she debated whether to wait, Marla rounded the corner of the cubicles in the open office space to Anna's right, her head not high enough for Anna to see her before that.

"You looking for me?" Marla said, her lowered eyebrows witnessing to the rarity of this visit from Anna.

Anna laughed, her nerves escaping in the halting puffs of air she caught in her throat. Her eyes danced all around Marla during this tension releasing laughter. But she finally focused on Marla's question and met the religion editor's deep brown eyes. "Yep. You caught me."

"You wanna come in? I was just wrapping up for the day," Marla said, easing her stout frame past Anna.

"You have a few minutes?" Anna said, trying to intuit Marla's response to this late intrusion.

"Sure. What's it about?" Marla headed straight for her desk chair, waving her hand at the chairs across the desk as she passed.

"Well, I don't know if you were aware that I'm doing a story on Beau Dupere . . ." she said, in what she knew was a mutant question.

"Beau Dupere," Marla said as she sat down. "Oh, yes—now that you mention it—I did hear that you were working on that. But I thought of it more as a celebrity piece than a religion story, I guess."

Anna snickered, still stretching her nerves. "Yeah, well it's been sliding from the one to the other for me, sorta." Again, she knew that her discomfort at the topic was handicapping her verbal abilities, which, of course, made her more nervous.

Marla picked up on the signs. "What's happening with you?" she said, assuming a lot more than Anna would have assumed in reversed roles.

"Happening with me...?" Anna said, looking for a good headline, or at least an opening paragraph. "You know, I think that's why I want to talk to you. I don't really *know* what's happening with me."

"You've met with him?" Marla said.

"Yes, and with his wife, Justine."

"Okay. What's your impression of them?"

Put so starkly, Anna hesitated to offer a summary impression, as if it would make her look naïve or suggestible. Some part of her also longed to please Beau and Justine, she didn't want to betray them in any way. She writhed inside, sinking into the center of the tangle that provoked this cry for help in the first place.

Finally, Anna tried an honest answer. "I have mixed feelings about them, and I guess I have more intense feelings than an objective journalist should have."

Marla leaned back and grinned slightly. "Well, let's set aside the idea of objective journalism. Are you feeling pulled in by them, like with a cult or something?"

Shaking her head rapidly, Anna said, "No, it's not creepy at all. I mean they seem like normal, very nice people. They seem to care a lot about me, especially when they can tell that the things they're telling me are freaking me out."

"Okay, like what things?"

"Like that Beau's youthful good looks, perfect teeth, golden tan and great hair are not the product of extensive training, surgeries or stylists. He says it all comes from being healed of everything, even stress. These people don't seem the least bit stressed. And this is with a crowd of people calling for their crucifixion outside their front gate." Anna surprised herself with the jet fuel behind her response.

"You believe his claims of healing?" Marla said, her tone even and revealing no prejudice.

If You Really Knew Me

Again, Anna aimed for honesty. "I actually do. And part of the reason I believe is the things I've felt when I'm with them. Like the first time I walked in the house, their daughter, Maggie, touched me and seemed to drive anxiety right out of my body. I didn't expect that at all. It wasn't Beau that did it, with his famous reputation, but just a teenage girl passing me in the hallway. I doubt that was just me being a pushover to the power of suggestion."

Even though Anna felt like she was chucking her guts out for Marla to scrutinize, she felt instant relief at being able to say these things to another person. Unexpectedly, she noted a tangent thought about what her *mother* would say if she told her.

Marla smiled a tight sort of smile that raised the prominence of her cheeks and overwhelmed her eyes. "You do sound like you've had some sort of spiritual experience." She held both hands out, palms up, her elbows on the arms of her chair. "Do you feel better than you did before you met them?"

Blinking and raising her eyebrows to maximum height, Anna answered, to her own surprise. "Yes, of course, I do feel better. Nothing they've said or done has harmed me in any way, and they've pushed stress and anxiety out of me more than once. My only negative feelings are just confusion, and maybe even fear, about what all this means."

"Fear about what it would mean if these people really could heal your soul or even your body?"

"Yeah." That was exactly what Anna feared. Wouldn't she have to change something about her life if these people, who claimed God lived inside them, proved it by the way they cared for her?

Marla chuckled. She was amused by the dumbfounded look on Anna's face, and excited at the positive review she was hearing about Beau Dupere. Marla's faith in spiritual things had never rested for long in any one religion. She not only thought of herself as open-minded, she had truly cultivated an appreciation for a wide range of spiritual experiences. Her estimation of Beau Dupere had elevated lately when she saw how much he was upsetting conservative elements of his own faith. Marla's openness to a variety of ways to pursue God tended to favor the fringe elements of any given religion. Pictures of Beau lifting a champagne glass with the stars, and possibilities that he practiced open marriage, endeared him to Marla, in exactly the opposite way he infuriated Dixon Claiborne and those who were even more conservative than him.

Marla stopped laughing and said, "Well, girl. Get as much good stuff as you can from these folks. Who knows, maybe they've found the map to the fountain of youth."

Though the religion editor seemed to be taking her experience more lightly than Anna would have liked, that levity relieved Anna of some of her fear. Maybe she could be like Marla, amused by Beau's eccentricities, without any deeper implications for her life.

Maybe.

Cold Comfort

Dixon Claiborne tried to resume the regular duties of a pastor, between the radio interviews, irate phone calls and confused visits from church members. The heaviest of those normal duties, of course, involved visiting the terminally ill members of the church.

For as long as he had been pastor of the church, Glenda Larson had faithfully attended, treading water through some rough changes and keeping her smile on throughout. Since her husband had died in the early days of the Afghan war, she had lived alone on the death benefits of the career Master Sergeant, supplemented by part-time work for the Post Office. She lived just past the outskirts of a little town called Kearney, ten miles from Parkerville. It was during a day when she substituted for one of the carriers that she first fell and broke her hip. At fifty-five, she was strong and healthy, not prone to the fragile falls of more senior friends and family. But, with the break, doctors discovered advanced bone cancer, which had weakened her femur and left it vulnerable to even a slight stumble, such as the one which left her lying face-down in the grass on the postal route. After weeping and crying out for as much as ten minutes with no help, she had passed out. A truck driver finally saw her on his way to deliver bottled water to a neighbor, perhaps an hour after Glenda fell.

In all the times that Dixon had visited her since that fall, never once had she mentioned lying on the ground for so long without help arriving. Never had she complained about the difficulties of a major injury, and then cancer treatment, for someone living on her own. She and Patrick had never been able to have children and Glenda had been an only child. Without family, people from the church had to step into the gap, though her distance from the population center of the church dissipated the amount of help she received. In a way, Dixon had been relieved when she was finally admitted to the hospital this last time, so he wouldn't have to worry about her being alone and in need.

"Well, hello, Pastor," Glenda said, her crinkly voice both weaker and older than her years.

Dixon strode across the hospital room with a pasted-on smile and great care at landing his steps softly, in deference to both Glenda's pain and the skeletal lady in the next bed, whose skin looked as if she was made of papier-mache.

"Hello, Glenda, dear," Dixon said, with the look of a man who smiled harder the sadder he felt. "How are you today?" he said, covering her left hand with his right.

"Oh, I'm feelin' pretty good today. I think you got me on one of my good days."

Throughout her convalescence, Glenda had traced the precarious path between refusing to complain and being dishonest.

If You Really Knew Me

By now, Dixon had learned to listen to her tone and ignore her words. The words didn't vary much from day to day. But her voice had been hollowed out by the extended pain, by the failed chemotherapy and by surgeries intended only to minimize her agony, with no hope of a cure.

Dixon didn't know it yet, of course, but Glenda had survived into her final week of life, still fighting to stay positive even as she resisted larger doses of medication. She seemed, to Dixon, to have begun to tip over the fence from tough to crazy. Maybe women really do have a higher pain threshold, but what he had learned from the doctors, and what he could detect in the changes to her glassy eyes and trap-tight mouth, convinced him that Glenda was enduring more than she should. He missed the sparkling face that smiled so easily and the woman that exuded compassion to others, compassion that she never would have tolerated for herself. Her terminal illness had already ended her ability to choose such things. She was at the mercy of strangers now. And the doctors and nurses who attended the shell of what used to be Glenda Larson didn't know what they were missing, and were too busy to dig deep enough to find out for themselves.

Dixon's silent stare in response to her usual game-face seemed to prompt unprecedented honesty from Glenda. She placed her right hand over Dixon's, still holding her left, and said, "I'm not going to be getting out of this place, this time."

Though this could have come as a complaint, or a mournful confession, Dixon knew it was rather a direct and brave embrace of reality.

"Tell me how to pray for you," was all Dixon could say.

Glenda relaxed her grip on the back of his hand and rested her head deeper into her pillows. He could see in her eyes the process of flipping through all the expected responses that she had practiced for over a year now. She sighed and said, "I just don't want to be any trouble to anybody. I know this is the end for me here. I just don't want to waste people's time and concern when I know it's already over."

If You Really Knew Me

These words nearly dragged Dixon to his knees in powerless pity for himself, and everyone else he knew, who would never be as selfless as Glenda. He cast about for some kind of response, some kind of reward suited to her faithfulness and courage. But he had none to offer.

Bowing his head, Dixon maintained his grip on Glenda's hand and started a weary, apologetic prayer to a God, who he imagined must certainly be tired of hearing from him on behalf of Glenda. All those prayers for her healing had used up what little endurance Dixon had for the attempt. All those "your will be done" prayers felt like a white flag surrender in the face of a ruthless enemy, who would only continue to be more ruthless as a result.

This time, in this last prayer with Glenda, before she would be unconscious and unable to hear what he prayed, he thanked God for her life and for her steadfast patience and faith. In essence, he thanked God that she was dying well, at least better than he would in her place. And that was the best he could offer.

It was nothing. Less than nothing. It was really a catalog of what she had offered to *him*, which was mostly an example of toughness without meanness. That example was, after all, something the former football player could appreciate more than most.

After a few words about funeral arrangements and contacting distant family, Dixon left as he had arrived, striding lightly, in consideration for the suffering of those around him. His silent retreat would do as much to defeat sickness and death as had his silent approach. Exactly nothing.

This had, of course, always been the case for Dixon. But this time, he actually felt it in his chest, like a wasp nest buzzing inside him, insisting that he leave it alone there, lest a swarm be unleashed—a swarm that would not only hurt him, but everyone close to him as well.

Dipping a Toe in the Deep End

Sara sat on her bed with her laptop in front of her, a posture unique to her generation, and one that would cause crippling pain to most people over forty. She stared at the Web page in her browser with an intensity worthy of a surgeon. About Beau Dupere and his friends and affiliates, she had become more than simply curious. The video she now watched in a small window, typical of shared public content, claimed to show a man's amputated finger restored. The healer was Kay Grayson, another product of Jack Williams's church. The fierce focus on Sara's face fled before a flash of wonder, as the stump grew into a whole finger before her eyes.

Of course, Sara had grown up with computer graphics enhancement to movies and videos. She knew that sort of thing could be faked. But, what would have been harder to fake than altering the video to show a finger growing into place, was the reaction of the sixty-year-old man who got his missing digit back, as well as his wife standing next to him. The wife, a head of cotton-like hair, a pointy nose and big smiling teeth, nearly fell over with the shock of it. She didn't look like an actress, but, if that video was digitally altered, she gave an Academy-worthy performance. The healed man laughed so hard that his round stomach heaved and shook, the definition of a belly laugh. He showed everyone around him his perfectly good finger, his brand new finger. Not very many adults have one of those, of which he seemed fully aware.

Sara paused and looked out her window, though not focusing on anything there, either on the glass or outside it. "What if this were real?" she thought, though, as it formed in her mind, the thought didn't fall together into one simple question. It was a hundred questions, questions about reality and perception, questions about faith and God, questions about her family and truth, questions about deceptions and liberation. A God who could do something like replacing that man's finger seemed much more interesting to Sara than the old guy she heard about in church, who seemed to live in some far country, one that had no extradition treaty with the United States.

She had never expected to see God. She had never expected to see God *do* anything.

At the age of eighteen, in the U.S. of A., in the twenty-first century, whether or not to take a chance in order to discover something inspiring is not even a rational question. Sara would find out for herself if this stuff was real. To begin, she stayed up past midnight watching videos on Web sites she had never heard of before, as well as on the most popular video Web sites of all. Though any number of the scenes could have been fabricated, she found it difficult to believe that so many absolutely convincing actors could be brought together to fake witnessing a healing, their own or that of family or friends. These people looked like people Sara knew. They acted like people she knew. At least, they acted the way she *imagined* they would act if they saw their father's glass eye replaced with a real one, or if they saw someone's leg grow out three inches in two seconds. She could only imagine.

And she dreamed. Sleeping late on that Saturday morning, she would have slept on until noon if Kim hadn't kept her word and finally called with information about where they could see Beau Dupere. The downside of that ring tone as her wakeup call, was that Sara had been dreaming all night of people getting healed, including a decapitated body getting a new head. And, of course, Beau Dupere—with his perfect, romance novel, good looks—featured in many of those foggy and fleeting scenes.

When she answered the phone, and heard Kim's greeting and bubbly details about the service the next day, in Sacramento, Sara couldn't sort out her dreams from reality for a full five seconds. Kim worried about the silence.

"Sara? Sara? Are you there? Did I call the right number?" she said into the stunned void of the mute cell phone connection.

"Kim? Oh, Kim." Sara regained her coordinates and engaged her vocal chords. "You woke me up, and I was dreaming of Beau Dupere holding my foot to heal it of something that I couldn't really explain, like I was just making something up so he would hold my foot." She streamed this account of the last dream she remembered, before considering whether she wanted Kim to know her subconscious thoughts about the famous billionaire.

Kim giggled. "Then you *definitely* wanna go see him," she said.

Sara focused her mental energy into the cell phone, feeling a light lift at the sound of Kim's giggle. It didn't sound like a ridiculing laugh. It hit Sara more like a sympathetic affirmation.

"Yeah, definitely. We gotta go and see him."

Counting to a Billion

Anna intended her conversation with Marla Kato as a security measure, a firewall against the brimming warmth and wonder she experienced when she merely *thought* of Beau and Justine and Maggie. Now, thanks to Marla's profligate appreciation for disparate faiths, Anna felt more open to the Duperes, and yet less vulnerable. She thought not only of Beau Dupere, with the quivering compulsion of a coquettish teen, she thought, instead, of Beau with Justine, with Maggie and with Luke.

"Who else was there?" she thought. She wondered about other offspring, about the mothers of those children. Had she seen those mothers around the pool? Bethany couldn't be one of the wives, could she? She was certainly beautiful enough for Anna to

If You Really Knew Me

imagine her with Beau. But, was external beauty something he desired, or was there more in his relationships with these women? When Anna thought of Beau with Bethany or with Justine, she couldn't find the same sort of salacious thrill she felt when she watched a sexy drama or comedy on Blu-Ray, or read a libidinous paperback alone in bed at night. She didn't *want* Beau more now. But she did want to know more about him.

The press, and general populace, often referred to him as "Billionaire Beau Dupere," as if "Billionaire" was his real first name, or perhaps a title granted him by the queen of something or other. Looking around their home, the only home she knew for sure that they owned, she had noticed a lack of the lascivious luxuries of the rich that she had observed in other Malibu mansions. Now she set about tracking Beau's finances, using the best public information available through the Web, and other news organizations, and using some contacts in the finance industry, where Beau had reportedly made his millions, and perhaps billions.

By Monday, the day of her next appointment with Beau Dupere, she had accumulated a pile of data, and managed to form it into a timeline linked to a spreadsheet. She used a Web site that allowed her to graphically navigate the data she input, to zoom in on details and zoom out for a broad overview.

Because the vast majority of his wealth was made and held in private funds, she couldn't be confident that she had found everything there was to know. But she had found enough to allow her to ask educated questions that afternoon at the Dupere home. What she found certainly did inspire questions, many of which would have seemed utterly bizarre to ask of any other rich investor. But, typical of how *atypical* everything about Beau Dupere seemed to be, some outlandish questions seemed necessary for Anna to assemble a true story of his wealth.

She felt confident going into the next interview that Beau had been a billionaire at one point in his life. Measuring the value of his investments and holdings at several points in time, in fact, she believed she could document at least a billion dollars in holdings as early as 2009. Before that, she doubted he had yet won the title "billionaire," but couldn't prove anything precisely.

Much of what she found came from adding pieces of circumstantial evidence, coincidences of timing. For instance, the rumor that Beau Dupere was the anonymous winner of a 2006 lottery jackpot led Anna to a big investment he made a month after that $140 million payout. Though he had already made nearly as much from "intuitive investment practices," which his former boss described, that lottery payout would have catapulted him a long way toward his first billion. This is true because he partnered in a new Web venture with some of that money, which multiplied more than twelve times in value over the next two years. He had not, however, put all of his new money into that investment, she knew, because he also funded an expedition that recovered the largest treasure of sunken gold in the Western hemisphere. Though the "intuitive investments" prompted three investigations for insider trading, no one could think of any way to charge him for being so lucky as to win a major national lottery and also recover a billion dollars of sunken treasure in consecutive years. In fact, Anna suspected that none of it was luck. She linked his investing "intuition," his pick of the winning lottery numbers, and his discovery of a fleet of sunken galleons, to his ability to "know things," as he put it.

As far as Anna could tell, no journalists had yet exercised the audacity, or gullibility, to ask Beau if he became a billionaire by listening to God whisper in his ear. She would be the first.

She didn't know if he would feel comfortable telling her about his finances, but then she couldn't imagine Beau being really uncomfortable about anything. Anna didn't think he would try to hide his finances any more than he hid his children with multiple women. The exception, however, might be questions about where the money had gone.

Anna didn't know how much the Dupere family's financial holdings were currently worth, but she suspected that they were no longer billionaires. She had discovered evidence of charitable

If You Really Knew Me

contributions totaling well more than a billion dollars. The balance sheet, as imprecise as it had to be, just didn't allow that kind of output without diminishing the status of "Billionaire Beau Dupere." "Multi-millionaire Beau Dupere," however, lacked the poetic ring, so she suspected people would be slow to adjust his title, even if she could prove he had lost it.

Of course, Anna wasn't interested in belittling Beau or his family. They had done nothing to raise such spite in her. She had, in fact, built her nascent career with insightful, but restrained, articles about the rich and famous. Access through the next set of eight-foot-tall mahogany doors depended, to some extent, on that reputation of restraint.

Others knew no such restraint. Hackers had infiltrated the Web site for Jack Williams's church and posted inflammatory photos and graffiti, aimed at "The Antichrist," or "The Devil," as the attackers had branded Beau Dupere. They supplemented these flames with, apparently altered, photos of Beau at a satanic ritual, or in sexually explicit poses with multiple women. No restraint there. At the same time that Beau's home church had to hire security consultants to protect their Web site, down in Malibu, the police had parked a car next to the driveway of the Dupere home, according to the latest news. They claimed they were responding to "credible death threats."

These vicious assaults stirred sympathy for Beau Dupere, Hollywood luminaries speaking out on his behalf and calling for moderation from those with a different opinion of the friend to the stars. Anna nodded knowingly, when she read these reports. She understood how Beau's sincerity, and quietly commanding presence, had won him a place among the super-rich and the super-famous.

When one o'clock arrived, Anna had dressed and packed her over-sized purse for another visit, wearing modest shorts and flip-flops. She was prepared this time.

What Are They Laughing About?

The night before Anna's interview, Beau had been away from home for a healing meeting, though not very far away. Sara and Kim, along with Jenny and Candy, attended that meeting. They made the two-hour drive to the state capitol, arriving at the church about a half-hour late.

The four girls had based their attire for the evening on Internet videos they had seen of these healing meetings. They simply dressed for a casual evening in Sacramento, in late May, none of the shiny shoes and stiff dresses they had worn to Sunday school as little girls. Because they had seen people passing out on the floor at Beau Dupere's meetings, they wore shorts instead of skirts. Because they were going to see a holy man at a religious service, they each independently checked that they weren't showing any cleavage.

The host church for the healing meeting met in a building formerly used by an organic grocery store and it still had the long row of windows on the front of the building, though the store sign had been neatly replaced and there were no food ads in those windows.

Once inside, all the girls except Kim stopped in the lobby. The wall of sound emanating from the sanctuary doors and the speaker system in the high ceiling above their heads dunned the uninitiated. To Candy, it sounded like a rock concert she would attend for the music and dancing. To Sara, it sounded like no church she had ever entered. To Jenny, it reminded her of the night her mother was healed. To Kim, it sounded like the sort of electric atmosphere she had long prayed would seep over into her Assemblies of God church. Kim waved the others forward, looking back at them with the smile of the knowing veteran. Clearly she was enjoying the stupefied faces of the newbies.

"C'mon, we haven't missed all the music," Kim said, leading the way.

Candy started dancing, swinging her hips and churning her arms as she fell in behind Kim. With a glance over her shoulder, Kim laughed and joined in. Jenny and Sara just looked at each other and followed, like little girls going to their first haircut.

A tall man with grey hair and glasses stood by the sanctuary door nearest them. He swayed with the music and sang under his breath right up to when the group of four bunched in front of him. The girls paused there as they would before wading into the ocean late at night. The man grinned at the new arrivals and made a dramatic sweeping motion with his right arm. "The meeting awaits you," he said with a chuckle that they couldn't hear over the guitars, drums and voices.

The equivalent of a ten-person rock band stood on stage under purplish lights, young men and women on instruments, half-singing, half-shouting into microphones. But their voices didn't overpower the singing and shouting of the congregation. If the crowd needed to be whipped up in order to get the healing flowing for Beau Dupere, the band was doing that job well.

When Sara began to acclimate to the temperature of this unfamiliar water, she felt disappointment pop up, as she realized that the size of this crowd meant that she would only see Beau Dupere from a distance. Two large projection screens above the right and left sides of the stage would offer a bigger video image, but it wouldn't be the same as standing next to the healer, or the healed, in one of those unbelievable scenes on the Internet.

By the time the four of them had located a place where they could sit together, much closer to the back than the front, the music had become more spontaneous and contemplative. As soon as they reached those four seats, Jenny began to cry, struggling to manage her sobs and internally baffled by the source of the tears. Was it the memory of her mother's healing? She didn't think so. Sara noted Jenny's reaction, and she thought she knew where it came from. To her, the air in the room felt charged with the same energy she had felt in sparks and splashes throughout her life. Here, that same emotional and spiritual energy seemed to flow over her in swimming pool quantities. She hadn't yet let it penetrate her heart as Jenny had. Nor did Sara let the weighty power charm her like it had Kim—her eyes closed as she danced an uninhibited slow dance with an invisible partner. Sara watched in fascination. She had never thought to hope for this much palpable divine presence, but she was beginning to wonder why not.

Candy, Jenny's best friend, avoided looking at Jenny sobbing next to her. She tried to join in the dance that had drawn Kim, but she wasn't feeling it, whatever *it* was. She looked over at Sara, who appeared to be capturing the sights and sounds for later playback. From Sara's example, Candy took permission to just stand and watch.

As the quiet music faded, Sara noticed laughter toward the front of the room. It didn't seem to fit into the massaging mood of the music. The people on the stage, however, appeared to ignore the interruption, standing still or swaying slightly with hands raised, or with a steady stroke of guitar strings. Then the video image on both screens switched to a hand-held camera in the crowd.

For just a second, this recalled to Sara the clipped up images she had seen at her father's meeting, images of Beau Dupere pushing people, appearing to ignore others and babbling incomprehensibly all the time. There, on the screen, stood Beau, leading a small entourage of people down into the congregation. He had just briefly touched a woman who had been one of the strange laughers. She fell to the floor as if shot in the head. Someone tried to break her fall, but otherwise no one seemed concerned. Now Beau slowed down so that a tech with a microphone caught up to him, but Beau pointed to the young man next to him and turned his own face away from the mic.

As Beau stepped between two oblivious worshippers he seemed to be speaking rapidly, and Sara thought she might be hearing him over one of the microphones. But the barely post-adolescent voice of a young man close beside Beau came over the sound system much more clearly.

"He's praising God about his love for you and his forgiveness. He's saying something about you being set free from all guilt and shame, especially about this accident. It wasn't your fault. He is praying freedom for you to let go, forgive, release yourself as God has released you, forgive the rider of that motorcycle and forgive the driver of the truck, the big green pickup truck with the name of a landscaping company on the driver's door. And now he is just praising God for your healing, delivered here by God's angels."

Along with this odd narrative, came the image of a young woman on the big screen letting crutches fall to the floor and throwing her hands in the air. She nodded her head vigorously, as if confirming what the young man reported about her accident. Suddenly Sara realized that the young man was translating the incomprehensible words Beau was saying.

"Tongues!" she said. She had never heard it so clearly, and had certainly never seen anyone translating it. Kim looked at Sara and laughed. She reached over and gently pushed Sara, standing next to her. Though it surprised Kim as much as Sara, that push resulted in two things. First, Sara started to shake uncontrollably, causing her to stumble and even to fall into the aisle on her knees. Second, she started laughing like a lunatic, as she thought about it later, a squeaky high-pitched cackling that she had never heard from herself, or anyone else she knew, for that matter.

Kim put both hands over her mouth and started laughing uncontrollably as well. Sara fell to all fours and then rolled to her back. She looked up at Kim for just a second and seemed to catch an increased dose of laughter, a convulsion that originated just below her belly button and wrapped itself around her stomach and up to her throat. The effect of this outburst was like an internal message, a very vigorous massage, that didn't hurt at all.

This is why Sara didn't get to see much of Beau Dupere that night. When she opened her eyes she mostly saw the lights on the ceiling. She did see him once, later in the meeting. Beau towered over her, where she lay sprawled on the carpet. Leaning down, he said, "Now you have tasted The Truth and no one can ever take it away from you." Then he was gone.

Behind him, Beau left Sara with a heart open like a blossomed poppy, feeling rain and sunshine that she never knew existed. Brief moments of self-consciousness about the spectacle she had become, collapsed repeatedly before surges of emotion that came like the power of a fast sports car expertly shifted into higher and higher gears. Though she hurtled past that embarrassment, she still noticed it each time her awareness included a noise from someone around her. She wasn't the only one laying in the aisle.

About half an hour after Beau spoke to her, Sara's mind settled on the memory of a painting that used to hang in her aunt's house, a painting of a young woman standing on the beach, with her shoes in her hands, turned away from the viewer, toward the ocean. She hadn't thought of that image for years. As a little girl, however, Sara had worried about the young woman, a faun-like teenager, whose story seemed incomplete. Sometimes Sara thought that the girl on the beach was there by herself. Sometimes she worried that she was about to run into the foamy waves and perhaps drown, maybe intentionally. She dreamed about that unnamed girl some nights. And she *was* that girl some nights.

As unexpected as this memory was, the way it served to scoop up her unpolished soul surprised Sara even more. She knew in an instant that some part of her still believed she was like that lonely girl, if not that she *was* the girl herself. And then she knew that she was not alone on that beach. She knew that the picture was the view of a lover who cared for the girl as much as the little nine-year-old Sara had cared. And the one watching was not prepared to idly stand planted on the wet sand while his beloved ran to her death in the sea. As soon as Sara knew these things, she heard someone call. That voice turned the girl around, and when she turned, the girl was Sara and she was crying. But her tears of despair turned to tears of relief and gladness when she saw who was there watching her, as if he were the one painting the picture.

Warm and strong arms wrapped around Sara and she leaned into the solid fortress of the love that both supported her and prevented her from rushing to her own destruction. Lying on the floor, Sara even opened her eyes briefly to make sure that no one in that room had actually touched her. She was alone, untouched, but only on the outside, only in that old hard reality that had once trapped her soul. Inside, on the beach, the warm breeze flirting with her hair, she was settled into ultimate safety and dizzy weightless. She could not drown. She would only float. She was always safe.

Meeting this part of herself, and seeing the rescue of that girl, left Sara sobbing there on the carpet for half an hour more.

Interview with the Devil

Anna stood in the three-story-high entryway to the Dupere home. Upstairs she could hear a woman reading a children's book, though all she could hear distinctly was the tone of the story and the occasional interruption by a child asking a question. In the distant background, she heard the shush and rest of the surf from behind the house, a windy day on the ocean elevating the volume of the waves. But, even with these noises around the house, Anna could hear the cadence of the protestors on the road in front of the driveway.

When she had slowed down fifty yards from the house to show her press credentials to a Los Angeles County Sherriff's deputy, she could see a neighbor across from the Duperes spraying a hose at the sign-waving protestors in front of her house. The police had tried to keep the protestors off the Dupere property, threatening arrest if anyone violated that line in the sand. But they had been less strict at keeping the growing crowd off the lawn on the opposite side of the road. The annoyed neighbor, whose cactus and palms had been trampled and scarred by clumsy men and women, finally decided to try dousing anyone venturing onto her property. The stiff breeze off the Pacific made being wet a bit uncomfortable for some, but for others the water was a welcome relief from the persistent sun. The cardboard signs, however, universally suffered from the confrontational stream of water.

As Anna slowly drove toward the driveway, a deputy jogging beside her car as an escort, she could see Malibu police conferring about what to do regarding the neighbor. Anna saw one officer turn his back to the commotion so he could release a laugh at the whining protestors. In the face of all that, Anna was glad to be a junior reporter for a small regional weekly, instead of a cop.

Turning into the drive, Anna spotted the usual security guards, augmented by two others. Though they carried no weapons that Anna could see, their sheer size intimidated her, and likely would intimidate any rogue protestor as well. One of the guards stepped out of the shade of an awning and waved her forward, recognizing her as she expected. Behind her, she thought she heard a wave of taunts that might have been aimed at her, given the repeated use of terms describing women of ill repute, to speak politely. Did they mistake her for one of Beau's women? That idea warmed her. And, in that glow, she completely missed the sting of her reputation being impugned by a damp protestor clutching a soggy sign.

Now in the entryway, Rhonda emerged from the hall to Anna's right, part of the house she hadn't seen yet. Looking more carefully assembled than when Anna saw her last, Rhonda's hair

If You Really Knew Me

bounced and shone as if it had been recently washed, and her clothes fit her more closely. Her face bore the rosy glow of someone who had absorbed just a little too much sun, and her light gray eyes seemed illuminated from within.

"Hello, Anna. Good to see you again," Rhonda said, with a welcoming smile that seemed to Anna to have migrated there from someone else's face.

"Hello, Rhonda. It's good to see you too."

Rhonda sobered. "*You* don't think Beau is the Devil, *do* you?"

"The Devil?" Anna said. "Did you hear the protestor shouting out front?"

Rhonda nodded. "I went with Beau and Maggie yesterday to a meeting in Sacramento. I saw the mob from the car."

"Were you afraid?" Anna said, not really sensing any emotion from Rhonda.

Shrugging slightly, Rhonda shook her head, glancing toward the street. "Not afraid, but sad. They're wasting a lot of time and energy on nothing," she said, tipping her head toward the faint shouts.

Anna picked up on something else Rhonda said. "So you went with Beau to a healing meeting?"

"Yeah, he always takes some of us with him if he can. We have different gifts that God can use in a big meeting."

"What's your...ah...gift?" Anna was unfamiliar with the language, but she was also distracted by Beau coming in from the kitchen with a boy about eleven years old.

"Oh, I can see things," Rhonda said simply.

"Like Beau sees things?" Anna said, casting a look at Beau as he stepped up next to Rhonda.

Rhonda glanced at Beau, but didn't hesitate to continue the conversation. "I see different things than he does some times. I tend to see spirits and angels more."

"Spirits and angels?" Anna said, again glancing at Beau. But again he remained patient, allowing Rhonda to answer for herself.

Here Rhonda turned to Beau and grinned. "He calls me one of the 'scary women,'" she said, with a little laugh. "'Cause we see in the spirit realm and can tell him things that are going on that he doesn't always see."

Here, Beau did step in. "She's being generous," he said. "I very rarely see the kind of spiritual detail that Rhonda sees, or Emma sees, or some others."

"Emma is one of the 'scary women' now too," Rhonda said, clearly as proud of her title as she was amused by it.

Beau laughed with her. "Yeah, kids see things more easily than adults. We just have to be careful to make sure they feel safe telling us what they honestly see, even if us grownups can't see it. Rhonda is especially helpful there. She can sort of translate what the kids are seeing and confirm it for me." He shook his head. "I still have some of those adult prejudices against trusting kids." Here he turned toward the boy next to him.

"Why do you look at *me*?" the boy said, elbowing Beau in the side.

Beau and Rhonda both laughed. Anna smiled uncertainly, on the outside of an inside joke, apparently.

"This is Adam," Beau said, introducing the blonde-haired boy, whose hair, narrow shoulders and light blue eyes showed no resemblance to the man standing next to him.

Anna shook his offered hand, and saved her question about the boy's relationship to the patriarch of the house for when she had Beau to herself. Before she could say anything, Adam spoke.

"Do you have any pain in your body?" he said.

As Anna stared for a second, Beau filled in an explanation. "He asks that of everyone who visits here. He can heal any pain you might have."

Anna hesitated at the thought that anyone could claim to heal every pain, but decided to give it a try. "I do have a sore neck, like a pinched nerve or muscle cramp, or something," she said, rubbing the right side of her neck with her hand.

"Can I touch it?" Adam said, asking politely, but with brevity that implied he had asked that question many times before.

"Sure," Anna said, her voice coming out more mousy than she expected.

Adam, a half a foot shorter than Anna, reached up and gently touched her neck near where she had been rubbing it. Anna straightened up almost immediately, as an electric buzz began beneath Adam's touch.

"It's buzzing," she said, her eyes wide and eyebrows arched.

Beau smiled and nodded, no hint of surprise on his placid face.

Rhonda whispered something into Adam's opposite ear, so Anna didn't catch any of it. Adam nodded.

"Tension, you go away right now," he said, with a tone that reminded Anna of a boy playing a game in which he was a commander of troops.

She didn't pause to ponder this odd tone, however, because the buzzing and the pain both disappeared immediately after Adam's command. Raising her right hand to her neck again, Anna began to twist and bend it. A surprise birthday party kind of smile spread over her face.

"That's awesome," she said, reverting to her teenage vocabulary in that unguarded moment.

All three of the others laughed. Adam dropped his hand to his side and looked at Beau.

Patting Adam on the shoulder, Beau teased Anna. "You look surprised. What did you expect would happen?"

Still bumping along with her wheels off their tracks, Anna blurted a question she had been forming since she first met Maggie. "Does this stuff just run in your family?"

Beau laughed louder. "You mean like a genetic healing gift?"

As far as Anna was concerned, there was nothing more absurd about that idea than the idea that an eleven-year-old could just tell pain to leave.

"It's not genetic," Rhonda said, as if she thought Beau was being too silly to provide a serious answer. "It's just what they're taught to try it as soon as they can speak their first words around here."

Beau did rein in his laughter, and said, "That's right. It's environment not genetics."

Anna nodded. She looked at Adam. "Well, thank you for taking care of that. It would have cost me plenty to see a chiropractor or massage therapist for that."

Adam grinned and looked at Beau again, with a sly smile.

Beau laughed again, but said, "No Adam, you cannot."

Anna furrowed her brow, wondering exactly what that was about, but suspecting it had something to do with requesting payment for his services. She knew Adam was kidding by the way he laughed back at Beau. Then Adam did something almost as surprising as offering to heal her neck. He slipped his arms around Anna and gave her a hug.

When he let go, Adam said. "That's all the payment I want."

Frozen like a mannequin, Anna offered half a smile in reply.

"Alright. You can go now, champ," Beau said to Adam. "Thanks for your help. Now stop flirting with my guest."

Adam pushed off of Beau's solid chest and sprinted for the stairs. "Hey, you can't have all the women in this house." And he bounded up the stairs two at a time, squealing with glee as Beau faked a chase.

That cheeky comment brought back Anna's question about Adam. "Is he your son?" she said, as Rhonda returned down the hallway from which she had emerged and Adam's stomping faded into the distance.

"No," Beau said, with a more subdued smile. "In spite of that last comment, not all of the women here are my wives." He motioned toward the huge living room to Anna's left and led the way as he talked. "Tammy is Adam's mother. I don't know if you met her. I think she was next to the pool the last time you were here." Beau swept his hand in a gesture that offered a variety of cream-colored couches and chairs on which to sit. As he waited for Anna to choose a spot, he continued. "We're still holding out some hope that Adam's father will take his wife and children back. Emma is Adam's sister." He added that last sentence when it occurred to him that he had heard something about Emma praying for Anna.

Anna set her purse on a glass coffee table big enough to sleep two adults and dropped her flip-flops as she pulled her feet up under her on a long couch that felt like silk against her bare legs. "So, how many children do you have, and how many live here now."

Beau grabbed a bulky armchair and tugged it around thirty degrees to face more in Anna's direction. He answered as he sat down. "I have eight children, five of them live here right now. My three oldest have moved out, my two boys, and Joanna is at Pepperdine, so she's not far, but she lives in a dorm. Maggie, I know you met her, is the oldest still at home."

"Right," Anna said, her throat tightening as she wound up her courage to press into the topic that had intrigued her most, before she met the people in that house. "And those are your children with Justine," she said, as if summarizing.

Beau nodded and pursed his lips. "Then there are the four younger ones," he said. "You met Luke, his mother is Olivia, who was probably with Gracie in the pool one of the times you were here before. Gracie is actually adopted. Olivia's sister died and left her custody of Gracie, whom I don't think you've met." Beau slowed down here because Anna was just getting her digital recorder settled on the table in front of her.

Seeing his hesitation, Anna said, "Oh, it's okay, isn't it?"

"Sure," he said. "Do you wanna test it though, to make sure it's working, and I'm loud enough?"

Clearly, he had done this before. Also clearly, he felt he had nothing to hide.

Anna picked up the recorder and rewound it to where she had turned it on, then played it back: *"probably with Gracie in the pool one of the times you were here before. Gracie is actually adopted. Olivia's sister died and left her custody of Gracie,*

If You Really Knew Me

whom I don't think you've met." His voice sounded clear enough.

"Do you want me to start again with the children?" Beau asked.

"No, I can remember most of it," Anna said. Then she started the recorder again and reviewed what he had said about his older children with Justine. He nodded that she had remembered correctly.

He continued. "Then there's Dianna's and my kids, Gretchen and Peter. I don't know if Gretchen has been around at all while you were here. Dianna works as a nurse at a hospital nearby and the kids often stay with her former partner during the daytimes."

"'Former partner?'" Anna said.

"Yeah, Dianna was in a lesbian relationship when I met her and she got pregnant with Gretchen. That was what started the whole expanded family we have here," he said, as matter-of-factly as everything he had said to her. "I had an affair with Dianna a little over nine years ago, and then came clean about it. I wasn't going to abandon her or the baby, and Justine wanted to take them in."

Seeing the look of discomfort on Anna's face—as if she just realized that she was sitting on a live animal—Beau paused, waiting for a question.

Anna waited a beat and then reached for clarity. "So, you had an affair with Dianna, while she was in a lesbian relationship, and she got pregnant. And Justine wanted to take her in?" Throughout her short acquaintance with the Dupere family, Anna had stretched and strained to try to hide her shock at things they said to her. She dropped the pretense here, her voice rising comically at the end of her question.

Beau smiled tolerantly. "I know it's unusual, but our churches really believe in forgiveness in a way that makes some unusual things possible," he said. As Anna sat, shaking her head, he went on. "Justine forgave me and accepted me back after that affair, and was able then to be really open and compassionate about what we should do next. Dianna's partner was not really a healthy influence on her, we all knew that, and Dianna was pregnant. We could've just supported her financially, in some condo around here, or something, but Dianna was really affected by the forgiveness she saw from Justine and wanted to change her life completely. She really needed someone like Justine to help her get free from old stuff holding her back, and she needed a father for her baby. It just made sense to make them part of the family."

Trying not to sound like a prosecuting attorney, nevertheless, Anna tried to clarify another fact. "And then you had another child with Dianna?"

"Yep, that's right. Peter. He's six, a faithful follower of Adam," he nodded his head in the direction of Adam's escape up the stairs. Here was the first time Anna suspected Beau was trying to avoid discussing something. She pushed against that awkwardness between them but got flustered with the number of unanswered questions she could pursue.

"So how did Olivia get into your family?" she said, only realizing too late that this left the topic of Dianna's second child with Beau an incomplete story.

"Olivia and Justine have been friends for about thirty years, although you wouldn't believe they met in college after I told you that." Beau smiled. "She was visiting us here after Dianna had joined us and was interested in pursuing a similar arrangement, the sort of extended family." His voice wavered very slightly with that last phrase, and Anna knew she had finally found a point of discomfort.

She took a breath, savoring a brief moment in which Beau's vulnerability made her feel more settled with her own. "So Justine and Dianna agreed to add a third . . . wife?"

Beau smiled. "Well, it's illegal in California to have more than one wife. So, of course, she's not a *legal* wife, the way the county measures such things." His grin seemed playful to Anna,

If You Really Knew Me

which annoyed her for the first time. Beau stepped into the void that her annoyance left in the conversation.

"When I agreed to this interview, we all felt that I should be free to tell you everything you wanted to know, with one exception. Justine and the others wanted me to promise that I wouldn't *give any information about things that go on here in the privacy of the bedroom*," he said, sounding as if he was quoting someone exactly. "That's why you heard me getting nervous there. I'm not used to holding back information, so I'm not very good at it." His smile turned boyish, and almost shy.

Anna nodded. Though she had, of course, been intensely curious about many details of their lives, she hadn't expected sexually explicit revelations. Just how much Beau could, and would, say was entirely unpredictable, but she knew the conversation would stay PG-13 or lighter. What she did hope to establish is whether the accusers were right in saying that he had multiple wives, or at least multiple sexual partners. That goal, however, did demand some frank answers about who sleeps where and when. Processing the conflict for a couple of seconds left Beau waiting for her in patient silence, a thin grin on his pursed lips.

"So, you're admitting to having children by three different women, all of whom live in this house with you, and with the full knowledge of the others, of course. But you're not saying you have three wives (or more) because you agreed to reserve sexual details for the privacy of the others, and because it's illegal in California to admit to having three wives while a reporter is recording you?"

Here Beau laughed again, a big Santa Clause laugh. "You know, Anna, I've seen you struggling to understand what's going on around here several times. But it sounds to me like you understand this part perfectly well." And he laughed some more.

Anna smiled and leaned back on a big, multi-colored Caribbean-style pillow that rested on the top of the sofa, against the wall. She tried to press down a bit on the facts she had gathered to make sure they fit into a whole story. "So it's just the three women?"

She imagined she could see Beau shuffling through the possible ways to take that question and the safest way to answer. What he might have been doing instead, however, is listening the that Truth inside himself.

"Yes. Just three."

Anna saw a look in Beau's eyes that reminded her of her brother-in-law on his wedding day, and she knew that it was fair to think of Beau with three wives, and no more.

"Okay," she said. "I think I understand you. And you seem to understand me. So, let's talk about something easy, like finances." Now it was her turn to grin at her own punchline.

Beau laughed and bowed slightly, as if granting her the point and the game.

Make that Two Billion

After a trip to the kitchen and the obligatory lemonade—strawberry this time—Beau and Anna headed out for the patio, with hopes that the wind had slackened enough to make it more comfortable out there.

"With Adam and me in the house, we can be sure that Bethany will be wearing something, if she's out here," he said with a wink. He held the door open for Anna as she blushed and ducked under his arm.

Around the pool, chairs and tables stood empty, except for one chaise lounge on the other side, in the shade of two palm trees. There, Maggie sat reading a book propped up on her knees. She waved at the new arrivals and returned to her reading. Beau selected a table on the same side of the pool, but at the opposite end. There they could sit in the shade of the pool house. All the umbrellas had been tied down because of the wind. Anna laid the digital recorder on the table next to her pink lemonade, glad for the pool house's partial shelter from the wind to make recording possible.

She started with one of her prepared questions. "I'm sure you're aware of the big town meeting up in Parkerville, where a group of conservative pastors warned their parishioners to stay away from you," she said. But she slowed to a stop when she saw Beau shaking his head with a curious crease above his brow. Anna looked at him. "You're not aware?"

"I know there are some people in churches around here, and elsewhere, that don't agree with things I say or do. But I don't know anything about any particular criticism."

Anna stared. Then she reached for her big bag on the ground next to her, pulling out her laptop computer. They both had to wait as she connected to the wireless network in the house and then to find the video that Dixon Claiborne's committee presented. When she found it, she and Beau scooted their chairs close together and Anna tapped the Play arrow. Beau watched calmly, the only change in his facial expression coming when Jack Williams showed up on the screen. He smiled mildly at the appearance of his old friend and pastor. Otherwise, he seemed no more impressed by the video than a tortoise is impressed by a tiny bird pecking at its shell.

"You've never seen that?"

"No. I don't pay attention to critics. It's something Jack taught me."

Ann looked at the video Web site. "It says over one-and-a-half million people have viewed that clip, and I know it's posted in some other places too, so that's not all."

Beau just shook his head. Anna scowled incredulously at him, trying to decide if he was being naïve or if he was truly uninterested in the opinions of others.

"Well, I was wondering what you say to their assertion that you get rich off your healing ministry," she said, returning to her intended line of questioning.

"I haven't ever needed to ask for money for healing meetings or conferences," Beau said. "If there's an offering at one of my meetings, it's always designated for the local congregation or for a local charity. I don't even use healing ministry to raise funds for my charitable organizations."

Anna nodded. She knew that he had been extremely wealthy before his ministry, and wondered how well-informed the financial analysis by Dixon Claiborne's people had been. Perhaps they had just placed Beau's billionaire reputation next to his healing ministry and assumed they were connected.

"You say you don't need to ask for money for what you do now. Can you tell me about where your wealth came from?" Anna pushed the recorder closer as the wind picked up again.

Beau, who had slid his chair a few inches away when the video ended, leaned in a little toward the recorder. "Well, the short answer, in terms of financial accounting, is that it came from various investments." He looked toward Maggie, but he seemed to be recalling or calculating, or both, instead of really looking at her. Anna glanced that way and saw Maggie flip her hair around to the side, in response to the renewed wind assault from the west.

"But that's only investments in the broadest sense of the word," he said. "It just means I didn't inherit any money and I didn't run any kind of company to earn it." He looked at Anna. "Do you know about the lottery win and about the sunken gold?"

Anna nodded slowly, surprised that he started with those specifics. "Yes, but those were unconfirmed rumors."

"Well, I can give you names of people who can confirm both of those windfalls," he said, as if she needed assurance that these outrageous stories were true.

"Great," Anna said, not wanting to appear as credulous as she was regarding Beau and his fantastic history.

Beau smiled and looked toward the ocean. Anna suspected that he knew she was only playing reporter in that last response. This game of hide and seek was beginning to unsettle her, but the obligations of her profession played in her head like a Greek chorus consisting of editors and publishers she had worked for past and present.

"But those things didn't really add up to the billions you're reputed to have," Anna said, returning to Beau's accounting.

"No, certainly, the gold barely amounted to a billion, and I paid a percentage of that to the captain and the divers, as well as taxes. No, most of my money came from more traditional investments, including some that built on those big paydays. I was a financial analyst and trader before all that, as you know. And my success there was controversial already. I was investigated a few times for insider trading. They just couldn't believe that I could pick big winners so consistently. One boss only finally believed me after I picked the winning lottery numbers. He knew no one could get insider info on that."

Anna backtracked to his reputation as an investor. "They never actually charged you with anything on the insider trading?"

"No, you can contact my old employer at Burns and Howell. There wasn't any kind of evidence that I got information from the companies before the trades, not anything even slightly suspicious. So they dropped it."

"So how did you get so lucky about picking winners?"

Beau looked at her with a slight tilt to his head, as if he was trying to decide whether she knew the answer and just wanted him to say it. "I told you that sometimes God just lets me know things. It's the way my healing ministry works most of the time." He considered Anna to see if she was following. "And, before I retired, it wasn't just people's ailments and such that God told me about. The only insider information I ever got came from him, but then there was no paper trail for that." He chuckled.

If You Really Knew Me

As with much of their conversation, Beau seemed barely interested in the details of his own extraordinary life, though patient enough to tell Ann what she wanted to hear.

"And the sunken gold, how did that come to you?"

For a moment, Beau's interest stirred, a crooked smile around his words and seaman's gaze toward the ocean as he remembered. "Well, that was pretty amazing. I had a dream about gold bars floating on the surface of the ocean, and me following them in a canoe, like the kids and I used to use when we went camping. After paddling toward them for a while, this train of floating gold bars, I noticed that the farthest one ahead of me just disappeared. As I looked more closely, the next bar sunk in the same place, as if the laws of physics had been suspended all along the calm surface of the water until they hit that point. Then they sank, just like gold bars should. When I reached the spot where the last of them disappeared, I saw numbers and letters printed on the surface of the water, like on a map." He looked at Anna with a full grin.

"When I woke up I could still remember the numbers and letters so I wrote them down, and I called Jack Williams that day. I told him the dream and he agreed that it must be the location of lost treasure, although neither of us had ever heard of God locating buried treasure for someone. I don't know if it ever happened before or since. I just knew at the time that this was what God was giving me. So I called around to find a captain with experience recovering sunken gold, including the guys that did the Titanic." He laughed suddenly, slapping his leg with one hand. "They sure thought I was nuts!"

Though he seemed content to remember and laugh, Anna wanted the story. "So how did you find someone to recover it?"

"Oh, there's always someone who's really desperate for money," he said, winding down his humorous convulsions. "I just had to pay a guy a million dollars up front, guarantee five million in expenses and give him a percentage of the haul. Although, since he was pretty sure there *was* no haul, he didn't negotiate very hard for that." Again, the memory sent him over the edge into a cascade of laughter and a loud sigh, even wiping a tear from the corner of one eye. Maggie looked up at him from the other end of the pool, oblivious to the content of the conversation. She just laughed at her dad's uninhibited jocularity.

Anna allowed a toddling chuckle to escape, before dragging Beau further into the narrative. "So how long did it take you to find it?"

Beau looked at her and raised both eyebrows. "You would think it wouldn't take long at all, given that I handed him the exact coordinates. But he insisted that I must be wrong, 'cause his charts showed that this area had been explored decades ago and nothing was found. I don't know what was wrong, his information or the methods of those who searched before, but I finally convinced him to anchor and drop the submersible exactly on that spot." Beau started laughing again, but sensing Anna's impatience, he throttled back this time.

"You know what they say about swearing like a sailor? You should ha' heard him when a drag-bucket brought up gold Spanish coins from hundreds of years ago." Beau let loose again, interspersing words with barks of laughter. "The funniest part...was each time he would say...some foul thing or other...he would stop and say, 'Oh, sorry, Pastor,'...and then just go on swearing and apologizing."

Anna surrendered to Beau's loopy laughter for a moment, though wishing she had something stronger than lemonade to get her to the level of intoxication Beau seemed to reach with his memory of the treasure hunt. When they both caught their breath, something occurred to Anna.

"Did you film all this?"

Beau shook his head, "Not the whole interaction with the captain and such," he said, "just the documentation of the actual treasure. I wasn't looking to get famous over that, I was just collecting the gold God had offered me. I couldn't see any advantage to making a sort of documentary about it, like we ac-

If You Really Knew Me

complished some great thing by our tremendous effort, or something."

"You didn't want anyone to know about your new found wealth?"

"Not particularly, and I didn't want people to get the idea that I could tell them where to find treasure, or how to pick winning lottery numbers. That could get really messy, I think."

Anna nodded slowly, trying to decide whether to probe deeper in what seemed another example of Beau trying to hide something, but again his manner seemed more disinterested than suspicious, as he settled back in his chair with the grin of a man who just finished telling a really good joke and getting the laughs it deserved.

"So, you weren't trying to hide how rich you were from other religious people who might be offended?"

"Naw, I got over worrying about what offends religious people years before that. It's like giving up smoking or some such habit that seemed enjoyable at the time, but really never satisfied. Just when you think you've covered your backside so as not to offend anybody, you discover another group who's offended by you saying words like 'backside.'" And that started another round of laughter, just as Maggie rounded the pool, headed for the house. She took a look at Beau's glass and joked.

"Did you slip something in his drink, Anna?"

Anna smiled at Maggie and answered half seriously. "No, he's just telling me about finding sunken gold." She said this before thinking about how much Maggie knew. at a mere sixteen years old.

Maggie laughed briefly. "Oh, that makes sense. Us kids used to get a big laugh out of trying to convince Dad to tell us what exactly the captain said when he saw the gold coins. But he never would."

Anna nodded and said, "Well, he wouldn't tell me either."

Maggie rolled her eyes and walked away shaking her head, a thin trail of girlish chuckles just audible over the wind, as she headed toward the house.

Again, Anna tried to drive into more serious territory. "So what did you do with all that money?"

"Spent it on rum," he said and laughed some more before sobering, with some effort. He put a hand over his mouth and looked skyward, in his effort to keep to the business at hand.

Before Anna could try again, Beau answered more seriously. "Oh, well, I couldn't tell you exactly where every dollar went. Even though God seems to shovel the riches my way, I've never been a great bookkeeper. I do know that we invested the proceeds for a while, paid the required taxes, and then set up a couple of new organizations for helping with homelessness in this country and food distribution in Africa. Justine is better at judging those things than me, including hiring good people to run the organizations. You'd have to ask her if you want more of the boring details."

Though she would have denied it in front of a jury of her professional peers, Anna didn't want any of the boring details, she seemed to have misplaced the carnivorous instinct required to push for more financial information. After leaving that day, however, she did contact Beau's accountant to get an overview of the flow of his funds, authorized by Beau, of course.

According to Steve Wickham, the senior accountant assigned to answer her questions, Beau gave general instructions about the money, and Justine monitored the execution of those instructions, but Steve did the day-to-day buying and selling for the Duperes. At least, he and his staff did.

"Their cash flow is considerable, though it comes in great waves sometimes, as you know," Steve said. "But I've gotten calls from Justine late in the evening with questions about small details that she noticed in reports I sent her. They're not obsessed with their money, but they do pay attention."

Anna sat holding her digital recorder, her legs crossed, a sandal dangling from her right foot as she rested her elbows on her knee. She wanted to ask whether Steve was connected to their church or their faith, but wasn't sure if that was relevant.

Uninterested in assembling any kind of conspiracy plot, Anna hadn't found any reason not to trust church members, as if they were all part of some Kool-Aid-drinking cult. She got her first hint about Steve's religious affiliations a moment later.

"So, miss Conyers, or can I call you Anna?" The tone of that preamble, along with the fondling foray of his eyes, rendered the actual words that followed completely obsolete. She was sure that no one from Beau's church would hit on her so crudely.

The following sexual overture, paired with her lack of suspicion regarding Beau and his money, wound the interview to an early close. Her adamant refusals and scolding looks prompted an innocent inquiry from the accountant. "Did I say something wrong?" His voice squeaked just slightly as he stood to follow her to the door of his office.

Ann just thanked him again and headed for her car.

The only other face-to-face interview she had planned was with Jack Williams, and she would have to wait another day to meet with Beau's mentor and friend.

We Don't Believe in that Sorta Thing

Beau went to pick up Adam from soccer practice, arriving early so he could see the boy in action. He found the team divided in half, scrimmaging on the full soccer field, red against yellow, eight on a side, including one of the assistant coaches. While standing on the sideline, his hands in his pockets, turning his head slightly to keep his hair away from his eyes, Beau caught Adam's attention. Adam smiled and then grew suddenly more serious. He lifted one hand waist high and surreptitiously pointed to Beau's right. Beau made a casual glance in that direction and then nodded to Adam the next time the boy looked at him.

From a minivan parked near Beau's Land Rover, a woman, about forty years old, was leading a boy who appeared to have Down syndrome. Maybe twelve or thirteen years old, the boy walked with feet flapping outward, clinging to the arm of the woman, who Beau understood to be his mother. Adam had spotted a healing target and aimed Beau in that direction. Beau guessed that Adam would have tried to heal the boy already, and perhaps met resistance or got no results.

After the mother and son had settled on the sideline, both shouting encouragement to a boy on Adam's side of the scrimmage, Beau sidled in their direction.

"So, you're Carson's mother?" Beau said, extending a hand.

The woman smiled and nodded, reaching out to take that hand. "Yes, I'm Alicia. And Adam's your boy?"

Beau nodded, not interested in precision on that point. He looked at the boy with Alicia. "Do you play soccer?"

The boy lowered his head and turned it side to side.

"He has trouble with his knees," Alicia said. She put a hand on the boy's shoulder. "This is Jamie. He likes to *watch* soccer. Don't ya buddy?"

Jamie looked at the field, a bit less enthusiastic than your average soccer fan. He stayed silent.

"I can make those knees feel better," Beau said, simply.

Alicia looked just past Beau, glancing in Adam's direction. "Your son tried praying for Jamie already. I guess he has a reputation for doing that among the boys. But we don't believe in that sorta thing."

"That's okay. You don't have to believe in it. It's starting to happen already," Beau said, looking at Jamie's knees.

Jamie looked down and then looked at his mother. "What's happening to my knees? They feel funny," he said. "I mean really funny, like I'm gonna laugh now." He put both hands over his mouth to hold the strange laughter in.

If You Really Knew Me

"Are you doing something?" Alicia said, firing a look at Beau.

If he were inclined to be intimidated by the wrath of a mother, that look might have robbed him of a couple of heartbeats.

"I think it's already done," Beau said.

As he said that, Jamie let go of his mouth and spewed a laugh that sounded a lot like a shout. He kicked his right foot in front of him and then the left. When he did that, his outward pointing feet each straightened to point more forward. Then he did it again, and his feet lined up quite normally. With his hands tightly fisted, Jamie turned and started to run down the sideline toward the corner of the field, his head down and a hoarse growl accompanying him there and back.

"I can run now, Mom. My knees feel great. 'Cept we don't believe in that sorta thing." He lifted his face to the sky and guffawed.

Adam had abandoned his midfield defensive position and drifted toward the sideline when he saw Jamie running. Beau met him with a grin.

Adam looked almost as concerned as Alicia did. "Did you just heal his knees?" Adam said, clearly disappointed.

"That'll do for now," Beau said.

Adam nodded at a lesson learned from the master.

Jamie bellowed, "We don't believe in that sorta thing," and he ran back toward them laughing and squealing some more.

Mourning the Loss of a Daughter

Exactly what the days ahead would contain for Dixon Claiborne lay beyond his grasp. He was used to that. Knowing that he would preach on Sundays—three times—meet with staff, meet with church members, lead committee meetings, etc. etc. was enough for him. Knowing that his daughter would graduate from high school, would begin her summer job at the swimming pool, and get ready for the big move to college in the Bay Area, left him feeling full. The schedule was full, and he was full of anticipation. But he would have liked to have known in advance about the revelation that would change the color of all that fullness, the way a hurricane rearranges schedules as much as it rearranges the lawn furniture.

Dixon didn't hear about Sara's visit to the Beau Dupere meeting until nearly a week later, the day of graduation. An unguarded moment between teenaged girls, caught in the spin of excitement before the robe-clad march into the gymnasium, started the avalanche that would bury Dixon's next few days. His expectations tumbled beneath what felt like a backlash against his effort to bring truth and righteousness to the wider church.

Jenny Washington's hair had been spun into a tight twist around her head, a golden slash of color wound in and around that celebratory quaff. Her eyes sparked and her lips shown with gloss recently applied. Holding her cap with one hand, she bounced at the sight of Sara, now more than just a cheerleading sister.

"Oh, you look so awesome!" Jenny said, in the piercing tone native to excited adolescent girls.

Sara and Jenny embraced, one arm each, caps held in place on top of special hairdos.

"Oh, I like the highlight," Sara said, returning the compliment.

Jenny lowered her voice, but not quite low enough for Kristen and Dixon to miss the mystery tempered elation of the words. "Do you feel totally different still? Is it still there?"

Sara glanced at her parents and turned away, nodding as vigorously as her headwear would allow. "I just can't stop praying, and when I do I either laugh or cry or...even pray in some

If You Really Knew Me

strange language. And I keep getting these shivers, like electricity. Why didn't anyone tell me about this?"

Perhaps it was an architectural accident—hissing whispers bouncing off glass and metal, the lobby full of people and noise—but, even facing the windows with her back turned toward him, Dixon grasped enough of what his daughter said to want an explanation. Not there, of course, that would be too public. But he would have to hear today, as soon as he could get alone with Sara.

That opportunity didn't come until much later in the day. Between Dixon's need and its fulfillment stood the ceremony in the gym—Sara graduating with honors—the reception at the house, a flux and flow of people from the church and the neighborhood all afternoon and into the evening. Then Sara disappeared for the primetime party hours. She was out of sight and out of the range of Dixon's reach in more ways than he would have imagined.

At Candy's house, Sara felt a freedom far beyond the release from all those years of public school education. Even the usual surreptitious offers of drugs or alcohol, as the night drove on, lacked both the temptation and the fearful condemnation Sara had experienced in the past. She looked at Denny Winslow when he flashed her the sight of a joint and raised his eyebrows in silent offer. How many times had she refused offers like this from Denny and his friends? But this time it was different. She felt as if she could do it. She knew she could say "yes," that she was free to choose. And she laughed. With such an expansive feeling of freedom, why waste it on something so stupid?

This felt like the first time she had actually chosen. Shaking her head at Denny, smiling without the usual biting disapproval of his offer, she simply said "no." It was her own "no" this time. As she walked down the hall, back into the living room, where clusters of teens huddled and laughed and even danced, she giggled. Anyone who had been watching might have thought that she had said "yes" to Denny, or to some other offer of mood-elevating substances.

If You Really Knew Me

Candy spotted Sara after the laughter subsided, but she recognized a radiance on Sara's face, her head raised proudly, her eyes surveying friends and acquaintances fearlessly. Near the fireplace, where three couples sat squished as close as possible, oblivious to the universe around them, Candy intercepted Sara's stroll through the room.

"Okay, I know you haven't been drinking or anything, but you look just like you have, only better," Candy said, having started talking before she knew what she was going to say.

Sara laughed, as if Candy's splash of affirmation granted permission for her to release the elation, like a bird uncaged. "You should try it, Candy. I'm sure it's better than drugs," Sara said, teasing, more than offering a formal invitation.

Candy just shook her head. "I guess I'm just not that kinda girl." She tried to joke, but felt the irony of her own admission. "I mean," she said, more seriously, "I think I'm just not ready."

Ready for what? Sara thought, as she looked at Candy's shifting brown eyes, cast now at the floor, looking for a place to escape Sara's shameless gaze. Her evening ended earlier than she had planned, as far as parties go, that is. Most of Sara's friends expected to be out all night. But Sara retired, saying goodbye with hugs for Candy, Jenny and the others. Kim had stayed away, accustomed to excluding herself from those sorts of parties. Was Sara becoming like Kim? Or was she just becoming more herself?

She sang aloud to the songs on her favorite Christian radio station on the way home, not conscious of choosing to sing worship music instead of trying to hook up with the hottest guy available that night, nor trying some new stimulant or other. She chose, but she did so without self-consciousness.

Floating like this through the kitchen door of her parents' house, Sara knocked into an obstacle to her bliss. Home early enough to find her dad searching for a snack in the refrigerator, Sara closed the back door and said a minor hello to the man in his sweat pants leaning into the fridge. After the party in the

If You Really Knew Me

house that day, the contents of the shelves and drawers in the refrigerator would be much more enticing than usual. But Dixon hesitated over suspicion at those enticements. "What would be healthy?" he was thinking, when the back door clattered open and Sara slipped in.

"Oh," Dixon said. "I was thinking you'd be out all night. I wanted to talk to you about something, but I didn't expect you home so soon."

Familiar with her father's tendency to process his thoughts aloud, Sara could tell that he was adjusting from a confrontation on the Sunday after graduation to one late on graduation night. Not a fan of confrontations, no matter their date or time, Sara was glad to get it over with as soon as possible.

"What did you want to talk about," she said, slipping her shoes off and picking them up, one red, short heel in each hand.

Dixon closed the fridge door, feeling that yielding to the temptations in there would diminish his authority in what followed. "Uh, well, I heard what Jenny said before graduation this afternoon, about you feeling different." He stopped there. The most disturbing words had actually come from the mouth of his own daughter, words about praying in another language. But Dixon enjoyed confrontation little more than Sara did and mitigated the pain of this one by glancing off of the real issue. He knew Sara would recognize his point of concern.

"Oh, you heard that?" Sara said. She didn't sound as surprised or guilty as both she and her father would have expected. The emboldening freedom she had danced with at the party seemed to have accompanied her home.

"Yeah, I heard what you said." Dixon slipped from targeting Jenny's revelation, to the one that really bothered him. Sara's upheld chin and steady, though gentle, voice provoked him to a more frontal assault on his daughter's *experimentation*. That's what he had labeled it, for his own sake, to contain the damage.

Sara increased her volume slightly and dug the knife in deep, in her effort to get this over. "We wanted to check out Beau Dupere for ourselves."

155

Dixon had intuited that there might be a connection, remembering their discussion about Jenny's mother being healed. He looked at his grown-up daughter, standing there, barefoot on the cool kitchen floor, still wearing her sophisticated red dress and holding those shoes like Audrey Hepburn in some old romantic film.

"Your mother's still awake. We should go and see her," Dixon said, his voice muted, as if speaking through a plastic bubble around his head. Sara followed him toward her parents' bedroom.

Kristen sat on the bed, one leg dangling toward the floor, her pale blue satin pajamas shining against the dark blue bedspread. She hadn't yet pulled down the covers and the news ran on the flat screen TV. With the sound turned down, the stories blinkied there neglected.

It occurred then to Sara that her parents had been preparing all day for this little talk. They must have been stressing about what to say, about what it all meant. She sampled a brief sympathy for their angst, though she could barely imagine exactly what it felt like to be a parent, to be responsible for the lives of young and vulnerable people who would eventually become independent.

"Oh, you're home," Kristen said. She glanced at Dixon and back at Sara, surmising the acceleration of the schedule for the planned parental intervention. She closed the newspaper she had been perusing for sales, and slid her folded leg free, turning toward her daughter and husband. She picked up the remote from behind her and clicked off the TV.

Dixon took up his place beside the bed, next to Kristen, his bare feet dug into the pale gray carpet as if needing the grip to launch his attack. His mind wandered to the leftovers in the kitchen again but he reeled it back in, forcing his resolve to latch down tight and stay with him. He looked down at Kristen and filled her in on the new information he had received.

If You Really Knew Me

"She went to a Beau Dupere meeting to see for herself," he said simply, no feeling betrayed in his voice.

Kristen didn't know what the right response to that was. She could understand why a teenager would follow her curiosity, especially after the unsatisfying confrontation a week ago. But she knew she dare not allow any sympathy to leak into her words. As a result, she said nothing, just turning her gaze on Sara, as if to prompt her daughter to account for her actions.

Sara took the cue. "I went with Jenny, Kim and Candy. We all wanted to see for ourselves." But that much explanation stayed clear of the point, like standing in the shower but avoiding the water.

"You know we don't believe this sort of thing," Dixon said, as if Sara had filled in the rest of the story, that she had not attended as a mere observer, that she had taken a taste of what was on offer there.

Sara furrowed her firm young brow against the "we" in her father's declaration. Had she ever been authentically included in that "we?" Based on her experience at the Beau Dupere meeting, and her continued sense of spiritual renewal, she concluded that if she had ever been part of her family's *dis*belief she had recently fallen out of it.

His daughter's silent scowl provoked Dixon to launch into a biblical and theological explanation for why he, and whoever he included in that "we," didn't believe in that sort of thing. A thorough explanation, with rebuttals and expansions would have been done sitting down at a table, with open Bibles and notes. Instead, Sara stood with her small red shoes in each hand, her toes crossed over each other, her graduation dress sagging at one shoulder. A father who was truly present in that moment, who truly saw his daughter—part woman and part girl—standing like that before him, would have hugged her, would have postponed the discussion and thanked God for such a daughter. Dixon would later wish he had been such a father.

Even as he spoke, Sara could tell that Dixon barely believed his own explanation for their opposition to the sort of spiritual manifestations she had not only seen but had imbibed. She had done it without planning to hurt her father, though she must have known such pain would result as soon as she inhaled the glory-laden air in that meeting. Sara hadn't been thinking about her father just then, however, just as it seemed to her that he wasn't thinking about her as he rattled through his umpteen points against speaking in tongues and related activities.

Shifting to standing with one foot fully on top of the other, her right leg bearing all her weight, her arms crossed in front of her now, Sara endured the meandering lecture until her father ran out of ammunition. She remained standing, as his smoking guns began to click, empty, harmless. She had survived.

Kristen looked at her husband as if to say, as she had wondered a week before, "Is that all you have?" From her, this was not a theological or exegetical critique, only a mother's disappointment that her other half had not lifted more of the load, more of the burden of keeping their family together.

Dixon stood still, even holding his breath for a moment. He let out that breath slowly. For a second, he allowed himself some curiosity. "Did the other girls have the same experience as you?"

Sara tipped her head a bit. Why would he ask that?

"Not exactly the same. Kim was already part of a church that does stuff like that, and Jenny had been to meetings like that before, when her mom was healed. Candy doesn't chew her finger nails anymore, after someone touched her at the meeting."

She didn't mention the healing from cancer, or Candy's freedom from that old habit, as evidence on her side, but Dixon took it that way. He aborted the refutation of modern healing, however, when he remembered how poorly it was received the last time. Without that response, without any response, he felt the life drained out of him. His voice sounded hollow, when finally, he said. "Well, I can't have you doing this sort of thing as long as you're living in my house."

Sara let that penetrate the late-night numbness that had deepened when her father attempted and failed at convincing her. "Can't have you doing this sort of thing." What did that mean? What did he want? It wasn't like he was forbidding her to smoke pot or sleep with her boyfriend in his house. It was prayer. But not the approved sort of prayer.

Beginning to nod, as if her head had cut loose from some sort of mooring, not fully invested in the gesture, Sara said, "Okay. I'll be out as soon as I can arrange it." And she turned and left the room.

She didn't know if she meant it, just as she couldn't be sure that her dad meant what he had said. But she knew that her life had changed forever on that graduation day. She had graduated from childhood to adulthood much more quickly than she would have guessed possible.

Hearing the sound her mother made when she declared her willingness to find other lodging, weakened Sara's resolve only a little.

That night, as she lay in her bed, trying to drain all the anxiety that had begun accumulating when she walked out of her parents' room, she heard an unfamiliar noise. But she knew what it was. It was the sound of her father weeping violently. Even as she allowed that arrow to pierce between ribs and lodge against the deepest chambers of her heart, she knew that she wouldn't be turning back. She wouldn't be staying. Even if they reconciled for some short period of time, she was now more a resident of some home she had not yet found, like Abraham looking for that land God promised to show him.

With these resolutions revolving around and around in her mind, she finally fell into a fitful sleep.

Practical Theology

In seminary, Dixon took a course entitled, "Practical Theology." The joke among the students, of course, was that the rest of the theology was entirely *impractical*. Privately, Dixon liked that title, and took it as a sort of endorsement of his fondness for keeping church practical and manageable. Because he believed that he was embarking on carrying responsibility for the spiritual growth of a whole congregation, he insisted, at least internally, that this task be manageable, that it come with easy-grip handles and a clear instruction manual, written in plain English.

When he met a young man in that seminary who admitted to coming from a church where people listened for the voice of God and genuinely believed that they heard that voice, he felt a tight discomfort, like the way his pants felt after Thanksgiving dinner. Instead of loosening his belt, however, he found relief by staying clear of that young mystic and any who sounded like him.

Spiritual experiences such as surrounded all the major historical revivals—weeping, falling on the ground, laughing, and even speaking in tongues—fell short of Dixon's requirements for orderly church governance. He didn't want to be stuck with responsibility for something so out of control. That was the sort of trap he felt clamping down on him when he worked for Tom Schaefer, a young entrepreneur who bought, rehabbed and sold houses when Dixon was a teenager. He once instructed Dixon to break up some furniture and drop it out the window onto the lawn, but was upset later when he found dust and slivers scattered across the hardwood floors, as well as the lawn. Throughout his life, Dixon had arched up against such unfair job descriptions, and he wasn't about to follow a lifelong career in a direction that included such impossibly contradictory obligations.

If he was going to be charged with the spiritual welfare of hundreds of people, he couldn't have them surrendering to powerful unseen forces all the time, even if they believed those forces to be of divine origin. As far as Dixon was concerned, the very disorderliness of what he called "holy roller" churches proved that those powerful forces were *not* from God. Certainly, God would not be like his summer camp supervisor, who insisted that Dixon control the behavior of fifteen ten-year-olds, without so much as a saber-rattling threat of violence.

Deeper than his disdain for disorderly behavior, and for emotionalism in faith and worship, was Dixon's suspicion that those emotionally expressive churches didn't believe in Christian obedience, at least not the way he did. In the early 1990s, when he was just finishing his seminary training in the upper Midwest, he suffered through half of a sermon/lecture/rant from a fellow seminarian who claimed a spiritual awakening, discovered at a famously enflamed church that was attracting curious and parched believers from around the world. As the emotionally unstable student gushed his new revelation for the gathered audience in the seminary commons, Dixon detected an irresponsible attitude toward both order and obedience. The teary-eyed young man spoke on and on about his intimacy with the God of all creation, and referred to his old way of thinking as graceless religion. Since Dixon had shared two classes with that student, before his reconversion, he knew that it was faith just like his own that his classmate now rejected, as if it were the equivalent to the legalism of the biblical Pharisees.

That cheap grace would infect a congregation with the notion that they could each do whatever they wanted, because God would love them no matter what they did, like a weak and permissive father. But that didn't sound like any father Dixon recognized, not his own father, nor the God of the Bible, who punished the wrongdoers and promised to discipline those He loves.

In Beau Dupere, Dixon found a vindication of his rejection of that kind of faith, having spat it out like a mouth full of rancid milk those many years ago. Now, decades later, it still smelled the same. He didn't need to taste it again to know that it was bad.

The Man Who Made the Myth

"So, young lady, what did you wanna ask?" Jack Williams sat behind his desk, his legs crossed and his hands behind his head, leaning back as far as one dared in a tilting office chair. The use of the phrase "young lady" was a grandfatherly habit, though Jack Williams was probably not quite old enough to be Anna's actual grandfather. And he didn't look it. His nearly shoulder-length gray-streaked hair covered most of the top of his head, and his jowly face sparkled with energy, his skin a golden tan. He looked at Anna through little rectangular glasses that one would expect to see on a European film director or trendy New York sculptor.

"Well, I'm doing this piece on Beau Dupere, as you know. I've interviewed him and Justine and a few others. He suggested I talk to you, as well, although I already had that in mind after seeing the video the pastors showed at the big rally in Parkerville, the video which looked like they ambushed you." Anna rattled all of this quickly and smoothly, nerves speeding her delivery but not hindering her tongue.

"Hmmm," Jack said, trying to remember the video.

"It's the one where somebody with a handheld camera caught you at the door of the church and asked you whether Beau had more than one wife or multiple sex partners, and things like that."

Jack nodded. "Oh, I'd forgotten about that. So it got on the Internet?"

As with Beau, Anna struggled to believe that Jack was entirely unaware of the movement started by Dixon Claiborne and friends. "It is on the Internet now, but initially it was shown at a big town-wide rally with national media present."

"And the point was to make Beau look bad?"

"To put it mildly," Anna said. "Some in the movement are calling him the Devil or the Antichrist."

"Really? That's a lot. And their reason is...his relationship with the rich and famous, or his healing ministry?"

Anna tried to decide how best to answer that, tipping her head and looking at her recorder for a second. "Personally, I think their motive is jealousy at his success. But they did a pretty convincing job of making him look very bad, in fact. For example, they showed a photo of him with three of his...wives, at a Hollywood party."

Jack nodded, but didn't immediately comment. He seemed to be listening to a voice that Anna didn't hear, looking just over her head. "And you want my comment on all this?" His low voice was edged slightly with the sort of squeak that comes from rubbing Styrofoam together.

"Of course. As his mentor and long-time pastor, I wonder if you endorse his lifestyle choices."

Jack leaned forward and set his elbows on the arms of the chair, his chin resting on the knuckles of both hands. "Well, I should start by saying that I don't know all the details of Beau's personal life these days. Our consultations recently have all been about ministry direction. Many years ago, I did premarital counselling for him and Justine, and I knew a lot about their relationship back then. I consider them a great team, a very good complement to each other. But I can't endorse or criticize his personal life now, because I don't know the details, and because I'm not in the habit of addressing the personal lives of my brothers and sisters in front of the press."

Anna grinned halfway, trying to look sympathetic. "I understand. But, just for the record, would you say you would allow a church member to have more than one woman living with him, with whom he has a conjugal relationship, even if they don't legally call it a marriage?"

"Ha." Jack let out a laugh and straightened up in his chair. "A hypothetical question?" Now *he* smiled sympathetically. "So this is the type of story you do about the stars and billionaires?" he said, returning to that grandfatherly tone.

Anna sighed. "Yes, I write articles about the lives of rock stars and lottery winners. I'm not particularly known for digging up the best dirt. But my readers do want to understand the personal lives of celebrities."

"And Beau is one of those celebrities?" This wasn't so much a question as a passive confrontation with reality.

"He is both rich and famous, and pretty good looking besides," Anna said playfully.

Jack laughed with full voice. "All right. I'll grant you all of that. But I should also say that Beau no longer works for this church nor any of its affiliated churches. He's still a member of the church down in Malibu, but not in leadership."

"And that means you have different standards for his behavior?"

"Well, biblically there are a lot more explicit rules set out for church leaders than for the members at large."

"But he's a public figure with a world-wide ministry."

"Sure. He has one of the most remarkable healing gifts in modern history. And I don't see any sign of that diminishing. In fact, with his children around him, I've seen *more* healing power lately."

"Doesn't that gift obligate him to some kind of higher moral standard?"

Jack shook his head slightly and made the face that goes with the word "naw." What he actually said, however, was, "You don't have to be a church leader to have a powerful gift. In fact, I respect the way Beau has stayed realistic about his gifts, not trying to be a pastor, or other church leader, where that's not really his calling."

"So, church members can have multiple wives in your church, or maybe multiple husbands?" Anna said.

Chuckling, Jack teased her. "You thinking of joining up?"

Anna snickered. Clearly, Jack was avoiding answering her questions transparently, but she felt as if this was more for the reasons he explained than to protect himself or Beau. If he didn't know the details, he couldn't comment on them, and it seemed wise to her to keep such things out of the public media, even if she represented one of those media.

She knew she had to be more serious, so she tried another tack. "He admitted to having children with three of the women he lives with, including Justine." Are you aware of those children?"

Jack looked at her over his glasses, his head tipped forward as if in contemplation. "Oh, I know about his affair. He confessed that to the whole church and then reconciled with Justine over it. I also know that they have several non-related residents as part of their household. But I haven't spent time with the whole family for several years. I don't know all of the kids."

"But you're not upset at the idea of him having children with multiple women?"

"Upset? No. As I said, I don't know the details. I haven't been in that kind of accountability with Beau for a good many years. I guess you could ask his current pastor, down there in Malibu, but I don't expect he would comment on the personal life of one of his members either."

Anna felt like she had missed an opportunity. She wasn't sure, however, that she really wanted to go back and catch it. She was curious, on the other hand, about something.

"Isn't it against the Bible for a man to have more than one wife?"

Jack grinned and raised his eyebrows, savoring the surprise he held for the young reporter. "Actually, the only thing the New Testament says about it is that pastors, or bishops—some would say—should only have one wife. And there's more evidence in the New Testament that you should stay unmarried, than about how many wives a man can have. And then there's the Old Testament. Solomon had thousands of wives and God let him build the Temple instead of his father David, because David was a warrior. And, in fact, David also had several wives, 'a man after God's own heart.'" He finished with a grin worthy of the class clown.

Staring at him for a moment, Anna had to adjust her expectations. "So why then are all these pastors accusing Beau of having multiple wives, as if it's the worst kind of sin?"

"It *is* illegal," Jack said, with a small shrug. "It also associates the accused with Mormonism, which is generally seen as outside of the mainstream among pastors like that. If I were to speculate, I'd say they were trying to appeal to popular cultural standards with that accusation." He raised his hands from the arms of his chair. "But then, this is the first I've heard of these attacks on Beau. I make it a point to ignore the critics."

"Yeah, that's pretty much what Beau said too." Anna looked tired, this article was cooking more calories than any she had written before. Jack sensed this.

"You seem pretty sympathetic," he said. "Are you a believer?"

Anna looked slightly startled. "In God? No, not really. But maybe I believe in Beau Dupere."

Now Jack was the one looking a bit startled, but he followed that look with a full belly laugh.

Apparently, he knew just what Anna meant.

No Place Like Home

Sara had texted both Jenny and Kim before she fell asleep that night of the confrontation with her father. Both of them said they would be glad to have her stay with them for a while, neither of them sure about a long-term arrangement, however. Uncertain about what to do, Sara stayed for two nights at each friend's house. It felt like a pair of extended sleepovers. She snuck home when she knew her parents would be at church meetings and gathered the clothes she needed, or picked up forgotten personal necessities. She didn't see either of her parents for nearly a week. Brett did catch her slinking out of her room the following Wednesday evening, however.

"Man you really did it now," he said, around a mouthful of ice cream. He stood at the top of the stairs when Sara stepped out into the hallway. She screamed from the shock of his voice smashing her guilty silence, and she dropped her purple gym bag on the floor.

"Brett! You nearly scared me to death!"

He grinned, a drip of chocolate stretching from his lower lip toward his little pointy chin. "Yeah, that's 'cause yer afraid to get caught, sneakin' in here." His grin only rested for another bite of ice cream.

"Well, things are complicated," Sara said, picking up her bag and squeezing past Brett with one hand on the railing. She descended the stairs like an athlete in training, feet fast and precise on each step.

Brett just turned around where he was and shouted after her. "Thanks for making my life easier."

Sara hesitated before making the turn into the kitchen. "How's that?"

Brett laughed. "They've been really nice to me since you screwed up. I can hardly do anything wrong. You just made life way easier for me." He waved his spoon at her, as if conducting his point for an invisible orchestra.

Sara just rolled her eyes, not surprised that Brett couldn't sympathize with either her or their parents. She also knew that his playful comment carried a detectable measure of truth. Perhaps she *had* made his life a little easier, stretching their parents' tolerance like a new pair of socks that has to loosen up a bit to be comfortable.

Somehow, word about her sudden exit from her family home seemed to follow Sara wherever she went. People at work, whom she hardly knew, had opinions for her. Many of these comments focused on how she was going to pay for college now that she had chopped down the old money tree. Most people didn't seem to realize that being both a pastor and a money tree was pretty much impossible. Sara's expenses for college would be covered by a combination of scholarships and loans, just like they would have if she had stayed in serene unity with her parents.

Sara had started to question whether college was, in fact, the next chapter for her to write. The spiritual revelations that had propped open her eyelids generated more passion than pursuing a degree in communications, even a degree from a prestigious private university.

In fact, girlish dreams percolated just beneath her consciousness. The adulthood which she had glimpsed on the horizon as a young teenager had finally arrived, only to point her back to childlike faith in unseen supernatural forces and a rescue by a heroic prince.

As the model Sunday school student, Sara had taken her Bible stories like so many vitamins and vegetables. So often repeated in her hearing, and even out of her own mouth, the stories had lost their fascination. But now, the stories of the early disciples sparked and flamed on the page. Their good news was now her good news. Their inexplicable words and actions now fit, and flowed into her waking and sleeping life.

She dreamed of Jesus riding to her like a conquering champion on a white horse, or strolling with her in a brilliant garden. At the same time, she lost her connection with the faith of her parents. The need for young adults to settle things into basic categories had not bypassed Sara. Her parents' faith landed now in the category of useless things, even harmful and ridiculous things. And her new discovery of unction beyond peer and family pressure lacked any continuity with her childhood faith, at least in those early weeks and months.

College seemed like part of that old life, lacking meaning in the context of dreams renewed and new dreams hatching every day. She would wait until she knew which of those dreams she would follow before she headed off to university. In the meantime, she needed to find a home.

An Article of Faith

Anna had published dozens of celebrity profile stories, though few of them started as controversially. That unusual genesis explained the article's treatment by the religion editor and the editor-in-chief, as well as her own section editor. They voiced numerous opinions and insisted on an array of corrections, especially of omissions of personal details about Beau's family.

Of course, a paper wants to sell copies. They want to satisfy subscribers that they provide real news; and they even want to make a little news themselves, breaking stories and revealing hidden truth. Anna knew all that. What she didn't know was the extent to which those ambitions would bend her story about Beau Dupere. If she had known, she would have concealed more of her recordings and notes from her senior colleagues.

"You can decide, Anna, whether you enjoy this job and want to keep it, or you can have your name removed from the story and we will publish it anyway." Dale Mattingly, the Editor-in-Chief, spoke to Anna as if she were a misbehaving teen. Marla Kato watched sympathetically, embracing the tension of Anna's situation, but doing nothing to relieve it. Anna's direct boss, Sandra Steinberg, looked stern, her pale cheeks shaded with tensed muscles, her eyes unmoving. Sandra seemed to feel no shame about ganging up on Anna. It was just business.

The young rebel that ducked and dodged in and out of Anna's consciousness, beneath her new shorter haircut, wanted to give them all the finger and storm out of the office, in full possession of her scruples and integrity. But she did like this job. It was this job that allowed her to meet fascinating people like Beau Dupere.

Finally, she decided that the implacable billionaire (or multimillionaire) would survive even the harshest telling of the true details of his life. They were not asking her to fabricate, only to reveal all that she had learned, or at least all the parts that would get people talking. That talk, of course, would include more accusations, and maybe even threats, from the religious people. But Anna told herself that she could ignore them just as Beau and Jack Williams ignored them. That's what she told herself.

The exposé that appeared in that weekly regional newspaper received more attention than any story they had ever published. Anna's fellow writers congratulated her jealously. But Anna had to resisted an occasional urge to plant her face on desk or floor in abject repentance for participating in the heartless persecution.

Readers, however, generally viewed Anna's story as sympathetic, even if it was salaciously revealing. Neutral eyes saw her admiration and acceptance of all that Beau Dupere had become. They could see that she indeed believed in Beau Dupere. But they could also see those nasty bits of laundry that stuck out of the sleeves and pockets of the lengthy story, including impossible claims to supernatural insight and freedom from the pain of public pressure. Readers could see that Anna believed in Beau Dupere. They believed Anna's story was sincere. But very few of them converted to Anna's faith.

In fact, the readership of that issue of the paper skewed to the political right of their regular audience. Opponents to the wealthy healer acquired bundles of copies of the issue, the story becoming their most effective pamphlet against the most famous charlatan of Los Angeles County. They had their evidence, even the secular press corroborated their accusations.

Though Anna didn't see the article through the jaundiced eyes of the haters of Beau Dupere, she knew that many who might have remained neutral would now turn against him, once they knew about the children by multiple women, once they knew how truly strange was this man who spoke in unknown tongues, believed he could read your very soul, and laughed at anyone who criticized him. He may have not turned out to be the creepy guru that Anna had feared, but he had shown signs of being just the kind of convinced religious person that nonbelievers can't tolerate. At the same time, he had shown himself truly vulnerable to the accusations of conservative leaders across the country, who now lined up in greater numbers to denounce him as an antichrist, if not *The* Antichrist.

Anna slept less than two hours a night for four days following the article's publication. She started an email resigning from the paper three times. She started an email apologizing to Beau and Justine twice. She sent none of those correspondence, choosing instead to continuing wallowing in self-loathing, and eating far too much chocolate.

The Blood of the Martyrs

Dianna waved goodbye to Justine in the kitchen and walked out the front door, where her small SUV waited her commute to work. As soon as she stepped into the open air in front of the house, she heard the shouting, mixed with satirical chanting. With her daily work at the hospital, Dianna traversed that angry battlefield more often than the other residents of the house. She had even accidentally seen a TV news report in one of the patient rooms, a handheld camera following the Seattle police, who were dragging away a man, found with a gun, trying to enter one of Beau's meetings in the northwest.

After that shocking story, Dianna had pleaded with Beau to hire security to travel with him, instead of just protecting the house. His cavalier response ignited a feeling of futility that she had known in trying to persuade him in the past. "Well, if someone does get to me with a gun, you just remember our deal on resurrections. I'm willing to come back." His careless grin ground her nerves like sand on sun-burned skin.

The gate opened as Dianna pulled down the drive. The police motorcycles stood ready for her. The first time they accompanied her through the vicious throng, she had wondered whether the motorcycle cops were just there to witness the crime, providing no protection from a stone or bullet if someone really wanted to hit her. But she shed those thoughts now and just focused on praying for the persecutors and driving carefully down the narrow path they allowed out of the house and down the block. The court order won by the neighbor across the street had stretched the crowd down the road farther, but had not reduced their numbers at all. In fact, it seemed to Dianna that the numbers had increased significantly over the last few days. She just shook her head at that observation and intensified her prayers.

By the time Dianna's southward drive reached Topanga, the sheriff's police generally pulled to the side and waved her on. But this time they accompanied her into Santa Monica, before waving and turning aside. As far as she knew, the difference was random, unaware of any increased threat to her, even after hearing of the assassination attempt on Beau. For a moment, she had to resist the temptation to turn on the radio, sensing that there was something that she should know. The chances that she would have actually heard any news relating to the rising opposition to Beau were still slim, as long as she avoided Christian radio stations in the area, a few of which had taken up the cause.

When she finally reached the hospital, her thoughts turned to work. As a nurse practitioner, her day would be a mix of the routine and predictable, along with the urgent and unanticipated. She prayed for patients that she knew she would see, some that she hoped had been released, and for those whose names she didn't yet know.

Finding a parking place out in the middle of the employee lot, she turned off the hybrid electric motor and gathered her shoulder bag. She stopped her usual exit routine, however, when she heard a text message reach her phone. She pulled the phone out of her bag and checked. It was from Gretchen, her nine-year-old.

Dianna unlocked her phone and blindly reached for the door handle, her eyes locked to the screen. She was trying to decipher some misspellings and wrong word substitutions in Gretchen's message. Her daughter was new to texting, and often just sent a message to say "Hi," and little more. This message, however, was a request for something that Dianna was having a hard time recognizing.

That's why she didn't see the man with the buckets running toward her. She heard his sneakers flapping on the pavement first, looked up and screamed as he dropped one bucket to the asphalt and seized the bottom of the one in his right hand, making a two-handed dump onto her chest and stomach. Bright red liquid dyed her pale blue scrubs to deep purple, stuck wet against her body. As she stood with her back arched, her hands raised in partial surrender, the man fumbled for the second bucket. Dianna recovered enough of her wits to turn and try to run away, but that only made her back the next target. Her pony tail whipped around her neck, propelled forward by more of the red liquid, which she hoped was not blood. She slipped slightly in the new puddle on the shiny black pavement but kept running.

Behind her, she heard the man shrieking at her, "Adulteress! You're going to Hell!"

If You Really Knew Me

She kept running, not looking back. A nurse and an orderly that had been smoking by the employee entrance, ran toward her when they saw the familiar looking woman soaked in what looked to them like blood. They slowed as they heard the man shouting again, this time on his way out of the parking lot. "Adulteress! Red is your real color!"

Dianna stopped running when she passed the other two employees, the male orderly with a cigarette still clenched between his lips, and the nurse waving her cigarette unconsciously wedged between two fingers. Seeing that it was not a medical emergency, such as they had assumed. they looked at each other in confusion. Even the catastrophic events training they had received failed to cover a situation like this one. They each threw down their cigarette, pausing to stomp them out, and jogged to catch up with Dianna.

"What was that about?" the orderly said, catching his breath.

The nurse scowled at him, knowing better than to satisfy the obvious curiosity prompted by the bizarre scene. Instead, she said, "Are you alright?"

Dianna turned back toward her two would-be rescuers and relaxed her shoulders. She noticed that she was still holding her phone, checking to find that it had avoided most of the dousing. Next she looked down at her clothes, plastered against her. She dropped her spattered tan shoulder bag and pulled her shirt free from her soaked skin. She sniffed the red liquid, which was obviously paint, and not blood. Then she thought of what the man yelled last, about red being the color of an adulteress.

"I'm just glad it's not blood," was all she could think to say to the other two employees.

"Yeah," said the nurse, her voice only half-convinced.

The orderly laughed briefly, before stopping himself.

Black and White and Red All Over

Dianna called the house to let them know what had happened, as a warning, in case any of them planned to go out. But she didn't call the police. The story leaked, however, from the other hospital employees who saw her before she found clothes to change into and managed to wash off most of the paint from her skin. She retained an added pink tone, but completed her entire shift, nonetheless.

Anna was driving in her car when she heard the news. At first, she slowed and swerved and then she found a place to pull to the shoulder of the busy, winding road. Then she burst into tears, taking the responsibility for the idiocy of others on herself. A few seconds of catharsis ended in a bitter resolve to drive directly to the Dupere home, to throw herself at their feet, begging for mercy.

Wiping her face with both hands, blowing her nose on her last tissue, and noting what a mess she looked in the rearview mirror, Anna checked for traffic and then pulled a tight U turn back toward Malibu. As she accelerated back up to speed, the little Honda pushing her into this impulsive visit, she asked herself just exactly what she thought she was doing. Was she going to apologize? To make amends? She shook her head in little movements that reminded her of her grandmother with Parkinson's disease.

No, she wasn't going to throw herself on their mercy. She was going to their house to hide, to find refuge with the only sane people she knew. She laughed aloud at this thought. The crazy, tongue-speaking, faith-healing, possibly-polygamous billionaire and his tribe of "wives" and children were the sanest people she knew? She slowed her car from escape speed to contemplation, letting the curves of the road pull her and push her, and weave her into a more reasonable state.

If You Really Knew Me

She couldn't just show up at the Dupere house. What would she say? Why was she there? Did she want to move in? With the older kids gone, were there enough bedrooms now? Again, her head started that unconscious shaking, as if her body disagreed with her spontaneous solution to her shame.

Anna surrendered her escape plan and turned the car again, this time a right turn that would take her another way toward her apartment. She suddenly felt very tired. Her shoulders sank and she sighed, as she watched the trees and houses through which she and the road dodged. Everything stood out in high contrast with the setting sun behind her. She arrived home just as white objects in sight had taken on the color of cheddar cheese. But neither rest nor food awaited her arrival.

A small cluster of reporters blossomed into action when she pulled into the parking lot of her apartment building. When her mind locked onto the idea that they were there to interview her, and that it must be about the attack on Dianna, she considered continuing around the asphalt lot and back out onto the street. Perhaps she did need sanctuary with Beau and Justine.

Anna's weariness, however, sapped her will even for a getaway. Or, maybe, she just knew that she had to face the questions sometime, from someone. After all, she was a reporter herself. Didn't she owe it to her fellow journalists to answer for her actions?

Her car fitted into a diagonal parking space, her emergency break ratcheted into place, she turned off the engine. The reporters stood in a line just next to her left rear fender. One of them had a TV camera. None of them seemed to be carrying buckets of red paint.

Anna opened the car door and swung her legs out. Her white sandals touched the pavement only briefly before she stood up and met the gauntlet that awaited her. A small injection of adrenalin subdued her weariness for a moment.

If You Really Knew Me

"Miss Conyers, Miss Conyers, Anna, Anna," several voices greeted her in chorus. But there were really only six people all together, no throng of reporters needing to vie for her attention.

"One at a time, please," Anna said, her voice cracking on that last word. "I can answer you, one at a time." She nodded at Barbara Stiller, a local newspaper reporter that Anna had met at press events.

Barbara said, "Thanks, Anna. Of course, we're here to ask for your reaction to what happened to Dianna Perry this morning."

Anna thought about her initial reaction to the news, which was still fresh in her awareness, as if her body hadn't yet recovered from the workout she had given it, trying to decide where to go and what to do. Then she answered more guardedly.

"I'm shocked, of course. I've been to their house several times and have seen the angry mob of people gathered there, shouting accusations, as some of you must have. And I can't say the crazy thing that happened to Ms. Perry is so surprising, when you see how exercised people are. But I really was shocked when I heard the news just a few minutes ago."

"So no one from the Dupere house, or from the police, informed you earlier today?" Barbara said, following up.

Anna tensed her brow and frowned. "No. Of course, not. They don't have any reason to contact me about an incident like that."

The young man with a microphone, accompanying the TV camera, piped in. "But don't you think that the attack was likely a response to your story published this week?"

Anna looked into the intense blue eyes of the reporter, whom she didn't recognize, wondering what she really did think. "I suppose someone could claim that, but there were already protesters and threats before my article, so it might be journalistic hubris to say that I affected things so much with one story." Or it might be *denial* to say I didn't, she thought silently.

"So you don't feel like your story could have incited more hatred against the Dupere household?" the young man said.

177

Anna tipped her head a bit to one side. "It certainly wasn't intended that way. I think it just confirmed what people believed already. I don't expect anybody who thought well of them suddenly decided to go and throw paint on one of them."

An older woman with one of the L.A. papers pushed forward. "Do you have a personal relationship with the family now, since you've been granted such intimate access to their home life and all?"

"Well, a personal relationship could be a lot of things. They did grant me access to much of their private life, but I don't think they count me as a good friend or anything," Anna said, feeling more vulnerable now, with the emotions raised by that question. It seemed a good time to cut off the interview. "I have to go," she said, pulling herself away as each of the reporters shouted questions at her. Anna almost laughed at what it felt like to be on the other end of those shouted questions.

Not Really What I Had in Mind

He was trying to reattach a loose shudder on his house, when Dixon Claiborne heard about the red paint attack. News radio had come on after the Giants baseball game and he heard the report as he sucked the thumb he had just mashed with a hammer...again. He noted the name of the woman, Dianna. Part of him thought it would be important to know who it was that Beau Dupere had swept into his web of spiritual deception. Part of him wondered how the woman was doing, intrigued to hear that she worked in a hospital as a nurse practitioner, when she lived with one of the richest men in California.

The realization that there were a lot of details about the Dupere disciples that he didn't know, meant to Dixon only that he was keeping a safe distance from the deception and corruption down there in Malibu. When he had heard about the would-be assassin captured in Seattle, he noticed mention of Dupere's sixteen-year-old daughter who was accompanying him. They left the girl's name out of that story, however.

Unlike Anna Conyers, Dixon assumed that none of this had anything to do with him, no sense of responsibility for stirring up opposition to Beau Dupere, no guilt keeping him awake at night. To him, it was all a matter of natural consequences for the actions of other people. There was Beau Dupere, whose lifestyle disgusted most Americans. And there were the crazies, armed with guns or paint. That whole cast would do what they would do, no matter what Dixon did to protect his church, his faith and his God.

Without any effort at all, Dixon turned to thinking about these things, instead of figuring out how to get the decorative shutter to attach to the house, where it had been ripped free, and the hole in the aluminum siding was left stripped and gaping. At least it seemed to be gaping compared to the size of the screw that had been used to mount it initially. His focus followed his worry back to the shutter. But the most worrying thing in his life did involve Beau Dupere, in a way.

He stared at the pale tan siding, textured to look like wood, but saw none of it. His mind had diverted toward his deepest fear. Had he lost his daughter? The weight and scope of that question suddenly made the repair work seem more attractive. He straightened the sagging shutter once again, noting an alternative spot for attaching a screw, as if ignoring the repair momentarily had freed his mind to see the solution. That didn't seem likely to work regarding the problem of Sara and her decision to follow another form of faith, however.

He worked at the problem with Sara in similar fashion to the way he had to wrench the nail free after his second attempt to reattach the shutter. He worked it back and forth until the new hole yawned wide enough to find satisfaction. Was Sara's deviance just a teenage effort at revenge? Or, maybe it was not revenge, but just independence, she sought. Maybe she would find out that it was all fake, and then she would come back to the real faith. Was it fake? Dixon reminded himself that he had adjusted his argument from fakery to...what? In his mind, deception was close enough to what he meant, what he now feared for Sara. Did he fear her deception, even captivity to unholy spirits? Or was it just the fear of losing one of the most precious things, one of the most precious people, in his life?

"Dad?" Brett said, from just behind Dixon.

Dixon jumped and dropped the drill he was holding. He had picked up the drill at some point to investigate making a new hole in both the aluminum shutter and the aluminum siding. When Brett startled him, Dixon dropped the drill on his foot after it glanced off his shin and left a stinging sensation to go with the embarrassment of being caught standing, staring at the side of the house.

Brett tried not to laugh at his dad's dance and efforts at not swearing in front of him. He recovered control momentarily. "Dad, are you okay?"

Dixon couldn't tell if the question was aimed at the bang on the shin and foot or the brown study Brett had interrupted. But, either way, every dad knows how to answer that question. "Uh, yeah, sure, everything's fine." He looked sideways at Brett, wearing his Oakland A's jersey. "You just startled me."

"What were you doin'?" Brett said, never one to allow an awkward moment to pass untortured.

Dixon took a deep breath. "I was thinking about your sister. Worrying really," he said, splashing two handfuls of truth into his own face. To Brett, it was an example of a man being real. Or so Dixon hoped.

"Is she joining a cult or something?" Brett was glad for a chance to ask a direct question, taking advantage of a vulnerable moment for his dad. The pastor seemed to feel that he was al-

If You Really Knew Me

ways on duty, always under observation, as far as Brett could tell. Maybe he could slip in a question at a time when an answer was looking for a way out, into the bright spring air.

"I hope not," Dixon said. He looked at Brett, thinking, maybe more honesty with Brett would prevent *him* from going elsewhere in search of truth.

"You think she can speak in tongues and stuff like that?" Brett said, crashing even deeper into this unexplored acreage.

Dixon stopped rubbing his shin and stood up straight. He looked at Brett, sure his son was asking a real question, knowing he was worried about his sister too, and realizing just then that Brett too would be curious. In that instant, Dixon entertained a crazy idea. Whether it was the bang on the shin, the frustration with the shutter—and life in general—or parental desperation at having a 50% failure rate so far, he proposed that idea aloud.

"Maybe you and I should go and investigate this guy for ourselves. Let's go and see for ourselves how creepy or fake he is."

Brett grinned shamelessly, something he would learn to repress when he became a teenager. "Wow, could we? Would we see Sara there? When can we go?"

While Brett's enthusiasm amused Dixon a bit, it also flipped red flags to a standing position in the peripheral vision on both sides. Was it dangerous? Could he really protect his second child in that context? Was he, himself, safe in such a setting? Right in the heart of the enemy camp?

Brett could sense his father's hesitation. "We wouldn't have to tell anybody we went. And even if someone finds out, you could just tell 'em you were investigating the guy for yourself. Or that you were just looking for your daughter who got captured by his cult."

Brett's childish problem-solving made Dixon smile. "Yeah, I don't think we have to worry about that kinda thing." But, inside, he worried about all of those things, though not as intensely as he worried about losing both of his children.

"I'll go look on the Internet for a meeting," Brett said, empowered in ways his dad valued, though in a context that Dixon could not help regretting.

"Okay," Dixon said. "No flights to Hawaii," he said, shouting over Brett's shoulder as his son headed for the kitchen door.

Brett raised one thumbs up, affirming that one limitation.

"Probably find one in Rio, instead," Dixon said to himself, muttering and then laughing quietly. He picked up the drill and made sure the bit was long enough to go through the tab on the shutter as well as into the aluminum siding. He hoped that would be enough to hold the screw, at least until the next typhoon.

Let the Children Come to Me

Though Beau was always looking for a chance to heal, his focus paled compared to Adam's. Wherever he went, Adam checked for physical ailments, particularly pain, his healing specialty.

On a sunny Saturday afternoon, Adam and Peter accompanied Beau and Luke to the park. After speeding through the gauntlet of spite at the end of the driveway, with the boys holding their hands over their ears, it was a short five minutes to a park with elaborate castles and bridges for the boys to conquer and defend. They liked it especially on a Saturday, when there would be lots of other boys and girls to join in their fantastic games.

Beau sat on a bench in the partial shade of a scrawny maple tree reading a biography of a powerful man in the U.S. tech industry, someone he had met once. Though his reading comprehension would suffer for it, Beau spent almost as much time watching the boys. He watched to make sure that Adam and Peter stayed close to Luke, who was still small for such a large and rowdy environment, and to see if Adam had spotted his next healing subject. Generally, it was a matter of when, not if, in a crowd of kids this size, especially kids that Adam didn't know, and whom he hadn't already tried to heal.

Engrossed in a description of the tech titan's family life, Beau stayed with the book for a few minutes uninterrupted, his right arm resting on the back of the wooden bench, the book cradled from below by his left hand. In the shade, a pink long-sleeve shirt unbuttoned over his blue t-shirt felt perfectly comfortable on that calm and sunny day.

An unusual silence in one section of the park awoke Beau from his reading. He looked up to check on the boys. When he located them he located the reason for the noticeable noise reduction. A little circle of children, along with a couple of parents, stood around Adam and Peter. Beau hoped Luke was there too, though he couldn't see the little two-and-a-half-year-old. Standing up calmly, noting his page in the book, he sauntered toward the action.

Children all over the walls of the castle and along the bridges had stopped to watch what was happening. Just when Beau got a glimpse of who was at the center of that circle with Adam, the whole impromptu gathering burst into cheers and applause. Between the running and jumping children, cheering or dashing to tell their parents what they had seen, Beau could see Adam and Luke focused on a six or seven-year-old girl. She held some small object in her hand and spoke animatedly to Adam. Luke looked up at her with the most satisfied smile Beau had ever seen on that little face.

When Adam saw Beau approaching, he said something to the little girl and Luke and then ran to meet Beau. Grabbing the hand not carrying a book, Adam towed Beau to the scene of his triumph.

If You Really Knew Me

"This is Deirdre," he said, gesturing much like he might when rolling dice on the ground in front of him. Adam was rarely self-conscious, in his excitement even less so. He bounced as he recounted what happened.

"Luke was trying to talk to this girl, Deirdre, and she said she couldn't hear him 'cause she had hearing loss in both ears. Luke didn't understand except that she needed healing, so he called me over." He paused to reassure Beau. "I was just up there where I could still see him. We were playing castle and he was out on the bridge."

Deirdre, not too shy to jump in, said, "I couldn't tell what he was saying when he pointed at Adam, but I got the idea I was supposed to wait, so I did."

A woman in a purple cardigan joined them. "Deirdre, what's going on?"

As if glad to finally be rid of them, Deirdre handed two small plastic objects to her mother, for that's who the woman was. "I can hear now," she said, looking up at her mom with the biggest grin her little blushing face could accommodate. She pointed at Luke and said, "It's 'cause of Luke and Adam."

Adam remembered his manners and stepped up to Deirdre's mother and shook her hand. He probably could have relieved her of her jewelry and shoes at that moment; the petite, dark-haired woman stood frozen and unresponsive to the world around her.

Beau noted the paralysis of the mother and decided to bypass that to get the story of how it happened. "So how did you do it?" he said to Adam. To Deirdre's mother, the intonation must have sounded wrong, because instead of asking, "How in the world did you do a thing like that?" Beau sounded like he was asking more of a methodological question. He did have a hint of a proud father smile about him, but no sign of surprise.

"Well, Peter thought that since Luke was the one who found her, maybe he was supposed to be the one that healed her, so I told Luke to put his hands on her ears," Adam said.

If You Really Knew Me

"I had to bend down for him to do it," Deirdre said.

"And I told him to tell deafness to go away, and he did," Adam said. His voice hopped as he said "he did," aiming a grin at Luke to accompany that declaration.

Luke sensed a cue for him, so he said it again, "Deafness, go away," as if to demonstrate how easy it really was.

Deirdre's mother had recovered her ability to speak by then. "You can hear? You can hear without the hearing aids?"

"Yes!" Deirdre exclaimed. "I can hear you, and I can hear the kids, and I can hear that jet flying overhead." Everyone looked up at a jet flying at least twenty thousand feet above, its engines barely breaking through the noise of a hundred children at play.

The mother blinked at her daughter and then at the three boys. She looked to Beau, perhaps hoping an adult could convince her that this was not just some sort of trick, or a child's game. Beau smiled at her and said. "God is good!"

She just shook her head, perhaps not denying God's goodness, but rather admitting her momentary loss of confidence that she knew anything for sure.

Deirdre covered her ears with her hands and then uncovered them, using her hands like flaps, opening and closing, to hear the sound come and go. "I can hear everything," she said, in a playful sing-song voice, an octave lower than normal.

Adam and Peter laughed, and Luke put his hands on his own ears to emulate Deirdre.

"So, God...did this?" Deirdre's mother said to Beau.

Beau nodded and introduced himself. "I'm the dad," he said. "Beau. And you are?"

"Deirdre's mom, Katie."

"Pleased to meet you. You wanna sit down and talk about this?"

Katie nodded, but failed to follow Beau back to his bench initially, still trying to find all the gears that had once driven her through her very normal and predictable life. Beau motioned for her to follow.

"Go, Mom," Deirdre said, pushing her mother toward where Beau had paused to wait for her.

Adam laughed at the comic contrast between Deirdre's lack of inhibition and her mother's stupefaction. Beau waited patiently. He had seen all this before.

Forgiveness for What?

The next morning, after Anna survived her first grilling by the press, she persisted in feeling responsible for what happened to Dianna. She carried this backpack full of guilt through her morning routine, from shower to dressing, to breakfast, to makeup. Not until she was driving to work did she decide she finally had to just do it. She turned her car toward Malibu and the Dupere house. She called the office to explain that she was going for a follow-up interview. She knew she had lots of leeway with her editor, given that her article had sold more papers than any other in the history of that publisher.

When she cut off the call on her Bluetooth earpiece, she settled back, thinking of what she would say, and how she would say it. Throwing herself to her knees, grasping Beau's feet, or maybe Dianna's feet, came to mind. Weeping seemed unavoidable. Her throat tightened every time she thought about her role in turning even more people violently against Beau and his family.

While she sat there on her knees, at Beau's feet, she wondered if she could offer herself, as penance. She would work for them, do anything they asked, because they were such good people and she...well, she was...

If You Really Knew Me

An accident along the side of the highway drew her out of her fantasy apology, or whatever that was. Attention to merging lanes, bumper-to-bumper traffic and mounting heat inside her inadequately air-conditioned car drained much of her ardent repentance and spontaneous resolve, such that, by the time she pulled down the long straight road leading into the Dupere's neighborhood she was second-guessing the direction her car was rolling.

What if they aren't awake yet? What if they aren't home? What if they laughed at her for thinking she could be forgiven for what she did?

That last notion made Anna cringe. That's not like them, she thought. Where did that idea come from?

She passed inspection by a sheriff's deputy and rolled toward the end of the driveway.

The crowd along the street, all the way down to the next intersection, was impressive for nine o'clock in the morning. She saw a sign with a picture of a nurse covered in red paint, and she knew the hardcore crazies where present and accounted for. And this renewed her momentum toward throwing herself at the mercy of the Dupere household.

In the driveway, none of the four guards looked familiar to Anna. This cast her entire enterprise into doubt. She didn't have an appointment and they wouldn't recognize her.

She pressed the button for the driver's side window, which crept down the rest of the way. A dark-haired young man, his muscular shoulders bulging against his black t-shirt, leaned down and looked in the window.

"Are you the reporter? Anna?"

"Yeah," she said.

"Okay, they thought you might be by today. Go on through."

The two-second delay between when those words entered her ears and when she next moved, to follow the guard's gesture toward the gate, was shorter than it would have been a few weeks ago. But, in all her anxiety over begging for forgiveness,

If You Really Knew Me

Anna hadn't ever paused to think that they might be expecting as much from her. Or was *that* what they were expecting?

Driving under the influence of overwhelming consternation is difficult, but not impossible, as Anna discovered. She coasted into her usual parking place, noting the absence of Beau's Land Rover and a couple of other cars she was used to seeing there. They were expecting her, but did they know when to expect her? As she stepped out of the car, she thought, maybe they *were* expecting me, and all ran away so they wouldn't have to see me.

Again, she noted how strange that thought seemed in the context of the people she had met in that house. Where were these thoughts coming from?

Anna had to ring the doorbell and wait. No one seemed to be poised at the other side of the door, politely waiting for her to finally get there, let alone had come outside to greet her and help her up the steps.

The front door opened and a young woman with very long, straight brown hair stood in a loose cotton dress and bare feet. Of course, her feet would be bare, Anna thought.

"Hi, I'm Anna Conyers. I was hoping to speak with Beau or Justine, or maybe Dianna," she said, assembling more words than she had planned.

"Come on in," said the young woman. "I'm Miranda McAllister, their administrative assistant. They're all out just now, but I can call and see when Beau or Justine will be back. Dianna's at work."

Anna hoped that her disappointment didn't show, but how could Miranda not notice the effect of such grand and fragile hopes popping and sputtering to the earth?

This time, Anna kicked her shoes off immediately when she entered. That spontaneous act felt like kicking off shackles, for reasons she couldn't even guess. She almost giggled.

Miranda led Anna toward a part of the house that she hadn't seen before, pushing a door open and gesturing toward a huge overstuffed couch, as she settled gently into a tall office chair

If You Really Knew Me

made of black mesh, curved to fit her back. "Have a seat, I'll get one of them on the phone and see when we can expect them."

Anna, still carrying the stunned silence that hit her at the news that all the protagonists were out of the house, followed Miranda's directions and took a seat on the couch. She lowered her shoulder bag to the floor and pulled her legs up under her, to avoid having her feet dangle a couple of inches above the floor. She felt vulnerable enough without that added evidence that she was just a child among adults.

The side of Miranda's phone conversations that Anna heard sounded like leaving messages on voice mail, both on Beau's phone and Justine's. Miranda hung up the second call and turned her chair toward Anna.

"I know they don't have big meetings or anything this morning. Justine was shopping and Beau was seeing a friend for breakfast. That leaves their times of arrival pretty flexible. How flexible is your schedule?"

Anna looked at Miranda, wishing she were as cool and unburdened as her hostess. We must be about the same age, she thought. How could she have it so together? Then Anna realized that asking questions was her job, so she would just do that.

"I know I didn't call ahead, so that's my bad," she said. "But I wonder if I could ask *you* some questions to follow up on my article, and some of the things that have happened since." She felt like she was faking it, but she hoped that she came across as professional and almost confident.

Miranda smiled. "Sure, no problem. Beau said you might want to talk to me, after I setup your meeting with Steve, the accountant."

It was news to Anna that Miranda had setup that meeting, but she did remember now that it was Miranda that she had talked with in her initial efforts to interview Beau. So this was the assiduous assistant that buffeted her early queries? Not what she had pictured.

"Great," Anna said, still maintaining the charade of unflappability. "How long have you worked for them?" she said, pulling a notebook out of her bag.

"Coming up on three years now," Miranda said, crossing her legs under her loose, flowing dress and leaning back a bit, as if she planned on enjoying their little talk.

"What did you do before?"

"I was the personal assistant to Maya Clark."

"*The* Maya Clark? The pop singer?"

Miranda laughed. "Yes, that's right."

"How did Beau get you away from Maya?" Anna said, remembering an interview she did with Maya a few years ago, before the young singer became a household name.

"Well, he made a very generous offer in terms of compensation, and I got a chance to see the family and observe their style and such. It seemed like a dream job for me, much less pressure than the pop music scene and the high-paced lifestyle of a twenty-something diva."

"So he pays you more than Maya did?"

"Yes, and the health benefits are unbeatable." Miranda's face lit up like a girl who wanted to tell a really good secret.

"Why are you smiling like that?" Anna couldn't figure out what could be funny about health benefits.

"I'm never sick," Miranda explained, still grinning.

"Never sick?"

"If I get any kind of negative health symptoms, I just have the family heal me. There's always someone around here that can cut an infection or injury short. I never have to go to the hospital or see a doctor." Her satisfied grin made sense to Anna now, though she was having difficulty believing what Miranda was saying.

"So, in three years, you've never taken a sick day?"

"Actually, at first, I did. But Beau sat me down and explained that I should always come to work, even if I'm sick, and they would take care of it. He even said, if I felt too sick to come over, he would send someone to come and heal me at home, or pray over the phone."

"That makes it sound so automatic," Anna said. "Haven't they ever found something they can't heal?"

Miranda grew a bit more serious, her grin fading and her tone more instructive. "Individually, I know that they have failed to heal things, but as a group, I have always seen everything healed by one or another of them. I'm at least two and a half years without a sick day."

Anna could feel herself getting mired in this point, and wanted to cover other questions, so she forced herself to move on, with a shake of her head and a little laugh.

"Well, as tough as all that is for me to absorb, I do want to ask you some other questions. So Beau pays better than Maya? That's surprising to me."

"He's a very generous man," Miranda said. "Justine, too, and all of them. No one here seems hung up on having stuff or keeping things for themselves. Actually, since I *am* so well compensated, I've followed their examples in how to deal with having more money than I need."

"Were you a believer when they hired you?"

"A believer?" Miranda said, measuring that word for its fit. "I went to church as a kid, and definitely believed that God was real. But I didn't really live like I thought God cared about what I did or would take care of everything I need." She thought for a second, her green eyes drifting toward the corner of the room. "I guess I was a believer to an extent, but not like now, after all the miracles I've seen and the way these people treat each other. It does feel a lot like another conversion."

"Conversion to something beyond the faith of your childhood?"

"Yes. Because the faith of my childhood was faith in a distant, and uncaring, God, who was mostly mad at me and everybody else. I mean, the God I grew up with was just someone you didn't wanna tick off, not someone who reaches into my life and loves me in every possible way."

Anna squirmed a bit in her seat, settling back down with her legs recrossed under her. Miranda's personal faith seemed different than what Anna had understood from other Christians. And even Beau didn't talk about his faith in the same fresh way that Miranda did. Perhaps it was just newer to the young assistant.

"I can see that what I'm saying makes you a bit uncomfortable," Miranda said. "I was like that when I started here. It was actually the only reason I hesitated about taking the job. I could tell right away that their way of loving God was so different from what I'd known that I would either have to shelter myself in some way, or I would end up giving in and accepting that love for myself."

Looking at her notebook, Anna cleared her throat slightly, then glanced at the map of the U.S. on the wall over Miranda's shoulder. She groped for a segue to more comfortable territory.

"Weren't you kinda put off by the whole family situation, Beau and all the women?" She still hadn't found her footing for addressing this issue after talking to both Beau and Jack Williams.

"You mean the extended household?" Miranda said, offering a pert grin and raised eyebrow that said, "*I know what you really want to ask about.*"

Anna nodded.

"Well, I didn't really understand when I started. They *did* tell me that things were non-traditional, but I wasn't really picking up on what they meant by that." She fanned both hands in front of her. "It was like I had no way of imagining the lifestyle they were leading, so I didn't hear it when they tried to tell me in polite terms." She laughed at herself. "You wouldn't think I would be naïve, coming out of working for Maya."

"When did you finally catch on?"

"Well, actually it took a while, because I mostly deal with their travel schedules and speaking engagements, healing events, things like that. So the dynamics of family life was all a bit beyond my focus. Since I work right here in the house, though, I was getting a bit confused about who all was living here and which ones were Beau's kids." Miranda laughed again, but not the uncomfortable laugh of embarrassment. She just appeared to be enjoying remembering her old self.

"Finally, when I seemed really baffled one day, Justine came in here, sat down and went through the relationships of everyone in the house. And I finally did the math, so to speak." She raised both eyebrows and grinned. "It turns out, it was a good thing I didn't understand at the beginning, 'cause I might have been too weirded out by all of it before I knew them. But, since I learned to trust them before hearing the whole story of all the relationships, I just kept trusting them, even where they were going beyond my comfort zone."

For Anna, of course, the path had been different, starting with the doctored video at the town meeting up in Parkerville and the accusations from the pastors there. She had followed Beau to find out for herself, but also to prove the accusers wrong. Proving religious people to be wrong seemed exciting at the time, even if in defense of others who lived a faith that she couldn't understand. The thing that annoyed her most about church people was how smugly they held onto their rightness. She liked the prospect of breaking that smugness open, even though she expected that Beau Dupere, and his cult, carried a similar self-righteousness. The irony, for her, was that Beau and Justine, and their family, seemed more convinced than their accusers, doubtless even. But they just seemed joyful, and not at all arrogant. The possibility that one could hold strongly to very particular beliefs, without being nasty about it, had not occurred to Anna before. This combination tempted her to consider whether this was something she wanted for herself.

Closing her notebook, and letting her bare legs dangle over the edge of the couch, her toes just grazing the plush carpet, she took a deep breath. "I didn't know what I was getting into when I started these interviews, but I'm beginning to take this all personally. I was all caught up in feeling bad that I might have contributed to the attack against Dianna. But now I'm thinking that, if faith is like what you describe, and what I see in Beau and his family, then I might be interested."

Miranda smiled and nodded, looking a lot like an approving mother, but without the anxiety that turns a mother's hair gray. "I'd be glad to talk to you about that any time," she said. "Off the record."

They both laughed. Anna liked the fact that Miranda didn't jump in to close the deal right then and there. She felt like she needed to give herself a bit more time before joining up, whatever that entailed. She was pretty sure now that offering herself as their indentured servant wouldn't be part of it.

And that's when Beau finally called Miranda back.

In Enemy Territory

With Brett riding shotgun, Dixon pulled into the parking lot of a big church near Oakland. Brett, the A's fan, had jumped on the chance to go to Oakland, even if it was to see the supposed healer, and expose him for what he really is. Brett didn't fill that idea with specific content, but hoped they would expose whatever it was the Beau Dupere had to hide.

They had to park a hundred yards from the front doors, the parking lot full of all sorts of vehicles, from little electric cars to big diesel busses. The pastor in the Toyota Camry couldn't help being a little jealous of the turn out on a Thursday night.

When he stepped out of the car, Dixon hesitated over whether he should wear a baseball cap and sunglasses in the meeting, to avoid being recognized. But that felt too creepy, once he pictured himself in that camoflage, skulking in and hunkering down. Brett waited like a boy who had to go to the bathroom, excited to get into the action, whether it was to bust this false prophet or to start speaking in tongues. It was really all the same to him, as long as he didn't have to move out of the house, whichever one happened.

Opting for going in without a disguise, Dixon put a hand around Brett's shoulders and they walked through the accumulating dusk, as the sun disappeared behind the church. He pulled his phone out of his pocket, and made sure it wasn't going to play "Bye, Bye Baby," the Giants' fight song, if someone called. He also noted the amount of battery power he had, in case he wanted to shoot a video of something incriminating. He supposed that recording was prohibited in the meeting, so he checked to see how he could hold his phone without being detected. That little side project ended when he nearly dropped his phone on the pavement. Brett looked a skeptical question at him as Dixon pocketed his phone.

"When do I get a smart phone, dad?" Brett said, thinking their little bonding experience might be a good time to seek some kind of reward.

"Oh, someday," Dixon said. His distraction about what they were heading toward practically erased Brett's question as soon as he answered.

Brett figured that out and decided to save that topic for a better opportunity.

A bald man, with a shiny brown head and glasses, greeted them at the door, a smile filling half of his face. Dixon nodded a reply to the greeting but missed the handshake. His nerves seemed to be flipping circuits in his brain somewhat randomly, making simply walking a chancy endeavor. He couldn't deal with complications such as shaking hands and pretending to be friendly just then.

Like water down a drain, people poured into the auditorium, leaving little choice for anyone not willing to fight to break free of the flow in that direction. Dixon and Brett were glad to follow.

If You Really Knew Me

The experience reminded Brett of being on vacation, when they would visit someone else's church for a change, where they would be strangers instead of the focal family. His pulse escalated at the knowledge that he wouldn't have seen and heard it all before, a feeling that recalled low-stress travel with his intact family.

Dixon troubled over a strange sensation when he looked at the Bay Area crowd. Finally, he identified what was clogging his filter. The racial composition of the crowd was as mixed as he had ever seen anywhere, especially in church. African Americans might have been in a slim majority, but the Hispanic and white communities were also well represented, not to mention Asians of all nations imaginable. He had never particularly wanted an interracial church, but something about that serendipitous mix stirred a hopeful feeling in him that he hadn't expected.

A pair of seats ten rows from the back was the best they could do in relationship to the stage, but the auditorium was slanted like a theater, and the view would be good enough. He sat down, remembering a movie about Jim Jones and the way he deceived people into believing that he could heal. Dixon wondered whether he would be able to spot a fake from that distance.

Both a band and a choir were on the stage now, and an African American man in his sixties headed for the podium, with Beau Dupere and two younger white people tagging behind. Dupere and his two associates sat down on a mini pew behind the podium, as the pastor of that church greeted the crowd. Dixon recognized him from the advertisement Brett had found on the Internet, though he guessed that the picture must have been about ten years old, from what he was seeing live.

With his head spinning in overdrive, trying to be something he had never trained for, Dixon barely caught a whole sentence of the greeting and invocation. His mind focused enough to stand up when everyone else did, as the racially mixed band, and nearly as diverse choir, started to fill the air with praise. No stiff conservative when it came to music, Dixon felt a lift with the growing momentum of the music. The instruments and voices performed expertly and naturally, but the verve of the music they made nearly overwhelmed him. The little governor in his brain, set there to warn him when he was about to get into trouble, seemed to have gone down, probably needing a reboot. He let the music catch him up and he followed the words on the screen, singing along as well as he could.

Brett checked his dad's engagement with the songs and figured that he was just playing along, so he did the same, trying his best to sing, to clap hands and even experimenting with raising one hand a little, until his dad let him know, with a cocked eyebrow, that that was too much blending in.

They sang and watched, sometimes distracted by the emotional responses of people around them, men and woman who seemed to sing the lyrics from their feet upward, from their hearts outward. Brett stared shamelessly at a woman lying in the aisle crying her eyes out, interspersing her sobs with, "Thank you, Jesus. Oh, thank you, Jesus."

Then the music wound down. The main event was not the jet-powered worship or the cathartic tears.

After forty-five minutes of music, Beau Dupere finally filled the large video screen. But only after the host pastor spent five minutes introducing him, a mini-sermon for a warmup, perhaps. Sweat glistened on the forehead of the white-haired pastor, when Beau approached the podium. He first whispered something into the pastor's ear and they exchanged a look and a laugh. Then Beau put his hand gently on that sweaty forehead, and the distinguished senior pastor collapsed to the carpet like a blow-up Easter decoration with a sudden air leak.

Beau turned to the congregation and smiled, perhaps shyly, perhaps apologetically, but he said nothing about what had transpired between him and the host pastor. Instead, he introduced his sermon, directing the gathered hearers to I Corinthians 2:1 – 5. He read the passage aloud, *"When I came to you, I did not come with eloquence or human wisdom as I proclaimed to you* the testimony about God. For I resolved to know nothing while I was with you except Jesus Christ and him crucified. I came to you in weakness with great fear and trembling. My message and my preaching were not with wise and persuasive words, but with a demonstration of the Spirit's power, so that your faith might not rest on human wisdom, but on God's power."

When he finished with the word, "power," the crowd burst into cheers and laughter. Some did so because they were watching the senior pastor rolling around on the floor next to the podium. Many cheered because they were there for the power, they were there to receive a healing miracle, as well as to witness the healing of many others.

The rushing wind of cheers and laughter sent several hundred people into delirious hilarity, way beyond any possible humor in the situation. Beau paused to explain, "That laughter you hear is dozens and dozens of people instantly losing their depression and anxiety disorders, their chemical imbalances, and their glandular conditions, with thyroid and other issues." Several women screamed and shouted from across the room, as if in confirmation of what he said. The room seemed to rock like a rickety train station gripping its foundation as the express roared through.

"I'm not a preacher," Beau said. He looked over the crowd. "I usually agree to speak before the healing begins, just to be polite." A few "amens" and a shower of natural laughter greeted this confession.

"God has made me a healer. Though some preachers are healers and some healers try to preach, I'm clear that I have little to say with my mouth, with my mind."

A seasoned male voice shouted. "Help him, Lord!"

"But I do bring the power of God's Kingdom, alive here on Earth, just as it exists in Heaven."

That passing train seemed to be replaced with a much larger model. Whether or not the rocking of that building was scientifically verifiable, most of the people there felt it. Dixon Claiborne felt it, and seriously considered climbing his way to the aisle and running for his car. Bret looked just the same as he did the last time he went to an A's game and saw them win by four runs in a ninth inning rally. His freckled cheeks bulged with pleasure around a toothy smile.

Then Beau changed his pace. "There's a woman here. Your name is Karen. You had a surgery that was supposed to be minor, but there was a problem and you nearly died. Now you have continued pain across your midsection near your belly button."

A woman with long red hair jumped to her feet to the right of the stage, twenty rows back. And just as soon as she jumped up, she collapsed into the arms of those seated around her.

"You're healed, right now, Karen," Beau declared.

Cheers, applause and laughter followed that declaration. At least a half dozen other women leapt to their feet clutching their stomachs. One, near Dixon and Brett, was saying, "I'm healed, my pain is healed!"

As if from a bomb blast where that woman stood, Dixon rocked and felt an electric shiver over the left side of his body, starting at his head and vibrating down to his waist. "Whoa! What was that?" he said aloud.

"What?" Brett said.

While they were distracted from the stage for a moment, Beau motioned for his two friends seated behind him to follow, and he stepped down the six stairs onto the floor in front of the stage. Soon after, a series of loud pops sounded and several people screamed.

To Dixon, this was just too much. The excitement had reached pandemonium, and he had to get out of there while he still had his wits. He grabbed Brett's t-shirt collar awkwardly in one hand, pulling him to his feet and heading for the exit. Dixon let go of his son's collar but found a hand and tugged that past a dozen people seated between him and freedom.

Just as he reached the blue carpet, a man ran past him at a full sprint. Dixon had to repress his old football instinct to run after the man. But he lost that thought when he realized that people at the front of the auditorium were still screaming and someone said clearly, "He's been shot! Beau's been shot!"

Her First Healing Meeting

A reporter for a state-wide paper for almost five years now, Anna was used to driving long distances to follow a story. And that's what her editor thought explained her drive up the coast to Oakland that day. Anna knew that Beau would be holding a meeting at a church on the south side of the city, and she figured it was her best chance to see him in action during the next month, based on the schedule Miranda had given her.

Some small part of Anna still wanted to find Beau and apologize for the article. But, mostly, she drove to that meeting to be close to Beau at his best, in a healing meeting with thousands of people poised to launch into a life transformed by the miraculous power that had made him famous, and infamous.

An accident on the way into Oakland delayed her enough that she arrived at the meeting ten minutes into the worship music. She had to park at an overflow lot down the street, next to a burned-out building. The contrast with Malibu flashed boldly, as she stepped carefully over broken glass in her thin sandals, on the way to the church building.

She could hear the music by the time she reached the main parking lot. Anna had seen Beau's meetings on the Internet, but had always skipped through the music when that was included in the recording. To a non-church person, that boisterous and callisthenic music session before Beau took the pulpit added to the mystery of it all. What were these people singing about? And how did they know it was all true, all worth throwing so much energy into it? As that non-church person, Anna assumed that all the people in that building believed it all and knew why they believed it. The forest looks dense from the outside, before you enter it and see the gaps between the trees.

Joining a few other stragglers, Anna had to satisfy herself with a seat in the balcony, up a winding staircase off the lobby. From there, she could see the churning and bouncing mass of worshippers on the main floor. She even had to step over a young man who lay on the carpet in the balcony, looking as if he might have fallen through the roof. Anna looked around to check how unusual the supine worshipper was. She found no one else looking around with similar questions and continued to assume that she was the only outsider there that night.

Even though she missed nearly a quarter of the music, Anna tired of the wall of noise that rose during each song, and sometimes flowed on between songs, with shouts and spontaneous singing. She felt more exhausted from enduring the heavy blanket of sound than the worshippers appeared to be from creating that sound. She was relieved to finally see the pastor step up to the podium and the choir leave the stage. She sunk to her seat in the fourth row of the balcony.

She could see Beau sitting with two people she didn't recognize at first. Then she realized that the young woman was Maggie. Anna was struck by how old Maggie looked from that distance. Suddenly, she flashed back to the condemning video she had seen at the town meeting in Parkerville. She was almost certain now that one of those photos that they claimed showed him with several of his wives, or sex partners, actually included Maggie, or maybe his older daughter Joanne, not a string of babes from his harem.

Anna mixed these ideas around in her head, instead of listening to the pastor's lengthy introduction, disguised as a short sermon, or the other way around. That other person, the young man, must be his interpreter. Anna shook her head and silently laughed at herself for having any room for this whole notion of someone translating Beau speaking in tongues while he healed people. Beau Dupere had proved to be as strange as she had expected, but in totally unexpected ways.

Now Beau was heading for the pulpit, a small tablet computer in his hand, so it appeared from where Anna sat. A large screen above the stage showed a close-up shot of the podium, so that she could tell clearly what Beau's collar and tie looked like, and how well trimmed and combed his hair was. On the big screen like that, sharp dark eyes, strong forehead and chin, a caramel apple tan and perfect white teeth, Beau looked like a winning politician, or maybe a TV anchorman. The lighting only made him look more handsome. Yet all he had to say was that he didn't have much to say.

When he talked about bringing power instead of words of wisdom, Anna wondered how that fit with the Beau Dupere that she had spent time interviewing and probing for his real story. Certainly, he had no trouble speaking to her. He wasn't shy. So what was he saying about not having profound things to say?

Then he did say something very striking, he called out a woman by name and described a medical condition in great detail. The fact that a woman reacted to this revelation very dramatically clearly led the gathered faithful to believe that Beau had learned this by supernatural means, like a psychic doing a stage show. Unlike any psychic Anna had seen, however, after demonstrating how much he knew about this woman, he claimed he healed her, and he did so from a distance of perhaps a hundred feet. Again, the gathered believers showed no sign of doubting all this.

Anna's thoughts turned back at this point, trying to assess how much of this she actually believed. She thought of each of the times people at the Dupere house had touched her and seemed to communicate peace or healing. That was power, she supposed. Was it real or just imagined? She hadn't expected any of it, so how could she have imagined what she didn't expect?

When three loud pops froze the animated crowd, Anna jumped in her seat and refocused on the front of the auditorium.

Beau was no longer on the stage, only the senior pastor, laying on the carpet shaking rather violently. No, Beau had done his usual move down onto the auditorium floor. She could see a man sprinting up the aisle, interrupted once by a man and his son who were attempting to use that same aisle for escaping what had begun to look like a mob in a panic. Then she understood what the pops had been, and what had stunned the crowd. Beau's interpreter stood up and gestured to someone. His yellow shirt was covered in blood. It didn't appear to be his blood. He bent back down over someone on the floor. Where was Beau? What had happened?

Seeking Another Touch

Just like Brett and Dixon, Sara Claiborne noted the meeting in Oakland as relatively close to Parkerville, close enough for her to attend her second Beau Dupere meeting—this time on her own. As if as another sign of her mantle of adulthood, she sloughed off the teenage girl's assumption that she should persuade some friends to join her in any endeavor, especially a road trip. This time, Sara felt that she wanted this experience for herself, neither interrupted nor hindered by any of her friends.

This road trip was possible because of the 1997 Toyota Corolla that Sara had received for her seventeenth birthday. Part birthday gift and part practical concession from her parents to having a third driver in the family, the slightly dented green sedan got her to school and back during her senior year. She hadn't, however, taken it on the Interstate very often. Nervous about driving on the six and eight lane freeways, Sara left plenty early to arrive in Oakland a half hour before the meeting.

Even after stopping to get something to eat, she arrived to join the crowd around the doors before they opened. Sara debated waiting in the car, thinking that waiting in the auditorium for the service to begin would be much too awkward by herself. But then she thought of how much she would like to be as close as possible to where Beau would be healing people. She knew that would be at the front of the auditorium, at least initially. She even pictured following him when he wandered away from the stage, wanting to understand what he did, what he *could* do. In part, she wondered about what had happened to her the last time she saw him. She harbored hopes of getting more of whatever that was.

Glad she opted for running shoes instead of sandals this time, Sara pushed through the doors with the hundreds of others hoping to get premium seats. It wasn't the sort of mob scene she had endured at the OneRepublic concert. This was more playful, and even polite, at least as polite as one can be while hurrying through double doors, across the lobby and down the sloped aisles. She landed in the end seat of the fourth row, in the middle section, next to a pair of laughing girls who regularly attended that church.

"Has Beau been here before?" Sara asked them when they had settled in.

The girl next to her, named Maleka, said, "You know, I don't think so. I know he was at the Assemblies church here in town. But I'm thinkin' he ain't been here at our church." She looked at her friend, Jessica, for confirmation, receiving an agreeable nod.

"You seen him before?" Jessica said to Sara. She chewed gum noisily before and after speaking.

Sara nodded, her gaze at her new friends wandering toward the ceiling as she thought of her first encounter with Beau Dupere. "My friends and I went to see him in Sacramento a few weeks ago." She laughed. "I never got knocked to the floor like that before."

Maleka and Jessica smiled and exchanged knowing looks. "You don't do that kinda thing at your church?" Maleka said.

Sara laughed again, her discomfort clear in her halting half-hearted tone. "The funny thing is, my dad is the pastor of the church I grew up in. And he doesn't believe any of this kinda thing."

Jessica looked a bit alarmed. "Does he know you're here?"

"No," Sara said, getting more serious. "I haven't seen him lately. I moved in with one of my friends for the summer, after my dad found out I went to that first Beau Dupere meeting."

"Ooooo, girl. We should pray for you now," Maleka said. "That you get all filled up and never have any bad stuff come at you from your father and his church."

Though she wasn't sure what "bad stuff" Maleka had in mind, Sara felt an unusual trust in these two strangers, strangers to her, but not to the ways of laying on hands and all that went with it. Pushing through the awkward closeness of her two new acquaintances, Sara did feel something when they put their hands on her, long red finger nails and all. But it wasn't anything like when Kim unintentionally knocked her down, or when Beau Dupere dropped his bomb on her. Instead of collapsing joints and a startled fluttering heart, she received what felt like a long drink of wine, burning slightly as it went down and lifting her mood toward rapture.

The most lasting effect of that impromptu prayer time was that the wait and the music part of the service flew by in a blur, a peaceful blur, that is. Sara felt as if every worry she had stocked up through the years had been surgically removed before the service. When it began, she floated with the music, and *that* ended far too soon for her.

For a moment, Sara worried that something was wrong with her, like she had low blood sugar, or something. When Beau Dupere stepped up to the podium and dumped the senior pastor to the carpet, this struck Sara as irrepressibly funny. She sat with both hands over her mouth, trying to muffle the laughter. She had no hope at all of actually stopping it.

This is when Maleka said, "That girl is drunk in the Spirit. Look at her laugh." Both Jessica and Maleka caught a mild version of what Sara had.

Sara stopped worrying about a medical condition and tried to relax into the dopey feeling that sat on her like a fat cat. She was too disconnected from the outside world by then to even want to shoo that big thing off her lap.

When Beau called out a woman in the crowd and healed her of surgical complications, Sara felt it, as if her best friend had finally escaped her suffering. This started her weeping uncontrollably, which seemed to set Maleka and Jessica into a more raucous humor. The whole experience made Sara feel emotionally dizzy.

At the point where Beau moved down to the auditorium floor and started to touch people in the front row, saying something to the young man accompanying him, Sara stood up. She found that maneuver surprisingly difficult, clinging to the back of the seats in front of her to keep from pitching over in any of four possible directions. Then a man in the front row said something harsh to Beau and seemed to reach out to him. Three loud bangs deafened Sara, even as her insides took a leap and a dive, before she collapsed to the floor in a dead faint.

The Big Bang

Maggie reached Beau's side just seconds after the stranger sprinted past her and up the aisle. Her thoughts slid away like a great sheet of ice hurtling off a glacier toward the ocean. She tried to slow her mind, to focus, to hear what she was supposed to do.

Her dad lay on the medium blue carpet, a dark pool growing around him, and three large crimson spots on his white shirt, his tie up next to one ear, his suit coat open so that she could see the custom label with his name on it. She knew he had been shot, but found herself struggling to not think about that, to not think. No, it wasn't to not think about it, it was to not panic, but think calmly, she told herself. People either edged away or lunged toward her, where she knelt on the floor. She maintained her place at her father's side even as others jumped in next to her, shouted instructions, cursed, cried, screamed and shoved others out of the way.

For a moment, Maggie recognized an unction of clarity. She pulled her cell phone out of her pocket and unlocked it. Her hands stopped shaking just long enough for her to locate her mother's number and to tap on it. She held the phone to her ear, noticing that her free hand was covered in blood. She just looked at it passively as she listened for her mother's answer. Somehow she knew Justine would answer.

And she did.

"Maggie, what's wrong?" Justine said, out of the little electronic speaker.

"It's Dad. He's shot. I think he's dead."

Three seconds of silence, and then Justine said, "You have to do it, Maggie. He knew this would happen, and he made us promise to bring him back. You know. Just tell him to come back, and he will."

Maggie Dupere had grown up in the home of parents who had travelled from believing that God *could* heal anything, to living as if God would definitely heal everything. Unlike so many others who attempted healing, Beau and Justine would get intensely angry when healing didn't happen. They believed in it that much. Where others would just shrug with regret and say, "I'm so sorry it didn't happen this time," her parents would launch a search for the culprit who dared block God's healing. They never blamed the person who didn't get healed, even if an argument could be made in that direction. But they never passively received failure like it was just the morning paper.

Beau Dupere had raised six people from the dead, verifiable resurrections in places where people knew the difference between being dead and being alive. People whose hearts had stopped beating, due to disease or trauma, came back to life. Six was the number of verifiable cases. There were a few others. One man, in Hong Kong had fallen to the floor while waiting for healing of his heart condition. No one was there to check his pulse and declare him dead. But, before Beau touched him and commanded him to come back, the old Chinese man claimed that he had seen Jesus standing in front of a bright light, telling him to wait a moment for his resurrection. That man counted himself as restore to life by Beau Dupere. But he wasn't one of the six.

"Maggie?" Justine said, unsure of the silence.

"Yes, Mom?"

"Get people to calm down, stand back and pray."

"Okay, Mom."

"Maggie?"

"Yes, Mom?"

"I love you, girl. You can do this."

"I know, Mom. Love you too." And she ended the call, slipping the phone again into the back pocket of her white pants, leaving a smeared red hand print on one hip.

Maggie stood up and spoke forcefully. "Everyone calm down. Please step back and give us some space. Start praying. I am going to bring him back to life."

People who have lost the connections between the various components of their minds, their will and their self-control, can be easily commanded into compliance. For some, perhaps it's a lack of clear direction in an unfamiliar situation. For others, it's an instinctual awareness that the situation requires utter cooperation, clarity of thought and action. Orders from someone who seems obviously to be in charge readily ignite action from people like that.

One of the assistant pastors of the church, a man about thirty years old with a short cut afro and a mustache, looked up at Maggie from his place on hands and knees next to Beau. He knew she was in charge, this sixteen-year-old white girl with whom he had never actually spoken. He knew she had command of the situation, and he knew he would cooperate with her instructions, even if those instructions included words connect in ways he had never heard before – "I'm going to bring him back to life."

Time to Get Up

The early Christian church has been said to have grown because it was watered by the blood of the martyrs. This means a couple of things. First, many of the early Christians died in ways that made it clear to those watching that these people did not fear death. That appealed to lots of people who *did* fear death. Second, many of the people who watched the Christians die knew that the ones doing the killing were the ones who had lost, driven to unmitigated evil by a lack of confidence in their own faith, their own reasons for living. The Christians were willing to die, knowing that their death would lead to ultimate victory, while their murderers would have to go on killing more and more people who didn't deserve to die.

The notion of surrendering your life for a religious cause has received the most press lately regarding believers in Islam. Those self-selected martyrs who make the headlines, surrender their lives with a bomb strapped to their torso, often under a layer of small metal objects that will launch out from their death to collect others to join them in what they see as their righteous departure.

If You Really Knew Me

The opponents of Beau Dupere couldn't find a willing suicide bomber. But they did find a veteran of the Afghan war, whose grip on his life after the military had become tenuous and painful for him. To use a bomb to kill one evil man was unnecessary, and would associate their cause with Islam, which, of course, they considered evil, in all its forms. To shoot a man in public, on the other hand, would put the man who pulled the trigger at risk. He might be seized immediately by the crowd of rabid followers who would see their messiah sacrificed before them. He might simply be caught by the police, just doing their job, not choosing between the available ways to be Christian in the world.

Most people would see assassinating Beau Dupere as a crime. When the network television anchors interrupted prime-time programming for a brief special bulletin, that healer and billionaire Beau Dupere had been shot and killed, most people were shocked. Very few were actually happy. Several news channels adjusted their coverage of the day's events to allow wide swaths of time to review the life of Beau Dupere, examining the controversy around his ministry, as well as the few facts they knew about his murder. Very few people thought of his death the way they thought of Jim Jones's death, along with hundreds of his followers in that South American compound, for example.

This was murder. Beau Dupere was the victim, not a criminal brought to justice. And the small coterie of his opponents that believed God would forgive them for murdering a man who clearly bears in him the Satanic power of the Antichrist, had to celebrate in secret...during the hour between his death and the announcement of his resurrection.

Network news producers had never reported on a resurrection before. They had, however, retracted stories due to further information received from reliable sources. So that's what they did.

When word had spread through the auditorium that Beau Dupere had been shot, many of the people present ran for the

If You Really Knew Me

doors, panicked, shocked. Many more, however, knelt where they were and prayed.

Anna Conyers fell into the back of the seat in front of her and then bounced into the lap of the man sitting next to her, before landing on the carpet below. Every fiber in her body screamed that she had killed Beau Dupere. She saw his face, she saw Justine, and the children. He was so naïve to trust her. She destroyed him with her exposé, a story that had been a tribute in her heart, but which was published to become more kindling for the fire of hate against Beau. She loved Beau, she knew that now. She had never met anyone like him. And she loved Justine, and Maggie, and Luke and all of them. She loved them. And she killed him, their husband and father, wounding all of them at the same time. These shocking realizations overwhelmed Anna such that she lost consciousness.

Dixon and Brett followed the man sprinting up the aisle, as if his momentum carried them. Not until they had nearly reached the doors to the lobby did they hear the first person say clearly. "Beau's been shot. They killed him."

"They?" Dixon thought.

"Dad? Did they kill him?" Brett said.

"Who?" said Dixon, to no one in particular. Then he thought of the man that had run past them. Wasn't he wearing gloves? Odd in the California summer. Was he carrying a gun?

Dixon stopped to look up at the TV monitors in the lobby. The camera had settled on a wide view of the stage and the area in front of it. The senior pastor had gotten up off the floor and now stood facing the camera, holding hands with the people on either side of him. They had begun to form a circle around the place on the floor where a young woman knelt. He could just see the crown of her head. Her golden hair reminded him of his daughter.

Sara managed to haul herself back to her feet two or three minutes after hitting the floor. She didn't appear to be injured. She stood shakily staring at the chaos in front of her, and then the sudden order imposed on that chaos, by a girl her age or younger. Sara could see between the remaining people in the rows in front of her, the ones who hadn't run for the exit or fainted to the floor. She thought that the girl must be Beau's daughter, the way she had held him and the way she now took charge of the situation. Sara felt her heart connected with Maggie's even though she didn't know that name, even though she didn't know really what that girl was doing. Though she didn't firmly settle on which it was, Sara assumed that Maggie was mourning the death of her beloved father. But, she also considered the possibility that, in spite of all the blood, the multiple shots at close range, that Beau was alive and his daughter was trying to heal him.

The people next to her on either side reached out and joined hands with Sara. And she knew that their hearts too had joined with the courageous young woman on her knees next to the fallen form of her father. Sara prayed, first silently, then whispering, then speaking out loud, and then beginning to cry and plead louder through her tears and the constriction of her throat, her mouth impinged by the severe emotions gripping her. A hundred people prayed aloud, some in English, some in unknown languages. The sound began to rush and roar like a mighty wind. And in the middle of that storm, one girl remained calm, in the eye of the storm, and in the eye of God.

Then Beau Dupere did the most surprising thing of his entire surprising life. He sat up. He propped himself on both hands stretched out behind him, like he had just been resting there and was now fully recovered. Dozens of people screamed on all sides, the senior pastor of the church shouted an alarming "Hallelujah," before collapsing backward, as if *he* had been shot. Several others fainted or fell to the carpet under the power of that miraculous restoration.

Maggie collapsed onto her father, wrapping her arms around him and knocking him back to the floor. Even in the pandemonium stirred by his rising, Sara could hear the hearty laugh of

Beau Dupere, the controversial healer, the billionaire, the friend to sinners...and now, the man raised from the dead.

In Search of an Explanation

Dixon and Brett heard the radio report of Beau Dupere's death as soon as they pulled onto the freeway toward Parkerville. They both remained silent. Even Brett was sober and contemplative. They exchanged a few trivial words about traffic and a place to eat, but they both needed time to process what they had just experienced.

It was an athletic stretch for Dixon to venture into that meeting under the guise of gathering firsthand information and even an experience of Beau Dupere. Way beyond that, however, he had just been present in a building, in a meeting, where a man was murdered. That was an ungainly load for which to find a resting place in his mind and in his soul.

Then there were those fringe elements in his mind, vying for a hearing in the center of his thoughts. On one side, a voice nudged at his conscience. Hadn't he encouraged people to hate Beau Dupere? Didn't he sow seeds that, in the right soil, would grow up into lethal plants?

On the opposite side, a small voice made satisfied sounds, relieved noises, and even slightly triumphant intimations. *This* would bring his daughter back to him. *This* would free his congregation from the temptation to follow that charlatan. This was good news.

But Dixon didn't allow either of those minority voices to take up the pulpit on the stage of his heart. They would stay in the shadows, in the overflow room, spreading doubts, distributing accusations, but only covertly.

Though he hadn't voiced his doubts the way Sara had, Brett wondered whether Beau Dupere was really so bad, so dangerous, as his father believed. Sure, he had been instrumental in Sara leaving home, but that wasn't really anything Beau had done intentionally. That just fit with the things that teenagers did to their parents. Brett was still reserving his vote on the subject—whether someone like Beau Dupere could heal people, and whether that healing expressed the will of God when it happened.

Brett felt the weight of the experience of being in the meeting where Beau Dupere was killed. Of all the meetings the famous healer had held, in all the cities he had visited, on all the nights that he did his thing, Brett had been there on that last night.

Back at the church, Anna rose from her place of purgation, down between the seats, when she heard that mighty wind rushing through the auditorium and swirling up to the front, where Beau had fallen. She leveraged herself to a standing position, with both hands and shaky legs, just as Beau sat up. Anna was one of those people that screamed. She narrowly avoided fainting again. Darkness had seeped into view all around her field of vision, like one of those old sepia movies with a fuzzy black frame around it; but the darkness had retreated in time to leave her standing, hearing the echo of her own scream. Then she laughed. She laughed for the same reason she screamed. Hysteria bubbled her brain, and relief relaxed her lungs and loosed her limbs. She laughed away the grief, and inhaled new hope more deeply than she had ever inhaled anything.

Then the news reporter in her awakened. What a story! What would she say? How could she tell this so that people wouldn't just dismiss it as religious nonsense? She grabbed her bag and climbed over bodies, scooting between people coming and going in the aisles and on the stairs. She was going to get to the heart of this story. And who cares what they will say about it, when she has researched and written all the facts? She shuffled down the aisle as fast as her feet, and the staggering people rising or falling around her, would allow.

With the whole death and resurrection scenario came a feeling like a flight in a small airplane that has lost its engine and begins diving toward certain death, only to be pulled up just before the ground can smack it, when the engine suddenly, and inexplicably, revives.

When Beau sat up, Sara jumped up and down. That's what cheerleaders do. Maleka and Jessica jumped with her, and they hugged each other and they cried on each other, and they made inarticulate sounds that made each other laugh. "Now, that's a healing service!" Maleka said, bursting into gales of unfiltered laughter.

Dixon Claiborne finished his ride back from the meeting around ten p.m. He and Brett had switched the radio a couple of times, away from the news, before finally turning it off. They both favored silence over more of the droning voices of people who were not there and did not see it themselves, did not see anything themselves.

Kristen was sitting up in the living room, the only other person in the world who knew of their secret mission, which is not to imply that she approved of that mission, beyond the slim hope it dangled regarding reuniting their family one way or another. Now, Kristen waited with the TV off, after seeing all the coverage of whatever it was that actually happened at the Beau Dupere meeting. After major news agencies retracted the death of Beau Dupere, deciding instead that he was simply severely, and then slightly wounded, video taken at the meeting hit one of the more sensationalistic cable news programs. The "slightly" wounded Beau Dupere took three large caliber shots to the chest, his body concussing with each bullet's "slightly" wounding him. And what of the blood-soaked shirt when he stood up finally at the end? What of that huge pool darkening the carpet? He was no longer as severely wounded as one would expect a man shot at point blank range. He seemed perfectly fit, though his shirt was clearly ruined.

If You Really Knew Me

A quartet of pundits on that channel commented on the story, bantering and debating until they concluded, in unity, that Beau Dupere had perpetrated a hoax, staging his own death and resurrection in order to convince his cultic followers that he was The Messiah come back to earth. When Kristen shut off the TV, no one yet had the footage of this latter declaration.

"Did you hear the news?" Kristen said, standing up to confront, more than greet, her two men.

"About Beau Dupere getting shot? We were there, we didn't have to hear the news," Brett said, youthful drama elevating his voice past the line where enthusiasm retains respect.

Dixon nodded knowingly, the veteran of a murder, the traumatized witness.

"You didn't hear that he's alive and well, then?" Kristen said, delivering her punchline with a stolid monotone.

"Alive and well?" Dixon said, trying to figure out where the humor was in such a joke.

"Resurrected, his followers are saying." Kristen raised her eyebrows and nodded sharply, her head providing the one last tap required to drive in that nail.

"Wait," Brett said, "you're saying he's not dead? You saw him not dead?"

"Alive." Kristen provided the adjective her son couldn't speak.

"No," Dixon said, his voice haunted with creeping disbelief.

Kristen nodded, this time repeatedly, as if to say it over and over –"It is true, it is true, he is alive, he is alive."

Though he had been driving for the past two hours, Dixon dropped into his big easy chair, in deference to his knees deciding that standing wasn't to be taken for granted.

"Some of the media, of course, are saying it's all a hoax, that he faked it to get attention, or to make himself look like Jesus."

"The media?" Dixon said. Hadn't he hoped to get the media turned against Beau Dupere? And now, he felt a protest rising in defense of Beau Dupere. Of course, the secular media wouldn't believe someone was raised from the dead. If they believed that was possible, they would have to believe in Jesus.

That rally proved short-lived, however. Dixon started then to absorb the opportunity the media was providing. Able now to look past the assassination, he remembered how uncomfortable the meeting had made him, like a teetotaler at a wine tasting. That discomfort turned now to anger. Of course, it had all been fake. Of course, this was a ploy to elevate the cult leader even higher. Dixon could see that. He could see the advantage of accepting that explanation.

"He won't get away with it," Dixon said, finally, rising from his chair, his bigger mission restored, and with new momentum. He looked at his wife and then his son and declared again. "This will be the end of him."

Seeing What You Want to See

Anna arrived at her office the next morning, notes in hand and speech prepared. Her editor would have to prove his commitment to true journalism, to man up and stand against the rising tide of disbelief.

"Disbelief? What do I know about believing?" she said to herself, providing her own editing, as usual.

Anna dropped her bag at her desk and pulled out her phone, pinning it against her steno pad on which she had scrawled shaky notes, in the adrenalin soaked air of the meeting the night before. Beau had laughed at her and her note pad when she arrived at the front of the auditorium. He was shaking hands with everyone, no one interested in hugging his blood-soaked shirt and jacket.

If You Really Knew Me

"You're here and on the story," Beau said, when Anna eased to a stop next to the surging, ebbing and flowing mass of arms and smiles around him.

She smiled back at him with closed lips and nocturnal animal eyes, not sure she believed she *was* actually there. "This is a pretty good story," she said, her voice diluted in the laughter and tears around them.

Anna began to ask people who had seen Beau shot, who had checked him when he was on the ground, what they had seen, what they believed happened. She collected seven accounts of the blood spattering from the bullet wounds, including one bullet that went straight through and embedded in the edge of the stage, twenty yards away. During her interviews, the police arrived, and then the FBI, who had been following a group opposed to Beau that they thought might resort to violence.

Special Agent Martin Parks focused on finding the shooter, leaning hard away from the question of how the victim could be standing, smiling and laughing, among the other witnesses. Anna marveled at the serious federal agent's tunnel focus on the only clear part of his job that remained.

Oakland Police took some statements but yielded to the half dozen FBI agents and investigators, who collected the bullet from the stage and took the necessary photos. One technician stood looking at Beau for a while, perhaps wondering what had happened to the other two bullets. Anna couldn't help laughing at that unprecedented investigative problem. The bespectacled crime scene tech just turned away, finally, swearing or praying in Spanish. Anna couldn't tell for sure which. The local cops interviewed several people, but avoided Beau, as if he might not actually be there. They certainly dared not be caught talking to a ghost.

Equally amusing to Anna were the emergency medical technicians who insisted on examining Beau. He wouldn't stop patting backs and shaking hands, tears in his eyes and in the eyes beaming at him from all sides. But he did let one stout thirty-

If You Really Knew Me

something EMT take his blood pressure inside his jacket. Beau didn't want to show off his blood stains, so insisted on keeping his expensive blazer in place. He also kept his shirt buttoned, still feeling like he was in public, and definitely not feeling a need for medical attention.

The paramedic just shook his head and said, "I don't know what to put on my report. There's usually more to show for it when there's such a big blood stain. He looked at the carpet in the taped off space in front of the stage and shrugged.

Like a party of partially drunk friends and neighbors, the group at the front of the auditorium milled and mixed, leaving only the bloody stain on the floor for the crime scene investigators.

At the end of the first row, Maggie sat by herself. Anna spotted her from the middle of the remnant of people who couldn't pull themselves away from the scene of the miracle.

Maggie looked less than miraculous. She seemed to be still recovering from her shock, her hair pushed back behind her ears, small looping locks stuck to her forehead where she had been sweating not too long before. Her pale yellow blouse bore the print of her father's blood from when she hugged his resurrected body.

Anna sat down next to her.

For a moment, both of them were silent. Then Anna said, "You know I want to tell the whole world what you did here tonight."

Turning briskly toward her, Maggie acted a bit like she had just woken from a vigorous dream. "You're gonna write about Dad being killed and then coming back to life?"

"Everyone else is saying you *brought* him back to life."

Maggie sighed. "He said he wanted to be brought back when someone finally got a clear shot at him. And it happened, just like he knew it would." The thin wires that had been propping up her appearance of unflappable composure snapped at that last phrase, and Maggie aimed her head at Anna's shoulder when the tears burst out of her. She sobbed into Anna's peach colored linen jacket, leaving a dark stain next to the lapel. Anna wrapped her left arm around Maggie's shoulders and held onto her notebook with the other, trying to keep it out of the weeping girl's hair.

Beau saw his daughter's breakdown and wriggled free of his well-wishers to kneel in front of Maggie. She switched her head from Anna's to Beau's shoulder.

"You won't ever have to do that again," he said, his muscular arms wrapped around her. "Let's get outta here, huh kiddo?"

Maggie nodded and sniffled harshly, causing a laugh of embarrassment and relief, as she stood up. Anna laughed with her. But she was thinking of one question for Maggie.

"Who did you call on the phone? People said you called someone."

"Mom," Maggie said, her tight smile quivering at the thought.

"I called Justine as soon as I got to my feet," Beau said. "I knew Maggie had called her and I wanted her to know I was alright."

Anna wanted to ask one last thing of Beau, as well. "While you were on the floor, and...you...were..." She didn't want to say "dead." But she still had her question. "What did you see?"

Beau put an arm around Maggie's shoulder as they started up the aisle. "Anna, that's one thing I'm not gonna tell ya. In fact, I don't think I can tell anyone for a while." He smiled as he said this, but a rock-hard resolve lay behind that cheerful veneer.

Now Anna wanted to know what he saw more than she wanted anything. Her inquisitive nature crossed paths with her hunger for contact with the mystery that sustained and animated Beau and his family. She even started to think that the driving desire she felt to know everything about Beau and Justine, might be leading her to know the one that they knew, the one that could raise the dead.

Lagging behind, after Beau and Maggie left, Anna noticed a young woman getting off the floor, makeup streaked from tears, her pony tail yielding a couple of odd lumps on the back and side. Anna felt like she had seen this girl before, but couldn't remember where.

Sara Claiborne smiled at the young reporter who stared at her just a bit too long to ignore, but she wasn't focused on who was staring at her, or why she might have attracted attention. Actually, she wasn't focused on anything. When Anna wandered toward her, Sara decided to talk to her just because her mind felt inverted and she couldn't think of anything else to do.

"You were talking to Beau. You know him?" Sara said to Anna.

Anna nodded, bypassing the sorts of answers she gave the reporters after Dianna's incident. "Yes, I've been reporting on him for the last few weeks, since a meeting up in Parkerville, where some pastors denounced him."

Sara's mind coalesced a bit at the mention of that meeting. Without wondering what it would mean to admit it, she said, "I was there. My dad was the one who called that meeting."

Hesitating for a second, checking her internal recording to see if Sara had said what she thought, Anna lowered her head, cocked it a bit to the side and said, "You...you're Dixon Claiborne's daughter?"

Sara was surprised that this reporter knew her father. "Yes. You know him too?"

"No," Anna said. "I just covered that meeting, and then followed Beau around for a while. One thing I asked him, and some of his friends and family, was how that meeting affected them. That kept your father's name in my head 'til now."

"Oh, yeah. That makes sense."

"Wait," Anna said, turning to the obvious question. "If you're Pastor Claiborne's daughter, what are you doing here?"

For the first time in the conversation, Sara wondered whether she should be careful what she said to the press. She didn't agree with her father about Beau Dupere, but she didn't want to embarrass him publicly. "Are you gonna write about it if I tell you?" Sara said.

"Not if you don't want me to," Anna said, still not the controversy-hound that some of her colleagues would be in such a situation. She felt some sympathy for this young woman. "I'm Anna Conyers, by the way."

Sara shook hands and tried to remember where she had heard that name before. Then it occurred to her. "You wrote that long story on Beau in that paper."

Nodding and tamping down a spark of pride at being recognized, Ann said, "Yeah, that's right."

"I really liked it," Sara said. "Oh, I'm Sara."

"Hi, Sara. I'm glad you liked it. I worried that it exposed too much of the Duperes' personal lives."

Sara pursed her lips a moment. "Yeah, I could see that. I don't think it helped any of the folks that didn't trust him already. But I loved learning more about him and his family. It made me feel more comfortable with some of what I was feeling from being in his meeting once."

"This was your second time in one of his meetings?" Anna said.

Sara snickered. "Yeah, I guess they're not all this dramatic, huh?"

Anna laughed. "I sure hope not." Then she took a chance. "I'm hungry. You wanna grab a bite to eat and compare notes. It sounds like you and I have been studying Beau for about the same amount of time. And I'd like to hear your story."

Sara shrugged slightly, liking Anna in person even more than her writing. "That sounds good. Now that you mention it, I *am* really hungry."

Sara collected her purse and followed Anna up the aisle. Anna had dropped her phone and notebook back in her bag, not planning on any more pictures or questions for her article.

She set aside her anxiety about whether she could convince her bottom-line beholding editor and publisher to show the world what really happened there that night. Their only motivation would be selling papers. Certainly, a good resurrection story would sell a few papers, she hoped.

Glad to Be Back

Beau and Maggie left early the next morning to catch a flight south toward home. They knew the family would want to see them as soon as possible, and they both felt like zoo animals in a glass display case. Beau wanted to escape more questioning by the FBI, feeling more like a suspect than the victim, after a meeting that morning. The vicious intensity of the arguments between federal agents, all clearly out of their depth, squeezed Beau out the door. The distractions of finger-pointing and damage control dropped Beau off their radar long enough for him to escape. Home would be the best place to think about what had happened, to recover from the shock of confronting death in such a startling way.

In the airport, Beau stopped briefly to read the subtitle to an article in the San Francisco newspaper. "Feds Say Dupere was Shot and Recovered." Of course, he hadn't dipped into the jet stream of speculations about what had happened, but Beau found that headline a very odd way to describe someone killed and resurrected. He failed to comprehend the political correctness that the FBI had risked, unaware of the prevailing opinion that he had faked the murder and the miracle.

Knowing Maggie's continued sensitivity on the topic, Beau didn't comment aloud, but thought of Anna and wanted to hear from her about what people were saying. To him, that approach held more promise than watching the news for himself.

Travelling anonymously had become impossible. While he had been a celebrity in certain circles before, Beau had generally travelled without attracting a crowd. If not for the perfect tan, perfect hair and perfect teeth, which added up to movie star in most people's minds, he might have never heard those common words, "You're him, aren't you?"

After the assassination, no one even bothered to ask; they just nudged the person next to them and pointed, unless they wanted an autograph. Beau had never signed autographs before, rarely ever asked for one. But, in the waiting area by the gate and even on the plane, a constant line of three or four people stood waiting for Beau to sign a copy of the newspaper, or any stray scrap. He refused to sign any body parts. Maggie shook her head at one such request, but said nothing.

Beau called to ask Miranda to send a limo with added security, to help them push through the crowd at LAX, expecting the spotlight to be even brighter on that end of the flight. Once they took off, Beau sat back in his first-class seat and reached over to hold Maggie's hand. He knew she needed some comfort and assurance from the father she had lost the night before. During the flight, his big hand on hers, he sent healing to that trauma. Maggie closed her eyes, alternately shedding silent tears and beaming a tight-lipped smile. Because of her lifetime of experience with healing, she was able to receive the restoration of her soul that coursed from her father's hand like a blood transfusion. Beau found a more cheerful and relaxed daughter at his side when they landed.

Going beyond his request, Miranda had sent a driver and two security guards to help Beau and Maggie get through the airport, but had also alerted LAX security. Miranda was not the only one to whom it had occurred that someone might just try to test Beau's rate of return, copying the assault of the night before. Just like the cops in Oakland, the airport security took the threat seriously, without addressing the oddity of having to provide protection to a guy because he had recently been killed and resurrected.

If You Really Knew Me

After her father's attention on the plane, Maggie laughed at the crush of reporters who had learned of Beau's arrival by some mysterious means. She felt like a Hollywood star, following security to her waiting limo with flashes and shouts all around her. The reporters called her name, as well as her father's, in their efforts to get a good photo. Just before the limo door closed, she heard someone shout, "Maggie, how does it feel to raise your father from the dead?"

Not since the last presidential election had the nation been so clearly and starkly divided as they were over the story of Beau Dupere's death and resurrection. Experts and pundits declared, without any shred of doubt, the impossibility of the story on one channel, and documented the extensive evidence that it had indeed occurred on another. Fortunately, for Beau and his family, they were already in the habit of ignoring the mass media and their manufactured crises and causes. On the other hand, they couldn't escape the crowd of protesters outside their own home.

Back in Malibu, through the limo window, Beau saw the multiplied mob, lining the street for several blocks now. Some held signs that read, "FAKE," among other new messages. He decided it was time to move the family to a new location.

For her part, Maggie ignored the furor outside the tinted windows, focusing on texting her brother in Argentina, instead.

Justine stood by the front door, her arms crossed over her chest, a broad smile on her face. It was one of those June days cooled by a breeze off the ocean, sunny and bright, and invigorating. Justine's face matched the weather. She hugged both her husband and daughter with the intensity of a catcher on a flying trapeze, but shed no tears, and eventually let go, so that others could get in on the action. Olivia, Peter, Luke and Emma waited their turn behind Justine.

Beau kissed and held Olivia for a half a minute. She didn't restrain her relieved tears, leaking the same sort of emotional trauma that Beau had sensed in Maggie. He knew then that it would be foolish for him to approach his death with such carefree boldness the next time. He could see the scars on his family, like the paths of erosion in loose soil after a heavy rain.

Riding into the house in the arms of his little clan, Beau was changed that day, and a brief exchange of eye contact with Justine told him that she knew it too.

Parting Ways

Even though Jonathan Opare had stayed at Dixon Claiborne's church through the early days of opposition to Beau Dupere, he couldn't get comfortable with so much open antagonism among Christians. But it was Treena, his apple-cheeked wife whose smile was famous in the church, who first declared her need to escape the tension between her faith and the culture that had grown up at their American home church. Not until the church's aggressive rebuttal of the resurrection story, however, did Jonathan finally agree to look elsewhere for an American church family.

Unlike many U.S. Christians, the Opares would not be content to simply slip into an empty pew and then slip out, reviewing the service like a movie or play on the way home. After researching their options, they scheduled joint or single interviews with senior church staff and asked preemptively what they thought of Beau Dupere and his resurrection story.

Winifred Whiting pastored a predominantly African American church on the north side of Parkerville. Though the congregation belonged to a denomination with ties to churches he knew in Ghana, Jonathan had learned that traditions faded in American churches faster than affiliations changed, so he assumed nothing when he entered Pastor Whiting's office late in June.

Winnie, as she liked to be called, had hair the color of steel wool and a round, almost girlish, face, which was a lighter, more golden brown, than Jonathan's. Her eyes, however, were the same deep brown as his, and her smile reminded him of his wife. She wore a traditional shirt from Zimbabwe, that Jonathan recognized.

"Are your ancestors from southern Africa?" he said, after they shook hands and each took a seat next to Winnie's desk, where four cherry wood and black leather chairs sat facing each other.

"No, I don't think so," Winnie said. "I don't know my detailed family tree, really. I acquired the shirt on a ministry trip with some folks from the church and an organization we support, one that works with local churches in areas suffering rampant poverty."

They talked for a while about that ministry, as a sort of social warm-up exercise. Jonathan knew that Treena had informed Winnie of their search for a new church when she set up this appointment. An economist by education and habit, he wondered how much of what this bright pastor said constituted marketing. He smiled on the outside while suppressing his critical graduate school habits inside.

After a pause in that pre-agenda conversation, Jonathan transitioned to the purpose for his visit. "As you know, my wife and I are looking for a church where we can be active and feel like part of the family," he said, initially leaning away from the particular concerns that had sent them on this search.

"So what are you looking for in a church home?" Winnie said, smiling in a way that felt to Jonathan like a practiced gesture. Again, he suppressed his instincts to analyze and critique.

"Well, we live here in town because my wife's job is here, and I am close enough to commute to school two or three days a week. So we want a local church that can be part of our connection to the people around us, here in Parkerville. We know that this limits the selection more than if we were to move to the bay area, closer to school. But we like the less urban environment here. So we're not looking for a perfect fit, just a place that shares what we value."

"What would you say is a value that your current, or should I say your former, church didn't welcome?"

Jonathan guessed that Treena had revealed some of the reasons for their transition, but he didn't think Winnie was asking a question to which she knew the whole answer, so he took her question at face value.

"We have a pretty good idea of what your church is about, we know some folks who attend here. But I want to hear you speak specifically to the current controversy over the ministry of Beau Dupere," Jonathan said.

Winnie's eyebrows shot up but the rest of her face remained placid. She did straighten her back and glance at the ceiling for just a moment, revealing a bit of discomfort with such a direct question. "Beau Dupere? Well, we don't have an official church position on his ministry. I suspect a few of our people are much more familiar with him than the majority are. We are *not* part of the group of churches vocally criticizing him, but neither are we in any way associated with him or the churches he's affiliated with."

That sounded like a good answer to a question from a newspaper reporter, as far as Jonathan was concerned, but it didn't reveal much about the heart of the pastor on an issue deeply dividing Christians that summer.

"Are you avoiding the issue in order to keep as many people as possible comfortable in your church?" Jonathan said, sounding more like a probing reporter than he had intended.

Winnie laughed uncomfortably, her smile diminishing quickly. "I supposed a skeptic might see it that way. But, I think I'm just being realistic. I don't know Beau Dupere. I've never even been in one of his meetings. I can think of two or three people in the congregation, however, who credit him with healing them of some significant ailment." She took a deep breath, having caught herself tensing over these questions and reminding herself that

If You Really Knew Me

she had nothing to defend. "Those healings, and other second-hand stories, lead me to think well of him, in general, as a healing minister. But that doesn't mean I endorse everything he does. Even if his healing is from God, not all of what he does is necessarily consistent with what God wants, I believe."

Jonathan paused, smiled at her and adjusted his tone of voice. "I'm sorry if I sound like a grand inquisitor trying to convict you of something," he said with a relaxed chuckle. "I don't know any more about the man than you do, I guess. But I do know that people aren't treating him the way they should, whether they know as much about him as they claim or are as uninformed as you and I." He shrugged and tipped his head slightly to the right. "I don't suppose you have an opinion on the truth of his resurrection story then?"

"Well," Winnie said, "actually, with so much heat being generated over the accusation that he faked resurrection, I have had to decide for myself, though I'm not speaking about it in front of the whole congregation."

Jonathan thought he knew her decision, but waited patiently to hear her finish her statement.

"I think it would be saying quite a lot about the man if he went so far as to so convincingly falsify his death," Winnie said. "I am definitely not inclined to believe he is such a monster as that. And I think Christians had better check themselves if they want to assert that resurrection is impossible." She punctuated her conclusion with a slow upward nod and slight twist of her head, aiming her right eye at Jonathan as if in challenge.

"I like the way you stay neutral about something even when others are flying off the handle on both sides, Jonathan said. "And yet you state so clearly what has obviously to be addressed. I think we will be quite comfortable here." He also suspected Treena would like this woman pastor for lots of other reasons too.

"I expect you will see Treena and I on Sunday," Jonathan said, standing and extending his hand.

Standing with him and shaking that hand, Winnie added. "Not all American Christians like to fight. It just seems like that on the news."

They laughed together and Jonathan nodded deeply, knowing exactly what she meant.

Party Splashing

When Anna finally saw the Dupere's again, it was a Friday evening in mid-July. She had received a call from Miranda, saying that Beau and Justine were going to a party and wanted her to accompany them. She had grown nervous while they stayed in exile during late June and early July, not sure that she still had their trust, or perhaps their friendship. When Miranda invited her to the party, Anna didn't assume it was time to set aside work and just accompany them as a friend. She seized the opportunity, instead, as time to follow up with Beau and his family, to finish her article on the assassination. She still assumed that her role in their lives was primarily that of reporter. That night, she would be a particularly well-dressed reporter, her favorite little black dress and spiked heels squeezed on for the party.

Having always considered herself a fairly plain girl, the idea of attending a Hollywood social event deeply intimidated Anna. As usual, Beau and Justine moderated that feeling as soon as they greeted her at their front door.

"Oh, Anna, you look beautiful." Justine said, hugging her as soon as she reached the porch. Beau stood behind Justine, smiling. "We missed you, and kept you in our prayers every day."

This intrigued Anna in so many ways that it left her speechless. She even forgot to doubt the sincerity of Justine's compliment on her looks. While Anna stood there, staring at Justine

If You Really Knew Me

with her mouth propped open half an inch, Dianna stepped out onto the porch, straightening her silky blue dress.

Justine glanced at Dianna and then back at Anna. "Dianna, this is Anna. Anna, Dianna."

Beau joked. "Wow, I hope you don't have to do that again. It nearly made me dizzy."

Dianna and Anna shook hands. Dianna spoke first. "I wanna start right off by letting you know that I don't blame you for any of the things people have been saying or doing." She smiled. "We can't control the way people respond, we just have to do what we're called to and let the results take care of themselves."

Beau stepped in again. "We all know that you've been taking heat right along with us, and without all the support we have around here."

Instead of apologizing to them, as she had longed to do for weeks now, Anna was receiving their sympathy. At this realization, she had given up on being able to untie her tongue for the rest of the evening.

Justine helped. "Okay, you two, you're embarrassing Anna. Let's just go to the party." She gestured toward the white stretch limo waiting on the driveway.

"They didn't have black?" Beau said, as the four of them clicked across the driveway in their dress shoes.

Justine shook her head and laughed. "No. Didn't you hear Miranda apologizing? She knows how you call the white ones 'televangelist cars.' She would have avoided it if she could."

They all laughed.

"Okay," Beau continued, holding the door for the women. "But if she starts making hair appointments for me at Big Hair R Us, I'll know it's a plot."

Again, they all laughed, though Anna's was the sort of laugh that follows the crowd, the sound of its uncertainty lost in the mix.

Not until they arrived at the gigantic mansion of an award-winning movie producer, did it occur to Anna that she was the third woman in Beau's usual string of female escorts. She

If You Really Knew Me

blinked over her contact lenses and assessed the other two women.

    Justine sat next to her, in a silky red dress and red heels. Her shiny tan legs and little bit of cleavage would fit right in. In contrast to Justine's golden coloring in that red dress, Dianna's skin was milky and her dark hair and eyes stood out in her happy, peaceful face. Both women were taller than Anna, even in her highest heels.

    These thoughts seemed to leak into the air around her. All three of the others got out of the car first and waited for her, the other two women each taking one of her arms, gently, but standing close enough for her to feel surrounded and safe. And they followed Beau's commanding figure into the ornate double doors of the classic Italian-style mansion. As Beau, Justine and Dianna took turns introducing her, Anna accumulated the feeling of being the guest of honor.

    When she had received the invitation, she paused to wonder whether Beau and the others realized how out-of-place she would be with their rich and famous friends. As a junior reporter on the celebrity beat for a small regional paper, she only interviewed minor stars of music or movies, and often, former stars, in fact. She thought she would be lost and smothered in the environment in which these people had learned to thrive. At least that's what her anxiety told her.

    Reality kept her reeling. She held onto her champagne glass without more than a small sip, feeling intoxicated already by her royal treatment, and by something else she couldn't identify. Whatever it was, made her feel warm and giddy. She said little, in an effort to hide this compromised state, but she was among people in search of listeners all evening, so they welcomed her girlish smile and occasional brief question of clarification.

    Whenever Anna found herself separated from the other three, within seconds one of them would swoop in and tow her to meet someone, or they would simply sidle up next to her and place a reassuring hand on her bare back. When Beau did this

If You Really Knew Me

once, the tingles that crawled up into her hair and ran down the backs of her legs nearly tipped Anna off her precarious heels and onto the custom marble floor. Justine rescued her that time, making a face at Beau that Anna couldn't decipher, perhaps a rebuke, but a humorous one, if that.

After about an hour of meeting famous people that she had only seen on screens, large or small, Anna noticed that guests kept pulling Beau into intimate conversation with plaintive looks on their faces. These were wealthy and well-known people that she had never seen look so child-like and needy, even if she suspected those conditions lay beneath the red-carpet waves and smiles she had seen on entertainment TV.

Finally, she happened to be standing on the second step of the central staircase, leaning on the polished mahogany railing and listening to a veteran actress expound to Justine on her recent theater work, when Beau put his hand on the forehead of the man who had won the academy award for best director two years before. Anna watched as Beau removed his hand and said something to the dark-haired man wearing small glasses, who nearly pitched over backward at those words. Beau's strong right hand caught the director's arm and steadied him. This maneuver brought the man forward so that his forehead pressed against Beau's chest.

Anna looked at the people around this scene. Half of them seemed deeply fascinated, studying every move, like it was a championship chess match. Others acted as if they had seen it all before, glancing at Beau and the wobbly director, and laughing, before returning to their conversations. It reminded Anna of those guys in college who would always come to the frat parties with illegal substances to distribute. Everyone knew who they were and no one was surprised when someone lost their balance after their ministrations. Beau was like a Holy Ghost drug dealer, she decided. Anna laughed aloud at the thought, and suddenly she felt extremely drunk, her arms and legs loose and rubbery.

Justine saw this transition, looked across the room to what Beau was doing, and smiled. She took hold of Anna, like the designated driver, and helped her to sit down on the stairs, a touch on her knees to be sure Anna remembered that she was wearing a short dress and sitting on the stairs in a crowded room. When she sat down, the angle granted Anna a look at Dianna sitting on the couch in the living room, near the entryway and the stairs. A woman that Anna didn't recognize was crying and wiping her eyes as Dianna listened with compassionate intensity.

"Is this what they do at these libertine Hollywood parties? Heal people and listen to them pour out their hearts?" Anna thought. It was like they were the priest and priestesses of the rich and famous. Anna started to sober a bit. She set down her champagne glass, still the original one and half full. She leaned both elbows on her knees.

Justine had been keeping her in view. "Are you okay, dear?"

Anna started to cry, as if the concern in Justine's voice delivered the dose of love that put her over her limit. "I wanna be like you guys," she said, blurting it like the time she admitted to her mother that her prom date had dumped her the day before the big dance.

Justine laughed quietly through her nose and glanced at the woman with whom she had been talking. The tall blonde actress nodded graciously and retreated to the living room. Justine took up a seat next to Anna, hip to hip, pressing her knees and heels together and resting her elbows on her bare legs in imitation of Anna. Anna had begun to recover from the sudden catharsis and sobbed quietly now.

"Do you wanna meet Jesus?" Justine said, as if she were talking about the host of the party, or someone in the next room.

Anna knew, of course, that God and Jesus would be involved somehow, but she hadn't expected to meet either of them just then, especially at her first big Hollywood party. She *had* briefly wished she would meet some rich and famous actor who found her charmingly attractive. But meeting Jesus was something she would have to consider...at least for a minute or two. Had any other Christians she knew offered this introduction, she would have assumed it was metaphorical. After what Anna had experienced with Beau and his family, however, she assumed this meeting would be anything but metaphorical.

After these considerations, Anna said. "You mean meet him here?"

Justine looked around and seemed to change her mind. "No, let's go out back by the pool."

Anna hadn't been given the grand tour, so she didn't know where the pool was, nor did she know why it would be better to meet Jesus out there. But Justine was the expert on these things, so she agreed. Helping Anna to stand, Justine stepped delicately off the shiny steps, holding the younger woman's hand as she led the way. Dianna had finished with the tear-soaked woman on the couch and was just getting up when Justine caught her eye. No words passed between them, but Dianna recognized something in Anna and fell into line behind her, on the way to the meeting by the pool.

As self-conscious as Anna had been about her appearance among the beautiful people, she forgot about all that as she walked hand in hand with Justine through the crowded hallways and rooms of the ornate house, tears still wetting her face, makeup beginning to sag a little, her hair damp from sweat, sticking to her forehead and temples in less-than-elegant clumps. All she could think about was meeting Jesus in her little black dress and high heels. It didn't seem like appropriate attire, nothing like the dress for her first communion, when she was a little girl, perhaps the first time she met Jesus in any real physical way.

Beau nodded slightly in their direction but made no move to join the train, perhaps aware that he was too big to be the caboose for that assemblage. He knew this was a crucial night for Anna. He didn't know how or why exactly, but felt certain that Justine and Dianna were leading her to where she needed to be.

The big outdoor pool looked over the coastline a mile below, darkness leaving room for the imagination about what lay in between, represented by occasional lights flickering yellow or white under the influence of the wind. Anna gulped fresh air, tasting the chlorine from the smooth blue pool beside her, and a hint of the ocean far below. Tall palms lined three sides of the tiled deck, in clusters of four or more, and a dark green hedge with fuzzy, copper-colored buds and white blossoms, like magnolias, added a sweet fruity scent. The lighted pool radiated a greenish glow under chins and noses, mixing with a golden light from a combination of torches and sleepy floodlights. Several couples stood talking near the railing on the ocean side, or sitting on white padded chaises and chairs. One pair had slipped free of much of their clothing and swam in the far end of the pool, speaking playfully, but their voices remaining just above the subtle waves stirred by their treading water.

In the dark, the pool seemed an enchanted place to Anna. Dianna and Justine also smiled at the beauty of the setting. Justine gently pulled Anna around to face her, near a table with unfurled umbrella—shading them only from the stars. Dianna tucked in close to them. The darkness, the captivating beauty of their surroundings and the intimate nearness of the other two women, left Anna feeling protected and private.

Without exchanging a word with Justine, Dianna spoke first. "Jesus is here to meet with you, Anna. He loves you and he wants you for his very own."

The romantic tone of Dianna's voice, the stimulating proximity of these two beautiful women, and something that hung in the air, mixed with the sweet scent of the flowers to send chills down Anna's back again. Then she felt a presence, just as if a fourth person had joined their little circle. This invisible person was electric. Her chills turned to shivering, and then to shaking. Yet she felt more peace than ever before in her life. Justine and Dianna simply stood by, propping Anna like the bride's maids that they had become to her.

To a stranger watching, it would have appeared that Anna swooned suddenly, losing consciousness and flopping backward, even as her knees buckled. Her trajectory would have landed her first on her rear end and then her back, but Justine and Dianna dipped quickly, tightening their subtle hold, to catch the petite young woman as she met her creator and her lover.

Justine pulled Anna's skirt straight, and laid her limp legs to the side, for modesty sake. Dianna pulled a chair around so that, when she sat in it, she shielded Anna from anyone more than a few feet away. Justine sat on the mosaic tiles, her legs bent around to the side, leaning over Anna to watch and wait with her.

When Anna was eleven years old, she and her father had been home alone one week, while her mother travelled to care for Anna's dying grandmother. Anna and her father soldiered through with carryout and questionable cooking, but they also played together. One night, it was a board game, another it was watching a softball game played by her father's company team. And one night, they stayed at home and listened to her dad's old collection of Motown vinyl records. Amidst the crackling pops and past the subtle hissing, she absorbed the romantic songs of love lost and love found. Then her father asked her to dance with him. She had always seen him as a romantic figure, conscious of his attentive ways with her mother, when Anna was around and especially when they thought their little girl wasn't watching. When he offered to dance with her that night, like a man at a club addressing a young wallflower, she knew he was sharing with her the romance of his love for her mother. The parents fought, of course, and ten years later they would divorce. But Anna soaked that night in the romance of their peaceful and agreeable times.

That night, long ago, she danced with her little feet on top of her father's brown dress shoes, humming along to Diana Ross and the Supremes, singing about love that lasts. Though her natural father had faded from her life now—with the acrimony of the divorce and his remarriage to a woman not enough older than Anna for her to feel comfortable with his choice—she still remembered the feeling of his strong hands and feet carrying her around the living room, under the light of two floor lamps and the glow from the stereo.

On the ground, next to the swimming pool, Anna experienced a moment with a living and passionate God, who swept her up with the warmth and romance of that daddy-daughter dance, and carried her far above any feeling she had ever experienced in any waking or dreaming moment in her life. She met Jesus, her dance partner, her true lover and best friend. After a half hour, when the experience started to fade, her most lasting thought was, "How did I miss this before?"

When Beau arrived next to the pool, he saw Dianna and Justine helping Anna off the ground and into one of the smooth, white-cushioned chairs. "Time for a baptism?" Beau said.

Justine looked over at Anna. "One thing we like to do, to get a fresh start with Jesus, is to be baptized in water. Basically, it's a sort of ancient ritual that says, 'I'm leaving my old life and taking up a new one with Jesus.'"

Anna had heard of baptism. She had seen it portrayed in movies. And she trusted this little congregation of people implicitly, like she would an old family doctor...times three. She looked at the pool. "Here?" She sounded just a little doubtful, but had lost most of her skepticism, at least temporarily, so she wasn't as doubtful as she would have been a month ago.

"Sure," Beau said. "No time like the present for a new start. And it's a way to make a sort of public declaration about it. I'm thinking this is public enough." He looked around at the wandering and philandering couples entering and lingering by the pool.

Dianna laughed, but said nothing. Anna got the feeling that she didn't need to say anything, because Beau and Justine already knew why she was laughing.

Still quite groggy from her intoxicating encounter, Anna felt no compulsion to ask about that joke. She just strained her neck looking up at Beau and said, "Will you baptize me?"

If she had been more calculating, more of a climber by nature, Anna might have asked this because Beau was arguably the most famous Christian on the planet, perhaps with the exception of the Pope. The Pope would have fallen into second place in California, however. But Anna asked, instead, because it seemed fitting that Beau would bring her into this wonderfully warm family, against all the nay-sayers and accusers. It was because of Beau, after all, that she even started to consider joining the Jesus people.

"Of course," Beau said. "It would be my honor." With that, he sat down to remove his shoes and pulled his jacket off to leave it on the chaise closest to the pool. Dianna left, striding toward the pool house, saying something about towels and robes.

Anna watched, a look of wonder and distraction on her face. Justine could see that she was worrying about something.

"You can just go in in your dress, I think. It's black, so it won't show too much when it's wet." She checked the tag in the back and said, "I don't think you'll do it any harm."

Anna kicked off the one shoe still on her foot, the other already lying under her chair. "So, I don't do this to get saved or anything, I just do this to say I'm following Jesus from now on?"

"Exactly," said Beau.

"She's not as drunk as I thought she was," Justine said, looking at Beau when she said this.

"I didn't even finish one glass of champagne," Anna said. But her voice tailed off at the end, as if she had just figured out that Justine was referring to something else.

Justine smiled. "Yeah, not that kind of drunk."

Anna nodded, standing up and looking at Beau to lead the way. He was back in bare feet, even at a fancy party, and so was she. He was going to get his dress pants and shirt wet. She almost felt some regret, but mostly a sense of ironic humor that she couldn't even translate into words. She just giggled as she watched Beau step down the stairs into the shallow end of the pool.

If You Really Knew Me

As she followed, Anna noticed Dianna returning with arms full of white towels and bathrobes. From behind her, as she stepped down into the warm water, she heard a man shout. "Hey, Vince, Beau's baptizing someone in your pool again." A more distant voice returned with a question. Then that first disembodied voice replied, "It's that new girl he brought with him." Another question followed, almost audible this time. "No, she's not one of his wives, I don't think."

By the time Anna had followed Beau into about three feet of water, her little black dress billowed upward only slightly. She turned around just in time to see the host of the party leading a dozen other elegantly dressed men and women. Here came the public part of her public statement.

Justine and Dianna each kicked off their shoes and sat down on the edge of the pool with feet playing languidly in the water. The host and company stood next to the shallow end, drinks in hand, and just watched, no comments, no looks of bafflement or disdain. They had seen this before.

"Anna Conyers," Beau said. "Do you declare here before this company, that you have met Jesus and would like to live the rest of your life loving him and being loved by him, even into eternity?"

It sounded like an appropriate religious ritual to Anna. She didn't know Beau was just making it up. "I do," she said, repressing a giggle at the wedding reference that her answer implied. Then her face took on a dreamy, watery-eyed smile that led Justine and Dianna to think that she had just gotten the connection between her intimate experience with Jesus and being a bride. She had never done either of these before, but the look of awestruck wonder on her face testified to her joyous acceptance of the combination.

Beau had to wait for her to stop laughing to give her instructions on how not to inhale the pool water on the way back up. She sobered a bit, held her nose and went over backward with Beau's left hand behind her, dipping her and lifting her again.

Though that maneuver was a bit odd for your average swimming pool at your average cocktail party, what Anna did when she came up out of the water really made a declaration.

As soon as the water had cascaded off her face, and before she had even wiped it away from her eyes, she was babbling in some unknown language, the words spilling out of her like little giggles, but with distinct foreign pronunciation.

"Oh my God," said one of the audience at the shallow end. "She's speaking Albanian, fluent Albanian, like my grandmother used to speak." The veteran movie actor who spoke up, had an East European accent that most of the party-goers would not have been able to identify, until now.

"What's she saying?" said the host.

"She's telling about how much God loves her and how much she loves God. How she was made to love him and will always be devoted to God. It's almost like a hymn, or poetry." The actor took a deep breath and sniffled. "I don't believe in any of this, though," he said, and then he laughed, and his laughter turned to sobs as he spun around and headed back to the house.

Beau was helping Anna back to the stairs, noting the hasty exit of one of the witnesses. Justine and Dianna stood up and met the pair with towels, as they rose from the surface of the water. The party guests applauded for Anna and she smiled shyly at them, hunkering into the warm towel with which Dianna was engulfing her.

Beau started bantering with the host of the party about finally getting baptized. Only after a minute or so did Anna realize he wasn't teasing.

"You know I can't do such a thing with all these guests here," said the A-list movie producer. "They would think I'd gone off my head."

Beau nodded. "Some of them. But a few would join you."

"What, after they see me coming up out of the water babbling in Albanian or something? No, I don't think so, Beau. Not tonight. Try me again another time."

If You Really Knew Me

Beau's voice struck a chord next that Anna had never heard, not even on videos of his healing services. "Vince, you know you're not gonna live forever. You gotta commit one way or the other, before it's too late."

The host lowered his chin and straightened his neck, his salt and pepper eyebrows shooting up his forehead. "You're sounding unusually desperate. What's gotten into you?"

"I just care about you, my friend. This is important, it's life or death, and it's for eternity."

"Sounds like you're trying to scare me into a decision. I don't think that'll work."

Beau nodded. "Yeah, I know." He finished toweling off, taking a large terrycloth robe from Dianna. He looked something like a boxer from the old days, only his face was just too pretty for that role. He looked at his friend once more and just smiled, saying no more.

In the car, on the way back home, Beau seemed pensive. Anna couldn't stand not knowing, and she hadn't acquired the ability to read his mind as Justine and Dianna seemed to.

"Why did you push him so hard?" she said, confident that he would recognize to whom she was referring.

Beau stuck out his lower lip and looked down at the floor, considering how much he could tell. "I wasn't supposed to tell him, but I'm pretty confident he's not gonna live past this weekend."

"Oh," Anna said, gasping. "Why couldn't you tell him?"

Shaking his head slowly, he said, "I don't always know the why, but I got my orders clearly enough."

Anna didn't recognize the rules to this new life she had entered. She certainly felt ill-equipped for it.

"Don't worry about the way we operate," Justine said, answering her thoughts. "You don't have to be like us to follow him. Just be yourself and he'll show you more and more of who exactly that is."

Anna's chest expanded for a big sigh, big for such a small person. The fluffy white robe overwhelmed her, pushed up over her ears as she sat in the tall leather limo seat. Not having to know all the answers seemed a grand relief just then.

A Bigger Bang

Dixon tossed the weekly newspaper onto his desk. He had seen articles from this Anna Conyers before. It was obvious to him that she had been brainwashed by Dupere and his people. Her detailed explanation of the alleged assassination reminded Dixon of the conspiracy theories around President Kennedy's death. She was reaching, as far as he was concerned. His conclusion, however, ignored the fact that much of her evidence came from the FBI, whom he could hardly accuse of being "brainwashed."

He sighed and then looked at his watch. Pushing away from his desk, he stood up and stretched. Sara was coming home for dinner that night and he wanted everything to be perfect for them, a welcome home, even though she had said nothing about moving back in. He stood, staring into the corner of the room for five seconds, sorting his hopes from what Sara had led them to expect. "Just a dinner," she had said. "Just a visit."

A knock on his office door startled Dixon to attention.

"Yeah?" he said, much louder than he had intended.

Connie opened the door slowly, as if afraid she might be attacked.

"Oh, Connie. Sorry. I was daydreaming and your knock startled me."

"Oh, *I'm* sorry," she said, trying to override his apology with her more vigorous and deserved apology.

"What is it?"

"Ah, well, your wife left a message while you were meeting with the Wilsons, and I almost forgot. She said to pick up some hamburger buns on the way home."

"Hamburger buns?" Dixon said, taking note and nodding. "Thanks, Connie. I'm heading home, so that was right on time."

"Okay, well, have a good dinner with Sara," she said. When she saw Dixon's curious look, she explained. "Kristen told me, of course. I'll be praying for you."

Dixon smiled down at Connie, who was still holding the door handle and looking like she was just starting to bow contritely. "Thanks for that. We can sure use it," Dixon said, his voice low and weary.

Dixon strode into the kitchen, doing nothing to avoid the appearance of running a quarterback draw up the middle, with the bag of buns under his right arm. He did stop short of stiff-arming his wife when she greeted him by the stove, however. If it had been Brett, the stiff-arm would not have been out of the question.

"Hi, honey," Dixon said, returning her greeting, dropping the bread on the counter and giving Kristen a little kiss. The sharp smack sound still hung in the air when Brett popped into the room from the opposite direction.

"Are you guys gonna lock Sara up and deprogram 'er?" he said, with a teasing grin. His parents looked at each other, both calculating the chances of getting away with that strategy, and also wondering where Brett had learned to ignore so many normal social boundaries.

"Not this time," Dixon said, his voice level and dry.

"Too bad," Brett said, as he opened the fridge and pulled out a whipped chocolate yogurt.

Kristen saw that acquisition and considered whether to say something. Having Brett well-fed and mellow certainly seemed the best approach to the dinner, so she held her peace, turning instead to encourage her husband.

"Go change, so you can start up the grill," she said.

If You Really Knew Me

Dixon looked down at his dress pants and button down shirt and knew she was right. He would have to change. But that was good news, it would keep his mind occupied while he waited. Finding clothes, visiting the restroom, getting undressed, turning on the TV, getting dressed, and then standing in the middle of the room staring into the corner again, took almost half an hour. Fortunately, he wouldn't have to explain exactly how so much time escaped. He went out the front door and around to the side of the house, avoiding questions from Kristen, and gathering the mail at the same time. He looked through the little pile of envelopes and flyers and thought, "Kindling."

That day in Parkerville had been summer warm from soon after dawn. The air hung hazy and torpid still at six p.m., when the grill reached the perfect temperature. Dixon waited for Sara to arrive before putting the burgers on, wanting to serve them fresh and hot, without the temptation to leave them on too long while waiting for someone to arrive. But his prompt daughter didn't disappoint him, arriving less than a minute after six, the time set by her mother.

"Oh, honey, it's so good to see you," Kristen said, following the slam of the screen door.

Dixon pulled his head out of the fridge, tomatoes and onions in hand. He dropped those on the counter next to the fridge and spun around to greet Sara. As they cheerfully exchanged hugs and hellos, Dixon couldn't keep the surprise off his face. His little girl looked like a woman, a grown woman. She looked so different than when he had seen her last. But that was probably because he had seen her last in his mind's eye, where he had substituted a picture of a skinny twelve-year-old with pig tails and braces. Add to that, the fact that she was working as a lifeguard again this summer, earning dollars by getting tan, he almost didn't notice the little rhinestone stud in the crevice next to one of her nostrils. His first thought was, "Did she have that before?" Followed by his second thought, "Not *my* daughter."

Kristen seemed to miss Dixon's telepathic suggestion of disapproval.

If You Really Knew Me

"Oh, that's cute. When did you do that?" she said, referring to the tiny bit of bling embedded in Sara's golden brown face.

"A couple weeks ago," Sara said, turning away, as if she could hide it from them now.

For Sara, the evening was like hopping on an exercise bike that was self-propelled. Without any effort on her part, she slipped right back into her place at the table, and in the family. Familiarity doesn't always breed contempt. Sometimes it breeds unconsciousness. Part of that sleepwalking feeling certainly came from Sara's clenched up nerves, restricting blood flow to her brain, as she hoped, against all probability, that they could avoid the religious divide between them, and also avoid the whole moving-back-in discussion. That *had* been the deal when she agreed to come to supper. She wanted to pick up some more of her things, but she also wanted to see her family, longing for a conflict-free evening of simply being together. That is, being together as a family which now included one grown child making her own decisions about her life. One can always dream.

"So, ya livin' on the streets these days, begging for quarters?" Brett said, around a mouthful of burger, everyone at their usual places twenty minutes after Sara's arrival.

Sara considered pretending she didn't hear or understand the question, but she didn't have to answer anyway.

"Brett! Behave yourself. No one needs you stirring up trouble," his mother said.

Dixon had decided ahead of time to go for a killing-with-kindness approach. He picked up on Brett's comment with a more serious question. "Is there anything you need done around your place? You know, handyman stuff."

Everyone at that table knew that Dixon was referring to himself as the handyman in question. They also knew that this was a very generous characterization of his skills with a hammer or screw driver. Sara appreciated the gesture, nonetheless.

"No thanks, Dad. It's nice of you to offer." She smiled at him briefly, internally sorting how dangerous it would be to discuss

If You Really Knew Me

specifics of her living arrangement. "The place is pretty new, and Kim's dad did a bit of work when we first moved in, you know loose hinges and drawer handles. Nothing serious."

Neither of her parents knew exactly how she managed to arrange the move into an apartment, including how the girls were able to sign a lease at eighteen years apiece. The mention of Kim's father, Will Crenshaw, introduced the likelihood that he had signed *for* them. Dixon tamped down an awakening resentment that the Crenshaw family was facilitating his daughter's delinquency. He glanced internally at that deprogramming idea Brett had mentioned, but shut himself down in that direction, as soon as he considered it. He cleared his throat and got up from the table.

"Anyone need any more to drink?"

They had each been allowed a soda for the meal. The rule in the house was one soda a day, and no more. Dixon's careless offer sounded as if there were no more rules.

"Sure, I'll have another root beer while you're up," Brett said, knowing an opportunity when he saw one.

Again, Kristen opted for silence, in the hope that Brett would behave himself if his stomach was satisfied. Dixon glanced at his wife and, hearing no objection, headed for the kitchen and a couple of cold sodas.

Brett thanked his dad, when he returned, and then asked for another bending of the rules. "Okay if I drink this in my room while I watch the A's?" He had a tiny TV with a color picture tube that was older than he was. But it worked well enough for an isolated Oakland fan in a Giants house.

"Okay, just this once," Kristen said, anxious to get Brett on his way, as if he was a ticking bomb.

"Great, thanks!" Brett said. He lifted his soda can for his sister to see and raised his eyebrows, reminding her of the new leniency he had described back when he caught her sneaking into the house.

As the other three rose to clear the dishes, Dixon made a suggestion. "Hey, why don't we watch a movie in the living room? We can watch something Brett would ruin with his moaning and eye-rolling."

"You mean a chick flick?" Kristen said.

Sara laughed. Her dad had tolerated far more romantic comedies than Brett could possibly bear. Though it was a generous offer, it wasn't unprecedented, as were so many other things that evening.

"Sounds good to me," Sara said, glad for something other than an evening of grilled daughter to follow the hamburgers.

Kristen and Sara agreed that Dixon could choose the movie from Kristen's collection of romances. These were all movies she liked, and mostly movies Sara liked, so it seemed safe to commission the man with the girl-movie selection.

Sara nearly laughed out loud when she saw that her dad had selected a movie featuring one of Beau Dupere's best buddies, Randy Cooper. Apparently, Dixon wasn't following Beau as closely as Sara was, so he must not have known of the connection. That realization was actually encouraging to Sara, a bit of hope that her dad wasn't totally obsessed with Beau.

"Oh, that's a good one. We haven't seen that for a while," Kristen said, when she saw Dixon's pick.

Sara looked at the cover, while Dixon setup the electronics. He and Brett were the only ones who knew the magic combination of remotes and buttons to switch the TV and sound system over from cable programming, or gaming console, to playing a movie. That was about as handy as Dixon was around the house.

The picture of Randy Cooper on the DVD case showed a much younger man than the one she had seen on Beau's Web site recently. The story there was of the often-rehabbed star finally going for the ultimate rehab and letting Beau baptize him in somebody's pool. Sara prayed a little prayer on Randy's behalf, hoping this latest rehab would be the one that sticks.

Sara sat sideways on the couch, her bare feet up on the cushions, leaning back on a small stack of throw pillows piled against the arm. Dixon occupied his usual easy chair and Kristen curled up at the other end of the couch with Sara. They could have sliced this scene out of any day three months prior, or from the future they had expected, as long as they didn't look inside the heads of each person in that room. The movie, no one's favorite, wasn't enough to distract any of them from the huge unspoken questions between them. It was, however, enough to keep them from talking about anything substantive, until Brett interrupted the movie near the end.

"Hey, did you guys hear about the bomb at Beau Dupere's house?" he said, startling them with his volume, before shocking them with his news.

All three of the adults said, "What!" in near unison.

"Where did you hear this?" Dixon said, over the noises of panic and confusion from the others.

"I forgot to turn off the TV after the A's game ended and the news came on. It just happened."

Dixon looked at the clock and then grabbed a remote to switch to the TV channels. In less than half a minute, he found a station that was broadcasting live from Malibu. Brett took a seat in the middle of the couch, next to Sara who had sat up straight at Brett's news.

The reporter on the scene was speaking. "The police aren't giving us any more specifics on that, but we did talk to a couple of the protesters who witnessed the explosion and what followed. At least two of them saw what looked like Molotov cocktails hit the north side of the house. One also said they saw a fire breakout at the location where the original firebombs seemed to be launched. This point was confirmed by the presence of an ambulance and emergency medical personnel working on someone about fifty yards from the house. And this is where it gets really interesting. Several bystanders say they saw Beau Dupere come running away from the house soon after the fire had been quelled by firefighters. He ran right to where we had seen emergency personnel treating someone away from the house. Those who were close enough to see, said that Dupere rushed in to where the injured person was and, within a minute, turned and walked back toward the house more calmly."

The anchorman in the studio interrupted the reporter at this point. "Rolly, have you found anyone who can confirm that Beau Dupere actually wanted to...ah...well, to help the injured person there?"

Rolly nodded vigorously and said, "Most of it is speculation, because officials won't comment, and Mr. Dupere is back inside the compound, and not talking to reporters. But bystanders did say that they heard that this was why he rushed outside, that is, to help someone who had been injured by that other fire which was witnessed by the crowd."

"Back to the damage on the house," the anchorman said, "do we know for sure that no one in the house was injured?"

"That's what we've heard from everyone we've talked to. The residents got out of the house itself, though they stayed within the compound, not coming out onto the street, where a large crowd of protesters is always present. The fire burned for about ten minutes and damaged one end of the house. People who have been watching the house, as part of the protest, say they think the firebombs were aimed at the master bedroom suite, which might have been where Beau Dupere and his...ah...his...his wife would have been this late in the evening. But that too is just speculation."

"And these firebombs were launched from some distance, is that right? Not just thrown by hand?"

"Right, launched by some kind of giant slingshot. The police captured the equipment, including unused bottles of flammable liquid. From where that equipment is in relation to the other fire, some have concluded that the second fire was the attackers accidentally setting off a firebomb close to their own position. This has led some to speculate that the person who was injured away from the house may have been one of the assailants."

If You Really Knew Me

The anchorman's voice escalated with incredulity. "But, then that would mean that we're hearing reports that Beau Dupere ran out to help rescue one of the attackers?"

Dixon turned down the volume on the report. "Sounds like all they have is a bunch of speculation." His voice sounded tight in his throat.

Sara ignored the missing details and vented about the attack. "Who is doing all of this? Do they really think God wants them to harm these people?"

She didn't consider her audience before blurting her reaction, but then her family was as caught off guard by the story as she was and didn't have their lines of defense in place either.

Kristen said, "Must be some really crazy people."

"Kinda like terrorists, right?" Brett said.

Dixon didn't like where this was headed and tried to moderate the prevailing attitude toward the opponents of Beau Dupere. "Well, people feel pretty strongly about their faith, and all through history there are people fighting for what they believe in, sometimes good people."

Even as he finished this unedited statement, Dixon regretted the impression that he might be defending the attacks. But he silenced the three-pronged racket of exasperated responses by turning up the volume on the TV and gesturing to the screen. "Looks like the police are making a statement."

They all turned to the screen, Sara seething at her father's sympathy for the attackers, but keen to hear something official about what actually happened.

"This is, of course, an ongoing investigation, so we can't comment on that," the police commander said. "I can confirm that the Dupere family are all safe, and the fire has been extinguished in their home. I can also confirm that a second fire was set by accident at the site from which the apparent firebombs were allegedly being launched. We have in custody a man who may have been part of the attack. He was reported to be severely injured, but is in good health now and on his way in to the station for questioning. We are assuming that the motivation for the attack has something to do with opposition to the sort of work Mr. Dupere does, but can say nothing further on what happened here tonight."

Reporters listening live to the commander exploded with questions as soon as he stopped talking. After several seconds, he managed to silence them and took one question.

"Is it true that Beau Dupere ran from the house and helped to heal the man who was injured, possibly one of the attackers?" the reporter said.

The commander shook his head. "We can't comment on that. We'll be investigating this further and will issue a more complete report as we gather more facts."

Sara, Kristen and Brett all moaned at the generic response from the police commander. Dixon looked at them, beginning to feel like a minority in his own home.

"Well, you know how these things go. People think they see something and then later you check it out and everyone changes their story, or the stories don't match up. They have to investigate to find what really happened," Dixon said.

Sara rolled her eyes and slapped both knees. "You just can't believe that someone could really go and heal a man that just attacked his family, just because you can't do anything even remotely like that."

Like her father a few minutes before, Sara regretted her tone and the spiteful accusation, as soon as she said it. The look on Dixon's face deflated her soul. His open mouth, wide eyes and face fading pale, revealed the shock to his own heart.

Sara stood up and dashed to the front door, running from her own anger as much as her father's intransigent opposition to someone she considered a hero of faith. She swung back to grab her purse, cast a look of forlorn disgust in her mother's direction, and spun back to the door. She couldn't even speak to apologize, and the tears in her eyes turned opening the front door into a desperate scramble. Her frustration broke out in frantic sobs that her family could hear even as she swung out the door and jumped off the porch, running toward her car.

Kristen made it to the porch as Sara started her car and began to back down the drive. "Be careful, Sara. Settle down before you drive home like that," she said, not knowing how to respond to what her daughter had laid on Dixon. Her immediate concern for Sara seemed the most clear of the dozen pulsing emotions she wrangled there in the warm summer air.

Heeding her mother's warning, Sara pulled to the side of the residential street a block from the house. Her gush of frustrated sorrow increased as she leaned her head on the steering wheel and let loose. Even as her entire body injected its energy into that catharsis, she recognized the fear that sparked her desperate response. She really feared that her father was condemning himself by siding with the wrong people, actually setting himself against God.

Back at the house, Dixon and Kristen sat in their usual places, stunned at the storm that had driven their daughter out the door again. Brett snuck out of the room, recognizing toxic air for what it was. When the news story switched to the unexpected death, by heart attack, of movie producer Vincent Corelli, known to be friends with Beau Dupere, they didn't notice.

The Cost of Caring

Dark clouds blew in over the ocean, the kind of clouds that seem to bulge with the weight of the water they carry. Yet, they hung on and left the coast dry again. Land so close to water yet so constantly dry reminded Beau of people that he knew. These would stand and watch as a partially blind person received perfect sight, close enough to the glory of God to reach out and grab some for themselves, yet they pushed back instead. They stay dry while people all around them pull the rain out of the clouds before letting them pass.

Beau sat on a chair with his pool behind him, looking out over the Pacific, the water nearly black under the stormy skies, dashed with white here and there, as waves foamed into the air, whipped by the wind.

Vince's death nearly smothered Beau's heart, a weight like a collapsed building pinning him, helpless. He knew the deepest part of that pain was not his own. He hadn't given *his* life for Vince, he hadn't known him from before birth, he hadn't watched him every moment of his star-studded life, nor hovered over his devastated soul. Beau could heal, but he couldn't save. It wasn't his failure. But it still hurt.

As he often did, when driven down by the weight of caring for people who could not grasp the treasure so freely offered to them, he remembered who he had been before fully grasping the reality of that grace. He remembered his struggles against the draglines of various escapes such as alcohol and sexual promiscuity, he remembered his weakness to resist. In those memories, he could understand the stubborn failure of those who refused to receive, even when they witnessed that grace given without a list of rules, without condemnation for the sins of the past, or even the present.

Along this path, Beau uncovered a memory of an early meeting he had with Jack Williams, just the two of them. Jack had seen a rough version of the healing gift that God had laid on Beau, but he knew that Beau needed help in carrying that much treasure in a corrupt and greedy world.

"You gotta give in completely," Jack said, sitting with his hands behind his head, leaning back on the couch in his living room. "If you just go half way, your gifting will eat you up, swallow you whole, and we'll never see you again."

Beau was a successful stock trader by then, making intuitive deals that made him lots of money, yet he found little excitement in the millions. He had looked elsewhere, into drugs and drinking and women, in search of something that did excite him. By this point he knew how hollow those options were and had returned to his childhood faith and committed himself to church.

"This healing gift that we saw again last Sunday, the way that guy's hand just straightened out right before our eyes," Jack said, "it's a sign of who God is and who you are in God. This is not isolated from the things inside you that drive you to look for something more, something better, something big. This *is* that something big, and not just the healing, it's the God who does the healing that's the big deal, the real deal. But you'll have to give up everything if you really want all of him."

Beau remembered looking at Jack, and knowing that he meant what he said. Beau had succeeded in business by being able to read people, and he knew that Jack was as real as the deal he was offering. This was not some super-spiritual sap, selling the usual religious formula. No, this was a man who feared very little, if anything, beside God. And he was a man more passionate about God than the traders he worked with were passionate about the deals and the dollars.

In the healing lines, Beau had felt the power of God at work through his hands, even before he understood what that gift was. In being healed in his own body, Beau had seen God give before he understood why his creator gave, and especially why he gave anything to *him*.

To the challenge Jack issued that day, Beau had answered, "Maybe later." He didn't ever say this explicitly, of course, but he showed it with his renewed efforts at work and persisting in his back row sort of faith. During those months and years, he advanced in his healing abilities, but only slightly, and most of the time Jack and others knew he was just going along with what they expected. He wasn't striving toward the mark set by a higher power than his own ego and his own ambition.

Remembering all this, eased the frustration for Beau when he thought of friends like Vince, that pulled away, instead of pushing in closer when they saw the hand of God at work.

Brushing his hair back to adjust a swirl drawn by a swift wind, Beau noticed Olivia rounding the end of the pool toward him. He smiled at her, in spite of his dark thoughts. Olivia smiled back, her red lips curving like the scrolling at the edges of an illuminated manuscript. Beau had always thought of her as an exotic beauty, unlike Dianna and Justine who looked like actresses or models. If Olivia were an actress, she would play the clever friend of the leading lady, the sidekick with a sense of humor and almond eyes that looked on with irony. She was wearing her hair in corn-rows these days, dangling earrings swinging in the breeze, where her braided brown hair left them free to catch the brunt of the approaching storm.

As she stepped up close, Beau knew that she came with purpose, and not just a friendly visit, or even a mundane message, like lunch being ready. He still smiled at her, even when he knew she came to offer a poke, a prod to keep his focus where it was supposed to be.

Olivia liked the way Beau could anticipate a difficult conversation. She had seen over and again that he used the forewarning from the Spirit to prepare his best response, not his best defense.

"You are an eternally brave woman," Beau said, greeting her by standing for a long hug that formed a brief shelter from the wind between them.

"Oh, you think you're so tough, do you?" Olivia said, the jousting tone of a tease tweaking her deep voice.

"I could have you for breakfast, little one."

"Ah, but it's way too late for your breakfast," she said, looking up at his face angled down toward her. He turned and pulled another chair close to his.

Olivia sat down, her thin legs—tinged a pale olive in the low light of the cloudy morning—leaned toward Beau's ruddier, hairy legs. She admired the contrast of their skin and their physiques, ever the admirer of God's works of art.

If You Really Knew Me

For a minute, they both sat watching the wind against the palm trees and across the tops of the waves, and they listened for the voice of the one that they both loved even more than each other, even more than their kids. From what they each heard individually, they knew how to speak to each other.

"It's about Maggie," Beau said, offering Olivia the stage only after introducing her topic for her.

"Umhmm." Olivia continued watching the surging sea, still listening for how much was hers to say.

"Should I go talk to her?" Beau said, his gaze in perfect parallel to hers, his voice smooth and sure.

"Not right away. She needs a bit more time. The firebombing just stirred up what the assassination laid on her. She *does* need to hear from you, but she needs to hear future assurances, not just present comforts."

"Ah," Beau said, "that makes sense. I knew I was missing the mark with her. A good long hug will usually cure as much as any number of words I try. But that wasn't working either."

Olivia nodded. Her brow was clenched, her lips pressed together. She was trying to push through the emotion that came with what she had yet to say. "The problem is," she said, pausing to tighten control of her voice. "The problem is that she knows it's going to happen again."

Beau nodded, rapid little motions with his head, his eyebrows curled down just above his dark eyes. He reached up and rubbed his right hand down from his mouth, over his chin, as if he still wore the beard he had when Olivia first moved in. With his other hand, he reached for hers and held on.

"I think," Olivia said, "that you should let us know more of how you'll miss the ones you leave behind." Her voice shook like loose shudders hassled by that wind.

Beau reached back and slipped his left arm around Olivia's right. She wrapped her left hand over their conjoined arms. This movement helped her to regain control of her emotions, but she felt him shaking next to her, sobs convulsing his whole torso.

She knew she had asked the hardest thing. She had asked him to allow his humanity to face what only the Spirit could endure, and she had asked it for her own benefit and for the children. The younger ones didn't know or understand. But Maggie, and perhaps Adam, could tell that something was coming, and they needed the affirmation of a role model doing the same thing they felt compelled to do, to mourn. Olivia, and the other women, needed this too. Without it, they condemned themselves for indulging emotions and ignoring the comforts of the Spirit. However, they were all human, no matter how much supernatural power pulsed through their hands and minds.

Beau sniffed long and hard, trying to regain control. He just shook his head with those little movements again, like his brain was caught between two immovable forces bouncing tensely back and forth between them. He too was still only human.

A Prisoner of Fear

When Anna heard about the firebombing at the house, she first drove over there, but the police wouldn't let her near. She had to wait until the next day to see Justine and Maggie and Beau, along with a few of the little ones. She seethed at the sight of the blackened wood and brick against the pristine paint of the unmarred sections. But she comforted herself with the safety of the residents.

Her next mission, as she saw it, was to pursue the attacker who was in custody, and whose life had been saved when Beau ran out of the compound to heal him. But she had to do this on her own time. The paper had tired of Beau Dupere, and wanted

If You Really Knew Me

Anna to work on another story, one about a double amputee training for the U.S. Olympic team, her usual genre.

She felt no remorse about using her press credentials to gather a story that she wouldn't be able to publish, at least in the short term. When she arrived at the Malibu police station, where the prisoner had originally been held, she found that she was a day late. The prisoner had been moved to a federal facility in Los Angeles, under FBI custody.

For six hours, in the maze of offices downtown, Anna talked with everyone she could get to listen, trying to schedule access to the prisoner. But the stack of policies between Anna and that goal was as tall as the Federal building in which she waged her struggle. When she was ready to give up, heading for the elevator at five p.m., an agent followed her down the hall.

The tall, dark-haired man in his thirties cleared his throat and prompted Anna to turn and see who was so close behind her. "Let's take the stairs," he said, motioning behind him. A half dozen people got on the elevator. A woman with a holster over her shoulder held the door until Anna motioned for them to go on. Something in the face of the man behind her set her at ease, in spite of the clandestine feeling that his invitation carried, his voice slightly hushed, his face neutral, as if avoiding calling attention to himself.

Anna followed him through the door to the stairs. They were ten floors up. It would be a long walk. She hitched her bag higher on her shoulder as the door closed behind them. The stranger stopped in the middle of the first flight and listened a moment.

"I just have a minute," he said. "I saw you trying to talk to that guy that hit the house in Malibu. He was on this slingshot thing lobbing Molotov cocktails at the Dupere house, and one of the bombs slipped loose and exploded at his feet, lighting him up. He wasn't gonna die, like the TV news said, but he was burned pretty much all over." The informant spoke steadily and clearly, intent on feeding Anna as many facts as he could in a brief conversation.

He continued. "The guy said that, while he was still waiting for the ambulance with some paramedics, this man jumps through a hedge and says he's there to heal him. He knew it was Dupere right away, but he was in shock, so he couldn't say or do anything. He says it was just a minute between when Dupere touched him and when he felt absolutely no pain and looked down at his arms and legs where the burns disappeared before his eyes." The stranger, stopped to take a deep breath. His eyes were wide, his pupils dilated. He was spilling this story like it was hot metal that he had to release into the air before it melted him from the inside out.

"You interviewed him?" Anna said.

"I was on the recorder when the lead agent was interviewing him. He was really upset. He's not eating. He thinks he has a demon or something now, 'cause he thinks Beau Dupere is the Devil. The prisoner is on suicide watch, he says he wants to die instead of be controlled by that man's demons."

Anna stared at the oval-faced man whose dark blue eyes darted to his left when the door opened. He quickly covered their conversation with a hastily constructed alternative.

"Ah, okay, I understand. Well, I guess I'm just not your type," he said.

Anna thought it was obvious that he was improvising, but the two agents tapping down the stairs past them just snickered and continued on their way.

"That's it. That's all I can say," the informant said, in a whisper. Unwilling to risk any more, he turned and followed the other two employees down a flight and opened the door to enter the floor below.

Anna didn't want to follow him, so she went down another floor before trying the door, only to find access denied. She had to go down three more floors before she could find an open door and take the elevator the rest of the way down. The whole time, however, she was replaying what the informant had told her. She wondered how much of that story would get out to the press. She could see why the feds had said so little about the prisoner. He presented yet another story for which they had no grid.

When she reached her car, her hands shook as she tried to fit the key into the ignition. Then she suddenly started to laugh. Apparently, she had found the grid in which that story made perfect sense to *her*.

A Little Help?

Sara monitored the news a lot more than she used to, before she first saw Beau Dupere in person. How ironic, that a man who ignores the press would be her motive to read papers and listen to the radio and TV. She was driving to meet with Claire Marquez, when she heard the story on the public radio station. The man Beau Dupere healed after he tried to burn down Beau's house, had committed suicide while in federal custody. The Justice Department had promised to investigate how the, still unnamed, prisoner could have acquired the drug overdose he used to end his life.

For Sara, the more infuriating question was why he would *want* to end it.

Arriving at Claire's house, Sara parked on the street and walked up the steep sidewalk to the front steps. Claire came out of the house, the heavy wooden screen door slamming behind her. She was full of smiles.

"Sara," she said, in a voice two octaves higher than normal. "Oh, it's so good to see you, girl."

They hugged at the bottom step and laughed awkwardly, both deciding whether to address directly the reason they hadn't seen each other. For Sara, this was the purpose of meeting with

If You Really Knew Me

Claire. Claire could only guess. She had been preoccupied lately with breaking off her engagement and testing other churches.

"How are you?" Sara said, offering an opening to that other unspoken topic, to allow Claire to vent as much as she needed.

"I'm fine," she said, shaking her head slowly. "I'm moving on, and have no regrets." Her slightly tempered smile hinted at a minor shadow of regret, her eyes a little more sunken, the lines in her face a bit more defined.

Sara waited to allow for amendments to that initial assessment, then, when Claire said no more, she released something she had kept pent up for a while. "I'm glad for you. I didn't think he was a great fit for you anyway."

Claire arched an eyebrow and turned her head a bit to the side. "*Now* you tell me. Where were you nine months ago?"

Sara laughed, half-embarrassed and half-relieved. The relief came from the obvious freedom with which Claire could joke about her cancelled wedding.

"Come on and sit on the porch swing," Claire said, hooking her arm through Sara's, and leading her up the uneven wooden stairs. "Mom is watching a program inside and it's such a beautiful day out here."

They thumped up the stairs and Sara looked at the front of the house. "How long are you gonna stay here?" she said, in a slightly lowered voice.

"Oh, I signed a lease for the beginning of the month," Claire said, smiling as if she was looking forward to moving out as much as Sara assumed. Claire was, of course, much older, and her living at home was as questionable as was Sara's exodus from home.

"Have you decided about college?" Claire said, taking one end of the porch swing, pulling a leg up and facing Sara at the other end.

Sara still faced forward, revisiting her own hours of struggle and late night prayer sessions over that question. "I know I'm going to get more education. But I just think I need another kind

If You Really Knew Me

of education right now." She turned to look at Claire. "I've found something so different from everything I knew about God as a kid in church, that I have to stop and take a closer look." She twisted around now and mirrored Claire, with one leg up on the dark brown painted swing. She dropped her sandal to the floor with a small clap sound.

"So how are ya gonna do that?"

"I'm signed up for a year of training up at Jack Williams's church, their course in *Miracles and Kingdom Living*. It's practically a full-time school, and I can work to stay alive while I find out more about what's out there," she paused, "or maybe what's in here." She tapped one finger to her chest.

"That sounds cool. I think you made the right choice." Claire pulled up her other leg and wrapped her arms around her knees. "So, you're moving up there?"

"No, I'm gonna make the long commute to the school and keep my apartment with Kim. She's perfect for debriefing the stuff I'm gonna get up at the church. Also, I can afford to live here with her and I can work at the Parks and Rec Department through most of the year."

Claire tossed her head to get her hair to blow back out of her face, hair she had been growing out in anticipation of a wedding. Sara, on the other hand had cut her hair short for the lifeguard job. There, the bleach and the sun had done their work to raise a golden shine to her pixie cut. Claire envied Sara's perfect little ears exposed by that hairstyle. But she turned her attention to more important topics that she had been saving.

"What about your parents?" she said, knowing that no road signs were necessary for the change of direction. She had already guessed that this was the reason Sara was sitting on that shady porch with her, late on a Thursday.

Sara took a deep breath and opened her soul. "I finally realized that I am really concerned about my dad. I had a hard time accepting it, but I have to admit that he seems to be lost. In all his confidence and outspokenness, he really seems lost, like he's rooting for the bad guys."

If You Really Knew Me

"Bad guys?" Claire said, her mouth and eyes neutral, but her head tipped a bit.

"I know that Beau Dupere is not perfect. I have no idea what's going on with him and his wives, or whatever. But it has to be clear to everyone who has a bit of sense that, even if he's got problems, it's not Christian to try to kill him, or burn down his house." Sara looked directly at Claire for a second and then continued. "And I was there when he was shot. It wasn't fake. It was real, and his daughter brought him back to life. People just have to deal with that, 'cause that's real."

Claire nodded, glancing to her left at two white butterflies circling each other over her mom's rose bushes. "Your dad's not dealing with that?"

Sara sighed like a weary old woman who had given too much and received too little in return. "He can't go all the way and really even confront me on things like that, like he doesn't really fully believe his side." She shook her head for a second and lowered her voice to a frustrated growl. "And what is my *mom*, doing? I know she doesn't buy Dad's denials and accusations, but she doesn't say anything, like she's afraid of what'll happen if she says the truth."

Sara's words held the atmosphere of the porch for a few more seconds, until Claire responded, though maybe it was not a direct reply to what Sara had said.

"I've been impressed lately with how much people are really motivated by fear in everything they do. It's like, if you could stop people and get them to tell the truth, without covering up, you could get them to trace each thing they do back to some fear of something." Claire's eyes strayed again, this time for more than a few seconds. She rested her chin on her arm, still wrapped around her knees, and looked at those roses again.

"It took courage to break it off," Sara said, knowing that Claire had been talking about her own engagement, as much as about Sara's parents.

If You Really Knew Me

Claire pulled her chin free of its resting place and looked squarely at Sara. "You know, part of what made it clear to me that Kyle wasn't right for me, was the way he just stayed with your dad's version of things, without even caring if it was true." She gathered her composure, after hearing her own words accelerating and her voice expanding. "He's smart, you know, that's one of the things that got me at first, smart and really responsible. But how can a smart person not care that the guy he works for is trying to ruin somebody, and in the name of God?"

Sara smiled a lopsided grin. "I should be insulted that you're talking that way about my dad," she said. "But that's exactly what I've been thinking about him and his whole staff, and the pastors of the other churches...everyone." She slowed herself, correcting her blanket indictment. "Well, not everyone. That's the good news. Darryl left for the same reason as me. I also knew *you* would see the wrong in what they were doing."

Again, Claire let Sara's words hang in place between them, fading slowly in the rising breeze. Then she said, "Now it's time to move on, to stop worrying about what other people are doing wrong. You have a whole lot of truth to discover, and you need to just focus on that." Claire's eyebrows stretched high, as she listened to herself, the wise counselor all the sudden.

Sara recognized the source of that surprised look. "I think that might be like a prophetic word for me, or something," she said. "I gotta learn more about that stuff, but I think that's what I hear in what you just said. Maybe even God speaking right through you."

Claire shook her head and snickered under her breath. "Well, no one ever confused anything I said with God's voice before, that's for sure."

Sara laughed. Then, suddenly serious, she said, "But, it's time to move on now, remember?"

Reality or TV?

As the summer rolled toward its dry and fiery climax in the California hills, Beau Dupere enjoyed a few weeks of peace. Though he wouldn't know it directly, no stories about him ran in the local or regional papers, and TV newscasters didn't say his name for nearly a month.

In the entertainment business, there is a line graph in the minds of the media gods, where fame has to arch downward to a certain level, but not below that, until it's just the right time to place a new bet on a famous name and face. Producers want a star that's hot but not volcanic. Someone judged that Beau had reached that point on his curve out of the limelight.

Miranda received a call one Monday morning from Bill Steinberg, a TV producer with a string of successful "reality" shows. She grimaced at his description of what he wanted, but knew that she had to tell Beau anyway. Later that morning, when Beau returned from a meeting at his local church, he asked Miranda about messages.

"A TV producer called about featuring you in a reality series called *The Healer*," Miranda said, managing to keep an editorial tone out of her voice.

Beau was looking at a pile of mail. "Oh, yeah. Who was it?"

"Bill Steinberg," Miranda said, consulting the note she had written.

Beau stopped his sorting through the mail and looked at Miranda. But she could tell that he wasn't really looking at her as he tried to think of something, or perhaps remember. "Bill Steinberg?"

"Yes. Is that someone you know?"

"No," Beau said. "But I'm supposed to call him back when he calls me."

"Supposed to?"

"I heard that yesterday when I was sitting down on the beach."

Miranda knew Beau liked to pray while sitting on the slim belt of sand at the bottom of the cliff, below the house. He often received his instructions for the day while stretched out in a beach chair, his feet inches from the foamy edge of the cool waves.

"I guess you have to call him, then," Miranda said, this time leaking a bit of her disapproval.

Beau laughed, looking at her for real this time. "You're not a fan of reality TV?" he said, his teasing voice pogoing in mock incredulity, from low to high and back again.

Miranda smiled. "I guess you could tell that, huh?"

"No surprise," said Beau. His eyes said he appreciated her reservations, but his lips remained silent on the subject. "Go ahead, and get him on the phone for me, please."

The next day, Beau and Justine met with Bill Steinberg, along with his assistant, Raylynn, and the director for the proposed series, Chuck Maxwell. They sat in their living room, spread out on the couches and oversized chairs, the director scanning the room as if looking for camera angles.

"This would be *your* show, all about *you*," Steinberg said, as if Beau were one of the ego-driven stars of his previous series, featuring prostitutes in one case and horse racing professionals in the other. "You would just do what you normally do. We would coordinate with your scheduler...ah..."

"Miranda," Justine said, providing the name for which Steinberg was searching.

"Exactly!" he said, as if Justine had deftly summed up the most important element of the show.

Neither Beau nor Justine annoyed easily, so they weathered the shoptalk between the producer and director, as well as the exaggerated strokes to their vanity, and sideways comments about ways to fix up the house. Beau was confident that God had instructed him to cooperate with Bill Steinberg until he received further prompting. This set him and Justine in a very cooperative mood, while waiting for some sign that they could cut and run back to their peaceful lives. The visitors picked up none of this nuance and the deal was turned over to the lawyers and agents.

Beau instructed his lawyer to make sure that he and Justine could shut the thing down as soon as the production stopped serving God's purpose. He didn't say anything about money or even how much time it would take, just wanting to make sure he could call it off when he needed to, as if he was certain that such would be the outcome of the venture.

Justine and he had seen situations like this before. They privately joked about God's mastery of the bait and switch, bringing people into their lives who thought they were there to make money or something, when the purpose was really for them to meet Jesus and perhaps get healed.

The first week of filming covered the last week of August, and would be boiled down to one show or two, about forty minutes of running time for each, allowing for commercials. The cooperation between the film crew and Beau's schedule ran smoothly that first week, and it seemed as if a television program featuring professionally filmed healing miracles was going to join the mid-season lineup of shows. They filmed Beau on the beach during his quiet time with God, they filmed him eating at the kitchen table with Adam, Peter and Justine, and they filmed him driving to meetings with celebrities or local pastors, or both. They followed him through three healing meetings, including one in which a woman with advance MS was totally healed and hopping up and down laughing hysterically by the end. At this stage, it truly seemed that God had instructed Beau to agree to the show because the show would demonstrate his loving power to heal.

The second week, starting after Labor Day, was more stressful. Chuck Maxwell wanted to get more film of the family, "more intimate footage," he said.

If You Really Knew Me

"What do you mean by more intimate?" Miranda said, when Chuck pulled her aside on Wednesday morning.

"You know, like how do they really live, what are they really like in private, that sorta stuff."

Miranda was waiting for Beau to finish a phone call to a friend in England. He had gone upstairs to get a clearer cell signal and she was left watching over the film crew. "You know what they've said about their limits for how much you can disrupt the rest of the family," Miranda said, only edging her words slightly with the defensive metal that she was getting ready.

When Beau appeared a few minutes later, Chuck tried a direct assault. "Hey, Beau, what do you say we schedule some filming for tonight, say the family settles down for the night, that kinda thing?"

Beau looked at Miranda and knew what was coming, sensing the ground she had already covered regarding the proposed intrusion. "Now, Bill, you know what we said about keeping the rest of the folks in the house out of most of this. I think you're looking at stepping over those boundaries."

Chuck saw his attempt batted away and changed his angle quicker than a cheetah in pursuit of an impala. "Oh, I just mean some sunset stuff. Maybe a kid kisses you good night and goes up the stairs, just some homey scenes like that. Of course, I wasn't thinking of filming in any bedrooms or anything."

Nodding, Beau recognized the retreat and agreed to the adjusted request, fully aware that this would not be the last time he fought this battle. The next week brought on the next round.

The family had taken a liking to Raylynn, who seemed the least calloused to their desires and needs. Though she hadn't been there for much of the shooting, she appeared one night right at sunset for more of the domestic scenes. Chuck had brought her in as his secret weapon, and potential infiltrator. Justine detected the smell of alcohol on Raylynn's breath and instantly wondered what it was that the lanky thirty-year-old was trying to numb herself against.

If You Really Knew Me

Chuck's assistant, Mike, had arrived fifteen minutes earlier with a large, dense chocolate cake, the bribe in the plan for that night. Dianna looked surprised at the arrival of the cake, but not as suspicious as Justine, who was starting to add up evidence that some covert operation was in the works. But not until Chuck plunked a can of whipped cream down next to the cake on the kitchen table did Justine pull Beau aside and share her suspicions.

Dianna insisted on cutting the cake, intent on managing at least the *size* of the portions for the kids who were present, Maggie, Gretchen and Luke. Somehow, Luke had never seen the spray-on whipped cream before and he laughed hilariously at the sight and sound of a little mound of white squirting noisily onto his small slice of cake.

"Do again!" Luke shouted and laughed, after Gretchen's cake received the same treatment. The crew was filming, but at times, they would get into the mix to stir things up a bit, counting on cutting themselves out of the footage later.

"You gotta do a big blast!" Chuck said, grabbing Dianna's hand as she held the can over Maggie's cake.

It appeared intentional to Justine that Chuck not only forced Dianna to spray far more of the whipped cream, but he turned the spout toward Maggie so that it drew a rough letter "c" on her chest. Maggie instinctively grabbed at her shirt in self-defense and modesty. Luke laughed louder and waved his plate of cake around in ecstasy, flipping his desert to the floor, a chocolate and cream pile. That stopped him in mid-motion. He stared down at the cake and then looked up at Dianna. "Oh-oh," he said with a little grin.

Beau was laughing, he scooped Luke up and whisked him away from ground-zero of the high calorie mess accumulating on the table and floor. This is where Raylynn stepped in, putting a hand on Maggie's back.

"Let's get you cleaned up, so we can put you back into the shot," she said, in a voice that Justine thought sounded much

If You Really Knew Me

too rehearsed. Maggie was dabbing at the smeary mess on her pink shirt with a dishtowel, leaving a dark pink stain behind. She looked at Raylynn and nodded, allowing herself to be led out of the kitchen, toward the stairs.

Maggie began to wonder why Raylynn had to come up stairs with her, but when she got to her room, Raylynn seemed to think the same. "You can take care of yourself, of course," she said. "What was I thinking?"

Making noncommittal noises, Maggie shrugged and watched Raylynn turn away, as she focused on getting a different shirt. That focus was what Raylynn, or rather Chuck, had counted on. With Maggie thinking Raylynn was headed back downstairs and the people downstairs thinking she was with Maggie, she snuck down the long hallway to get some digital photos of the various bedrooms, using a tiny camera with which Chuck had armed her. But, just when she found what looked like the newly-repaired master bedroom, Justine reached the top of the stairs.

"Raylynn? What are you looking for?"

Raylynn spun around, tucking the little camera in her right hand jacket pocket when it was away from Justine. She opted for a half-truth.

"Sorry, just being nosey. Maggie and I both realized that she didn't need my help. I was just sorta looking around before heading downstairs."

As plausible and honest as that sounded, Justine knew that it wasn't the whole story. But she felt as if she had done enough and didn't pursue any more of the truth. She waited for Raylynn to join her at the top of the stairs, following the nervous production assistant back to the first floor.

When they returned to the kitchen, Justine could see the exchange of looks between Chuck and Raylynn, and she knew that she had interrupted something. What occurred to her was that they might have planted a hidden camera in one of the bedrooms, though that idea hadn't occurred to Chuck...yet.

This was just the one of several attempts to get deeper into the sleeping quarters, and deeper into the lives of the family.

Chuck showed less and less interest in the healing meetings and spent more and more of his credibility trying to make excuses to film at the house. Finally, Beau, Justine and Miranda met with the production team to air out the conflict.

They met with Bill Steinberg, Chuck and Raylynn again, but this time in the production offices. The first episode was to air in a couple of weeks, an episode that featured more of the family and less of the healing than Beau and Justine had hoped. As an introductory episode, that didn't seem unreasonable, but they suspected that the change signaled an attempt to redirect the series.

"Anyone want coffee, latte or anything?" Bill said, as they settled into his office, which looked as if someone had dumped the contents of an electronics workshop into a luxury executive suite. Chuck fiddled with an old digital camera as he sat on the couch next to the door, Bill behind his desk, and Raylynn in a puffy chair with her feet up on a coffee table. She had moved aside two laptops and a stray camera lens to find room for her feet. The guests sat in chairs arched around the front of Bill's desk.

Bill aimed for the heart of the discussion. "Chuck tells me you have some hesitation about the direction of the program."

Nodding, with his lips pursed, and a brief glance at Chuck, Beau replied. "We do. It seems that *The Healer* is less about healing than we had hoped."

Bill nodded, an exaggerated gesture meant to emphasize his total understanding of Beau's concern. "I know that you all want the world to know about the healing and all that stuff, and I appreciate that, I really do. But our market research has shown that our best bet for getting people to watch is the family. They want to know more about the family, and aren't completely sure that they believe in the healing stuff."

Beau raised his eyebrows. "Is this a change from what you found before you pitched the program to us?" He knew enough about show business to catch Bill in a corner.

"Well, not a big shift, but there is definitely a shift. In our earlier research, we were focused on whether the public wanted to know more about you, and that answer was clearly 'yes.' We didn't get so much into exactly *what* they wanted to know." He picked up a tennis ball that had been sitting on his blotter and began to squeeze it. "But don't get me wrong. There are plenty of people that wanna see the healing stuff, and we're gonna show it. We've got some pretty spectacular footage already, and we can cut in more, of course. But I think we have to pull people in with a more personal perspective at first, then hit 'em with your message."

Beau thought he knew the answer to the next question, but felt he had to ask what Bill was afraid to say. "What exactly is it that Mr. and Mrs. America want to know about our family?"

Bill tossed the tennis ball back and forth between his hands, his elbows resting on the arms of his tall desk chair. "You know, they're fascinated, of course, with how someone lives who has such an extraordinary gift. But, to be honest, we're getting the most intense interest over some of the more nontraditional aspects of your...ah...family arrangement."

Justine jumped in. "You want footage of Beau in bed with his harem of wives."

Bill stopped tossing the ball and stared at Justine, glanced at Beau, and then looked back at Justine. He seemed to be assessing how to take her statement, but couldn't detect any sign of humor in her face.

Raylynn shifted uncomfortably, pulling her legs back and trying to sit up straight in a chair that invited her to slouch. Chuck busted in, thinking a more honest approach would work best with his stars.

"That's exactly what people wanna see," he said. "And, why not? You're not ashamed of how you live. Why not let the world see how good life can be?"

Beau and Justine looked at each other. Miranda cleared her throat, raised one eyebrow and cocked her head at Beau. Her face seemed to say, "If you don't wanna say what has to be said, I will."

But Beau had no problem speaking for himself. "Well, Bill, it seems to me that we have come to exactly that parting of the ways that we had anticipated when we wrote up the contract. We're not gonna be your holy-roller version of the playboy mansion. We're not interested." He stood up, towering over Bill's desk. Justine and Miranda followed.

Bill just stared up at Beau, looking more nonplussed and intimidated than anyone in the room would have expected.

Justine grinned. "It was nice to meet all of you," she said, looking from one to the other of the three stunned people still seated.

"I'll walk you out," Raylynn said, standing up and avoiding eye contact with either Chuck or Bill. This added to Bill's shock, the whiff of mutiny in the air prolonging his silence.

When they had begun padding down the wide, carpeted staircase to the ground floor, Bill finally reached his door, and found his voice. "You sure there's not some room to compromise on this?" He still held the tennis ball, and his fingertips showed red and white from his tight grip on it.

Beau stopped and looked at Bill with the patience of a seasoned therapist. "No, Bill, we expected this all along. But we felt we were supposed to give you a chance until it happened. No compromise on this one. You know how to reach our lawyers." He smiled slightly, no sign of tension, let alone animosity.

Again, Bill fell into stupefied silence at the unprecedented collapse of one of his shows. "But, they seemed like such nice people," he finally said, to no one in particular, after Beau and the three women had disappeared down the stairs.

At the bottom of the stairs, Raylynn spoke in huffing spasms. "I'm so glad you guys figured it out. I'm glad you called it off. It was driving me mad, all their tricks and schemes." Her lower lip quivered and she ratcheted in a halting breath.

Justine reached over and took her arm. "You come by any time you like, Raylynn. You'll always be welcomed."

The tall brunette looked like a little girl receiving her first puppy, her eyebrows arching above her angular nose, a tilted grin skewing her long chin. "Thanks, Justine. I will come by. I won't be able to stay away."

Still standing in the ornate lobby, her brown flats slightly pigeon-toed on the caramel and white marble floor, Raylynn watched them swing through the large glass doors trimmed in brass. She suddenly felt that she knew how so many women came to live in that house.

The Meeting

Instead of celebrating the approaching debut of their new show that weekend, Beau and several family members joined old friends for a healing service at the church that still felt like their spiritual home. As it turned out, that Saturday night healing meeting up at Jack Williams's church would be referred to around the movement as "The Meeting," for months, and even years, afterward.

No one knew for sure how many times Beau had presided at healing services in Jack's church. The first time had been nearly ten years ago, when Beau was new at leading a whole meeting himself. And this would be the last time.

After a flowing and climactic worship set which already knocked dozens to the floor, Jack took the stage with his tiny lapel microphone clipped to the collar of his green flowered Hawaiian shirt.

"I gotta tell you," he said, a tipsy drawl to his voice that few had ever heard before. "I have a feeling that this night is gonna be really special." With that, he collapsed to the floor and began to laugh hysterically.

Though this sort of thing happened in that church every week, in almost every meeting, it didn't happen to Jack Williams. No one would accuse him of being resistant to the influence of the Holy Spirit, but that influence rarely sent Jack flat on his face in front of a full house. A mixture of laughter and hushed awe greeted the sight of the world-renown senior pastor rolling around on the stage in hysterical laughter. Beau took Jack's indisposition as his cue to mount the stage and start the healing.

He had already discovered what Jack was trying to say, that something unusual was in the air at church that night. Five feet from where Jack lay cackling on the floor, Beau rocked for a second, an uncharacteristic wobble for him. It looked as if a very localized earthquake was tossing the stage in waves. He looked out at the crowd, which had settled into a whispery buzz. Later, those present would claim that they felt something waiting to explode before Beau brought down the house. Some even reported hearing the people around them suck in their breath, expecting all Heaven to break loose. And some claimed to see a golden cloud descend on the first twenty rows or so, when Beau made the pronouncement which would ring on as his most memorable words.

"Let the unstoppable healing power of God Almighty fall on this room, right now." He chopped with his right hand as he said, "now," and several hundred people fell to the floor simultaneously. The Internet video—which would be seen by tens of millions of viewers within weeks—showed an uncanny coordination of individuals from one end of the room to the other. From the stage, it looked like a large hand suddenly pressed down on the crowd and flattened a quarter of them. Then the hand lifted and squashed another large section. The third press from that hand wasn't necessary, because the vast majority of those still standing keeled over at the sight of so many being knocked to

If You Really Knew Me

the ground in front of them. The room rang with the sound of relieved laughter, shouts of deliverance and howls of rejoicing.

By Jack Williams's count—from the video record, interviews, and written testimonies—nearly two thousand people were instantly healed of an extreme spectrum of physical, emotional and spiritual ailments. But he missed all that when it started, because all he could see at the time was the carpet on the stage.

After Beau made his famous declaration, he stumbled forward a step and then appeared to be blasted off his feet by the same force that flattened the first wave of people being healed. Microphones worn by both Beau and Jack seemed to pick up a primal sort of howl that arched through the air as Beau left his feet and skidded into the drum shield. The drummer tried to get up to help Beau, but he too flew backward, doing an awkward three quarter flop that left him on his face as well.

Sara Claiborne was not one of the inflated number of people who later claimed to be at that meeting. But she did happen to be watching on her computer, from home. Her work schedule had demanded that she return to her apartment from the church, instead of sticking around for Beau's meeting, as she sincerely wanted to. When the first wave of people crumpled to the floor in unison, Sara fell off her bed, toppling over and landing nearly squarely on her head. The first miracle was that she didn't break her neck, or even raise a bump on her head. The second miracle was that an uncomfortable lump, that regularly swelled and dissipated with her monthly cycle, had disappeared from her lower abdomen. She lay laughing on the floor for nearly two hours, her only break coming in slow seasons of weeping.

The first few waves of power that flattened the room and freed so many people at once were not the end of the meeting. For hours, people lay on the floor, some completely unable to move, others undulating like a pile of prone dancers, accompanied by intense tears or drunken laughter. When Beau managed to stand, he helped Jack to his feet, and the two began to stagger around the room, propping each other up, and adding more

If You Really Knew Me

healings and miracles to the first layer that had landed on the room.

During this tottering tour of the room, many people reportedly were relieved of medical devices, replaced by healthy limbs and eyes and audio nerves. Hundreds of these claims were later corroborated by doctors. Perhaps the most startling healing miracle, one that was partially captured on video, was the restoration of an Iraq War veteran's amputated arm. Both Beau and Jack fell to the floor crying like babies as the man stood feeling his face with his new fingers and clapping his two good hands together in front of him, a huge grin on his face and a glassy glow to his eyes.

Anna Conyers had been unaware of the meeting scheduled that night. But a friend at the church she had begun attending texted her soon after the seats in Redwood had been emptied by that invisible hand. Her friend had been watching via Internet since another friend of *hers* had texted her from the floor of that meeting.

On Anna's laptop, the video image of hundreds of people lying among the chairs, in the aisles and even on top of each other, initially baffled her. Her friend had alerted her to check it out, but without any explanation of why. The young reporter assumed something had gone wrong, even stretching to try to imagine what sort of weapon could have knocked so many people unconscious at once. But, when the rocking camera angle settled on a pair of young girls lying on the floor with euphoric looks on their faces, Anna remembered her baptism experience. Something had not gone wrong, something had gone amazingly right, she decided. And she watched for two more hours, as people lay crying, laughing, or singing worship songs. One of the musicians managed to stand at a microphone with a guitar to accompany the holy circus with familiar songs of praise.

Anna was, of course, most fascinated with the stretch of video showing Beau and Jack, their arms around each other like wasted drinking buddies trying to find where they had parked

If You Really Knew Me

their car. Along the way, they seemed to find spectacular miracles, tipping them off their ledges with outstretched hands and tear-filled healing commands. She laughed as the audio engineers kept changing their mind about whether to mute the microphones attached to Beau and Jack. The uneven volume and often incoherent speech of the two men mixed over each other and added a comic bent to the situation, at least for the Internet viewer. Anna stopped laughing several times during their staggering mission, however, to cry. She was the wonder of a woman with a glass eye receiving a new natural eye, a boy with severe nervous system disabilities jumping up from his wheel chair, and the man with the missing arm received a genuine replacement. She swore aloud and then clamped both hands over her mouth, embarrassed by her lack of self-control, and unhinged by the impossibility of what she saw with her own eyes.

Anna stopped watching when she fell to the floor, overcome with the warm caress of a loving presence in her apartment. She eventually fell asleep on her living room rug, after hours of listening to a voice from deep inside herself singing over her, and pledging his love to her forever.

For Jack and Beau, the evening didn't end until they had each spent another hour on the floor weeping and laughing, each in a separate pile of stunned and healed meeting attendees.

Four hours after the meeting began, Beau was back on his feet. The video stream had been shut down. Half of the people who had been lying on the floor had left. And he found a restroom where he could wash his face and comb his uncharacteristically wild hair. By this time, news of the outrageous healing event had bounced around the world and back to secular news outlets. Half a dozen reporters crept into the building during the latter stages of the meeting.

One reporter, after hearing stories from twenty or thirty people, found Beau and asked him, "Are you the greatest miracle worker in the world today?"

Beau laughed, stopped his search for Jack Williams, and looked squarely at the man. He said, "Miracle worker? When it comes to miracles, I'm not even the greatest in this country. That would be Bobby Nightingale. And that doesn't account for the rest of the world."

Several of the reporters and groupies who heard this statement began researching this Bobby Nightingale over the following days.

Beau finally found Jack, who ushered a very boney woman with a pale face toward him. He assumed the woman needed healing from something, perhaps AIDS or cancer.

That woman was Willow Pierce, who lived in Palos Heights, Colorado, near Boulder. She had travelled to the meeting to deliver a message to Beau, not to receive healing. Jack was familiar with Willow, such that, when he received a call from her earlier that day, he planned to link her up with Beau at the end of the meeting. But, when Jack saw Willow late that night, he barely recognized her. She seemed shrunken from when he had seen her four years ago. Her eyes glistened out of sockets that looked like small craters in her sallow face. Jack's first thought was that she was terminally ill, also thinking of AIDS. Then a thought landed in his head, that she had been fasting from food and had not slept well for a long time. This revelation accelerated Jack's pulse, and tightened his neck and shoulder muscles, as he connected her wasted condition with the message she had for Beau.

"How are you, dear?" Jack said to Willow, when they met at the front of the auditorium around midnight.

She smiled, knowing why Jack asked. "I knew there would be times that I would have to deliver a hard message," she said, bowing her head as if it was too heavy to keep upright for more than a few moments. Her skeletal frame jerked with sobs for two seconds and then she recovered. "But I'm glad God didn't tell me *how* hard it would be."

Willow's weakened state spurred Jack to urgently search out Beau, both to relieve her of the message she was carrying, and to hear what this terrible news might be. He had known of her for decades and had first met her about ten years before, introduced

If You Really Knew Me

by a mutual friend. At that first meeting, Willow had prophesied the huge expansion of miracles and increased attendance at Jack's church. This was before the acceleration of Beau's healing ministry and the subsequent multiplication of Jack's churches into several more. Jack had come to rely on the accuracy of Willow's messages from God.

Beau saw Jack, and seemed to know he was looking for him. He recognized Willow, but couldn't remember her name, their acquaintance being scarce and his clarity of thought muted. When he saw the look in both Jack's and Willow's eyes, however, Beau sobered and prepared for what he had coming. He knew Willow had an important message for him.

To Jack, it appeared that Willow suddenly became inflated with life, when she finally stood facing Beau. She stood up straighter and her eyes opened wider. The wracking sobs he had witnessed just minutes ago, made no return, as she reached the end of a very long journey with this message.

Beau took a deep breath. Jack made introductions.

"You know Willow Pierce, don't you Beau?"

"I think we've met," he said, automatically offering his hand.

Both Beau and Willow seemed surprised by the electric current that passed between them when their hands made firm contact. Again, Jack saw Willow infused with more life and strength.

"You know that the end of your time here is coming," Willow began, as if reading Beau's mind. "And you must also know that, this time, Father isn't going to let you come back. It is your final exit from this life."

"How soon?" Beau said evenly.

"Timing is always hard to understand," Willow said. "But it is not months, though it seems like more than just days."

Beau looked at Willow with the eyes of a loved one who fully appreciates the cost of a gift he has received. Though he didn't know her well, he felt he needed to embrace her. And Willow stepped into his enfolding arms, allowing her body to rest against his.

Only Jack could see one of the strangest effects of this mystical embrace. Willow's hair appeared to drink new life from the air. At the same time, her whole body seemed to be fueled with strength that further straightened her back and lifted her head. When Willow pulled away from Beau, he and Jack both saw that her face had shed years of age in that half minute of contact with the healer.

"David killed the messenger," Willow said, referring to an ancient biblical story. "But you heal her."

Beau smiled. It was exactly the sort of surprising thing he had always loved to be part of.

Jack tried to reflect Beau's smile, but he found no heart for such an expression of contentment and peace. He turned to Willow and patted her on the shoulder, nodding, without a word to say. Whether you knew him as a pastor or even an apostle, no one knew Jack Williams to be without words.

Adopted

Just as Justine expected, Raylynn showed up at the house. She arrived two days after "The Meeting." As far as Beau and Justine were concerned, Raylynn was the profit earned from their little reality TV venture, which made it a good investment of time and frustration, according to their accounting standards.

What Beau, Justine and Miranda didn't realize about Raylynn, was that the woman they met was a different Raylynn than her mother had known. Born in a small town in the Ozark mountains of Arkansas, Raylynn Joyce Collins, she had known more pigs than people by the time she graduated from high school, and escaped her shameful back-woods childhood. At

If You Really Knew Me

least, that's how she thought about it, looking back from Hollywood, California, ten years later.

That's about how long it took her to lose her hillbilly accent, and learn to speak proper California English. Again, that's how *she* calculated her transformation. From feeding chickens on her uncle's farm to attending parties hosted by famous actors and directors, she had transformed herself, even saved herself. That's what she thought.

Then she met the Dupere family. In their presence, she discovered that, as high as she had climbed out of her past, she was still in the foothills. She hadn't even reached the mountains yet, the ones that she really wanted to conquer.

When Raylynn was six years old, her father jumped in the family pickup truck and took off for points south; Houston or New Orleans, the adults speculated. When she was eight, her mother died of cervical cancer. A good-hearted man, her uncle on her mother's side adopted her into his family. But she always knew she was adopted. She never forgot. She kept a secret copy of *Cinderella* in her plywood toy box, beneath the eyeless dolls and cracked plastic tea cups. She *was* Cinderella. None of her cousins worked as hard as she did. And that was because she was adopted. She was sure of it. Her aunt and uncle hadn't brought her into their family to love and comfort her, but to harvest her labor, to put her to work earning her place in the corner of the ten-by-ten bedroom that she shared with two cousins.

Raylynn was too smart to get pregnant and married, like her cousin Brianna. Instead, she graduated at the top of her high school class of eighty students and grabbed hold of a scholarship to the University of Arizona, like the ladder rung she often gripped to pull herself out of the pig sty and up into the main level of the barn.

She studied hard and worked two jobs much of the time, earning her degree and her self-respect out in the bigger world, beyond her rock-strewn and cheerless beginnings. It was hard work that landed her production assistant jobs in Los Angeles and then in Hollywood. The young men and women against whom she competed for those prized gateway jobs didn't know anything about hard work, compared to Raylynn.

Though her body still stood tall and straight, and she never even thought to complain about the long hours and low pay, she had grown weary inside, where no one tried to enter. And she dreaded days off, alone in her little apartment in Venice, alone in the crowds on the beach, alone in her heart.

This is what drew her to Beau and Dianna and the kids. She wanted to be really adopted, the way Justine had invited Dianna in, and the way Rhonda and Bethany had found a home full of compassion and rest.

That first evening, at dinner with the mixed collection of women and children present for that meal, Raylynn couldn't finish eating. Peter looked at her over his spaghetti and said, "Are you gonna be adopted into this family?" That broke her open.

Olivia and Dianna exchanged a look, as their guest sobbed into her white cloth napkin, and each finished their food in a few quick bites. Still chewing the last of her salad, Olivia stood up, excused herself, and then took Raylynn by the shoulders and helped her to stand and stagger toward the back patio. Dianna said something into Emma's ear and the little girl nodded, skipping dessert to go and help the new lady get well.

Insightful observers have said that we are a society and a generation of orphans, children longing for the love of father and mother. For Raylynn, an orphan in the literal sense, this culture of emotional poverty had its hands stuffed into its empty pockets, offering no hope. When she thought of attaching herself to the household in Malibu, Raylynn felt a twist just above her stomach at the thought of being the odd guest, or the thought of her hosts offering obligatory tolerance.

Wrapped in Olivia's long, strong arms, with Emma's head resting on the opposite shoulder, Raylynn lost that twisted feeling, a feeling she had climbed over to risk rejection one more time. As she sat there weeping, she remembered the men she had scared away, their eyes wide and feet fast for the door, fleeing her need to cling, which they discovered after they pressed in close enough to flip her from shy to dependent, as they sometimes did.

She cried that history right out of her, both the clinging urge, and the shame of disgusting so many men—surfers, nerds, starving actors and hipster musicians, united in their flight away from her.

With Emma's cooing consolation in her ear, Raylynn's old self peeled off like thin white curls of birch bark. Softly, easily, she sloughed off loneliness, fear and shame at the cost of one long evening and a hundred wadded tissues. That was just the beginning, of course. But, adoption *is* just the start, after all.

Gone Again

Anna didn't understand the invitation she received from Miranda near the end of October. The gathering at the Dupere home was personal, mostly family, it seemed. The difficult piece for Anna was understanding her place among them.

With protestors still lining the street, though fewer than even that first time Anna visited the house, Anna had to park outside the Dupere compound. The driveway was full of cars, both inside and outside the gate. Four black-clad guards stood along the line between the street and Beau's property. One of them that she hadn't met before asked for Anna's I.D. But one of the more familiar young musclemen spoke up for her. "She's invited. I know her," he said.

Anna thanked him and passed between the defensive line, her high heels clicking on the pinkish paving stones of the long drive. Ahead of her, Anna could see a couple approaching the

If You Really Knew Me

front door of the house. When the man turned toward the woman to say something, she recognized Jack Williams. She wondered if he would remember her. Then she recalled the video of him staggering around with Beau, at the dramatic healing service, and she repressed a laugh.

Anna followed Jack and his wife into the house, and was greeted by Olivia at the door. Anna had only met Olivia briefly during one of her later visits to the house, but hadn't had time to interview her, nor to get to know her personally.

"Anna, I'm glad you could join us. Beau was very determined that you should be here," she said.

The look on Olivia's face reminded Anna of an elementary school teacher she had, or perhaps of a compilation of teachers. Olivia's eyes warmly embraced her without self-consciousness. This freed Anna to ask the question she had been rubbing in her mind all day.

"Why did he want me here, especially?" she said. "I mean, of course, I want to be here, but I'm not sure I fit into even the broadest category of family and friends."

Olivia wrapped an arm around Anna's shoulder. "Well, you have to remember that around here, some of the most significant things happen where eyes can't see and ears can't hear." Wading into the crowd milling in the foyer, as throughout the house, Olivia could feel Anna's confusion through the tension in her shoulders.

"To Beau and Justine, you're like an adopted daughter," she said, "and it's important for them to have you with us for a big family celebration." They stopped at the living room and Anna stared, with her brow curved in continued question.

Olivia persisted. "It's not just your conversion, or the baptism, or any of that. It's also the way you shared in their suffering around the attacks on Beau. They feel like you paid a price that you weren't really warned about, when you took the time and effort to be honest about what you found here."

Anna mostly recalled the self-recriminations she survived around each of the attacks on the family. "Thanks for explaining all that, Olivia." She looked at the willowy woman and felt like she knew her beyond her ability to explain. Then she realized that Olivia had that same spirit about her that had welcomed Anna into that house from the first. That spirit apparently blurred things, like the lines between inside and outside, even regarding who counts as family.

All of Beau's children were in the house for one of the few times since Luke was born. Anna met the older sons, had her first real conversation with Joanna, and even spent some time sitting on the carpet in Peter's room, surrounded by a dozen other little ones playing with Peter's toys. He didn't seem to mind the strangers playing with his things, and even displayed a gift for intuiting which toy each child would like most, when they entered his room.

Beau found Anna there, her shoes off, her head resting to one side as she listened to Luke explain what the men in his truck were doing.

"Hello, young miss. I heard you were here, but hadn't seen you. Hiding with the kids?" Beau said.

Anna stood up, with her shoes in one hand, as gracefully as she could. "I've made the rounds, met your grown sons and Joanna, and a bunch of your friends. I feel so lucky to be included in all this."

Looking down at her like a proud father, Beau's warm smile gradually wore away under the weight of sorrow he had been hiding all day. "As usual, you haven't really been briefed on exactly what's going on here. Not everyone knows, of course." He put an arm around her, his large tan hand resting gently on her pale shoulder. She let him lead her out of the room.

"A woman Jack knows, named Willow Pierce, was sent to give me a message," Beau said, leading her toward the master bedroom suite.

Anna's disorientation about what Beau was saying erased the realization that she was heading toward the only part of the house she hadn't seen before. The door stood half open, a lamp in the corner keeping the approaching darkness of the fall night from invading the entire room. As they pushed through the door, Anna first noticed Dianna and Maggie sitting close to each other on a window seat in the far corner of the sitting room. Beau smiled at them, but continued talking to Anna.

"She said I wouldn't be allowed to come back this time," he said, stopping in the center of the room and releasing his soft embrace from her shoulders.

"Come back?" Anna said. But, as soon as she said it, she knew what the answer was. She had recognized a sort of intuition rising in her in recent weeks. But, just now, she ignored the wonder of this new ability, focusing instead on Beau's news.

"Did she say when it would happen? Is there anything you can do to prevent it?" Anna said, realizing that she was talking like the other people who lived in that house, allowing the unspoken parts of a conversation to mingle with plain old words.

"It's soon enough that I called all my kids home for one last family time. We're heading out this weekend to our place in the mountains, just me, the kids and their mothers. This is goodbye," he said. And for the first time in Anna's experience he looked both sad and resigned to that sadness.

She tried to ask another question, but it stuck in her throat. She could hear Dianna's ardent but gentle tone as she spoke with Maggie on the other side of the room. Anna could guess the subject of their conversation, in light of the news she had just received.

Beau continued. "It wasn't a warning, like when someone tells you to duck. It was more like advice to see my loved ones before succumbing to a terminal illness." His smile lacked the aggressive joy that she had always felt from him.

"But the kids, little Luke," she said, protesting in fragments.

"Yeah, that's where the sadness comes from. But even that's selfish, as if I'm the one they really need. God will take care of them in ways I never could. And my absence will make way for others to have a bigger place, a bigger reward."

Anna looked now at Maggie. She seemed more solemn than Anna had ever seen her.

Beau glanced toward the window seat and said in a hushed tone, "She really felt it deep when she sat over my bleeding corpse. She took the weight of bringing me back to life fully on herself. It left a mark," he said. "It cost her a lot." He took in a gulp of air and released it quickly.

Anna understood the reason for the party, but she also understood something that no one had spoken. She suddenly knew why Maggie was going to walk away from all this. She knew Maggie had seen the whole price and didn't want to be so close to suffering again. And she knew that, while Maggie didn't get to choose the sacrifice of being robbed of a loved one *this* time, she would checkout before there was a next time.

After absorbing this revelation, Anna looked at Beau. "I know things. Like what you told me about yourself, and the others."

Beau smiled, that proud father look returning. "You're one of the family now."

Two weeks later, after Beau returned with his family from a teary and inspiring retreat to their cabin in the Sierra Nevada, he sat in his Land Rover, thinking about all the grace he had seen in his life. His car was parked on a quiet commercial street, just off the main thoroughfare in Parkerville, where he had met with some old friends for the last time. When he turned the key in the ignition something sounded strangled. The always-reliable vehicle failed to start.

He looked up and noticed a man walking toward him, down the street, looking like he knew him and wanted to talk. Lost in wondering who the man was, Beau tried the ignition again. And suddenly he knew why the car wasn't starting.

Darryl Sampras had heard that Beau Dupere was in town, visiting someone just down the street. Two women gossiped about it in the drug store where Darryl was picking up a prescription. Since his resignation from Dixon Claiborne's church, and the tense and gray days following, Darryl had grown thankful that Beau had been an unknowing catalyst in his liberation from a religion that was smothering his soul.

He paid for his daughter's medicine and headed out the door, hoping to briefly introduce himself, and to thank, the famous man. Using an overheard conversation as his direction seemed a tenuous plan, but Darryl felt driven to see Beau in person. Though he told himself this urge was to thank him, part of him doubted that was the whole reason for his desire to see Beau.

From more than a block away, Darryl saw a man who looked just like he imagined Beau Dupere would look in person. He had walked out of the café to which Darryl was headed and climbed into a dark green Land Rover. Darryl stopped at the corner to allow a compact car to buzz past and then sped his pace toward Beau's car, hoping he could get the driver's attention before he drove off. The sound of a failing ignition nudged a bit of added hope into Darryl's heart, as he increased his step to meet the man that he now saw clearly through the windshield of the Land Rover.

As Beau let go of the key after his second try, he simultaneously lifted one hand toward the man approaching, who stopped dead still as if frozen to the cement. At the same time, the world around Beau lit up white and orange and blue all at once. And his faithful old ride exploded around him, transporting him to another world, like Elijah in *his* fiery chariot.

At about fifty feet from the car, just when Darryl was beginning to raise his free hand to flag down Beau Dupere, he noticed a disturbed look overtake Beau's face. Then Beau looked squarely at Darryl and quickly raised a hand toward him, as if to bar him from coming closer. And it seemed to work. Darryl felt his feet anchored to the ground, though he wasn't sure whether it was the natural reaction to Beau looking at him and putting up his hand, or some supernatural brake applied to his feet. Before he could even finish that question, however, the Land Rover lit up. A ball of orange flame enveloped the top half of the vehicle. Beau Dupere disappeared. And the entire car leapt two feet off the ground.

Darryl heard glass breaking all around him and felt the push of a vicious wind knock him over backward. He tried to catch himself with both hands, his white paper bag from the drug store flying behind him. He managed to keep his head from slamming into the pavement, pain instead shooting up both arms and into his shoulders and neck. When his head did land on the asphalt, its impact had been moderated by the sacrifice paid by wrists and elbows.

As he lay there looking up at the pure, blue California sky, the world seemed to go silent, except for a ringing, like a church bell that wouldn't stop. And Darryl collected one thought from the shock of what had just happened.

"They really killed him this time," he said to himself, before blacking out.

Passing it On

People of a certain mindset like to insist that their funeral should be a celebration. Beau Dupere had never said anything like that, as far as anyone could remember. He knew that his death would not cost him anything and would benefit him eternally. But he also knew that his death would cost a lot of people more than they would like to pay.

None of the churches in Malibu were big enough for the funeral. Jack Williams figured this out with Justine and the others, and found a suitable venue in Los Angeles, a colossal church with a long history. That church had hosted Beau and his healing

If You Really Knew Me

ministry several times over the previous ten years, and Jack was well acquainted with the senior pastor.

At one point in his sermon, Jack commented, "Of course, if we wanted to have Beau's funeral in a building that would accommodate everyone he impacted deeply, with some life-changing healing, we would be disappointed. No building in all the earth would accommodate that many people." Though Jack was an aficionado of such details, he didn't even try to speculate about the exact number.

When a religious leader dies of cancer, or in a plane crash, or from old age, those that he touched are saddened. But when a man like Beau Dupere is assassinated, his name becomes associated with martyrdom; and his friends and followers, who don't surrender to anger, see in that death a call to push forward all the harder.

The FBI found evidence from the bomb site that pointed to the same sort of domestic terrorist groups they had been tracking since before the first assassination. That this was the work of more than just one disturbed individual was undeniable, given the video footage of the man who shot Beau, the body of one of the firebombers at the house, and several men and women whom the Feds had brought in for questioning, as persons of interest. But no clear suspect emerged in the first few weeks of the bombing investigation.

Darryl Sampras recovered from his injuries, and from a brief stint as the lead suspect for the bombing. This latter connection ran through Dixon Claiborne's church, of course, but failed to produce any solid evidence. The bomb blast did no lasting damage to Darryl's body, which didn't suffer any broken bones, and only a temporary loss of hearing. But he did discover something about that day which changed his life even more than the trauma of watching a man murdered in a flaming explosion.

Not finding new employment as a pastor, Darryl had settled into a job in a cell phone store at the mall. Even with overtime, he and Susan relied on relatives to help meet their financial obligations. Their one-year-old, Betsy, could stay out of daycare as long as those relatives helped, and Karen could stay home with the baby. Karen did earn a little money, buying things at garage sales and selling them via the Internet, but that barely paid for Betsy's diapers and baby food.

Counting their coins as usual, Darryl and Karen debated whether to take Betsy to the doctor over a runny nose she had suffered for about a week. Their health insurance was affordable because of its high deductible, which made these small medical decisions much more monetary in nature than the conscientious parents would have liked. It was really out of frustration one night that Darryl put his hand on Betsy's warm and damp little head and prayed. "O God, please, we need your help. Please heal Betsy, so we don't have to spend the money on a doctor." And then he backed down a bit. "At least let us know whether we really need to go to the doctor."

The next morning, Darryl rolled over in bed and glanced at the clock; 7:17 it said. Karen greeted Darryl with a relieved smile, up already, and bouncing Betsy in her arms. She spoke in the high-pitched voice she used to channel what she was sure her little daughter would like to say.

"Hey, Daddy, you need to get up and play with me, 'cuz I'm feeling all better now," Karen said,

Darryl looked at Betsy for a moment before he registered what Karen had just said. "Wait, she's feeling better?"

"She's feeling *completely* better," Karen said in her own voice. "She just fed more than she has in over a week. I'm thinking it's about time to increase her solid food intake."

"No more cold?"

"No sir," Karen said, sitting on the bed and handing Betsy to Darryl. "I'm feeling full of spunk this morning," she said, speaking for Betsy again. And Betsy confirmed that assessment with a laugh at her dad holding her in the air. She pulled her fist out of her mouth and just missed him with a string of drool. Her full-faced grin made Darryl laugh as he settled Betsy into the crook of his neck.

"You think it mattered that I prayed last night?"

Karen rolled her eyes. "Why else do you think she's suddenly all better?"

Darryl looked at Karen and squinted slightly, trying to decide how much to make of the coincidence. Then he made a surprising connection. Before his mind's eye he saw that moment that Beau Dupere reached his hand toward him, as Darryl stood frozen to the ground. This time, however, that memory wasn't about reliving the trauma of seeing a man trapped in an exploding vehicle. This time, Darryl saw the power in that hand, the power that stopped him from getting any closer before that bomb ignited.

Though Darryl couldn't say it aloud to Karen just then, he suddenly knew that Beau Dupere had left something with him before he took off. And, because of that hasty departure, Beau wasn't able to do more than just leave a piece of himself to a stranger, a stranger who would be forever grateful.

Trying to Walk on Water?

After Beau died, no one moved out of the house immediately. They all stayed together. They all needed each other.

When Tammy, Adam's mother, received divorce papers from her husband, she was glad that she already had a new life, and new props to hold her up. She worried about her kids, however, when this second strike hit them, a second loss of a father.

Working as a legal aid most of her adult life, Tammy had worked to live, and had lived primarily for her kids, until her husband left her for a woman from his real estate firm. Then her kids were the only thing keeping Tammy from ending her life.

In that condition, she attended an evening service at the church in Malibu where Beau, Justine, and the whole family, attended when not travelling. Olivia approached Tammy during the worship music and invited her to come and sit with the family, a strange invitation, but one that Tammy had no reason to refuse. That she had returned to church after her husband, the deacon, had betrayed her, witnessed to her desperation. She hoped to find someone to help her hang on to life, like a woman fallen overboard, clinging to whatever buoyant flotsam she could reach. But Olivia, and her extraordinary family, offered more than a slippery bit of floating junk, as Tammy could tell immediately.

Later, Justine and Olivia had confided to Tammy that they had both worried that she would not survive through that Sunday night, if they didn't scoop her into their orbit of peace and hope. When they met Adam and Emma as well, later that week, the family knew they had found more of their members, if only temporarily.

Tammy cried uncontrollably when she saw how Beau wrapped his smile, and a strong arm, around Adam. Her own longing for a father's love had multiplied her desire for her children to find a dependable and loving father figure. Only when she later discovered the intimate connection between Beau's family and their father in Heaven, did Tammy find what she had really been seeking.

For his part, Adam had found a role model as influential as a father and as awe-inspiring as any man he had ever heard of. Better still, Adam discovered the gateway into the purpose for his life. He attached himself to Beau as a disciple in healing, but he also stretched beyond Beau to the God who gave him power. Adam's first night sleeping in the Dupere house, he had run down the hallway shouting for Beau, who had just begun to get ready for bed himself.

"What is it, Adam?" Beau said, though something in the level set of his eyes alerted the boy to the possibility that this miracle man already knew what he had seen.

"I saw shadows on my wall, shadows shaped like angels," he said, breathless from the fright more than from the running.

If You Really Knew Me

Beau gripped his shoulders, leaning down to look into Adam's eyes. He was looking for the effect of the visitation, not for signs that the boy had been dreaming. "They're there to welcome you to this house, and to protect you for the work God has for you." He said this in the same tone of voice other men would use to explain a thermostat or hot water faucet to a visiting foreigner. His excitement rose only to the height of Adam's, and his satisfaction grew to greet the boy's apparent insight into the world that remains unseen to most people in the technologically advanced world.

Where Adam and Emma both excelled at spiritual sight, Emma excelled even more at faith. She accepted all of what Justine or Maggie told her about God's love, and his purpose for her and the people she met. And she spread that faith with her sincere prayers for family, friends and strangers alike.

Even as her children embraced the supernatural lifestyle of their new family, Tammy considered herself too old for such mystical belief, and focused on getting her heart healed from the wounds of a fifteen-year marriage and its tectonic fracture. For a time, she had lashed her gasping soul to the hope of becoming part of Beau's family, as Olivia and Dianna had, but Justine and Beau resisted any movement in that direction.

Over the two years since moving into the Dupere house, Tammy had settled into the hum and rhythm of her temporary home, which felt more homey than any she had lived in permanently. She adjusted to having Beau Dupere act as surrogate father to Adam and Emma, and as master artisan to Adam's apprenticeship in "the things of the Spirit," as they used to say in her old church. And she adjusted to the nurture and practical training of both Justine and Beau.

Her biggest adjustment, however, was watching her little boy approach adolescence with a full-grown faith in the supernatural world of the Bible, and of Beau Dupere. She ricocheted from fascination to fright within a single conversation, many times each week, as she listed to Adam's dreams about angels, nighttime struggles against attacking demons, and experiences of healing people of major illnesses, both with and without the help of Beau. In her heart, Tammy looked up to Adam as a sort of spiritual prodigy that she could only admire from a distance, though externally she maintained her motherly role in his life.

After Beau's death, and a few days after she had met with her lawyer about the final settlement of her divorce, Tammy spied Adam out in the Pacific, a dozen yards off the beach, up to his waist in cold water. She ran down to rescue him as fast as she dared, down the steep wooden stairway to the sand.

Adam heard the panic in his mother's voice as quickly as it registered that his mother was calling to him. He watched as she huffed and puffed down the stairs, careful of her footing and glancing at him as she called. The cold water had already made its point, that he was not welcomed there, and Adam was nearly out of the water when his mother reached the driftwood-strewn sand.

"What were you doing out there?" Tammy said, grabbing a towel that Adam had left lying on the beach.

Adam finished his assent out of the water and wrapped his arms around himself, his long-sleeved red t-shirt like a second skin now. Salt water dripped from the teal, knee-length swimsuit that Beau had bought for him on his last trip to do healing meetings in Hawaii. Adam's teeth began to chatter, as if in answer to his mother's inquiry. But he knew that she wanted more. "I didn't mean to make you worry," he said, trying to keep his voice steady and submissive amidst the shivering.

"Well, I think I'll worry anyway, young man."

Adam nodded, as he leaned into the welcomed wrap, and rapidly rubbing hands, of his mother. He had chosen this navy blue towel for its volume and warmth, even though he had hoped not to need it.

"I was just trying something," he said, his youthful optimism about avoiding full disclosure still intact.

Tammy tightened her arms around him and drew his head up under her chin. "Trying what? To freeze to death?"

If You Really Knew Me

"I was hoping not to get wet," he said, hearing how silly it sounded even as he said it.

"Not to get wet? Walking out into the ocean?"

Adam hunkered into his mother's embrace and silently prayed for wisdom. "I thought I could do it," he said, his voice smaller and lower.

"Do what?" His mother asked, even though she was beginning to suspect she knew the answer to that question.

Adam looked up at her and knew that she had guessed. He just nodded his confession.

Standing on the slim strip of beach, Tammy pulled back and stared at Adam, as if searching for other symptoms that the dual traumas of Beau's death and her husband's divorce had shattered her son's sanity. Adam smiled at her, recognizing her worried mother look, her light blue eyes turning darker, her thin red eyebrows pulling together, and her freckled forehead bunching up.

"Beau came to me in a dream," Adam said. "He was walking on the water, out there." He pointed a shivering hand toward Catalina Island. "He said I could go out and join him when I was ready." Adam looked at Tammy, to check how she was taking this. "It wasn't scary, or anything. It's not about me dying. It was just him telling me what he always did, that I could do whatever God asked me to do, even the things that Jesus did."

Tammy weighed her words during a two-second pause and then said them anyway, in spite of the hollowness she heard in them. "Maybe he didn't really mean walking on water," she said. And the "maybe" grew larger after she said it.

Adam sensed the faith limits his mother still felt throttling her soul, and didn't want to challenge those further. "Maybe," he said.

He yielded to her tug, allowing himself to be the little boy again, kept warm by his mother. They walked to the rustic wooden stairway up the sandy cliff toward a warm and welcoming home.

A Vigil of Thanksgiving

Sara Claiborne cried for hours the night she heard the news. The next morning, she started up her Toyota Corolla and drove south until she reached the hills above Malibu, winding down toward the shore on the last fumes of gas. Only the cruelly impaled grief imbedded in her heart kept her from worrying about how she was going to pay for gas to get back up north to her apartment.

When she found the house at the address listed for Beau Dupere on one of the protest Web sites, she found no protestors. One broken sign leaned against a split rail fence across the road from the house, but there was no one left to hold that sign, or to shout or chant.

Sara had to park a quarter mile past the house and walk back, however, because of the crowd. Strangers hugged her when she paused to look at the medical records they held up in protest of a murder, and in testimony of a life surrendered. Mothers, with children grown now, still remembered the doctor's diagnosis of a slow painful death for their boy or girl. X-rays, charts, and test results witnessed to the suffering. Tearful smiles told about the healing.

Moving slowly, listening to one and then another tell the story of their own healing, or that of a friend or parent, Sara drifted into Anna Conyers. They hadn't spoken since that day in Oakland, both forgetting their promise to stay in touch.

Without hesitation, Anna ran into Sara's arms and they stood together crying. The cheerleader hugged the reporter and they both knew that they weren't crying for Beau, but for themselves and for the family, and for the world that suffers every day in sickness and in pain.

A bulwark of flowers had already accumulated against the white wall next to the gate. A flickering crowd of candles surrounded that fragrant and colorful memorial. Dozens of people just stood looking at a large photo of Beau that someone had planted in the middle of the wall of flowers. The wind covered the sound of sobbing, but could not conceal the curses and screams when grief became too much to contain inside a lonely mourner.

Anna and Sara stood arm in arm at the memorial, watching a man lead a young woman, perhaps his wife, away from the silent vigil, her cries and questions opening vents in souls all around her, grateful that she said the words that they had thought, that they too had felt.

Or Just Wading In?

Maggie looked over the cliff, down to the beach, and found Adam where she suspected he would be. She could see the wind rearranging his straw-blonde hair from above, the brightness of his head contrasting with the steely dark of the water. He stood at the water's edge for a full minute while she watched. Then he started out over the waves. From where Maggie stood, it seemed that he was actually doing it this time, as if he had found a place where the surface of the water was as solid as the stone tiles on which she stood watching. After several steps on top of the waves, he finally fell through the surface to the bottom, wet now up to his waist.

Adam threw his hands into the air, and Maggie could hear his shouts over the waves and wind, all the way at the top of the cliff. He jumped up and down and spun, splashing water with his hands and feet in celebration.

The swells on the ocean rolled toward the shore, looking like long limbs sliding under dark satin sheets. Taking a deep draft of the salty air, Maggie sighed, turned away from the distant scene of celebration and shook her head. With her face the same stony mask that she had worn at the funeral, she headed back to the house, beginning to plan her departure from that house.

An Answer

Dixon Claiborne stood in his office, looking at the letter in his hands, a mile-wide smile on his face. On the professional letterhead of a large church in a burgeoning young city an hour away, he had the offer for which he had been waiting.

The month before Beau Dupere's funeral—that event in another universe that Dixon had only visited once—he had received an invitation to come preach at a big, prosperous church. He knew that invitation was the equivalent of a major-league tryout. And he had preached his best sermon ever, full of emotion, full of scriptural revelation and practical application. It was a touchdown, to return the metaphor to a more familiar field of play.

Ten or more meetings and two months later, he had the offer in his hands. He laughed. He punched the air, and said, "Yes!" in that squeezed sort of voice one uses to shout a celebration without alerting the neighbors. He *would* have to tell Connie soon, but not today, not right away. His awareness of his secretary outside his office door helped stop him from dancing a jig in the middle of the carpet. Instead, he uttered a spontaneous thanksgiving.

"Thank you, Lord!" he said, forgoing any formalities, such as reverently folded hands. "I know I don't deserve this. And I know this is by your grace," he said, confessing magnanimously, out of his joy. "I'm counting on you to help me all along the way," he said, dropping his hands to his side and shaking his head in wonder.

"I will help you, and I will also show you some new things."

That two-pronged phrase rose up so clearly in Dixon's head that he turned around, as if he might find the speaker sitting at his desk. He stopped, standing statue still, only his eyes moving, his gaze rolling across the room, both high and low. Had he actually heard a voice? Or, maybe it was just a random thought that bounced through his brain. He usually didn't hear voices, and most random phrases just bounced past without catching his attention, without sending that electric charge up his spine.

What was the message? He tried to remember. "I will help you . . . I will show you something new," he thought, trying to reconstruct it.

"Did you say that, Lord?" he said, his voice clenched, a haunted feeling growing inside.

He jumped as his cell phone rang.

The ring tone was from Sara's favorite song. His daughter was calling.

When Dixon had preached the first time in that big new church, Kristin and Brett accompanied him, solidifying his résumé for the potential employer. Sara's absence would have been easy enough to explain, she was college-age now and the school year was underway. But no one asked, of course. They didn't know Sara, nor did they know about her escape into scary new territory, at least scary for Dixon. Of all his insecurities, the questions Dixon feared most in the interviews were ones about why his daughter hung out with people who spoke in tongues and claimed to have healing powers. Those fears bordered on paranoia, he knew. But that didn't keep them away.

That he had survived the vetting process, been invited back to preach a second time, and now held the offer letter in his hand, felt like grace to calm his fears and ease his suffering at the revolt of his daughter.

If You Really Knew Me

He and Sara had talked a few times over the last several weeks, but Dixon was surprised to see her face on his phone, his grown-up girl calling him in the middle of his work day.

He tapped, "Answer Call" and raised the phone to his ear. "Sara?" he said, surprise tuning his voice.

"Dad?" she said. "I know this is gonna sound strange…" She paused, as if trying to decide whether to continue.

"Yes?"

"Well, I think God wants me to tell you something. I think He wants me to tell you, 'Yes, I did say that.'"

Dixon again stood bronzed to the floor. He might have even stopped breathing.

"Dad?"

"Yeah," he said, his voice clamped and breathless.

"You okay?"

"Yeah."

"Did that make any sense to you?"

"Uhhh, yeah."

Sara breathed relief into the phone. "Good. I guess I'm not just imagining this one."

"This one?"

"Yeah, at school I've been learning about hearing God's voice, and giving others messages from God sometimes."

Someone inside Dixon's head distinctly said, "But we don't believe in that." Since Dixon was having trouble engaging his voice, however, all he said was, "Okay, thanks."

Sara said, "Love you."

Dixon echoed that sentiment.

And they ended the call simultaneously.

All Dixon could think was, "What if God really did say it?"

ACKNOWLEDGEMENTS

The biblical quotation in Beau's Oakland sermon is from I Corinthians 2:1-5, in the New International Version, 2011.

Thanks again to Erin Brown for teaching me a lot about publishing a novel.

Thanks to Dave, Cheryl and Valerie for reading an advanced copy and helping me fix some broken pieces to the story.